PHANTOM MONEY

a novel

S. ALEXANDER O'KEEFE

GREENLEAF
BOOK GROUP PRESS

Published by Greenleaf Book Group Press
Austin, Texas
www.gbgpress.com

Distributed by Greenleaf Book Group

For ordering information or special discounts for bulk purchases, please contact Greenleaf Book Group at PO Box 91869, Austin, TX 78709, 512.891.6100.

Design and composition by Greenleaf Book Group
Cover design by Greenleaf Book Group
Los Angeles city night Bokeh; Beautiful sunset of Los Angeles downtown skyline and palm trees in foreground; grunge style abstract background image of textured metal surface, used under license from Shutterstock.com

Publisher's Cataloging-in-Publication data is available.

Print ISBN: 978-1-62634-764-9

eBook ISBN: 978-1-62634-765-6

Part of the Tree Neutral® program, which offsets the number of trees consumed in the production and printing of this book by taking proactive steps, such as planting trees in direct proportion to the number of trees used: www.treeneutral.com

TreeNeutral

Printed in the United States of America on acid-free paper
20 21 22 23 24 25   10 9 8 7 6 5 4 3 2 1
First Edition

Acknowledgments

I want to thank my wife and children, and my mother, brothers, and sisters for their love and support. I particularly want to thank my now deceased father for insisting I read *A Tale of Two Cities* by Charles Dickens, *The Count of Monte Cristo* by Alexandre Dumas, and *Scaramouche* by Rafael Sabatini when I was ten years old, which I reluctantly did. Thousands of books later, those are still three of my favorites.

I also want to thank the talented editors and technical experts who advised, guided, and assisted me in so many critical respects. I am honored by, and deeply appreciative of, your invaluable assistance.

PROLOGUE

Heroica Matamoros, Mexico

eclan Collins sat in the darkness, staring through a hole in the tattered window shade at the narrow street three floors below. His eyes were fixed on the two men walking toward the Hotel Especial, a misnamed one-star hotel on the outskirts of the city. The flickering light from the cerveza sign atop the bodega on the corner illuminated the killers as they strolled by.

The man in the lead, Nacio Leon, was wearing a white linen suit, a matching Panama hat, and a pair of sunglasses, despite the darkness. He was holding a gun in his right hand. Although Collins couldn't see the weapon clearly at this distance, he was certain of the make and model—a Beretta 92FS. Nacio had pressed the business end of the gun against Collins's head less than a month earlier. The killer had been denied the pleasure of pulling the trigger, because Collins had been deemed a necessary asset then. Now he was a liability.

Collins didn't recognize the second man. He was shorter and broader than Nacio and wore an oversized black T-shirt and jeans. Tattoos covered his bald head and the muscular forearm grasping the deadly looking twelve-gauge shotgun resting on his right shoulder. Collins recognized the weapon—a Kel-Tec KSG. It held twelve lethal shells in its dual tubes when fully loaded.

The two men made no effort to conceal their approach. They didn't need to. It was two in the morning, and the third-floor room registered under the name of Declan Collins was on the other side of the hotel. The clerk at the front desk would also have told them that Collins had gone to bed hours earlier with a bottle of Johnny Walker Red. Collins couldn't blame the old man for his lack of discretion. Dying to protect a guest wasn't in his job description.

As Collins watched the two men cross the street, the surreal chain of events leading to this deadly rendezvous raced through his head like a movie watched in fast-forward. Three months ago, Ramon Cayetano, the head of one of Mexico's oldest drug cartels had demanded the impossible: transform one hundred million dollars of illegal drug profits into clean, legitimate funds through a single money laundering transaction. In spite of the network of laws and the legions of law enforcement personnel tasked with thwarting exactly this kind of scheme, Collins had succeeded. Now the drug lord intended to pay for his services in lead instead of gold. Collins walked over to the Glock 17 and the three spare magazines lying on the bed across the room. This alchemist did not intend to go quietly into the night.

ONE

Los Angeles, California

Gregorio Pena looked out the window of the limousine at the skyline as the car traveled through the thinning traffic on the Pasadena Freeway. The cell phone on the seat beside him vibrated, and he quickly picked it up. Keeping Ramon Cayetano waiting was not an option.

"Good evening, sir."

"When are you meeting with the lawyer?"

"Within the hour."

"Where?"

"At a club here in Los Angeles."

"This a waste of time! You will bring this man to me."

"Sir, my relationship is with his friend, Esposito, the securities broker. I—"

"Nacio says this man is a fool. We don't need him. We need the lawyer."

Cayetano's casual reference to Nacio Leon was not just a rebuke. It was a threat. Nacio was the drug lord's most feared enforcer—a proficient killer who thoroughly enjoyed his work.

"Sir, in the end, we may not need him, but the broker is the contact point. I need to use him as a bridge to the lawyer. I also need to ask the lawyer a number of questions. The scheme he devised is clever, even ingenious, but it is also complex. I need to make sure it is . . . viable."

The phone was silent for a long moment. Gregorio knew the drug lord was weighing his options. Cayetano had a team of men in a van outside the club waiting for the go-ahead to kidnap the lawyer and bring him to Mexico—the option urged upon him by Nacio. Although Cayetano had kept the operation a secret, Gregorio had discovered it through his own sources within the cartel.

"Very well, we will do it your way for now. Call me in the morning with a report."

"I will, sir."

Gregorio rested his head on the soft leather headrest and exhaled slowly, trying to relieve the anxiety his doctor said would kill him if he "continued to work in such a high-stress profession." Gregorio smiled ruefully when he remembered the comment. Working for Ramon Cayetano was not a profession; it was an involuntary servitude, one that ended, more often than not, with a bullet and an unmarked grave. Gregorio was all too familiar with his predicament. He knew he was running out of time.

Ramon Cayetano was the scion of a wealthy Mexican family whose father had squandered most of the family fortune before he passed away. Cayetano had used what was left to enter the illegal drug trade. Over the past forty years, he'd made over a billion dollars in profits through a network of suppliers and distributors stretching from South America to the streets of Chicago—a network personally loyal to him.

When the younger, more violent drug lords had threatened Cayetano's business, the cartel lord had played the new entrants against each other and used his extensive law enforcement resources to thwart their shipments. Although profits had waned during these struggles, over time Cayetano had always come out ahead. But in the last five years, the game had changed. Natural selection had left only two other cartels, and one, the Nauyacas had decided the road to supremacy lay in the confiscation of Cayetano's empire.

In the past year, the Nauyacas had killed more than half of the suppliers and distributors in Cayetano's network, and many others had switched allegiances to stay alive. The drug lord's losses in the realm of governmental influence had been equally devastating. The army of judges and bureaucrats who'd served at his beck and call for decades had sensed Cayetano's coming demise and become unresponsive, or they'd joined the ranks of the enemy. Just a month earlier, a judge under the control of the Nauyacas had issued an order seizing one of Cayetano's largest cash accounts. Ramon Cayetano had received the message: It was time to get his remaining hoard of cash out of Mexico.

The drug lord still had sufficient resources to accomplish this end—bankers, lawyers, accountants, and a host of other minions— but none had been able to offer him what he so desperately needed: the perfect money laundering scheme. Cayetano's acres of cash were the problem. Large cash deposits invariably activated the international regulatory regime designed to track terrorist funding and drug money. What Cayetano needed was a scheme that would enable him to move cash from his warehouses in Mexico to safe, reputable depository institutions in the United States without drawing regulatory scrutiny and seizure.

The drug lord had tried laundering these funds through check cashing businesses, small retail stores, casinos, and, most recently, Blackpool Studios, the film production outfit where Gregorio served as the general manager. These efforts had only been marginally successful. Three million dollars had been laundered, but the process had taken over two years, and the costs, in the form of taxes, bribes, and acquisition-related fees, had consumed over 40 percent of the incoming cash. Worse, several months ago the excessive cash deposits from one business had sparked an investigation by the United States Treasury Department, resulting in the loss of the cartel's entire investment.

Gregorio's intimate familiarity with Ramon Cayetano's problems, and the measure of trust he'd been accorded by the drug lord, had a long and painful history. His mother had worked in the drug lord's household as a maid, and Cayetano had groomed her precocious child as a future cartel asset without her consent. In time, the drug lord's investment had paid off. Gregorio had graduated magna cum laude from Harvard, and he'd obtained an MBA in accounting from Wharton. After spending two years working for a top international accounting firm after graduation, Cayetano had ordered his indentured minion to return to Mexico and work exclusively on Cayetano family matters.

At first, Gregorio's work had been limited to routine accounting matters, but as the cartel's existential crisis grew more severe, his responsibilities had steadily increased. A year ago, he'd been assigned the ultimate task: transport the family's hoard of illegal cash from Mexico to a safe venue and convert the cash into legitimate investible funds.

The choice of where to move the money had been an easy one—the United States. Laundering the money had been more difficult. The US financial system was not only highly regulated, but industry players were constantly audited by a series of federal agencies looking for illicit cash contributions. Then Gregorio met Matt Esposito.

Every year, the top players in the film industry attended a private party at a twenty-thousand-square-foot mansion in Malibu. Not surprisingly, Blackpool's executives were not on the invitation list. A fifty-thousand-dollar bribe had upgraded the company's industry cred, securing an invite for himself, Nacio, and Adriana. The price had been steep, but the investment would be worth it if Blackpool could gain access to the more lucrative content opportunities. Once the company achieved a modest production track record, it could begin to record millions in phantom profits on its books and records—profits backfilled with Cayetano drug money.

Matt Esposito had also found a way to obtain an invite to the party, although Gregorio suspected he'd paid far less than Blackpool for the privilege. The broker had cornered Gregorio just as he was about to leave. After a few pleasantries, the broker had launched into a description of the "killer" screenplay written by his best friend, a lawyer named Declan Collins. The story was woven around a money laundering scheme involving bankrupt corporations, phantom profits, and the manipulation of net operating losses.

Although Gregorio had listened politely to Esposito's pitch, he'd initially dismissed the complicated scheme as implausible. The next morning he'd reread the script Esposito had given him and investigated the lawyer's background. He decided Declan Collins was a most clever man, but he was not convinced. Then he'd received a call from Nacio that changed his mind.

As the limo approached the nightclub where the meeting was scheduled, Gregorio hoped Collins was as talkative and boastful as his friend Esposito. He needed to get the lawyer to explain his money laundering scheme in detail, without arousing his suspicions. If the scheme was viable, the Cayetano family could well have the lifeline it needed.

"Your life, Mr. Collins, is about to get . . . interesting," Gregorio said aloud with a hint of regret.

The phone vibrating in his hand interrupted Gregorio's thoughts. "It's Adriana. Where are you?"

Adriana's tone was curt and impatient, but then, as a member of the Cayetano family, she considered herself royalty, whereas Gregorio was just the hired help. He ignored the insult. In Ramon Cayetano's world, Adriana was no more than a useful tool, like him. Her role in tonight's drama, that of an attractive and potentially available temptress, confirmed this status. Gregorio suspected Adriana's antagonism was driven, in part, by this realization.

"I will be there in a moment. Where are you, Adriana?"

"In the Maserati, a block away."

"Good. Pull up to the valet. I will be right behind you."

"You had better be."

Gregorio smiled wistfully at the threat in her voice. *Arrogant fool, if we fail tonight, both of us may end up in the same grave, in spite of your foul lineage.*

TWO

Los Angeles, California

The line of people waiting outside the nightclub was over forty yards long, and most of the would-be patrons looked like they'd just walked off the catwalk of an elite fashion show. Declan Collins wasn't surprised. It was a Friday night, and four of the top five LA entertainment blogs had recently designated the Arezzo the hottest nightclub in the city.

Collins eased the black Porsche Panamera into the private lot behind the club and parked it beside Tony Lentino's red Lamborghini. Lentino had opened the club six months after the jury in his tax fraud case had deemed Collins's defense more persuasive than the case presented by the prosecution. Had it gone the other way Tony would be sitting in a ten-by-twelve cell for a decade instead of making fifty thousand a month running a nightclub.

Collins nodded to the six-five, two-hundred-fifty-pound bouncer outside the club's back door and walked up the stairs to the suite of offices on the second floor. He stopped in front of the mirrored door at the top and stared at his reflection. The lean six-foot man returning his stare through a pair of striking blue eyes was wearing a dark gray suit, a white button-down shirt, and a dark magenta silk tie. At thirty-seven, Collins still had a full head of brown hair and a face that would have been considered handsome but for the scar under his left eye and the twice-broken nose—souvenirs from two decades of ice hockey. His last girlfriend had affectionately called him ruggedly attractive.

The prominent dark shadows under his eyes bothered him, but Collins decided it could be worse. He'd just finished his third tax fraud trial in six months—another acquittal despite the fact his client was as guilty as sin. The verdict didn't bother him. In his mind, keeping a tax cheat out of jail wasn't the same thing as putting a murderer or rapist back on the streets. His clients paid millions in taxes; they just didn't pay as many millions as the government demanded. This course of conduct was criminal if the underpayment was the result of an intentional fraud, but reasonable minds could always differ on the element of intent. After all, the Internal Revenue Code was over six thousand pages long. Who could fault a taxpayer for failing to understand all of its complex nuances?

Collins had never been uncomfortable in this morally relativistic world until yesterday when he'd found a photograph on the windshield of his car. It was a picture of two teenage girls lying in a pool of blood. Their throats had been cut. There was a handwritten note on the back of the photo: "The handiwork of your client Igor Bykov. These girls were killed in Budapest a month after YOU set him free. By the way, Bykov's one of the biggest human traffickers in Eastern Europe. Interpol says he's done this before. Live with that karma." The note was signed by Sarah Dubois, the prosecutor on the losing side of Bykov's tax fraud case.

Collins had initially dismissed Dubois's accusation. *Bloomberg* and *Barron's* had described Bykov as a Russian oil and gas oligarch with a billion-dollar net worth. Yes, the Russian had always been accompanied by a beautiful young woman when they'd met, sometimes more than one, but that wasn't unusual. Billionaires attract beautiful people.

Contrary to Dubois's unspoken accusation, Collins had not known Bykov was a human trafficker. He wouldn't have represented him if he had. Dubois's moral zinger also ignored the fact that Collins wasn't the only top draw legal gun in Los Angeles. If he'd passed on the case, Bykov would have found another expensive defense lawyer and the result could well have been the same.

Collins had considered throwing the photograph in the trash but found he couldn't do it. It was still in the right pocket of his suit jacket. He unconsciously started to reach for it when the door in front of him suddenly opened.

"Declan! What the hell are you doing out here? I've been watching you on the camera. You've been staring at the door for five minutes!"

Collins looked up at Tony Lentino, one of his oldest friends from Boston. Tony was five-eight, 170 pounds, and his face looked like the bust of Julius Caesar in the Louvre—strong, formidable, and intense. He routinely boasted he was in better shape at the age of forty-two than he'd been when he was in the Marines. Collins was skeptical, but he knew Tony was in better shape than he was. They'd both run in a 5K charity race last month, and Tony's nineteen-minute time had bested his own by ten seconds.

"Sorry, T. Just tired, I guess."

Tony opened the door for his friend and held out his hand. "You look beat. Hell, I thought you was one of those raccoons that used to run around the old neighborhood on garbage day."

Collins smiled and shook Tony's outstretched hand. "Relax, T. I'm good."

Tony pulled Collins into a bear hug and guided him to a door down the hall. "That's BS. Get in here."

Tony pushed open the door and waved him into his office. The walls were plastered with sports memorabilia interspersed with pictures of Tony posing with various celebrities. Tony took two bottles of Birra del Borgo out of a refrigerator, handed one to Collins, and pointed to the leather couch across from his own oversized leather chair.

"Sit and tell me what's going on, and don't give me that 'I'm okay' BS."

Collins eased back into the cool dark leather and stared up at the New England Patriots logo on the ceiling.

"You remember the Russian guy I represented a while back?"

"Yeah. You got him off, just like me, but I betcha he paid you a whole lot more than I did."

Collins nodded. "Yeah, I did, and he did. And then he flew back to Europe and killed two teenage girls."

Lentino leaned forward. "Are you shitting me?"

Collins shook his head. "No, I'm not. The US attorney on the other side of the case put a photo of their dead bodies on my windshield yesterday with a note. Apparently, the guy was a big trafficker. I tell you, T, I didn't know. I wouldn't—"

"That's crap. You just did your job. You're not responsible for what happens after that. No way."

Collins stared at Tony for a moment. "Yeah, I know, but I also know the guy was guilty, and I'm the guy who got him off. If . . . if those were my kids lying in that alley, I'd see it differently."

Tony looked away for a moment. When he did, Collins remembered Tony had a daughter on the other side of the country. His ex-wife had obtained sole custody, due, in no small measure, to the skills of a cunning lawyer like Declan Collins.

"Hey, Tony. I'm sorry about bringing this up."

Tony chuckled. "Relax, I've been listening to your crap for thirty years. Don't worry about it. By the way, Esposito's waiting for you in the reserved section. Says he's got big news. He wouldn't tell what it is. I'm sure it's more BS. That guy's full of it."

Collins smiled, finished the rest of his beer, and stood up. Tony stood up as well and slapped him on the shoulder.

"My dad used to say, 'Life isn't fair; it just is.' Never made any friggin' sense to me, but there it is."

Collins chuckled as he walked out the door. "Your dad was a great guy, T—whatever it means."

As Collins started down the stairs to the main floor of the club, his eyes strayed to the dance floor where a twenty-something couple right out of the pages of GQ magazine were undulating inches from each other in perfect rhythm amidst the sea of dancers. He envied their escape from reality, however momentary.

The bouncer at the bottom of the stairs gave him a friendly nod as he removed the golden chain barring access to the second floor. Collins returned the nod and looked over at the reserved section of the club, where a decent table went for a grand on a Friday night. Matt Esposito had taken one of the prime spots on the raised level in the back. Matt would have asked for the spot using Collins's name, without permission, knowing Tony's guys wouldn't say no.

Matt's family had lived three doors down from Collins in Boston, and the two of them had been friends since grade school. Matt's dad had worked for Boston College, driving the Zamboni machine around the ice rink during the hockey games and on weekends, when the arena was rented out by club teams. After the games were over, the two of them would spend an hour or two racing up and back on the ice, playing a two-man hockey game. That ice time and a passion for the game had made them the two best players in the metro league every year. Boston Latin had taken notice and given them both scholarships.

The two of them had made the All-State hockey team in their junior and senior years, but Matt had always been the better player. His skills as a goalie had earned him the nickname "The Fly Catcher." Boston College had offered him a full ride. The head coach had made noises about making Collins an offer as well, but Collins had known it was only available if it was a package deal. Matt was the real prize. When he'd accepted an invite from Harvard, the awkward situation had been laid to rest.

Collins knew the well-dressed bodybuilder-type standing near the entrance to the VIP section, but Matt called out to him anyway. "Yo, Donny. He's with me." The bouncer smiled and waved him past.

Matt pointed to the seat across from him. "Take a load off, old man. I ordered you a beer and a shot."

Matt was about the same height as Collins, but he was broader and carried an extra thirty pounds in the waist. He had an impressive square jaw, a full mouth, a broad prominent nose, and a full head of perfectly coiffed black hair. His charcoal gray bespoke suit was way outside even Matt's lavish clothing budget, but since the tailor was a friend, an accommodation had been reached. With Matt, there was always a side deal of one kind or another.

"Your beneficence is appreciated," Collins said with a hint of sarcasm, knowing Tony comped the drinks.

As he sat down in the chair, a waitress in a skin-tight black dress put a glass of beer and a shot of whiskey on the table. Collins nodded his thanks and took a drink of beer.

"You know me, always looking out for the common folk."

Collins smiled. "Yeah, right. So, what's the big secret? Another party in Vegas? If it is, count me—"

Matt scoffed. "Don't worry. I wouldn't invite a bum like you to one of my parties."

"So, the last time I crashed the party and paid for it too?"

Matt chuckled. "Relax, I'll pay you back. I'm getting a big commission next week. That being said, you owe me big time, or you will, soon."

Collins took a drink, preparing himself for one of Matt's convoluted arguments that always ended with the same conclusion—Collins owed Matt "big time" for something or other.

Matt smiled and glanced around the room as if expecting a wave of adulation from a wider audience. "I sold your screenplay! I mean our screenplay. I was a contributor after all."

Collins raised a skeptical eyebrow. "You suggested the title, Matt, that's it. And by the way, this is the fourth time you allegedly sold it."

"Yeah, but it was a kick-ass title—*The Alchemist's Run*. I think that's what drew the guy in."

"What guy?"

Matt leaned forward as if communicating a secret. "This guy I met—"

"At a party on the West side or downtown or in Vegas—"

Matt rapped his knuckles on the table. "Hey, how about a little respect, and the party was in Malibu, wiseass. Now, listen to me. This is the real deal. The guy is coming here tonight."

Collins threw back the shot of whiskey and shook his head in derision. "Matt, the guy just wanted a VIP pass to the club! And you got him one, right?"

Collins could tell by the look on Matt's face that he did.

"Look, Matt, I'm beat. You do the pitch. I'm going—"

"I can't do it, Declan! *You* have talk to the guy. He went to Harvard about the same time you did. He was in the MBA program. I told him all about you. When we spoke on the phone yesterday, he wanted to drill down on the tax and finance nuances of the scheme in the screenplay. He had questions I couldn't answer. He needs to talk to you."

Collins shook his head. "Matt—"

"Listen to me! The studio this guy works for, Blackpool, is real. It's new, but it's real. They have options on five or six other screenplays. I checked with a couple of guys in the space. Gregorio—he's an executive VP with Blackpool—is going to be here in five minutes. Spend an hour with him. That's all, okay?"

Collins hesitated for a moment and then raised his hands in submission. "Okay, okay. An hour it is, but no more."

Matt stood up, visibly relieved. "Great. I'll be back. Nature calls."

Collins watched Matt ease his way through the crowd to the men's room. His friend was about forty pounds over his college weight, but he still moved with the ease and grace of a natural athlete. In his junior year, Matt had been ranked as one of the top three goalies in the country by the pros, and then the accident had happened.

The two of them had left a bar in Chestnut Hill at 1:00 a.m., a week after the last game of the season. There had been a foot of snow on the ground, and Matt had bet Collins ten bucks he could beat him to the car, which was two blocks away. They'd hit the second street at a flat-out sprint, when a truck had come out of nowhere. Matt, who was a step ahead of Collins, saw the threat a half-second before Collins did. Instead of getting out the way himself, he'd slowed and shoved Collins toward the sidewalk.

The fender of the old truck had clipped Matt just slightly as it passed, but it was enough to knock him off balance. He'd crashed full speed into the bumper of a parked car. At first, Matt shook it off and said he was fine, but the next morning he could hardly walk. The X-ray at Mass General showed a fractured hip. The injury kept him off the ice for his entire senior season and took him out of the pro draft. Although Matt had worked hard to get back in shape, after the accident he wasn't on the pro teams' radar. His pro career had ended before it began.

When Collins had tried to thank Matt for saving his life, his friend insisted he'd been trying to push him under the truck so he could win the race. Collins knew otherwise. But for that shove, Collins would have been the one hit by the truck, and Matt would have been a professional hockey player. Collins suspected Matt was being played by this Gregorio, but Matt was his oldest friend, and he did owe him, big time.

————

As Matt returned from the restroom, he caught the eye of a tall blonde woman who appeared to be in her early thirties. She was sitting at the bar talking to another woman about the same age. The woman was attractive but not beautiful. The dress she was wearing was expensive but not stratospheric, and she didn't have male company. These characteristics placed the woman in what he called the potentially available category. He nodded and smiled at her. She returned the smile but kept talking to her friend. Matt considered it a good sign. He had a similar exchange with two other women before he returned to the table.

Collins raised an eyebrow as Matt sat down. "Marking our territory, are we?"

Matt smiled and held up his hands in mock protest. "Just being friendly."

"Right."

Matt glanced at the women he'd made eye contact with and noted that the blonde at the bar was looking in his direction. She looked away when their eyes met. He smiled. If she was still there when the meeting was over, he intended to pay her a visit.

His eyes strayed to a couple walking through the VIP entrance on the far side of the club, and he turned to Collins, a broad smile on his face.

"Take a look at the couple coming through the VIP door. It's Gregorio, the studio exec. The gorgeous babe with him is an actress, Adriana. I met her at the party. See, this is the real deal."

Collins looked over at the approaching couple. The tall, svelte man in the lead was in his early thirties, but his conservative hairstyle and dignified mien made him seem a decade older. There was hint of a smile on his face as he glided through the lively crowd, nodding politely here and there to the patrons who glanced in his direction. For a moment, the man's bearing, handsome features, and the traditional cut of his dark gray suit elicited a mental comparison—he reminded Collins of a Hispanic Cary Grant.

Collins only caught a glimpse of the woman in the man's wake. It was enough. She was a seductive beauty who seemed to revel in the power she held over the lesser men and women staring at her voluptuous body, flawless bronzed skin, and mesmerizing face. When her eyes found Collins, there was a hint of recognition before she smiled and looked away.

As a trial lawyer, Collins was in the sales business as well as the legal business. His customers were judges and juries. Over time, he'd learned a critical skill: the ability to quickly take the measure of people. His read of the man and woman approaching the table was they were after something, and they intended to get it. He was still skeptical, but he decided there was at least a chance they really had an interest in the screenplay.

As Collins stood up to greet Gregorio and the woman, Matt cuffed him on the shoulder. "Admit it. You're a believer."

Collins gripped the table for a moment as the two beers and the shot of whiskey caught up with him. "Let's see what they have to say."

Matt strode over to Gregorio and engulfed the smaller man's hand in his own as if they had known each other for decades. "Gregorio! Great to see you again."

Gregorio smiled warmly as he shook Matt's hand. Collins sensed the other man's display of pleasure was a well-practiced façade, but he was unable to gain any insight into what he was really thinking.

"It is good to see you as well, Matt."

The man turned to the woman on his right. "Adriana, you will remember Matt Esposito. We met—"

"At the party in Malibu. How could I forget?"

The woman's tone was warm and welcoming, but she wasn't as skilled as Gregorio at masking her inner thoughts. Collins could sense an element of scorn within.

Matt started to reach for the woman's hand, but she deftly evaded him by walking around the table toward Collins, as if she'd missed the gesture. Matt called over her shoulder, "Adriana and Gregorio, this is Declan Collins, my oldest friend and the smartest attorney in LA."

Collins smiled politely. "I'm not the smartest lawyer in LA. Not even close. However, it's a pleasure to meet you."

Adriana responded with an alluring smile. "The pleasure is mine."

The subtle invitation in the woman's eyes led Collins to check an internal box. Adriana wasn't Gregorio's date. She was there to help him get whatever he was after. For some reason, the thought was unsettling.

During the first round of drinks, the conversation roved over a number of topics, and Collins found himself impressed by Gregorio's intellect and charm and his ability to deftly guide the conversation to the topics he wanted to hear about.

"So, Mr. Collins, what induced a lawyer to write a screenplay about a money laundering scheme?"

Collins smiled. "Call it a confluence of fate. I took a class on writing screenplays during a summer session at Harvard. I needed the credit, and it just happened to fit into my schedule. I liked it but never thought about it much until a year ago when I had to defend a client against a money laundering charge. The scheme the client employed was simplistic, but he got away with it for years. After the case was over, I decided to come up with my own scheme and write about it."

Matt jumped in before Gregorio could ask another question, his eyes on Adriana. "The title of the screenplay was my idea."

Gregorio smiled and nodded in his direction. "Very impressive."

"Did you win the trial?" Adriana asked.

Collins glanced over at her. "The jury acquitted on all charges but one. It was a minor offense. He spent a year in Lompoc instead of a decade or two in a less . . . accommodating venue."

Gregorio pulled a golden pen and a small notepad out of his suit pocket. "Do you mind if I take notes, Declan?"

"Go right ahead."

Gregorio made a note on the pad before continuing. "If we take this to the next level, I will have to pitch your screenplay to a group of investors. That constituency will have a lot of questions about the viability of the scheme in the story. When you answer my next series of questions, I want you to assume the screenplay gets made into a movie and the first showing is to a theater full of the government regulators charged with thwarting this kind of scheme. With that qualifier, tell me why the money laundering scheme you came up with is plausible?"

Collins leaned back in his chair, wishing he'd ordered coffee instead of another round of drinks. "Because the scheme in the story walks the money through the least likely doorway."

"And that is?" Adriana asked.

Matt pounced on her silken inquiry. "Through one or more corporations in bankruptcy, right?"

Collins nodded. "Yes, corporations operating under the protection of Chapter 11 of the bankruptcy code."

Gregorio tapped the notepad in front of him with the pen as he spoke. "I read the screenplay, but can you give me an example of how the scheme would play out in real life?"

"Sure. Within the next ninety days, a large retail firm is expected to file Chapter 11. Let's call it Retail One. The company has over five hundred stores, and it's currently generating about nine hundred million in sales annually. Unfortunately, it's also losing about fifty to one hundred million a year in cash. When the company is dumped into Chapter 11, the case will become a liquidation, not a reorganization."

Collins took a drink from his half-full glass of beer. "In this kind of big retail case, the bankruptcy lawyers will get court approval to run a going-out of-business sale. The people who run these sales are masters at pushing massive amounts of cheap product through the existing distribution platform in a short period of time—say two or three months. They advertise like crazy using a blood-in-the-water marketing strategy. Customers pour in looking for a once-in-a-life-time bargain."

Collins tapped the table with his index finger. "That's the magic washing machine used in the screenplay. In sixty days, hundreds of million dollars will pour through Retail One's stores. A high percentage of those transactions will be in cash. Accounting mistakes are made during these giant sales. Everyone expects it. A skilled operator in control of a company like that could easily book fifty million dollars in bogus sales. This same operator would then bring in fifty million dollars in dirty cash and dump that money in the company bank account. As long as the incoming dirty cash ties out to the bogus cash sales booked on the accounting system, those dollars become clean legit money."

Gregorio stared at Collins for a moment, as if pondering the concept. "What about taxes? Corporate tax rates in the US are high. Does the script deal with this . . . problem in any respect?"

Collins waved his hand in a dismissive gesture. "Taxes are not a problem. Retail One, like most companies in bankruptcy, has huge accrued net operating losses. These NOLs will wash out any federal or state tax liability attributable to the bogus sales. The issue isn't perfectly clean, because of the change in control rules, but there's a . . . workaround. I only mention this in passing in the script, but it's there."

"What about sales taxes?"

Collins shook his head. "Can't do anything about that. The party laundering the money has to eat the sales taxes on the bogus sales."

Gregorio's next question was posed a moment after Collins finished: "Any other costs?"

Collins nodded. "Possibly. It depends on how you manage the thing."

"Enlighten me . . . and the money people. These are the kinds of questions they will ask. It's the plausibility issue."

Collins pulled a silver pen out of the inside breast pocket of his suit jacket and drew a circle on the white paper napkin next to his beer and labeled it "secured debt."

"To do this kind of deal, you'd have to get control of the secured debt position in the case—the claim held by the lender financing Retail One's inventory and receivables. A good negotiator could buy this position for a steep discount."

He drew a second circle on the napkin and labeled it "lawyers." He tapped the second circle with his pen. "While you're in the process of cutting your deal with the secured lender, you have to concurrently cut deals with Retail One's bankruptcy lawyer and the lawyer representing the unsecured creditors' committee in the case. Ideally, you want to have those locked down before you invest your dollars in the discounted secured note."

Gregorio nodded slowly.

"The film version of the screenplay won't get bogged down in the minutiae. However, to assuage the inquiring minds of the accountants who may represent the capital source on this production, can you provide me more . . . clarity on this lock down, as you say?"

As Collins took a drink of his beer, he glanced over at Adriana without turning his head. Her eyes were watching the dance floor, but she made a small smile, without looking in his direction, letting him know she'd noticed the glance.

He put the glass of beer down and tapped the napkin with his pen. "Yeah . . . sure. Let's use some numbers to put a finer point on it. Assume the bank with the senior position in the Retail One case is owed one hundred million. If the company completely craters, the bank will be lucky to get thirty cents on the dollar, and then only if they spend a lot of time and money picking up the pieces. That's not what banks do, so getting rid of the loan will be job one for whoever's in charge of the credit. This gives the money launderer a golden opportunity. He offers to buy the bank's position at thirty cents on the dollar—cash payable in thirty days. That'll get the bank's attention. The bank counters at eighty cents, and you negotiate it out at forty. However, you tell the bank the buyout is contingent upon you cutting a deal with the unsecured creditors' committee."

Gregorio shook his head, a confused look on his face. "If the lender has a lien on all of the company's assets and it's about to take a haircut on the loan, the unsecured creditors are out of the money. They're not entitled to anything."

Collins chuckled. "Now, you're getting down into the minutiae. Here's the reality: You're right, but the lawyers representing Retail One and the unsecured creditors won't accept that."

"What? Why not?"

"Because they won't get paid.

"But there's an easy fix. You tell the lawyers you'll set aside a pot of money to pay their fees, and you agree to leave enough money on the table so they can promise a small dividend to unsecured creditors. Stated otherwise, you bribe them to buy peace."

Gregorio pondered the concept in silence for a moment before nodding his understanding and gesturing toward the napkin in front of Collins. "Let's get back to the plausibility factor. The money people—the people who we both need to do this deal—will point out the big hole in your scheme. If I'm the source of the dirty money being laundered, I'm going to want to stay out of the limelight, but at the same time, I'm going to want to retain control. How do you thread that needle? Please, walk me through the details of the corporate control mechanisms."

Collins flipped the napkin over and drew a circle and wrote the letters *HF* in the center. "First, you need to buy the senior position through an entity that appears legit. You do that by reactivating the shell of a defunct Cayman Island hedge fund."

Gregorio shook his head. "It won't work. Any decent analyst can check out the owner of the fund and trace the illicit source of the funds. Then it's game over."

Collins nodded. "That's if they look. Remember, this is bankruptcy land. The regulatory folks don't go there. But let's say someone in the SEC or Treasury takes a passing interest. A good lawyer can create a daisy chain of corporate entities that will make the ownership of the hedge fund so murky—"

Gregorio shook his head again. "Someone, a person, has to be at the end of that ownership chain, and—"

Collins held up a hand. "There will be someone, Gregorio. But he or she will be unknown. You see, the ticket is to put a Panama corporation with bearer stock at the very end of the corporate daisy chain."

"Bearer?" The question came from Adriana.

"Yeah," Matt answered. "The stock is issued to the bearer, as in whoever is bearing or carrying the stock certificate at any point in time. So whoever physically holds the stock owns the corporation at that instant in time. If this napkin is the stock," he said as he ceremonially handed it to Adriana, "I just gave you title to the corporation. If you hand it to Gregorio, he's the new owner. And so on. That's how it works."

"Why would anyone want a corporation like that?" Adriana said skeptically. "Anyone could steal it by stealing the stock."

Gregorio answered: "Anonymity. Ownership can be moved constantly."

Adriana leaned back in her seat, a look of understanding on her face. She gave Matt an enticing smile. Matt returned the smile, but Adriana's eyes had already returned to the dance floor.

"What is the next step, Mr. Collins?" Gregorio asked.

"Once the hedge fund acquires the bank position for forty mil, you advance ten million to Retail One through the bank line as part of a court-approved financing deal. The order not only recites the terms of the loan, it also approves the deal with the committee. That deal allows the money launderer's management people to take over Retail One's top management spots—so you can control the accounting data."

Gregorio nodded. "So now I'm out fifty million, plus the money set aside for the lawyers and the unsecured creditors. How do I get my money back and, more importantly, walk new money through this washing machine?"

"The going-out-of-business sale will generate the cash. During the sixty-day sales push, the firm running the sale will double or even triple the company's normal sales volume. Between the inventory on-site and the new inventory dumped into the mix, you should have no problem generating enough cash to pay operating costs and repay yourself the money you advanced. As for the bogus sales claimed on books—those sales are backfilled with the dirty money."

Gregorio jotted down notes as Collins spoke. After several moments he leaned back in his chair, spinning his golden pen between his thumb and forefinger for several seconds. "How do you manage the bogus sales?"

"Remember, the court order approving your deal gives you control of the books and records. Any decent computer expert can make that happen. You selectively gross up the inventory numbers at each of the store locations and add extra sales to the daily accounting entries. No one will see it except the people who control the accounting system—your people."

Gregorio leaned back in his seat and smiled slowly. "A very clever hypothetical, Mr. Collins. But a few more questions, and I know I'm wading into weeds, but humor me. I'm a former accountant. What about the IRS? What if they audit the books three years later and find this overstatement of revenues?"

Collins shook his head. "It won't happen. Before the end of the case, Retail One will file the final tax returns on behalf of the bankruptcy estate. Those returns will be hundreds of pages long, and the IRS will have sixty days to object. If they don't, and they almost never do, Retail One is in the clear. The IRS and the state agencies are bound."

Gregorio shook his head. "Mr. Collins, a skilled team could change the electronic records, but the paper records, the purchase orders, invoices, receipts. . . . When someone comes to look at them, those records—"

"Will no longer exist," Collins said. "The order confirming Retail One's plan of reorganization will incorporate a standard provision allowing the company to destroy all paper records to reduce storage costs. This will leave only the electronic records, and they'll say just what the money launderer wants them to say."

Gregorio was silent for a moment. It was as if he were struggling to find a hole in the scheme. He raised a finger as though he'd found the defect. "How would the money launderers get their money out of Retail One?"

Collins shook his head. "They don't need to. Under the deal with the committee, the plan of reorganization pays the five-cent dividend to the unsecured creditors, cancels all Retail One's common stock, and new stock is reissued to the hedge fund. At the end of the day, the bad guys will control a hedge fund with a bucketload of clean cash. All they need to do is change the corporate name from Retail One to Investment One and start investing in new businesses, or whatever else it is they want to do. I think I mentioned this in the screenplay."

Gregorio wrote furiously on his notepad for several moments before looking up. "One more question. Is there a potential sequel here?"

Collins shook his head in confusion. "Sequel?"

"Yes. Assume the film is picked up by Netflix or one of the other streaming services and they're looking for a season two. In your hypothetical, the bad guys launder fifty million dollars of drug money. What if we increase that number to one hundred million? Would one transaction work, or would this be something where the same group might have to come back in season two to finish the job through a second transaction?"

Collins answered the question without thinking about the level of specificity in the inquiry. "You could do it in one fell swoop with a big case like Retail One, particularly if the sale ran during the holiday season. But you wouldn't. Too much risk. Better to walk the money through two or three bankruptcy cases over a period of a year or two. So, yeah, if the bad guys have to launder one hundred mil, you might need a sequel or second season."

Gregorio leaned forward, his eyes on Collins when he asked another question. "But a one-shot deal over a two- to three-month period *is* a possibility?"

Collins glanced over at Matt, whose eyes pleaded with him to say yes. "Yeah, sure. It's possible."

Gregorio stared at Collins for a long moment, and a satisfied smile came to his face. "Thank you, Mr. Collins. That was very enlightening."

Collins waved off the comment, but he was surprised at the relief in Gregorio's eyes. "You're welcome."

Collins was even more surprised by Gregorio's next question: "Oh, and by the way, would you and Mr. Esposito have time to meet with the money people in Mexico to discuss the sale of your rights, if they decide to go forward with the film?"

Matt jumped on the possible invite. "Sure, we can get down there. Just say when."

THREE

Los Angeles Gun Club

Steve Mantle, the range master at the Los Angeles Gun Club, watched the woman eject and deftly reload the magazine of the Glock 19 after firing fifteen rounds into the paper target at the far end of the range. The shots were fired at one-second intervals. This was the fifth time she'd replaced the target and emptied the magazine downrange.

After the woman packed up and left, Mantle walked over to the trash can and pulled out the paper targets. The bullet grouping was dead center, every hole within a three-inch circumference. He dropped the targets back into the can and walked over to the sign-in sheet and glanced at the name of the shooter—Anna Torres (Guest). Under the employer section she listed the FBI. Mantle glanced toward the exit door and whispered in appreciation, "You can shoot at this range any time you like, Agent Torres."

Los Angeles, California

Anna Torres walked over to the reception desk on the ground floor of the Los Angeles office of the Federal Bureau of Investigation and held up her badge to the middle-aged woman behind the desk. "Good morning. Agent Torres. I'm here to see Michael Sontag, the SAIC."

The woman pulled up a screen on her computer and shook her head. "Sorry, Agent . . ."

"Torres."

"I don't see you on his calendar."

"I'm from the Dallas office. I know I have a meeting at 8:30 a.m. Can you call and check?"

The woman reluctantly picked up the phone and dialed a number. There was a brief exchange, and the woman turned back to her. "Mr. Sontag is waiting for you on the fifth floor."

When the door to the elevator opened, Michael Sontag, the special agent in charge of the Los Angeles office, was waiting there. Anna recognized him from the bio she'd pulled up on the bureau's website. The SAIC was fifty-one years old, six-two, and a lean 190 pounds. His short-cropped blond hair framed a handsome face dominated by two piercing blue-gray eyes. Sontag smiled and held out his hand. "Agent Torres, I presume."

Anna took his hand and shook it firmly. "Yes, sir."

"Very good."

Sontag stepped past her and pressed the elevator button and gestured for her to enter when the door opened.

As she stepped past him, Anna noted the scar running just above Sontag's left eye. It was referenced in his bio but not the one available on the bureau's website. Two years out of the academy Sontag had been involved in a shootout with a white supremacist group in Washington State. The scar was from a Remington 700 Tactical fired from a half a mile away. A fraction of an inch to the right and SAIC wouldn't be standing there. The agent next to Sontag had not been so lucky. The next round had killed him instantly. Sontag had patched himself up and continued to return fire until the shooter was taken out by an aerial sniper.

When they entered the elevator, Sontag waived a key fob at the security screen and pressed a gray button on the left side of the panel. The elevator started upward, passing the twenty-fifth floor, which Anna understood to be the building's top floor.

The door opened a moment later, and Sontag turned to her and smiled. "Utility floor. Access is restricted, but rank has its privileges."

Anna followed the SAIC past the generators and exhaust vents to an open space by a window that was rarely cleaned. A folding table with four chairs was pushed up against the window. Sontag gestured to one of the chairs as he walked around to the other side of the table.

"Please, sit."

Anna glanced around quickly as she sat down, confused by the location of the meeting.

Sontag looked across the floor at the maze of machinery, ducts, pipes, and electrical conduits that filled most of the floor. "The domain of the anonymous men and women who keep this building running every day. This is where they eat lunch when they're working up here. I make a point of having lunch with them every now and again. There are over one hundred FBI personnel in this building, which makes it an attractive target for our enemies. If I wanted to do something untoward to this fine edifice, infiltrating the maintenance crew would be an ideal place to start."

When his gaze returned to Anna, he smiled disarmingly. "Relax, Agent Torres. This floor was swept this morning for anything untoward, large or small."

Anna smiled. "Understood, sir."

The SAIC glanced quickly at his watch. "You probably want to know why you were reassigned to this office. Don't worry. It's only temporary, and it has nothing to do with your past performance. You come with glowing recommendations. What you bring to the table, along with your particular linguistic skills, is anonymity. You're going to be working with a special unit located in the city of Chula Vista. It's about two hours south. The bureau is running an undercover operation there, a top-secret operation. You will report to the agent in charge of the operation, Tony Ortega, in three hours. This is the address of the meet." Sontag slid a small piece of paper across the table.

"It's a parking garage next to a commercial building in the downtown area. Park on the third floor. Agent Ortega will be waiting there for you in a white van. He's easy to recognize—looks like a fire hydrant with a bald head and mustache."

Anna smiled at the description as she stared at the address. She committed it to memory and then pushed the paper back across the table to Sontag.

"I will let Agent Ortega brief you on the specifics of the operation and what your role will be. You are not to discuss this assignment with *anyone* other than Agent Ortega, the other members of the unit, and me. And yes, that includes the SAIC in the Dallas office, if he asks."

"Can I ask you a question, sir?"

"You can ask," Sontag said evenly.

"Why am I being briefed here?"

Sontag hesitated before answering. "A very sophisticated listening device was discovered in the office yesterday, and for reasons I cannot disclose, we have reason to believe it may have been smuggled into this building by the people who are the target of the operation in Chula Vista. You are being briefed here because, as I said, I know this particular spot was electronically swept an hour ago."

Sontag's answers and the location of the operation gave Anna a pretty good insight into the undercover unit's focus—one or more of the Mexican drug cartels. She spoke Spanish fluently, her master's degree was in Mexican and Central American history, and she had written a report a month ago about the rise of the Nauyacas Mexico's newest and most violent Mexican drug cartel. Sontag's last comments before they entered the elevator confirmed this assessment.

"One other thing, Agent Torres. Actually, make that two. Dress down a wee bit for this assignment. You want to go for the anonymous, mobile look. Second, you will carry at least five magazines for your service weapon at all times."

Anna nodded. "Yes, sir."

FOUR

Punta Maldonado, Mexico

The Beechcraft Premier taxied over to the small hangar at the east end of the small airstrip where a dark gray Suburban was waiting. Gregorio was sitting in the first row of seats just behind the pilot and copilot. The copilot's left hand was resting on the butt of the Smith & Wesson 357 that was tucked into the webbed pocket on the right side of his seat.

The moment the jet came to a rest, a man stepped out of the SUV on the passenger side but remained behind the protection of the door. Gregorio recognized the man, and apparently the copilot did as well. His hand eased off the revolver. Eduardo, the man next to the SUV, was one of five men who'd been recruited by Ramon Cayetano from the Fuerzas Especiales, an elite unit of commandos within the Mexican Navy, after an assault on the Cayetano family's walled compound in Mexico City by another drug cartel.

The early morning attack by five heavily armed assailants clad in body armor had taken the guards by surprise. Two had been killed in the opening exchange of fire, and a third had suffered a disabling wound, leaving only two effectives. Then Nacio Leon entered the fray. The killer walked through the mansion's shattered front door dressed in his trademark white linen suit and took out two of the assailants with head shots. The third had wheeled in response to the muted cough from the suppressor affixed to Nacio's Beretta 92FS and avoided the same fate, at least for a moment. Nacio put five shots into the man's chest. Although body armor stopped the bullets, the impact knocked the man off balance, giving Nacio time for a third head shot. When the two men attacking the rear of the house realized reinforcements had arrived, they fled through the back gate.

Although Cayetano's sister and Adriana, the only two family members in the house, had hidden in the steel-reinforced safe room once the assault began, their reprieve would have been short-lived had the assailants' mission succeeded. A week earlier the family of another drug dealer had died in just such an impregnable room from smoke inhalation when the house was burned down around them.

Gregorio knew Nacio was unhappy about the employment of the Especiales, although technically the new men were not invading his space. Nacio was an assassin. Managing a security detail, even Ramon Cayetano's detail, was a task Nacio considered beneath his specialized skill. Still, the killer didn't like the idea of new muscle coming into the organization that he didn't control. Cayetano, who undoubtedly knew of Nacio's feelings, had given him a three-hundred-thousand-dollar cash bonus for stopping the assault on his home, but it was also to soothe his ruffled feathers.

After scanning the surrounding area for a moment, Eduardo waved to the cockpit. The copilot waved back, walked back to the cabin area, and lowered the ramp to the tarmac before turning to Gregorio.

"The car's waiting."

Gregorio stood and smiled at the thin balding man he'd come to know through his frequent trips back and forth from the United States.

"You mean it's safe, Eduardo."

"Yes, my friend. It's safe."

Chula Vista, California

Anna Torres pulled into the parking structure next to a four-story commercial building and drove the rented Toyota Camry up to the third floor. The white van she'd been told to look for was parked by itself. She parked in an open space next to a black SUV on the other side of the garage, grabbed her keys, backpack, and phone and eased out of the car.

Anna glanced down at her outfit before walking over to the van. She hoped the combination of dark running shoes, jeans, and a long-sleeved gray Sahara shirt met the "anonymous and mobile" criteria mentioned by the SAIC. Satisfied that she had everything, she walked toward the white van, slinging her backpack over one shoulder.

The man behind the wheel of the van, who was wearing a pair of sunglasses and a black baseball cap without a logo, didn't look over at her as she approached. His eyes were scanning the rest of the garage. She opened the passenger side of the van but hesitated before getting in.

"Agent Ortega?"

The man glanced over at her. The combination of the bald head, sunglasses, broad flat nose, and the heavy mustache was almost a perfect caricature of the word *sinister*. For a moment, Anna felt like laughing when she remembered Sontag's description, but she suppressed the feeling.

"That's me. Hop in."

Ortega's voice was a friendly baritone, but Anna sensed an undercurrent of tension. As soon as she closed the door and put on the seatbelt, Ortega eased the van out of the space and drove down the ramp toward the exit. She decided to keep quiet and let Ortega make the first move.

About halfway down the ramp, he slowed, leaned forward, and glanced to his left and right repeatedly. For a moment, Anna was confused, but then she realized that he was scanning the lower level of the garage they were approaching through the gaps in the concrete supports. The intense expression on Ortega's face suggested the exercise wasn't for effect. He was worried about a threat, an imminent threat.

Anna lowered her backpack to the floor of the van and moved her right hand closer to the holster clipped to her belt. The shirt she was wearing was just a little larger than what she typically wore, and it was untucked. The style wasn't the most flattering, but it hid the Glock and allowed easy access.

As the van turned down the next ramp, Anna glanced in the side-view mirror and saw movement on the floor above them. It was only a glimpse, but she was able to catch sight of two men racing down the staircase carrying guns.

"Agent Ortega, I saw just two men carrying—"

Two projectiles slammed into the windshield, cutting off the warning. Big white circles appeared in the glass at the point of impact. Ortega jammed on the brakes, threw the gearshift into park, and drew his service weapon. Anna drew her Glock, sprang out of the van, and prepared to return fire, using the door as a shield. When she glanced around the edge of the door, she saw two men wearing baseball caps. They were firing at the van from just inside the concrete doorway that led to the stairway. One of the men leaped back into doorway when three rounds smashed into the wall two feet from his head. Anna glanced over at Ortega. He was in the same position she was on the other side of the van, returning fire.

When she glanced around the door again, a bullet slammed into the window just above her head. She flinched, but kept her eyes on the doorway, waiting for one of the men to pop out again. A moment later, one of the men appeared and fired off two shots in Ortega's direction. Anna drew a bead on his head and began to pull the trigger but hesitated and instead targeted his exposed thigh. There was a scream of pain a moment after she pulled the trigger, and the shooting stopped.

She started out from behind the door, but froze when Ortega yelled, "Stay behind cover and keep your weapon at the ready. It could be trap."

She waited impatiently as the sound of footsteps running down the stairs grew more distant.

Ortega dodged between the parked cars on his left and moved to the wall of the parking garage where he could see the ground below. A moment later, he ran back to the van and jumped in.

"Get in. They got away on bikes. We need to get out of here, now."

Anna could hear the sound of sirens in the distance. She jumped into the van, and Ortega sped down the last ramp. He hesitated at the exit, looking both ways before racing down the street.

"Shouldn't we go after—"

Ortega shook his head as he yanked the wheel to the right and roared down another side street.

"No! And we can't stay here and wait for the locals. My orders are clear. We are to stay completely off the grid until we are told otherwise, no exceptions. I'll connect with HQ at the Bureau. They'll deal with it."

Ortega pulled into a crowded parking lot two miles from the site of the shooting and glanced around before pulling into an open space at the back. Anna scanned the area as well. She didn't see any threats.

He stepped out of the van and turned to look over at her before he closed the door. "I need to call this in. Keep your eyes 360."

Anna nodded. She holstered the Glock but kept her right hand on the grip.

Five minutes later, Ortega returned to the car.

"We can't bring the van back to the safehouse," he said. "It's obviously been identified, and forensic wants the bullets lodged in the door. They're bringing us a new ride."

Ortega drove south on a series of side streets for about two miles, scanning the rearview mirror constantly, before pulling into a parking lot alongside a small municipal park. For a minute he watched the street, then turned to Anna and held out his right hand.

"Teo Ortega."

Anna shook his hand. It was like gripping a bear paw.

"Anna Torres." Her voice was friendly but reserved.

"Everyone on the team calls me Teo, but it's up to you," Ortega said, raising his hand in gesture of surrender.

Anna nodded. "Teo works."

He nodded toward the empty trail running around the perimeter of the park. "Let's take a walk while they do the swap. I'll fill you in on what's going on."

Teo placed the keys on the floor of the van and left the door unlocked. He didn't say anything until they reached the deserted walkway encircling the park. Then he glanced over at her. "Are you okay? You did great back there, by the way."

Anna nodded and exhaled as if she'd been holding her breath. "Yes, I'm good."

Teo stopped in the middle of the path and stared at her. "Is that your first shooting? If you need to see a counselor ASAP, we—"

Anna waved off the invitation.

"It's not my first shooting, Teo, and no, I don't need to see a shrink. That said, I will be adding an extra prayer and a glass of wine to my nightly routine . . . when the time is right. By the way, who was trying to kill us and why?"

A slow smile came to Teo's face. "I intend to do the same, but I'll substitute a glass of scotch for the wine. I'm also going to thank the guy who armored up that van. But for that bullet-resistant glass and the extra plating in the doors, we might not be going home tonight."

He started down the path again. "Let's keep walking."

Anna matched his pace and repeated the question Teo had not answered. "And what about the who and the why?"

Teo held up a placative hand. "I'm getting there. However, I have to give you a few admonitions before I do. This briefing and—in fact everything about this operation—is top secret. This is the real shit, Anna, excuse the French. You can't talk to *anyone* about what you're told or what you see or hear. The only exceptions are me, the other members of the team, and . . . Sontag. Any disclosure will get you booted out of the agency. It could also get you and the rest of the team killed. That's no BS. I don't mean to lean on you about this, but I have to. It has to be totally clear."

"It's clear, Teo. Crystal clear," Anna said. "No talking, no leaks, and I can only talk to you, the team members, and Sontag."

Teo nodded. "Good. Okay, then let's get to it."

He raised his right hand as if he was about to make a point, lowered it, hesitated a moment, and raised it again as if he'd made his decision.

"I know you've heard all about the drug war raging in Mexico and its effects on US border cities, but I need to . . . to give you a little more insight into that nightmare. You gotta understand the scope and intensity of what's going on to appreciate how critical our piece in the big game is. You also need to know this stuff, because you are about to wade into a real scary swamp."

Anna just nodded. That seemed to satisfy Ortega, because he resumed his steady pace and continued talking.

"You're probably familiar with a lot of this crap, but here are the numbers. Last year Mexico reported over sixteen thousand drug-related killings. The real number is more than twice that. So, think of it this way—that's the equivalent of three US combat divisions being wiped out *in one year*. Not wounded—killed."

Ortega shook his head slowly as he spoke, as if trying to mentally grasp the bloody import of the data himself.

"You might say, 'Yeah, yeah, Teo. There's a lot of violence and killing. I get it.' Let me tell you. It's worse than that. Do you remember those contractors that got caught by Al Qaeda in Iraq?"

Anna nodded. "Yes. They found their bodies burned and strung up on a bridge." She noted Teo's right hand brushed against the bulge of the holster underneath the dark brown shirt he was wearing.

"Those poor guys were brutally tortured and people were shocked and pissed off about that, as they should have been. That kind of stuff is common with the drug gangs. These dudes try to outdo each other. Last week they cut someone's face off, sewed it on a soccer ball, and played a game with it! Two weeks ago, a bus full of folks making their way up to the border were executed—men, women, and children—when they refused to agree to work as slaves for these monsters. My point is these folks have no boundaries. None. They will kill anyone, anywhere, and do it in the most horrific way possible to send a message. Or just for fun."

Ortega slowed to kick a rock off the trail and glance over his shoulder. Then he raised his right hand again to punctuate his point.

"Okay, so how does this relate to what just happened in that garage? Well, some people on this side of the border, particularly those folks in Washington, seem to think the gangs wouldn't dare take on the old US of A. Let me be more specific. They think the gangs wouldn't dare to catch, torture, and kill a couple of FBI agents like Teo Ortega and Anna Torres. Let me tell you, that's BS. They haven't done it yet because they don't need to. We're not stopping enough of the drug flow for them to waste the time. However, if we ever do seriously cut into their money flow, then you can be sure San Diego, El Paso, and Tucson will become war zones."

Ortega glanced over at Anna, as if expecting her to challenge his analysis. She kept her face neutral.

"I know, you think I'm overstating the case. I'm not. The Mexican mafia—that's the distribution arm for the gangs in the US—has over forty thousand soldiers pushing their crap in SoCal alone. That's four divisions. Sorry about the military stats. I served with the 2nd Marine Expeditionary Force in Desert Storm. Besides, the nomenclature fits. These folks have an army in this country. They may not get up in the morning and put on a uniform and march in unison, but they get the job done, selling billions—yeah, billions—of dollars of drugs from San Diego to Boston. All that cash flows back to the cartels in Mexico and Columbia. Each year they get bigger and more powerful."

Anna interrupted Ortega's monologue. "So how do we fit into this picture and why did—"

"You mean, nightmare." A smile eased the tension on his face. "Yeah, let's get to that. Most of the assets in the drug war work on interdiction—keeping the poison out. That's not us. We're after the money."

Anna was momentarily confused, so she kept quiet and let Ortega continue.

"The drug gangs have a problem. They're too successful. They have, and I mean it literally, tons of cash, as in greenbacks. They have crates of twenty, fifty, and hundred dollar bills stacked in ware-houses and basements and packed away in private vaults all over

Mexico and Central America. Their problem is they can't use it, at least not the way they want to.

"They can buy or build big houses south of the border and buy expensive cars, jets, and that sort of thing, but that's just pennies. To spend the big dollars on things like shopping centers, four- and five-star hotels, that kind of mainstream investment, they need to launder the money."

"There are banks that take their cash, Teo. A bank was just sanctioned in—"

"Latvia," Ortega interjected. "Yeah, there's a few. Most of them are smaller outfits in places like Russia, Kazakhstan, Mongolia, and a few East Asian countries, but the price is steep, and these small outfits are not trustworthy. The heads of cartels want their money in American and European banks. They want to get a statement in the mail every month telling them their hard-earned cash is safe, accessible, and earning a decent yield."

Ortega pointed across the park at a Boston Terrier chasing a tennis ball with feverish intensity. "I had a dog like that as a kid. Great dog."

Anna smiled, watching the dog bounding across the grass. "Pugs are my favorite."

Ortega nodded. "Yeah, I had one of those too. Feisty bastards."

He watched the terrier racing after the ball again for another moment before continuing. "Right now, these folks are kinda like that dog going after the ball. They have *got* to have this thing—a safe place to park their money. And they will get it, unless we stop them."

He smiled as the terrier seized the ball and raced back to his master for another round.

"How do they do it?" he asked. "They can't just walk into a bank with a sack of cash and open an account. Every US bank sends Treasury a notice whenever they receive a cash deposit of ten grand or more, or any sequence of cash deposits that smells like someone is trying to get around the 10K reporting rule. So, how do they do it?"

Anna assumed the question wasn't rhetorical, so she answered it. "They need to funnel the money through one or more legitimate businesses so it comes out on the other side clean and reputable."

Ortega nodded. "Yeah, that's the ticket. But it's not easy. To do it, they either have to start a business from scratch, using small dollar investments that won't hit our radar, or coopt your local businessman and use his business platform to get it done. So far, they've been working the second option but not too successfully. These boys have a problem with blending in. They don't understand business, and they have no patience. Every time there's a hiccup, they whack someone and the whole thing blows up."

As they came around the corner of the park where the terrier was chasing the ball, the dog started trotting toward them. A call from his master sent the dog racing back in that direction.

A wistful look came to Ortega's face, and Anna couldn't help smiling.

"Missing someone?"

Ortega chuckled. "Hell, yeah. That was a great dog. Okay, back to the money. In the past couple of years, the game's started to change. The cartels have recruited, or home grown, a class of uber-educated financial gurus. These dudes have MBAs and law degrees from top American universities, and they're using this knowledge to clean and reinvest the hoards of cash the cartels generate into legit US business. Our job—your job—is to stop these folks. DC doesn't want one of the cartels owning the next Google."

"Okay, so where do I fit in, and why did they try to take us?"

"Here's where you fit in. Our unit is intercepting and monitoring communications from a bunch of sources on both sides of the border. We have phone taps, computer bugs, sonic intercepts—the whole spectrum. Intel is pouring in the door. Almost all of it's in Spanish, and you—"

"Speak Spanish," Anna finished.

Ortega smiled.

"So do I. We have plenty of Spanish speakers, Anna, and they're going through most of the data. You bring a lot more than that to the table. I'm told your parents are rather famous Mesoamerican archaeologists who spent a good part of their lives, with their daughter, in Mexico. I'm also told you went to school at an elite private high school in Mexico City, graduated at the top of your class at UC Irvine, and worked in the State Department on cartel-related diplomatic problems after graduation. In fact, as I understand it, this last experience is what led you to join the FBI."

Anna nodded. "It was."

Ortega chuckled. "There's one other big thing. I was told you were a top-drawer shooter, and now I can confirm that fact. In this assignment that counts for a lot."

"And now—" Anna began.

"I'm going to answer your question. We work with an elite Mexican police unit in Tijuana. It was hit by the Nauyacas this morning."

"The Nauyacas!"

Teo nodded. "They tell me you know a bit about these folks."

"Yeah, I did a paper on them at State. It's an up-and-coming drug gang named after a poisonous snake. They're incredibly violent, and they don't respect any boundaries."

Teo glanced over at her. "You got that right. They wiped out everyone in the Mexican Unit—except one guy. The survivor was either a rat or the Nauyacas grabbed him and made him talk."

"And the parking garage?"

Teo exhaled heavily. "It was one of four meet-up locations. When their top guys came across, they'd leave their transport in the garage, and we'd take them to a safe house. I didn't find out about this morning's attack in Mexico until ten minutes before you showed up and—"

"You didn't have my cell number."

"No. LA didn't either. You need to get that to me and to HQ in LA as well."

Anna nodded. "Sorry. I just arrived from Dallas yesterday, and Sontag told me to come down right away—no data forms, no meet and greet—nothing."

"That sounds about right. This is a joint operation with the CIA, and to a lesser extent with a special unit within the Pentagon. We're not just playing in a different game; this is a different league."

Anna stopped, and Teo stopped as well. She pointed at Teo when she spoke. "Those shooters were there to finish the job, weren't they? They were sent by the Nauyacas to take out the US half of the operation."

"That's my read."

Teo's cell phone vibrated. He walked away from Anna and took the call. His face was grim when he came back. "The good news is they caught the shooter you wounded. The bad news is he's dead. His own men cut his throat before crossing the border."

FIVE

Punta Maldonado, Mexico

The Cayetano family's ten-acre compound was situated on a steep bluff overlooking the Pacific Ocean, about two miles south of the small town of Punta Maldonado. The main residence was a palatial Italianate villa with a broad semicircle drive in front. Two smaller adobe structures used by the servants were hidden behind a hedge on the north side of the villa.

As the SUV eased toward the eight-foot stone archway in the center of the wall, the steel gate barring the entrance opened, and the driver of the SUV pulled into the courtyard on the other side. A guard carrying an Uzi submachine gun gestured for the SUV to stop and approached the driver's side window, while a second guard armed with an AK-47 kept his distance. The first guard scanned the occupants inside the car and waved them on.

When the SUV pulled in front of the main house, Alex Sanchez walked past the two guards standing in the driveway facing the vehicle. Sanchez was dressed in his signature gray suit, white shirt, and tie, despite the informality of the meeting. Like Gregorio, Sanchez was not a member of the Cayetano family. His mother, Leya, had been one of the two nannies who'd served at the beck and call of Ramon Cayetano's two sons, Ignacio and Raul. Gregorio's mother, Selene Pena, had been the other.

The two boys had lived on the grounds of the estate in the servants' quarters with their mothers. When they had shown promise in school, the drug lord had paid for their educations. Sanchez had received an accounting degree from the University of California at San Diego and spent three years working in Mexico City for a large accounting firm. A year ago, Cayetano had ordered him to return and join Gregorio as one of his financial advisers.

Neither man had the option of saying no. Leya Sanchez and Selene Pena's servitude had ended years earlier, but they now served a different role—that of hostages. Their lives ensured the loyalty of their sons, a point Cayetano reinforced by sending the two women gifts of cash four times a year and by periodically asking Gregorio and Sanchez about their mothers' health and welfare. Although this familial tie would be severed when the two women passed away, Gregorio and Sanchez knew Cayetano anticipated he would have a new crop of hostages to harvest before their demise—their wives and children. Both men had vowed not to let this happen.

In the past year, the focus of Gregorio and Sanchez's services for the drug lord had become singular: to transmute the Cayetano family's vast hoard of cash drug profits into legitimate investment dollars available for use in the United States. Although the two men had managed to successfully launder three million dollars of illicit cash through a series of small businesses during the past two years, Cayetano had dismissed these accomplishments as insignificant. Six months ago, he'd given them an ultimatum during one of his fits of rage: Find a way to evade United States law and launder the money, within a year, through a single transaction, or die.

Until a week ago, Gregorio and Sanchez had concluded the task was impossible, and they'd secretly begun working on an escape plan. Then Declan Collins's money laundering scheme had thrown the two men a lifeline. After his meeting with Collins, Gregorio had called Sanchez, described the scheme in detail, and told him he intended to bring it to Cayetano for approval. When Sanchez had begged him for time to research its viability, Gregorio had given him twelve hours. The dark shadows visible under Alex's brown eyes confirmed he'd used every minute of the time afforded to him.

As soon as Gregorio stepped out of the SUV, he put his hand on Alex's shoulder and cut off any attempt at conversation in front of the guards. "Let's talk in the study. The meeting with Mr. Cayetano is not for another hour."

Alex looked furtively around and nodded his head solemnly. "Yes, yes. Excellent idea."

Gregorio walked up the stairs and through the main door, which was being held open by an elderly servant, into a large circular foyer. Bianc Carrara marble laced with blue and gray striations covered the floor and the walls. The domed ceiling was clad in dark blue mosaic tiles embedded with over a thousand white semiprecious stones. The sunlight pouring through the glass-encased circle at the top of the dome reflected off the white stones and illuminated the magnificent fountain in the middle of the foyer below.

A statue of Our Lady of Guadalupe carved from Italian marble by one of Mexico's foremost sculptors was the centerpiece of the fountain. It had been a gift from Ramon to his deceased wife, Portia, the mother of the two boys whom Cayetano had expected to be his heirs, Ignacio and Raul. To the right of the fountain, a broad stairway led upstairs to the second floor. A series of French doors, which led to the villa's great room, lined the far side of the foyer.

Gregorio walked down the narrow hall on the right side of the stairway. He poured himself a glass of water from the silver pitcher resting on the table in the center of the room and walked to the window overlooking the north side of the property. Two small worn casitas were just visible over the top of a hedgerow forty yards away. Gregorio stared at the modest buildings in silence for a moment before speaking in a quiet voice filled with regret.

"They suffered so we could live a better life, my friend. We must honor their sacrifice."

"Yes, Gregorio," Alex said in a whisper as he glanced over his shoulder at the open door behind them. "Yes."

Gregorio's mother, Selene Pena, was the daughter of a respectable Mexican family. She'd fallen in love with the son of a wealthy Brazilian diplomat when she was in her junior year at Barnard College. Her Brazilian lover had been in his senior year at Harvard. Despite his professions of love, Gregorio's father had returned to

Brazil the day after he'd received his degree, seven months before Gregorio's birth.

When Selene's family discovered the pregnancy, they'd refused to continue to pay for her tuition, and she was forced to return to Mexico. After the child was born, her parents gave her a choice: put the child up for adoption or make her own way in the world. Selene had refused to relinquish the child. A friend, Leya Sanchez, who served as a maid in the home of Ramon Cayetano, had introduced her to Portia Cayetano, and she was hired to teach their two young boys English and serve as their nanny along with Leya.

During the summers, the Cayetano family had lived in the grand villa, and Selene and Leya had lived together in the small casitas, with their two young sons, Gregorio and Alex. Selene had worked as a maid each morning alongside Leya and taught the young Cayetano boys English each afternoon. Life had been bearable until Portia Cayetano and the two Cayetano heirs had died in a plane crash.

A week later, Gregorio and Alex had been sent away to a boarding school where discipline was harsh and the academic burdens were demanding. Although the boys had struggled at first, they'd endured and graduated at the top of their class. Leya Sanchez and Selene Pena had suffered a far worse fate, one that would continue for over a decade.

Alex looked across at Gregorio. "You need to get some rest. You've been chasing this thing nonstop for the past two months."

Gregorio turned to his friend. "I cannot. There is no time. Now, tell me, is Mr. Collins's scheme viable?"

SIX

Los Angeles, California

Declan Collins glanced out at the sun setting over the Pacific Ocean from the window of his office on the fifty-first floor of the US Bank tower. He started to reach for his iPhone to take a picture of the scene when Matt, who was sitting on the black leather couch on the other side of the office, interrupted him.

"We need to talk percentages, bro."

Collins took a picture of the scene before turning around.

Matt was wearing his standard workday outfit: a dark gray Brioni suit, white Prada dress shirt, and a red tie. Collins considered the white gold cufflinks and the thousand-dollar Italian shoes a bit excessive, but then again Matt was almost always over the top. His own gray pinstriped suit, sans tie, and black loafers looked shabby in comparison.

"Percentages? What are you talking about?"

Matt smiled. "My percentage of the big bucks you're gonna get for the screenplay and the film rights. The way I figure it, 15, maybe 20 percent is fair."

Collins walked over and sat down in the leather chair across from the couch, his eyes glancing back at the sunset.

"And why's that?"

"Because I reeled in the big fish, and maybe because you're a pain-in-the-ass client. Or both."

"We haven't won the lottery yet, wise ass, and in all likelihood, we never will. I looked up Blackpool Studios on the web and pulled a Dun & Bradstreet report. There's not a whole lot out there on this outfit. The corporate entity exists—I checked, there's several press releases about options on screenplays, and there's a little bit of noise about a possible film in the future. That resume doesn't fill me with confidence. As for Gregorio, he's listed as Blackpool's general manager with the Secretary of State, and he checks out at Harvard and Wharton, but there's not a whole lot more on him either. In sum, I'm not holding my breath on a possible big-bucks movie deal."

Collins's eyes strayed to the photograph on the wall of himself, Matt, and Matt's sister, Sienna. "Tell me about something that matters, like Sienna. What's this about a mission in Mexico?"

"Sienna?"

"Yeah, you know, your kid sister. The only Esposito kid worth a farthing."

There was an eight-year age gap between Matt and his younger sister. She was in her third year at Westmont College, in the premed program, and last year she'd knocked out a 3.9 GPA.

"Didn't I see a mass email about something in Chiapas?"

Matt took a drink from the beer sitting on the table beside him before answering. "Yeah. The kid's amazing or nuts or both. She's working as an intern with Doctors Without Borders. The clinic's in southern Chiapas, out there in the boonies. She sent me pictures of the place yesterday in an email. What a dump. They couldn't pay me enough to go there. Sienna, on the other hand, volunteered."

"Like I said, the only Esposito—"

"Screw you. When was your last Peace Corps gig?"

"I would have signed up but keeping your butt out of trouble is a full-time job. Hey, tell Sienna I said be careful."

A brief look of concern clouded Matt's face for a moment. "Yeah, I'll do that."

To the extent Matt had a soft spot for anything, it was Sienna. Matt and Sienna's dad had died when she was ten years old, and Matt, who was eighteen at the time, had appointed himself to serve as her lord protector. Although Sienna loved her older brother, she rarely needed his guidance and often found it more than a little irritating. When Sienna's mother had died ten years later, the roles had been reversed. At twenty years old, Sienna was the more mature sibling and often scolded Matt about his frat boy lifestyle. Collins smiled when he remembered her oft-repeated admonition, "Matt, you need to grow up."

"She'll be fine, Matt. Unlike you, she's not in the habit of running amuck—"

Matt scoffed. "I never run amuck. Now, let's get back to those percentages."

Collins shook his head in frustration. "Matt, I'm not wasting time—"

"It's not a waste of time anymore, bro," Matt said, a smile coming to his face.

Collins leaned forward in the chair. "Okay, Esposito, what are you hiding?"

"You're dead wrong about Blackpool. We struck gold! I got an email from Gregorio an hour ago. The guy who's funding the movie wants to meet us on Friday night. He wants us to stay the weekend."

"Next Friday? That's not a lot of time. Where's the meet, Mexico City?"

"No. The money guy lives just south of Acapulco and get this— he's sending a private jet to pick us up at LAX. This guy must be nuts about the screenplay! So, as for that percentage . . ."

Collins pretended to stroke his chin in concentration before answering. "How about 5 percent?"

"No way! You owe me big time, Collins."

Chiapas, Mexico, Doctors Without Borders Clinic

Sienna Esposito looked at the mound of disparate medical supplies in the backroom of the concrete building serving as a rudimentary clinic, medical supply dump, and residence for the five-member Médecins sans Frontières team. The two local guards assigned to protect them lived in the two-room adobe building next door.

They'd refurbished the old building using materials left over from the construction of the clinic.

The team had two doctors, a husband and wife from Ireland, two nurses from Mexico City, and Sienna, the intern, gofer, and chief of the supply room. The MSF team was there to provide basic medical services and inoculations to the people living in a remote part of southern Chiapas.

The clinic opened at seven each morning and closed at four. The long line of people waiting for treatment began to form an hour before opening. Sienna worked in the clinic each day, interviewing patients before they were seen by the doctors or nurses, keeping records, and assisting the doctors with medical procedures when the nursing staff was overwhelmed. Today she was tasked with attempting to organize the mound of disorganized medical supplies delivered yesterday.

The temperature in the back room was almost a hundred degrees and sweat stains marked the back of her dark gray T-shirt and the knees of her hiking pants. All of the women wore hiking gear. It was synthetic, light, easy to wash, and almost indestructible. It was also asexual, which was the look Sienna and the other female members of the team wanted. The nearest *policía* station was fifty miles away, and Sienna, in particular, had been advised to do whatever was necessary to disguise her voluptuous five-nine figure, long honey blonde hair, and pretty face.

After sorting through the last box of supplies, she listed the contents in bold black letters on the outside and then lifted the box, with some difficulty, onto one of the long wooden shelves. She scanned the room with satisfaction and announced, "Now that job is what Matt Esposito would call a 'real bitch.'"

"And what would Sienna Esposito call it?"

Sienna turned in surprise, a smile spreading across her face. Stephen O'Brien, the tall, fiftyish doctor nominally in charge of the MSF unit, was standing in the door that connected the storeroom to the clinic. O'Brien looked more like an old boxer than a doctor, which he'd been during his college and medical school years. As he'd explained one night over a pint, "Fisticuffs paid my way through medical school."

O'Brien appreciatively scanned the now organized room.

"A magnificent job, lass. Now can I ask you to scrub up quickly? I need you to help me sew up a wee lad who's had a bad fall. No rest for the wicked and all that."

Sienna sighed and then laughed aloud after Dr. O'Brien left, thinking about what Matt would have said in response to the doctor's quip: *Who you calling wicked? Come over here; I'll give you a slap.*

SEVEN

Chula Vista, California

When they returned to the parking lot, the white van was gone. Teo pointed at the dark gray utility van at the far end of the parking lot. "That's our new ride."

As they drove out of the lot, Anna looked over at Teo. "Have we had any luck identifying new money laundering operations?"

Teo's jaw muscles relaxed and a satisfied smile cross his face. "Yes. A source says one of the older cartels is about to move big dollars into the US. The word is they've either found or made a hole in the regulatory system."

Anna raised an eyebrow. "Which one?"

"The Cayetano cartel. Ramon Cayetano's fief. It appears the old butcher is getting squeezed out by the other cartels. In the last couple of years, the Nauyacas have become Cayetano's personal nightmare. They tried to cash him out in a raid about a month ago—hit his compound in Mexico City real hard."

"How did we get inside information on the scheme?"

"By mail, if you can believe it. A letter arrived at the LA office addressed to Sontag. It said Cayetano was trying to launder a massive amount of cash through a scheme being set up by a lawyer in LA.

"Sontag assumed it was BS, but he sent us the letter anyway. Two days ago, we received more intel from another undisclosed source on the Mexico side. The source said a big-deal lawyer was meeting with one of the Cayetano's money guys. That was it."

"Any idea who sent the letter?"

Teo shook his head. "No. It's gotta be someone inside the cartel—"

"Or someone playing a game," Anna finished.

Teo nodded. "Could be, but we caught a break. When Cayetano's limo was stuck in traffic in Mexico City, the van tailing him intercepted a part of a call he made to a guy in LA."

Anna raised an eyebrow. "What did we get?"

"The audio is sitting on your new desk. The quality's not good, but the consensus is they were talking about some kind of big-ass money laundering operation. The guy on the other end mentioned he was meeting a lawyer whose best friend is a securities broker with the last name of Esposito. We ran a search and came up with a guy named Matthew Esposito, a big-time securities broker. His best friend is Declan Collins, a lawyer in LA."

"It's thin, but it's something. What's the deal with the lawyer?"

Teo turned down a street lined with old warehouse buildings. Most of them were surrounded by tall fences with barbed wire scrolls running along the top. It looked like her new work location was going to be a bit different from downtown LA.

Teo shrugged his shoulders. "We don't know. Legal in LA say the guy's an ace. Big cases, big clients, and big fees."

"Doesn't sound like a guy who needs to launder money for a drug cartel."

Teo nodded as he pulled around to the rear of a worn, four-story brick building with faded white letters painted across the front. The windows on the first and second floors had been filled in with brick at some point, but the outlines of the old openings were still visible.

The rear of the building was surrounded by a twelve-foot concrete wall topped with barbed wire scrolls. The solid steel gate allowing access through the wall was just wide enough to allow one full-size vehicle to pass through at a time. Cameras on the right and left of the opening provided whoever was inside the building a clear view of the entire access point.

When Teo pulled up to the gate, it rolled out of the way on a steel track with surprising speed. It closed just as quickly behind them when they drove into the small parking lot in the rear of the building.

Teo glanced over at Anna. "Welcome to the fortress."

"Fortress," Anna said with a nod, "is the right word."

EIGHT

Los Angeles, California

Sarah Dubois finished her review of the first draft of the appeal brief in the Racine case and pushed the document aside. Kate O'Regan, the newest attorney in the office, had written the draft. Although Dubois knew it was a good first effort, she had no intention of saying anything of the kind to O'Regan. The newbie needed to sweat for a while.

Dubois turned to her computer and started typing an email to O'Regan citing the deficiencies in her brief, when someone knocked on her door and opened it before she could answer. There was only one person in the office brave enough to risk incurring Dubois's wrath through such an improvident move: Ed Danson, the US attorney for the Central District of California. Danson was six-four, 210 pounds, and his stern, handsome face and full head of iron gray hair conveyed a sense of dignified power.

Although Dubois considered Danson a bit of blowhard, he'd been appointed by the president of the United States, which meant it didn't matter what she thought. He was the boss.

"Good morning, Sarah. Two agents from the FBI will be here in about ten minutes. You need to meet with them this morning. I meant to let you know earlier, but the AG called in the interim. I checked with Debbie. She said your calendar is open this morning."

Dubois made a mental note to set Debbie, the admin she shared with three other attorneys, straight. Her calendar was never "open." As far as Dubois was concerned, she was the busiest attorney in the office, and anyone who wanted a minute of her time had to pay a hefty price for it. Dubois yearned to set Danson straight on his failure to appreciate her busy schedule, but that was not an option.

"Of course, Ed. What's this about?"

"I can't tell you much about it. The underlying operation is very . . . sensitive. What I can tell you this: Declan Collins is going to be the topic of conversation. Regge Carlton is lead on the criminal case, so he'll be the master of ceremonies."

The phone in Danson's hand belted out an old jazz tune. He glanced down at the screen. "Gotta go."

Dubois knew Reginald "Regge" Carlton all too well. Everyone in the office did. He was the Central District's top criminal prosecutor, a status he never let anyone forget. He'd prosecuted mobsters, terrorists, serial killers—the worst of the worst—and he'd never lost a case. Whenever Washington had a big name "no lose" prosecution, Carlton was added to the team, or he found a way to get on the team.

The Boston WASP had graduated from Yale law at the top of his class and taken a job with the United States Attorney's office in Manhattan. The understaffed and overburdened office had given him the opportunity to try cases almost immediately. Two years ago, he'd moved to the Central District of California to be closer to his fiancée, a top fashion model who lived in West LA.

If Carlton was on the case, it had to be a big deal. Collins's involvement in the equation, on the other hand, stumped her. She didn't like Collins, but she didn't think he was dirty.

The phone buzzed on her desk. "Ms. Dubois, Mr. Carlton is waiting for you in conference room A."

"I'll be there in a minute."

Dubois thought about making Carlton and the FBI agents wait five minutes. It was her practice to make everyone wait, except Danson, but she wanted to hear what Carlton had to say. She grabbed a yellow pad and a pen and walked down the hall.

When Dubois walked into the conference room, Carlton was the only one there. He was standing at the far end of the glass conference table looking out the window. Sarah noted the Boston Brahmin hadn't added a pound to his spare, six-one frame or lost the wavy head of hair and regal good looks women were so taken with. Sarah also noted his smile had the same welcoming but slightly condescending quality she found more than a little irritating.

Carlton eased around the table and met her in the middle of the conference room. "Sarah, so good to see you. I hope all is well?"

She ignored Carlton's question. "Good to see you too, Regge. How can I help you?"

Carlton's smile widened. "Of course. Right to business."

The comment, like most things about Carlton, rubbed Dubois the wrong way, but she didn't react outwardly.

"Very well. Let's get right to it, shall we? But before we get to the essence of the matter, let me draw some boundaries—inflexible boundaries that cannot be crossed."

The comment annoyed Dubois, and her irritation grew when Carlton failed to elaborate. Then she realized the chair he'd pulled back from the table was for her, not him, and he was waiting for her to sit down. She remembered another one of his character- istics she found so disagreeable: his self-appointed status as Mr. Etiquette.

After Dubois sat down, Carlton took a seat as well.

"Here are the boundaries."

Sarah interrupted him. "Are the FBI agents coming?"

"Here? No. They'll dial in. We don't want any of the agents working on this case to be seen entering this building or talking with any known member of the Justice Department until this operation is over."

Carlton glanced at his cell phone. "First, the operation we will be discussing is to be treated as a national security matter. You will not discuss this case with anyone other than myself and, if he asks, Ed Danson. That rule is inviolable. One mistake in that regard could get people killed . . . including, quite frankly, both of us."

Dubois almost rolled her eyes, but she restrained herself. "Regge, come—"

"That's not BS, Sarah. The Mexican affiliate of the FBI unit was wiped out, as in to the man, two days ago. Are we clear on this?" The intense look on his face surprised her. She nodded, stunned by the disclosure. She hadn't seen anything in the news about a massacre. "Understood."

"Second, this will probably be the only time you will interface with the operation. However, the part that you are about to play right now is critical, and Justice needs you to be a team player on this."

Carlton's cryptic statement didn't mean anything to Sarah until she heard the "team player" reference. She had something Carlton wanted, and he was letting her know if she didn't give it up, it could affect her career.

"And what, Regge, does that mean?"

Carlton steepled his fingers, hesitating before answering. "We . . . believe Declan Collins may be laundering money for one of the drug cartels."

Dubois looked at Carlton skeptically. "You have evidence of that?"

Carlton looked up at the ceiling. "I can't go into that."

"So, you don't. Look, Regge, I'm not sure what you're after, but it's not clear to me how I can help you, as a team player or otherwise."

Carlton's eyes met hers. "Actually, you can. When I put the two agents on the phone you can advise them that, in your opinion, Collins is the kind of character who might well aid and abet a money laundering operation."

Dubois stood up. "Actually, Regge, I can't. I don't like Collins, but I don't think he's your guy on this. He's too smart and too successful. This guy is already raking in the big bucks. I can't see him doing something stupid like laundering money."

As Dubois started toward the door, she could almost feel Carlton aiming a verbal gun at her back, and then he fired. "Sarah, after the Bykov debacle, I would think—"

Dubois spun around and exploded. "That case was prosecuted by the book. I am not responsible—"

"For the two dead girls in Budapest that Bykov killed a month after the trial was over. No, but the *LA Times* might see it differently. Make the right choice, Sarah."

Carlton pressed the speaker button on the phone in the middle of the table. "Put Agents Ortega and Torres on."

NINE

Chula Vista, California

Anna leaned back in her chair and perused the ten-by-ten office that was her new domain. Three of the walls were unpainted plywood supported by steel frames at the edges. The fourth wall was the external brick wall of the building, and although someone had tried to patch some of the crumbling pieces of mortar holding the bricks together, the job was only half-finished. It wasn't the walls, however, that bothered her. It was the ceiling. The cardboard tiles above her head had a yellow cast, and quite a few of the tiles showed evidence of past moisture damage. She suspected the other side of those tiles might be covered in mold.

Calling the furniture in the room utilitarian would have been charitable. Her "desk" was a six-by-three piece of wood resting on top of two small file cabinets, and her chair, although comfortable, was an ugly gray affair. The laptop and the thirty-inch monitor on the desk, on the other hand, were new, and the computer had every program she needed. All in all, she decided it was a bearable arrangement.

During her first three days with the unit, she'd listened to hours of chatter picked up by the NSA and reviewed transcripts and listened to tapes of chatter picked up by intel sources on the other side of the border. The agent she was working with on the data, Eric Hanson, was from the Bureau's Chicago office. He'd spent the last year tracking drug shipments being transported from Juarez, Mexico, to the streets of the Windy City by the MS-13 gang.

Hanson stood six-five, carried 240 lean pounds on his frame, and had the strong features and blond hair that would have made him the perfect extra in a B movie about Vikings. The first time he'd spoken Spanish with a Minnesota accent during a call with a Mexican border agent Anna had almost burst out laughing at the incongruous contrast. Hanson had chuckled and said, "I know, get it all the time."

Teo knocked on the open door before walking in. There was a smile on his face. "We got the affidavit from Dubois. Things are going to get interesting real fast. We're having an all-hands meeting at three in the conference room. Mattson and Calder will be there. They're finally back from their romp on the other side of the border."

Anna could hear the disapproval in Teo's voice.

"Bring your iPad. Our CIA brethren are going to show us how to hack into one of those things, which may be just what we need."

Anna smiled. "I'll be there."

It was clear from Teo's comments that he didn't approve of Mattson's judgment, and he may even have suspected the CIA man was running his own game on the side. But when she'd asked about the background of their CIA counterparts, it was clear that Teo respected their abilities.

Mattson had served with the 5th Special Forces group for about fifteen years, spending time in Somalia, Afghanistan, and Iraq. To quote Teo, "The guy has done some heavy-duty stuff." The CIA had invited Mattson to join their club about ten years ago. According to Teo, Mattson "had the Deep South passive-aggressive thing down to a science."

At 2:59 p.m., Anna walked down the hall to the conference room with her iPad and a yellow legal pad. She was the first one in the room. Eric Hanson walked in next, followed by Teo.

Eric waved. "Hi, Anna. Whaddya think so far?"

"Great. Just working through the mounds of transcripts and recordings."

"Yeah, there are plenty of those."

As Teo glanced down at his watch, an African American man in his late forties or early fifties walked into the room followed by a second man. Mattson was about six-two, 180 pounds. Anna had run a general search on the web before the meeting and discovered he'd played tight end for Ole Miss in his college years and earned All-American honors.

The second man, Jason Calder, was about five-nine, 170 pounds, with a full head of black hair. His reserved gray-brown eyes, which showed evidence of both Asian and Caucasian ancestors, were complemented by a perfect nose, a dimpled chin, and a flawless complexion. Calder nodded to Teo, Hanson, and Anna and moved to a seat at the far end of the table, where he focused on setting up his laptop. Anna remembered Teo saying Calder was a genius when it came to surveillance tech.

Mattson's face didn't fit the image Anna had developed from Teo's description. She'd expected a special forces, hard-ass type with a cagey attitude. The man across the room was handsome, in an urbane understated way, and his easy smile and large brown eyes were inviting and friendly. Mattson walked over to Teo and gave him a friendly slap on the shoulder.

"It's a scorcher on the other side of the river today, chief. Yes, sir. However, the good Lord was merciful. Mr. Calder and I were able to find a friendly cantina offering a decent view and cold cerveza."

"Glad to hear it," Teo said without emotion.

Mattson walked over to where Eric was sitting and gave him an even more enthusiastic slap on the shoulder. "Good to see ya, Minnesota. Everything good?"

"Same here, Gabe, and yes."

Then Mattson stepped past him and stopped in front of Anna, the easy smile on his face widening. "Now, you must be Anna Torres. Why, it is my sincerest pleasure to make your acquaintance, ma'am."

"And mine as well, Mr. Mattson."

"My dad in Tuscaloosa is Mr. Mattson, Anna—God bless his ornery soul. Please call me Gabe."

Anna returned his infectious smile. "Gabe it is."

"And does Anna work for you?"

"Perfectly."

"Magnificent. Then I suggest we get this show on the road right quick, because there's a whole lot of folks who will need to get operational really quick if we're gonna grab us some valuable intel."

Teo, who was watching the exchange, took the cue. "Right. Let's get to it."

Anna, who'd been watching Calder try to find an opening to introduce himself, quickly reached across the table before Teo began the presentation.

Calder's hand met her halfway. "Jason Calder. Welcome to the team."

"Anna Torres. Thanks, Jason."

Teo nodded to everyone at the table and began. "Okay, here's the deal. On Friday, a guy who we know to be affiliated with the Cayetano cartel met with two men in LA—Declan Collins and Matthew Esposito. Collins is a lawyer. Justice says he's heavy duty. Specializes in criminal tax fraud cases. Esposito is a securities broker. Sells private placement deals to high-net-worth people.

Eric, who was furiously taking notes, raised his hand without looking up. "What's their—"

"Getting there," Teo said and glanced down at his notes before continuing.

"The guy Esposito and Collins met works on the money side of the Cayetano's drug empire. We have a partial transcription of a phone call this guy made to Ramon Cayetano, the big boss."

Eric raised an eyebrow and Teo answered the unspoken question. "Take the legalities up with our CIA brethren."

Eric looked over at Mattson, who shrugged his shoulders in mock innocence.

"Here's the transcription," Teo said and pushed four stapled documents over to Anna, who passed them around to everyone else at the table.

For several minutes, the table was quiet as each member of the team read the transcribed exchange. Eric was the last to look up.

Unlike the other members of the team, Anna had listened to the audio of the call before the meeting. She remembered the younger man's polite but cryptic summary of his meeting with the lawyer and Ramon Cayetano's repeated interruptions. Two things had come through loud and clear from the audio exchange: The two men were discussing a scheme for bringing drug money into the United States, and Ramon Cayetano considered this a matter of utmost urgency. What was not clear was whether or not Collins and Esposito had agreed to implement the scheme and, more importantly, the details of the scheme.

"Sounds to me like these folks may have found a washing machine for some of the money those cartel folks have been stockpiling down there," Mattson said, as he leaned back in his chair and looked over at Teo. The two men's eyes met, and Teo nodded slightly. Calder spoke without looking up from his laptop.

"The combination of the broker and the lawyer gives us a pretty good clue as to how they're going to do this thing."

"A private placement deal, I suspect," Anna said.

Calder gave her the thumbs up, again without looking up from his computer.

"Now, why don't one of you two bright young folks enlighten this old man on just what y'all are talking about?" Mattson asked.

Teo responded to the question with a raised eyebrow. "They didn't cover that sort of thing in your CIA training?"

"Must have missed that lecture, chief," Mattson said with a smile.

Hanson weighed in on the topic. "Here's one possible version of what they are considering. The lawyer puts together a private placement deal that raises money to buy defaulted credit card debts from banks at three cents on the dollar. Then they hire a bunch of badass debt collectors to harass the people who owe the debts with the hope of recovering say, fifteen cents on the dollar, overall. If it works, they make a 500 percent profit."

"So, where does the bad money come in?" Mattson interjected.

"Instead of reporting a profit of one million, which is what really happened, the lawyer reports a profit of six million. Five million of drug cash is dumped into the pot to make up the difference between the real one million profit and the bogus five million profit reported to the IRS. So, voila, the bad guys just converted five million of illegal drug money sitting in a warehouse in Juarez into five million dollars of legit, clean usable dollars."

Calder raised a finger but didn't look up from his computer. "Only if they pay the tax on the bogus profit, which kinda sucks—I mean for the bad guys—but that's the price of admission."

Mattson looked over at Teo. "Damn, Teo, I may just have to persuade Ms. Torres to go into that line of biz with me. Why, with Anna's language skills and connections, we could set up a shop in Mexico City and have a line out front in about fifteen minutes."

"Yeah, and get blown to shit in twenty," Teo said gruffly.

Mattson chuckled. "Well, there is that."

"Okay," Teo said, "we need to find a way to get ears, and if possible, eyes into this lawyer's office and home. So, let's talk about that."

Eric shook his head. "We only have bits and pieces here. Yeah, it looks like they may have talked to the lawyer, Collins, about a conceptual scheme, but I don't see any execution here. This is just . . . talk."

"The Justice Department in LA thinks otherwise," Teo said, waving away the objection before continuing. "Here's the deal. A private jet will be picking up Collins and Esposito on Friday and taking them to a private airport outside Acapulco. We think they're going to meet with Ramon Cayetano and the higher-ups."

Eric started to interrupt, but Teo held up his hand. "The big dog, Cayetano, has a compound on the ocean about an hour south of Acapulco, and we just happen to know he'll be there this weekend."

Eric nodded slowly and returned to his notes, scribbling furiously.

"We have to get a warrant authorizing us to electronically surveil Collins and Esposito. If we're right, and there is a meeting with the big guy, this may allow us to get a set of ears into that meeting."

Anna looked up from the notes on her iPad and turned to Teo. "That's a death sentence for those guys. The cartels sweep—"

"Yeah, I know, but—"

"You're right," Calder said, looking up from his computer for the first time. "The room will be swept, and so will Collins and Esposito, but we have some new tech that changes the game. We're told Collins takes his iPad everywhere, and the agency has developed a surveillance program that hides in the iPad's clock function. The software alters a few basic subroutines so the audio and recording functions operate even when the machine is off. The data is then recorded as a hidden file.

"The software can be programmed so it runs during a fixed time frame and then stops. A bug sweep won't pick it up, and as I said, turning off the iPad won't stop it. And one other thing, unless they have an elite team of techs standing by ready to search the iPad, with a couple of hours to spare, they'll never find it. It's a thing of beauty," Calder finished, a smile on his face.

Eric whistled. "Wow, that's a serious piece of tech."

"It is," Teo said, "but let's remember the judge issuing the warrant limited its use to this one event. So as soon as this meeting is over, our electronic surveillance of these guys is at an end."

Calder nodded. "One and done; I get it."

"Now," Teo said, "what's the plan for getting this program installed on Collins's iPad within the next seventy-two hours without his knowledge?"

TEN

Los Angeles, California

Collins looked up when he heard the quiet knock on the door. A moment later, Michaela Stewart, Collins & Associates' receptionist, stuck her head in the door. The twenty-three-year-old blonde was wearing her standard outfit—jeans and a T-shirt sporting the logo of a local surf wear company.

"I know you don't want to be interrupted, Mr. D, but I just got a call from the parking garage. They think someone may have hit your car. I can go down and check, but they asked for you."

Collins leaned back in his chair and shook his head. "Of course someone did, and today of all days. No, I'll go down. I need a break from this. Can you tell Donna I may have to take her car to court today?"

"I already have."

Collins followed Michaela out of the office and walked to the elevator bank in the corridor. He was flipping through the emails on his phone when the elevator door opened, and he started into the elevator without looking up.

"Good morning, sir. Can we just step past you with this ladder before you hop on?"

Collins looked up into the face of an attractive Latino woman in her late twenties dressed in a building maintenance uniform. A handsome Amerasian man was standing behind the woman, dressed in the same uniform, holding a small stepladder.

"Yes, of course. I'm sorry."

Collins stepped back, and the woman smiled her thanks.

Collins stepped into the elevator after the two of them started down the hall and pressed the button for the lobby. He turned back to his phone, but something about the woman made him glance up. He watched her walk down the hall toward his office as the door closed. At the last moment, she glanced back at him, and their eyes met.

He continued to stare at the closed elevator door for a moment and then murmured aloud, "Cute."

When the elevator opened, he walked across the lobby to the bank of elevators that serviced the underground garage area. A bald Latino man in a gray suit walked over to the same elevator and stood beside him. Collins nodded to man and said, "Good morning."

The man answered with an easy smile that changed his otherwise dour face. "So far."

Collins nodded. "Good point."

When the elevator doors opened, both men entered, and Collins pressed the "P1" button. Seconds later, the door opened on the underground floor where the valet desk was located. He walked over to the elderly man behind the counter.

"Excuse me, my office received a call about an accident involving my car. Who would I talk to about that?"

The man looked at him, without understanding.

Collins tried again. "Someone from the garage called my office and said my car had been hit."

The man looked down at the screen in front of him for a moment and then looked up, shaking his head.

"I'm sorry. I don't know anything about that. Arturo might know. He's on P3. He'll be back in a minute."

"Okay, I'll wait." He walked over to a wooden bench several steps away, sat down, and continued to scan the emails on his phone.

The old man turned to the Latino man who'd been in the elevator with Collins. "Can I take your valet ticket?"

"No, I don't have one. I'm getting picked up here."

"Oh, okay."

After responding to a number of emails, Collins looked up. The parking attendant was still the only one at the valet stand, and the Latino man was still waiting to be picked up. He started walking toward the valet stand when his cell phone rang. He looked down at the number. It was his office.

"Hello."

"It's Michaela. Good news. The parking garage just called. It wasn't your car."

"Well, I guess I can't complain about that."

As the doors to the elevator to the lobby closed, Collins glanced over at the Latino man, who was still waiting for his ride. He was on the phone.

Chiapas, Mexico, Doctors Without Borders Clinic

Sienna Esposito returned the stare of the unicorn mantis clinging to the screen covering her window for a moment before continuing to edit the long email on her laptop screen. When she looked up again, the mantis had been joined by a companion. Both of them were staring at her.

"And just what do you find so interesting?" she mused aloud.

The sound of knuckles rapping on the door to the room drew her attention away from the green bugs. It was Dhanya Kumer, the nurse practitioner whose room was down the hall. The oversize green scrubs she was wearing seemed almost comical on the Indian woman's diminutive frame, but the concerned look on her face froze the smile on Sienna's face.

"Sienna, they just received a call on the SAT phone. It was from the American embassy. They said your brother, Matt, was injured in a car accident. His friend Declan . . . I'm sorry, I forgot the last name . . . hired a helicopter to take you to Centalapa. From there you can catch a flight to Mexico City and then to LA."

Sienna was stunned. "An accident? How bad is it? Did they—"

Dhanya shook her head. "Arturo took the call, Sienna. As you know, his English is not . . . great."

"A helicopter? I'll get my stuff packed. Is Dr. Stephen here?"

"No. He won't be back for a few hours. A boy broke his leg jumping from a wall about twenty miles west of here. It's bad—a compound fracture."

"Thanks, Dhanya. I better get—"

"Yes, go. Let me know if there's anything I can do."

"Thanks. I'm okay."

Sienna looked around the room, trying to focus on what she needed to take with her instead of on how badly Matt might be injured. She walked over to the large hiking backpack hanging from a hook on the wall and started stuffing it with clothes and personal belongings. In what seemed like just a matter of minutes, Dhanya came back into her room.

"Sienna, Arturo is out front. He says the helicopter will land any minute. Are you ready?"

Sienna nodded and threw one strap of the backpack over her shoulder.

"Do you have your passport?"

"Yes, I have everything I need. I can't carry any—"

"Don't worry. Anything you leave I'll ship out if you don't get back, but . . . I'm sure you will. Your brother will be fine, Sienna. I will pray for him."

Sienna turned and gave the Indian woman a quick hug, struggling to keep her emotions in check.

When Sienna walked out of the building, she was surprised to see that the sun had already set. Arturo was waiting beside the dirt road that ran past the small collection of buildings. The portly, middle-aged Mexican man who served as the clinic's general handyman pointed to the open grassy area where local kids played soccer on the weekends.

"It will land there. Stay on the edge of the field until it lands, Miss Sienna."

Sienna nodded. Moments later, she heard the sound of a helicopter in the distance. Arturo ran to the soccer field and waved his flashlight slowly back and forth in the air and then pointed the beam at the center of the field. The helicopter pilot circled the field slowly several times, scanning its length and breadth with a searchlight, before slowly descending. Arturo jogged to the far side of the field, away from Sienna and Dhanya. As soon as the chopper touched down, a man in a perfectly tailored suit stepped out of the helicopter, scanned the area for a moment, and then walked across the grass to where Sienna was waiting. A smile came to the man's strikingly handsome face when he shook her hand.

"Ms. Esposito, I'm with the American Embassy in Mexico City. Please come this way. We must hurry so you can catch the next flight to Los Angeles."

As Sienna walked over to the helicopter, she noticed the man was wearing sunglasses, despite the time of night—glasses with a tiny gold panther head at the edge of each lens.

ELEVEN

Los Angeles, California

Collins glanced at his watch before walking over to the black limousine pulling up in front of the building. This was a first. Matt was never on time. Collins walked to the rear of the car, and the driver, a white middle-aged man, met him there.

"Can I take that, sir?"

Collins suspected he, not the driver, should be lifting the overnight suitcase, but he didn't want to offend the man. He compromised by lifting the bag up to the level of the trunk and allowing the man to lower it into the compartment.

Collins retained the smaller bag with his iPad and walked over to the rear door of the car, which Matt was holding open, a big smile on his face.

"Not bad, eh?"

Collin's nodded. "Not bad at all."

Getting through LAX's Private Suite terminal was a painless ten-minute experience, and the Lear 45 waiting for them on the tarmac was a thing of beauty.

About thirty minutes and two drinks into the flight, Matt leaned back in the plush seat across from Collins, a smile on this face.

"I could get used to this. You're going to have to get off your ass and write another screenplay for me to rep."

Collins slowly surveyed the palatial interior of the jet, noting the plush swivel seats, the two refrigerators, and the full-size television screen. "Indeed."

Matt leaned forward and pointed an accusing finger at Collins. "But? I recognize that look. Out with it."

"Look, I don't mean to be a spoiler, but this . . . it doesn't make sense. Why is a small, unknown production outfit putting out this kind of cash? This ride alone costs 10K."

Matt threw up his hands in mock frustration. "Because they think they're going to make a bundle, because I'm the best salesman in the world. What do you care? Have another drink and shut up."

Collins stared at Matt for a minute, ignoring his self-satisfied grin, before closing his eyes and easing back into the cool comfort of the leather seat. He had to admit that taking a private jet to a resort in Mexico was not such a bad thing. He opened his eyes and looked over at Matt. "Okay, Esposito, maybe you did good thing, but—"

"No friggin' buts. This is going to be one of the best weekends you've ever had. Why, Mr. Harvard U might even wake up with a tattoo."

Collins chuckled. "Not a chance. Grab me a beer from that fridge, Mr. Agent."

Two hours later, the Lear landed at a private airport and stopped thirty yards from a black limo. Gregorio was waiting by the vehicle. He was dressed in dark gray linen slacks and a casual white shirt.

Matt enthusiastically shook Gregorio's hand but omitted his trademark slap to the shoulder. "Gregorio!"

"Mateo, welcome to Mexico, my friend. How was your flight?"

"Awesome, totally awesome."

Gregorio eased past Matt and took Collins's hand in a firm but respectful grip. "Mr. Collins, welcome to my fair country. May your stay be . . . safe and happy."

Collins sensed an undercurrent of unease in Gregorio's tone as he turned to the chauffeur.

The chauffeur, a small Mexican man dressed in a black suit, picked up the two overnight bags from the tarmac, placed them in the trunk of the car, and then opened the rear passenger door.

Gregorio gestured toward the car. "Please, my friends, come."

As he approached the car, Collins noticed a second man standing beside the front passenger side door, which was open. Like the chauffeur, he was dressed in a black suit, but he was younger and in better physical condition. His eyes were focused on the road leading to the airstrip. His right arm was held in an unnatural position in front of him, as if he was shielding something from sight. The pieces came together as Collins slid into the capacious rear seat of the limo beside Matt. The other man was a guard, and he was keeping the gun held in his right hand out of sight. Mexico had become a more dangerous place in the past decade, but it seemed as if the man was prepared for an imminent attack at the airfield. If this risk existed, why did Blackpool bring them there? Despite Matt's assurances, the entire situation didn't add up.

Gregorio entered the car last and sat across from Matt and Collins in the rear-facing seat. He seemed to relax when the door closed, but the undercurrent of anxiety was still there, despite his polite camaraderie.

"Gentlemen, the party has already begun, and I don't want you to miss another moment of this bacchanalian experience. So, if acceptable to you, we will go there first."

"Let's get to it," Matt responded enthusiastically.

Collins forced a smile. "Yes, indeed."

TWELVE

Acapulco, Mexico

Collins took a sip of coffee and stared out at the magnificent view from the balcony. The five-star resort was built on a cliff overlooking the coast, and he and Matt were staying in two spacious villas. Although Collins enjoyed the over-the-top accommodations, the equation didn't add up. Gregorio didn't need to spend over ten grand on a weekend junket to get the rights to the screenplay.

Collins googled the name of the private club they'd left about six hours earlier on his iPad—La Velocidad. Gregorio's description of the party as "bacchanalian" had been an understatement. The interior of the club had been palatial, and the clientele had exuded power and wealth. It was as if the top slice of Mexico's rich, young, and beautiful had gathered in one place, all of them drinking and dancing the night away in one epic soiree.

Matt had jumped into the fray with both feet, drinking enough tequila for three people. Collins, however, had been more circumspect. The party seemed too perfect. No money changed hands, except in the form of cash tips, and yet the tables were full of exotic foods, expensive wines, liquors, and ice-cold beer. And then there were the women. Club owners in LA often encouraged a limited number of high-end call girls to frequent their club, but this was different. Collins suspected half of the women in the club were in the sex trade. Three of them had discretely approached him, and he'd politely declined their invitations.

When he added up the variables, he came to one conclusion. The price of admission to that party must have been steep, which led him back to the same question he'd posed to Matt on the jet: Why? What did Gregorio expect in return for all of this largesse?

"Whaddya doin' up so early? Damn, I feel like shit."

Collins looked over at Matt, who'd just walked through the front door. He was wearing a dark blue hotel bathrobe, white boxer shorts, and a pair of black socks.

"You look like shit too. By the way, how did you get into my villa? I thought I was paying big bucks to keep degenerates like you off the premises."

"Who are you calling a degenerate? Come over here; I'll give you a slap. And by the way, bozo, they're adjoining villas, remember? I can roam wherever I please."

"I'll have to speak with your buddy Gregorio about that."

Matt sat down at the table and poured himself a cup of coffee from the silver pot. "You got any aspirin or Motrin? It feels like my Uncle Vito's jackhammer is going off inside my head."

Collins pointed to the bottle of aspirin next to his computer. "Yeah, drinking tequila all night will do that. It's over there."

"Are you telling me you don't have a hangover? Can't be."

"I'm half Irish, remember? And unlike you, I drank judiciously."

"Judiciously, my ass. You quaffed your share."

Collins chuckled. "Yeah, I guess I did. But I drank two bottles of water and took four aspirin before I hit the sack. Works every time."

Matt threw three aspirin down his throat and washed them down with the coffee. Collins scanned the search results on his computer and clicked on an old blog post. The blogger claimed to have attended a party at La Velocidad. Membership interests in the club were allegedly fifty thousand per year, and a reserved table was two thousand dollars a night. No wonder they didn't charge for the drinks and the women. Collins shook his head.

"What's your problem, Collins?"

"You know what my problem is. There's something wrong with this picture."

"Jeez, why don't you just—"

"Listen, Matt, you need to think about this equation."

"Why—"

"You know what I'm talking about. I've done some research. A killer screenplay that's written by a big-name writer can sell for seven figures, but that's a rarity, and I'm not coming to the table with either of those attributes. And no, Matt, don't give me this 'It's because I'm such a great agent crap.' If you add up the cost of that flight, the party, and this hotel, we're talking big bucks. Let face it, they didn't need to spend that kind of money to get the rights. I would have been thrilled to get a check for a hundred thousand plus a tiny piece of the back end."

"Relax. Uncle Matt has it all figured out."

Collins scoffed. "You are so full of—"

"Just listen! Two minutes, then I'll shut up."

"Not likely, but go ahead."

"I've got clients in the entertainment industry. When I asked them about the best way to sell your screenplay, they gave me the usual crap—it's a waste of time, you gotta know someone, get someone with a real name to sign on as the coauthor, and on and on. But there was one thing they all agreed on—the hype factor. If one outfit is chasing after a screenplay, all of the others will sit up and notice. If two or three are after it, it becomes a frenzy. My read is this: Gregorio's spending these dollars for show. He wants the big players in the space to think he got his hands on a hot piece of property. If he gets there, they'll line up to get a piece of the game. Worst case, he flips the screenplay for a hefty profit."

Collins stared at Matt and nodded slowly. "Could be, could be. At least it makes sense."

Matt took a sip of coffee and almost choked on it. "Glory be to God, he agrees with me. Of course it makes sense! I know about these things. And if I'm wrong, we'll know in two hours. And by the way, if they send us back with nada, so what? It's been a great weekend, and we didn't have fork over a penny for anything!"

Collins glanced at his watch. "Two hours? What are you talking about?"

"That's why I stopped by. I got a text from Gregorio. He says we're meeting Mr. Big Bucks for lunch in two hours, so we need to get the suits and power ties on."

"Where?"

"A seaside villa about an hour or so south of here."

Matt groaned as he stood up but managed a big grin. "I'll be back in thirty minutes. Be ready! I'm gonna make you rich, Collins, even if you don't wanna be."

Chula Vista, California

Anna walked into the conference room at the far end of the hall five minutes before the meeting Teo had scheduled an hour earlier. Calder was already there working on his laptop. He pointed at the fifty-five-inch television monitor on the wall behind him without looking up. The inside of a large red umbrella was visible.

"If a few things come together, we just may get to watch something . . . interesting."

"What do you mean by interesting?"

Calder nodded at the computer screen. "Like, hell yeah, interesting, assuming all the tech stuff and human intel—"

A voice with a distinct Southern drawl interrupted him. "It will. Said my prayers last night."

Anna turned around. Mattson was standing in the doorway with an amused look on his face.

"Good morning, Anna. Is the big boss on his way?"

"Good morning, and I'm sure—"

Teo and Eric appeared in the hallway behind Mattson.

"Why, here he is and the big guy, too. Come right in and take a load off," Mattson said as he walked in and took the seat next to Calder.

Teo and Eric sat in the chairs across the way. Teo's expression was guarded. He just nodded to Anna and looked over at the monitor on the wall.

Eric smiled at Anna and waved.

Anna returned the wave. "Eric."

"What's going on?" Teo said.

Mattson nodded toward the screen on the wall. "Mr. Calder tells me the app he put on Mr. Collins's iPad is doing its job. Collins and Esposito just had a little conference, and we just got the feed. The video's not good, but the audio's great. So, let's all take a listen."

Anna could tell from Teo's body language he didn't like Calder and Mattson having control over the intel being gathered in Mexico, but she suspected he couldn't do anything about it. Although it was a joint FBI and CIA operation, she sensed Mattson and Calder either could not, or would not, share control over their sources in Mexico.

Calder tapped a key on his computer and looked up. "Collins and the broker are staying at a resort in Acapulco. I looked the place up. It's totally high-end, and these guys are staying in the private villas on-site. We're talking real big bucks. The iPad is on the table on the balcony of Collins's room. What we're seeing is the inside top of the red umbrella over the table on the balcony. What you'll hear is a piece of a longer recording, but this is the . . . relevant part."

Anna glanced across the table at Teo without moving her head, and he returned the glance. She understood the message. They needed to hear the entire recording.

A voice on the screen brought her eyes back to the monitor.

"Whaddya doin' up so early? Damn, I feel like shit."

Calder pressed a key on his computer and the recording stopped. "That's Matt Esposito. The next voice you hear is the lawyer, Declan Collins."

When the recording finished, Eric pointed at the screen. "How are you getting that signal out?"

Calder nodded. "The app searches for open networks and sends out data in short bursts. In this case, it used the hotel's Wi-Fi."

"How is it activated?" Anna asked.

"It's triggered by incoming sound within a certain tonal range— basically the high and low of most human voices. If the sound app goes on, the camera app begins to record as well."

Teo interrupted Eric's next question. "Mattson, are we going to be able to get eyes and ears in on the meeting with the money guy?"

"Don't know for sure," Mattson said without waiting for Calder to answer.

"Well, if the iPad's in the room—"

Mattson shook his head. "It won't be if the meet is with Ramon Cayetano. Everyone is searched and scanned beforehand. Nothing electronic gets into a room with him. That being said, we have a game in play. We'll let you know once—"

"Can we have a word outside?" Teo asked.

The country boy smile appeared on Mattson's face. "Sure. Let's do that."

Ten minutes later, Teo returned alone. "We'll reconvene here in twenty minutes. Anna, can I see you in my office for a moment?"

Anna nodded and followed Teo back to his office, which was a wood-and-brick box similar to her own, but larger. Teo had a laptop and stack of manila files on one side of the desk and a picture of his wife and two young boys on the other. An old fan in the corner of the room slowly swiveled back and forth, fluttering a piece of paper sticking out of one of the files.

Teo closed the door and gestured to one of the two chairs in front of the desk.

"Okay, here's the deal—and this is coming from Mattson—they're pretty sure the meet is with the Ramon Cayetano, and it's going to be a big deal. I asked him about the source of the intel, but he didn't give me much. He said it's an agency asset, and the folks above his lowly pay grade don't want any more details released without their say-so. I think it's bullshit, but I can't do anything about it. The good news is we may have a set of eyes and ears in that meeting, as in real-time audio and visual feed."

Anna was stunned. "How? That's incredible. This could—"

"He won't say. Same excuse, but if he's got what he says he's got, we may have the keys to the kingdom."

Anna shook her head. "I don't see how that's possible. I read the write-up you gave me on Cayetano's outfit. A top security firm sweeps all of their secure locations once a week and before every big meeting. If Collins or Esposito try to get any tech into that meeting, they're going to get killed."

"Yeah, or worse," Teo growled, "but they can't be the inside source. You heard the back and forth between those guys. They have no idea what they're walking into. It's gotta be someone else—someone the CIA turned a while ago."

Anna leaned forward in her chair. "What about the Mexican national, Gregorio? Could he—"

Teo shook his head. "I don't think so. If he was the source, we wouldn't need the lawyer and his friend. We'd already be inside."

Anna nodded reluctantly. "Do we have a picture of this Gregorio?"

"So far, no. We only have a first name and a partial facial. We're running a query through Homeland Security. We'll see what comes up. The bottom line is we take what we can get from Mattson and Calder and work with it. I'll need your insight. I suspect most of the back-and-forth will be in English, but Cayetano and his advisers may talk among themselves in Spanish. The guards may talk as well. We may even get a visual on a document. Once it's all over, I'll get you a recording of the feed, and you can go over it as many times as you need to. I want as much insight into these people as I can get."

Teo glanced at the clock and stood up. "We have about five minutes before game time. I'll see you then."

THIRTEEN

Acapulco, Mexico

C ollins stepped out of the limousine and scanned the impressive Italianate villa and the surrounding grounds. A picture-perfect lawn ran from the edge of the circular drive to the fifteen-foot perimeter wall encircling the property a hundred yards away. Although flower beds were interspersed throughout the green expanse, none of the flowers were taller than six inches, and there were no trees, hedges, or other plants on the grounds that offered any shade or cover. As he walked toward the rear of the car to get his computer bag, Collins noted the plethora of quasi-hidden cameras on the outside of the building. The spartan landscaping and the cameras suggested to him one thing: Whoever lived in this house took their security seriously.

Gregorio's voice interrupted him before he reached the rear of the car. "Mr. Collins, Jorge will get the bags. Please come in. The staff has set out a light lunch on the rear deck. The view is magnificent."

Matt answered for both of them. "Sounds great. Maybe they have something that will cure this hangover."

Gregorio smiled. "They just might, Mateo. Come, please."

Collins followed Gregorio and Matt through the front door of the grand residence. He nodded to the middle-aged Mexican man wearing a black bow tie, white shirt, black pants, and polished black shoes holding the door open. The man's answering nod was stiff and almost imperceptible.

The floor, walls, and domed ceiling of the massive circular

foyer were clad in marble, and a column of light poured into the room through the circular window in the top of the dome. The room reminded Collins of a miniature version of the Pantheon in Rome.

Gregorio's voice interrupted his thoughts. "It's . . . striking, don't you think?"

Collins looked across at Gregorio, who was waiting under the stone archway on the far side of the room. He detected a hint of scorn in the comment.

"Yes, it is."

"Come. Matt is already out on the loggia."

Collins followed Gregorio down a long hall and through a room with fourteen-foot ceilings. Two massive French doors on the far wall were open, revealing the grounds in the rear of the house.

Gregorio walked past Matt, who was staring through the open doors at the stunning vista of the Pacific Ocean. A grand stairway in the center of the red marble loggia led down to a broad stone path bordered on both sides by flower gardens. The path split the downward sloping semicircular lawn into two perfect halves. A large white gazebo overlooking the ocean was located at the terminus of the path. The seaside edge of the lawn was bordered by a five-foot wall.

Gregorio gestured to the gazebo. "Come. Please. Lunch is served."

Matt and Collins followed Gregorio to the ornate octagonal structure, which was supported by four Doric columns. The gazebo's occupants had an unobstructed view of the Pacific Ocean and the stretch of white beach one hundred yards below. Collins stared at the magnificent vista for another moment before joining Matt and Gregorio at the circular table in the center of the space.

Two attractive Mexican women in their early twenties, wearing black skirts and white blouses, were standing in the shadow of one of the columns. Collins nodded politely to the women as he sat down at the table. He was surprised and somewhat disturbed by their reactions. They returned his nod, and then they glanced quickly at the open door to the house, as if they feared this simple act would bring retribution.

The table was covered with a white linen tablecloth, and three ornate silver plates were laid out with matching silver utensils. Each plate contained a ceviche salad in a silver bowl, ringed by an assortment of small sandwiches. The presentation was a work of art. Gregorio pointed to each of the four silver pitchers in the middle of the table.

"This one is iced tea, with the perfect mixture of vodka, tequila, and rum; this one is also iced tea, but minus the enhancements; this is lemonade; and the last is purified water."

Matt reached for the iced tea pitcher with the vodka and filled the crystal glass in front him to the brim. Then he turned to Gregorio. "Can I fill your glass, sir?"

"Yes, thank you."

After filling Gregorio's glass, Matt turned to Collins and raised an eyebrow. "Let me guess. Too early in the morning, right?"

Collins reached for the pitcher of plain iced tea. "Something like that."

Collins ate half of one of the sandwiches and drank a glass of the iced tea, as he listened to Gregorio and Matt banter about the view, the house, and last night's bacchanalian revelry. Once the two men finished eating, Collins tried to turn the conversation to the impending meeting.

"Gregorio, I'd like to know what your objectives are before we meet with the client. Specifically, is this meeting in the nature of a pitch or is it really just a meet-and-greet?"

Gregorio nodded and smiled politely, but his expression seemed feigned, even forced.

"Yes, of course. Let me try . . . to—"

"Relax, old son." Matt, who was already working on his second glass of iced tea, slapped Collins on the back. "Just let Matt the pitch-meister do his magic."

Collins brushed off Matt's comment. "I'd like to hear from Gregorio. I want to know what the game plan is *before* the meeting."

Gregorio nodded slowly and looked down at his hands. Collins sensed Matt was going to interrupt again, and he raised his hand to cut him off. "I want to hear from Gregorio."

Gregorio reached for the glass of water he'd poured during the meal. Collins noted Gregorio's glass of leaded iced tea was still three-quarters full. After taking a drink in the uncomfortable silence, Gregorio answered the question. "Mr. Collins, the client will do the talking. We will listen, and he will communicate his . . . demands. As far as my objective, it is very simple: to meet those demands. My expectations for you and Matt are the same.

Gregorio glanced down at his Rolex and eased out of his chair. "And now, gentlemen, it, as you say, is 'game time.'"

Matt took a final drink from his cocktail as he stood up and slapped Collins on the back again. "Suit up, chief. We need a hat trick today."

Gregorio smiled stiffly at the comment and started down the pathway back to the house. He stopped just outside the door to the house and turned to Matt. "Mateo, one . . . point. The investor is a man of great power and wealth. We must treat him with the utmost respect at all times or we could lose . . . the deal."

Matt ignored the quiet intensity, even fear, in Gregorio's tone, but Collins didn't. Gregorio wasn't just worried about losing a potential big deal. He was afraid of whomever they were meeting with.

Matt, put his hand on Gregorio's shoulder and nodded in mock seriousness. "Relax, paisan. This isn't my first rodeo."

Gregorio nodded politely. "Of course."

Collins watched the exchange. Gregorio almost winced when Matt put his hand on his shoulder, despite the smile on his face.

For a moment, Collins considered pulling Matt aside and telling him they needed to get out of there, but instead he suppressed the thought. If this investor was a major source of capital for Gregorio's employer, he had reason to be trepidatious. As for Matt, Collins knew he could be an incredibly persuasive salesman, and most clients liked his confident, gregarious personality. But some did not. Matt was so confident and competitive he had difficulty taking no for an answer, particularly when a big payday was on the line. Collins suspected Gregorio feared that Matt's informal bonhomie wouldn't play well with the money guy.

Collins stepped toward Matt with the intent of advising him that he would take lead, but Gregorio stepped in between them and gestured toward the residence. "Gentlemen, it's time for our meeting." There was an undercurrent of urgency in Gregorio's voice.

As they walked back up the path to the main house, Collins noticed a figure sitting on a stone bench at the far end of the loggia watching them. He was wearing a white linen suit and dark glasses. Although Collins couldn't see the man's features clearly from this distance, he seemed familiar. Gregorio noticed Collins's glance, and he looked in that direction. He visibly stiffened when he saw the man, and neither man acknowledged the other, which Collins considered odd.

When they entered the villa, Gregorio pointed toward two formidable-looking double doors at the end of a dimly lit hallway to the left. "We will be meeting in the conference room through those doors."

Then he pointed at a side table against the far wall. "Please place all of your electronic devices on this table—everything. We will be scanned before we go into the meeting. I know it seems excessive, but business is done . . . a little differently in Mexico today."

"I'm good with that," Matt said. "I have a lot of clients who are spooked by recording devices and cameras."

Collins didn't say anything. He just followed Matt's lead and put his iPhone and iPad bag on the table.

Gregorio glanced at his cell phone as he laid it on the table and sighed in exasperation. "I'm sorry, my phone is running out of power, and I have to take a call right after this meeting. I will be right back. I am going to put it on a charger."

"Sure," Matt said and walked over to Collins. When Gregorio was out of earshot, he whispered conspiratorially, "Do you think I'd be outta line if I asked Gregorio for one of those leaded ice teas to go after the meeting? Damn, they were good."

Collins turned, stepped closer to Matt, and spoke in a low whisper. "Let's just get through this meeting."

Matt chuckled. "Pregame jitters? Relax, ole Matt has it covered. I'll sell—"

"Matt, listen to me. This is how we're going to play this—they talk, we listen. Then I'll respond to what they said, clear?"

Matt made a dismissive gesture with his hand. "What? No way. We're not selling a bunch of legalese to a half-asleep jury, chief. We're pitching a screenplay to a big-money guy. I'm the salesman—I mean agent, remember?"

Collins glanced around quickly and then stepped closer to Matt and whispered, "Something is not right here! Let me take the lead on this."

Matt's eye's widened. "What are you—"

"Gentlemen? Is everything okay?"

Collins froze and wondered how long Gregorio had been listening. He shook his head. "Matt was just telling me about a problem investor."

Gregorio nodded in sympathy.

Matt followed Gregorio to the door at the end of the hall. As he followed Matt down the hall, Collins glanced into a darkened room on his left and hesitated for a moment. It was a small yet lavishly decorated memorial chapel. A large black-and-white picture of a beautiful Mexican woman holding two small boys was located at the foot of a life-size bronze crucifix affixed to the wall. Fresh red roses lay in front of the picture. The room was obviously a shrine to the woman and the children.

"Mr. Collins?"

Collins turned. Gregorio was standing at end of the hall holding one of the double doors open. Collins walked through the door into a small, brightly lit anteroom where Matt was waiting. When Gregorio closed the door behind him, Collins noted it was made of a heavy composite material and the rubber trim at the bottom of the door made a perfect seal when it closed.

He glanced around the room. The walls and ceiling were bracketed by two steel strips about two feet wide—a metal detector. Gregorio walked over to the heavy wooden door on the far side of the room and waited. There was a muted click, and he pulled the door open. Apparently, whoever was monitoring the anteroom was satisfied they weren't carrying any metal or electronic devices. Gregorio gestured for Matt and Collins to walk into the darkened room on the other side of the door. Matt strode into the room, a confident smile on his face. Collins followed but stepped to the right just inside the doorway and hesitated long enough to allow his eyes to adjust to the relative darkness.

The conference room was impressive in a dark, ominous way. The twelve-foot-high ceiling was coffered with dark mahogany squares inlaid with gold. The walls were clad in a lacquered wood so dark it was almost black. Two four-by-six glass cases, backlit by a series of hidden LED lights, were embedded in the walls on the left and right sides of the room. The case on the right side of the room held a painting of a beautiful Mexican woman with voluptuous features and flowing black hair. It was the woman in the memorial chapel down the hall.

The glass box on the other side of the table held the flag of Spain, but not the current version. The flag in the case had a dark black eagle standing behind a shield—the Spanish flag during the reign of the dictator, Francisco Franco.

The wooden conference table in the center of the room was as old as it was magnificent. The two small lamps set in the center of the table cast a cone of illumination on the two heavy wooden chairs located on opposites sides of the table. The crystal goblet set in front of each chair made it clear their host expected his guests to sit in these assigned seats.

As Collins's eyes adjusted to the darkness, he noticed a figure sitting in the chair at the opposite end of the table and the three men dressed in dark suits standing behind him. A fourth man was lounging in a chair to his right. It was the man in the white suit Collins had seen on the loggia. He must have entered the room through a second door.

Gregorio, who was standing behind Matt and Collins, pointed at the chair with the goblet on the left side of the table. "Mr. Esposito, please sit here."

Then he turned to Collins and pointed to chair on the opposite side of the table. "Mr. Collins, please take this chair."

Collins glanced over at Matt. His friend had just noticed the man at the other end of the table and the guards who were with him. Matt stared at them in confusion for a moment before walking stiffly to the seat on the left side of the table and sitting down. Collins walked over to the other chair, his feet sinking into the plush Oriental rug spanning the length and width of the room. When he reached the heavy chair, he pulled it several feet away from the table and angled it toward the man sitting at the opposite end of the room before sitting down.

Collins could now see the basic features of the man sitting at the head of the table. He was wearing a black smoking jacket with red lapels and a white dress shirt, open at the collar. He had a full head of gray hair, a prominent brow, deep-set eyes, a broad, flat nose, and cheeks noticeably pockmarked by acne scars. His broad shoulders, large hands, and hard mien made him seem larger than he was. Collins suspected the man was no taller than five-ten. He estimated his weight to be in the 190-pound range. As the man's features came into focus, Collins realized he was returning Collins's stare. There was no hint of welcome in his cold, merciless eyes.

The three men standing behind the man had three common characteristics. They spent a lot of time in the weight room, they wore their hair in a short military crop, and their posture made it clear they were there to protect the man sitting in front of them.

The man in the white suit lounging in a chair behind him was an enigma. He was dressed casually, his hair was long and stylish, and unlike the other four men, who were staring at Matt and Collins, he seemed disinterested in the meeting. He was examining the nails on his right hand, as if deciding whether he needed a manicure.

Collins had walked into all too many meet-and-greet meetings with the US Attorney's Office that turned out to be "shock and awe" setups, packed with hyper-aggressive prosecutors and FBI agents. He knew from experience the smart game in that kind of preplanned kill box was to keep quiet, learn as much as much as possible, and get out. Collins suspected he and Matt were now in a similar but potentially far more lethal box, and the man with his finger on the trigger was sitting at the head of the table. They had to play their cards very carefully in the next few minutes, or they might not leave Mexico alive.

Collins reached for the glass of water in front of him with his left hand and intentionally bobbled the glass slightly to draw Matt's attention. When Collins and Matt had played hockey together as kids, Collins had played the right-wing position, and Matt had played the left. Two fingers meant Matt was to take the last pass and make the shot on the goal, three fingers meant Collins was the shooter. As Collins steadied the glass he placed the first three fingers of his left hand against the back of his right hand and glanced over at Matt, without turning his head. Matt's thumb eased slightly off the table. He'd gotten the message, although the look on his face made it clear he wasn't happy about it.

For a long moment, the room was silent and no one moved. Then the man at the end of the table spoke. "Good morning, gentlemen. My name is Ramon Cayetano. You will call me Mr. Cayetano."

"Good morning, Mr. Cayetano," Collins said politely. Matt nodded.

The man kept his eyes fixed on Collins through a long silence.

"Mr. Collins, I have need of your services," Mr. Cayetano finally said. "I am told you have the means to orchestrate the transfer of a large sum of cash from Mexico to the United States under conditions that will convert what your government deems illicit funds into legitimate funds. I am also told you have the means to do this without the imposition of an unduly harsh surcharge on my funds. The amount of money I need cleansed in this way is . . . not less than one hundred million dollars. I will need this done within four months. In return for these services, I will pay you and your friend the sum of six million dollars. You can divide this fee however you like."

The man's words, which were spoken in a low guttural rasp, were slow and deliberate. Although there were uncomfortable pauses between each sentence, Collins instinctively realized that interrupting him could have fatal consequences. He feared Matt might not see it the same way. As he waited for each pause to end, Collins unconsciously held his breath, anticipating an outburst from Matt.

Collins also realized the man at the end of the table wasn't making them an offer. He was telling them what they were going to do. Although Collins had no intention of complying with the man's demand, he also had no intention of defying him until he was free from his control. His game plan was simple: Say and do whatever was necessary to get the two of them out of there alive.

Collins waited until he was completely sure the man had finished what he had to say before he responded. "I assume you are talking about the scheme in the screenplay, Mr. Cayetano."

The man at the end of table blew a puff of smoke from the cigar into the air. "No, Mr. Collins, I am not talking about the screenplay. I am talking about reality—a reality *you* are going to bring to fruition for me."

Collins spread his hands out on the table in a placative gesture. "That is a very generous offer, Mr. Cayetano, and I—we—would like to meet . . . achieve your objectives; however, there are systems in place in the United States, systems designed to prevent this kind of scheme from succeeding. The screenplay is just a story. To bring about what you are talking about would—"

Collins stopped talking as soon as the man made a dismissive motion with his left hand.

"Gregorio!" The man's cold gaze never left Collins when he uttered the command.

Gregorio, who was standing at the opposite end of the table, nodded respectfully and spoke in a voice that bore little resemblance to the cultivated jocular banter Collins was used to hearing.

"Mr. Collins, the resources you will need to implement this . . . operation will be provided, and I am quite sure you can and will accomplish what must be done within the four months requested by Mr. Cayetano. You told me yourself, just a week ago, it could be done."

"We were talking about a hypothetical scenario," Collins said quietly.

"I would respectfully disagree. The distressed company you referred to in your hypothetical—Retail One—is a very real corporation called PriceStar, Inc., and the financial distress this company is experiencing is also very real."

Collins didn't outwardly react to the Gregorio's statement, but he felt as if a noose were tightening around his neck. As Gregorio continued his recitation, Collins realized the trap they'd walked into had been planned weeks, if not months, earlier.

"PriceStar is what is known as a ninety-nine-cent store in the United States. It generates over eight hundred million dollars in sales annually, and a very high percentage of those sales are cash transactions."

Gregorio hesitated for a moment. "The company makes its headquarters in Irvine, California, and it has stores in every major city in California. PriceStar is within weeks of filing a Chapter 11 case and during this proceeding it will almost certainly be liquidated through the kind of going-out-of-business-sale you described to me. This filing has been delayed for one reason—a lack of cash. The company has been unable to reach a deal with what you refer to as a debtor-in-possession lender to fund its post-petition inventory purchases and cash needs. The few bidders seeking this position are demanding a very steep discount from PriceStar's senior secured creditor, Bank of America, and they are offering the unofficial committee representing the unsecured creditors a penny-on-the-dollar distribution.

"As you explained to me in great detail, this is the ideal situation in which to implement a money laundering scheme. But then, you know all this. So, you see, providence has offered you and Mr. Esposito the means to achieve Mr. Cayetano's ends and . . . to make a handsome profit in return for your assistance."

Collins stared at Gregorio. His mind raced past the obvious fact that Gregorio had carefully orchestrated this setup using Matt as the means to get to him to the more frightening issue. These people would not have laid their plans on the table without knowing they had ironclad leverage over him and Matt—leverage to keep them in line once they returned to Los Angeles. When Collins looked from Gregorio to Cayetano, he knew the man realized exactly what he was thinking. When he didn't say anything, Collins decided to put the issue square on the table.

"I see. And if Matt and I go back—"

"Gregorio," Matt interrupted, "what is this bullshit? Is this some kind of game?"

Collins tried to regain control of the exchange. "Matt, let me—"

"Screw that. I brought you into this bullshit. I want to know what this is about."

Gregorio looked down at his hands as Collins turned to Matt. "Let me deal with this!" His voice was quiet, but it carried a desperate intensity. Matt turned and stared at him, his rage barely under control. For a long moment, Collins feared he wouldn't listen, and the situation would spin out of control. Then he relented.

"Go ahead." Matt's voice was a restrained growl.

Collins turned his attention back to Gregorio, who was still looking down at his hands. "I assume you have some reason to believe Matt and I will comply with your demands once we return to LA?"

The room was silent for a long moment. Then Cayetano leaned back in his chair, his eyes locked on Collins. "Yes, Mr. Collins, I do," Cayetano said, his raspy voice barely above a whisper. The man in the white suit smiled and reached for a television remote sitting on a small table to his left. A moment later, the massive television screen behind Cayetano, which had been hidden in shadow, came on.

The video feed playing on the screen was second rate, but Collins could see the woman sitting at the far end of a table. It was Sienna, Matt's sister. The muscular Latino man with tattoos covering his arms standing behind her was holding a Colt Python .357 Magnum three inches from her head.

The man in the white suit gestured casually to the man on the screen behind him. "Juan, have your guest nod her head. I want to make sure the audio is clear."

The man standing behind Sienna spoke to her gruffly. When she didn't react immediately, he barked out the command again, and she began to nod frantically. The fear in Sienna's eyes was like a knife in Collins's stomach.

A moment later Matt sprang out of his chair and lunged for Cayetano. Collins watched the scene as if in a trance, momentarily overwhelmed by the video of Sienna and the sudden explosion of violence.

The two guards on Cayetano's right side had been expecting Matt's reaction and intercepted him before he could reach their boss. Cayetano slowly drew a cigar from the vest pocket of his smoking jacket, unconcerned by the threat. An amused smile played across the face of the man in the white suit as he watched the scene. It was as if he had been looking forward to this sporting event.

The sight of the shiny brass knuckles on the raised fist of one of the two guards grappling with Matt unleashed the rage simmering within Collins. He vaulted onto the conference table, took two quick steps, wheeled, and drove the heel of his right foot into the head of the guard. The force of the blow drove the man into the second guard, who had Matt pinned to the wall, and the two of them fell to the floor.

The vibration of the tabletop gave Collins a moment's warning of the attack by the third guard. The man, who easily weighed 200 pounds, leaped onto the table with the intent of crashing into Collins from behind. Collins dropped to one knee, lowered his head, and pulled the onrushing man over his own body. Then he stood up quickly. The man flew off the table and crashed into the wall, his legs flying over his head.

Collins wheeled and jumped off the table, landing beside Matt. He froze the instant his feet touched the floor. Matt was down on one knee, unmoving. The man in the white suit was holding a gun to his forehead. Collins recognized the weapon—a Beretta 92FS. There was an amused smile on the man's face. When their eyes met, Collins realized, with absolute certainty, the man intended to kill Matt as an object lesson. Cayetano believed Matt was expendable, and he knew having Sienna in custody was a sufficient threat to keep Collins in line.

Collins turned to Cayetano, who was examining the Cuban cigar he'd lit in the midst of the fight. The five rings on his right hand gleamed in the light from the tip of the cigar.

"I need him," Collins gasped in a hoarse voice. "He has the relationship with Nigel Kendrick, the Brit who controls the hedge fund in the Caymans. We have to reactivate the fund to do this deal. Without it, we have no conduit to bring your dollars into the US."

Cayetano didn't react.

"He's right. We need that conduit," Gregorio said quickly from the far side of the room.

A flicker of irritation crossed the brow of the man holding the gun to Matt's head. Cayetano raised a hand from the table. For a moment, Collins feared the man in the white suit would ignore the command and kill Matt anyway, but instead he turned to Collins, his smile fading. The look in his eyes promised another lethal reckoning.

"There *will* be another day," the man in the white suit said. He wheeled around, stepped over the two guards on the floor, and eased into the chair he'd left moments earlier, as if nothing had happened.

Cayetano leaned forward, placing his arms on the table as he puffed on the cigar. "So, Mr. Collins, you can do this deal after all."

Collins slowly exhaled, nodded, and looked up at Sienna. She was staring back at him. Tears were running down her cheeks. The fear in her eyes bordered on hysteria. A dozen potential angles and options screamed through Collins's head as he assessed the situation. None of them offered a solution. He and Matt were in an ironclad box as long as Cayetano had Sienna under his control, and although Cayetano wouldn't kill her until he had what he wanted, his men could make her wish she was dead in the interim.

Collins had to try to buy her a measure of protection, but what? How? Collins's eyes fixed on the picture of the woman in the glass case on the wall.

His eyes then met Cayetano's. "Yes, I . . . Matt and I can get it done, but time is short. Matt will need to get on a plane to Grand Cayman today, if a flight is available, and I need to get back to Los Angeles. The bankruptcy firm that controls the PriceStar case, Pace Cohen, has been trolling for a lender to finance Retail One's bankruptcy case. I . . . I need to get into that acquisition contest. Once we lock up that position, we control the case, including the going-out-of-business sale that will serve as the washing machine for your cash."

Collins hesitated, his mind racing through the hundreds of hurdles he'd have to sequentially overcome to give them a shot at making this insane deal work, while concurrently trying to find a way to keep the three of them alive. He raised his right hand slowly, as if trying to get them to understand the magnitude of what had to be done.

"Matt will need to cut a deal with Kendrick . . . a deal giving us control of the Cayman hedge fund he ran into the ground last year. We—"

"Wait!" The interruption came from Gregorio. Collins had to control his rage when he looked over at him. "Why will Mr. Kendrick be so accommodating?"

Without looking over at Gregorio, Matt answered as he slowly stood up and brushed away the stream of blood oozing down the side of his face. He spoke in a monotone, as if the life had been sucked out of him. "Because he's an alcoholic, and he's broke. If we pay him a stipend of at least ten grand a month, he'll do whatever I want."

"What about the other shareholders or investors who owned interest in the fund?" Gregorio asked quietly.

Matt kept his eyes on the television screen as he answered. "The fund, CerTrust Limited, was a wipeout. I had clients in it. There was a litigation settlement. They returned their shares to the fund in return for a cash payout. A bunch of brokerage firms and D&O insurers funded the pot to make it happen. There are only two shareholders in the fund now—Kendrick and me. We'll transfer the shares to whatever entity you . . . plug into the ownership daisy chain."

"Explain," Cayetano said curtly.

"We need to keep a certain number of corporate blinds between you and CerTrust; otherwise the scheme will be discovered," Collins said. "We will . . . we will probably park the fund's shares in a Cayman Island entity and put the shares of that entity in a Panamanian corporation, with bearer stock. Whoever holds that stock will control the Cayman entity and the hedge fund where your money will be going. I'll get the Panamanian entity set up with a lawyer I know in Panama City on the flight back. You'll need to have someone fly down there to get the stock certificate."

Collins hesitated. "To have credibility with the Pace Cohen law firm and with Bank of America, the holder of the debt we need to buy, I need to show them that the cash for the deal is in CerTrust's bank account. I'll need to have ten million wired to that entity within a week."

Cayetano eased back in his chair and spoke in a cold, threatening voice. "You do your part, Mr. Collins, and I will do mine. The money will be there. Now, I suggest that you and your . . . friend get on your way. You have much to do."

"There's one more issue," Collins said, his eyes locking on Cayetano.

The drug lord slowly leaned forward, placed his forearms on the table, and eased his fingers together into a steeple. "And what would that be?"

"Our side of the deal is this: Matt and I convert at least one hundred million of drug money into clean, legit, available funds and—"

"And what?" Cayetano said coldly.

Collins glanced up at Sienna, who was staring at him, rendered mute by the tape across her mouth. He raised his hand and pointed at the woman in the picture on the wall. "I want you to swear on the grave of this woman that Sienna will be protected from all harm or abuse, sexual or otherwise, until the deal is done."

For a long moment the room was deathly silent. Collins's eyes were locked on Cayetano.

The drug lord's steepled fingers slowly locked together, and the tips turned white. The man in the white suit glanced over at Collins, a smile on his face. Then Cayetano broke the silence, speaking slowly and emphasizing each word, in a voice as cold and hard as steel. "I swear. Now go."

FOURTEEN

Maijoma, Mexico

ienna stared at her older brother through the television monitor as Declan Collins guided him out of the dark conference room. A stream of blood was running down the side of his face from a cut just above his right eye, and he was hunched over at the waist, but that wasn't what shocked her. It was the look on his face.

Matt had always been Sienna's larger-than-life protector and mentor, even when she wished it were otherwise. Everybody in the old neighborhood had respected her older brother—the All-State, All-American goalie with a golden ticket to the NHL. Although the accident had taken that dream away from him, Matt had recovered and climbed to the top again as a securities broker in LA. She still remembered the day he picked her up at LAX in his red Ferrari and drove her to college in Santa Barbara. The indomitable protector Sienna remembered was not the man she watched walk out of the room on other side of the screen. The look on Matt's face was a mixture of shock, desperation, and, worst of all, despair.

When the man standing behind her turned off the monitor, the full realization of her situation hit her. She was being held hostage by a merciless drug cartel at a remote location somewhere in Mexico. Although the man in the conference room had promised she wouldn't be harmed, what was that worth? And how long would his protection last? Once the cartel no longer needed Matt and Declan, she was dead, and they were probably dead too.

For a minute she was unable to breathe. When she felt someone touching her wrist, she shot out of the chair and spun around. The chair fell to the ground behind her. A Mexican man in his early sixties wearing a worn long-sleeved shirt, jeans, and a dusty pair of boots was staring at her. His worn, sun-bronzed face, which was framed by an unkempt tousle of white-gray hair, showed a mixture of surprise and irritation.

"*Cuidado!*" The man's tone was gruff but not threatening. He held up a key in one hand. "I take those off," the man said, pointing at the handcuffs on her wrists.

Sienna hesitated for a moment and then nodded. She turned her back, bent slightly at the waist, and extended her wrists toward the man. He fumbled with the lock for a moment before removing the handcuffs. When she turned back toward him, he pointed to the gag over her mouth.

"You can take that off. Is okay. Then you follow me."

Sienna removed the gag and placed it beside the blindfold she'd been wearing when they had escorted her into the room. She glanced at the blank television screen and scanned the room before turning back toward the man behind her. The walls were made of stained corrugated metal, the floor was concrete, and the ceiling, which was about twelve feet high, was formed of stained white ceiling tiles held up by a metal infrastructure.

"Come."

Sienna turned to follow the man, but she stopped, as did the older man, after two strides. A second man, who was standing just inside the door, held up his hand and spoke in a quiet voice laden with menace.

"A moment, Arturo. I want to establish a few ground rules so there will be no painful misunderstandings in the future."

The man stepped uncomfortably close to her and stared at her for several moments with cold disdain. His short, neatly trimmed hair framed a thin face dominated by cold, dark eyes, a hooked nose, and a striking scar that ran from his right cheekbone to the tip of his chin. Unlike the older man behind her, the second man was dressed in expensive clothes. He wore a black silk shirt, designer jeans, and highly polished western boots. He also carried a large handgun in the holster on his hip.

Although the man's words were matter of fact when he spoke, the lethality of the threat he communicated to her was crystal clear.

"You are being held in a secure facility in the desert. The nearest human being is over sixty miles away. There are no phones or other communication devices of any kind in this compound, so you cannot get a message out to anyone. You will stay in your room at all times, and that room will be locked at all times, with one exception. You will be allowed to eat in the kitchen with the cook three times a day. She does not speak English. Do not attempt to escape or violate these rules. If you do, your punishment will be harsher than you can imagine."

When he finished, the man nodded curtly to Arturo, who walked past him quickly and gestured for Sienna to follow.

She followed the older man into the building and down a long hallway. The walls on either side of the hallway were made of the same corrugated steel. A row of intermittent lights hanging from a wire ran the length of the corridor, providing just enough light to see ahead and behind. Sienna heard muted voices speaking Spanish that seemed to be coming from the dark expanse above her head, but she suspected the voices came from another part of the metal structure, and the sound waves were being carried along the metal roof.

The older man stopped at the end of the corridor and opened a door on the right, stepped back, and gestured for Sienna to enter. She glanced back down the corridor before walking into the room. A silhouetted figure stared back at her. It was the man in the black silk shirt with the gun.

The room Sienna entered was similar to the one she'd just left, but it contained a small bed, a dresser, and a table with one chair. A plate with a sandwich covered by a napkin, and two bottles of water were sitting in the center of the table.

One part of the room, which had been partially walled off with concrete blocks, had a toilet, a sink, and a narrow shower stall. The long fluorescent light hanging down from the drop ceiling illuminated the center of the room with a flickering halo of yellow but left the remainder in shadow. She noticed, with relief, her backpack at the foot of the bed.

The man behind her shuffled his feet, and she turned to look at him. He didn't meet her eyes when he spoke: "This is your room. You stay here."

As the man closed the door, he whispered in a voice filled with equal parts warning and fear, "Do not cross Matias, the man in the black shirt. He's likes to hurt people . . . almost as much as he likes to kill them."

A moment later, Sienna heard the heavy bolt slide into place on the opposite side of the door.

Acapulco, Mexico

Matt stared out the window as the jet flew north, oblivious to the golden halo cast over the magnificent beaches below by the last rays of the setting sun. The image of Sienna's terrified face as he left the room hours earlier was all he could see. It haunted his thoughts, bringing waves of rage, fear, frustration, and despair—waves that crashed within, leaving him feeling hollow and broken. *How could this have happened? How could I have left Sienna in that terrible place? How can I save her?*

He had never felt so helpless and overwhelmed. He loved challenges, and he'd always come out on top whenever he decided the contest was worth the effort. Even after he lost his shot at the NHL, he knew he would get up off the floor and climb to the top of another mountain. It was just a question of which one and when. But this was different. This was his worst nightmare.

His dad had made him promise to take care of his sister, no matter what it took, as the old man lay dying of cancer in a second-rate hospice facility. It was the one charge he'd always faithfully honored, until three hours ago.

As the private jet banked east toward Mexico City, he remembered a scene from the old neighborhood. He'd just gotten off the bus after hockey practice, and Sienna was waiting for him. She was sitting on an old bike that he'd spray-painted pink to make it somewhat palatable to the feisty seven-year-old.

She pointed an accusing finger at him and said, "You're late. Mom already has dinner on the table."

He waved at the departing bus. "What am I supposed to do, make the bus drive faster?"

"Maybe. I'll race you home."

She'd won the race, because he'd let her. He always did.

A year after his father died, Sienna caught a severe case of the flu. She spent two days in the intensive care unit at the local hospital. He remembered the prayer he'd said over and over again as he waited for news from the doctors: "God, if anything bad has to happen, take me instead of Sienna."

Matt had not prayed in a long time. He decided it was time to start again.

FIFTEEN

Chula Vista, California

nna was working through another gig of emails and documents when Teo knocked on the door to her office. He walked in, closed the door after him, leaned back against it, and ran a hand over his bald head.

"Calder said it was a no-go on the meeting. The iPad was left outside the room, which we suspected would happen. These outfits know what we can do, or most of what we can do."

"Okay. What's the next step?"

"The higher-ups have decided we need to get someone inside Collins's office. He's going to quarterback whatever's going to happen. He runs a small shop, but we think we've found a way in. His office manager uses a contract paralegal service when Collins needs help on bigger cases, and he's looking for help now."

"That's a great idea. That will put us in the middle—"

"Put *you*." Teo pointed at Anna.

"Me?" she said, incredulous. "Teo, I've never worked undercover, and I'm not a paralegal."

Teo made a dismissive motion with his right hand. "On the first, don't worry about it. You'll do great. On the second, we're gonna get you trained up. You will be meeting with a top paralegal every night for the next week—four hours a night. The Bureau will also have an experienced paralegal on call. You can email her questions, and she'll be standing by ready to draft anything you want. The bottom line is we need someone in that office, someone from this team, and you're the only one who fits the bill."

Anna was about to make another argument when Teo turned around and opened the door. He stopped in the doorway, as if he'd just remembered a small detail. "One other thing—you have two hours to get back to LA for your first four-hour paralegal training session. I'll text you the address."

She stared at the closed door in shock for a moment, then stood up and grabbed her backpack.

Mexico City, Mexico

The private jet ran into a patch of turbulence about ten minutes after taking off, but Collins barely noticed it. He was making a mental list of the steps he'd have to take in the next seventy-two hours just to get in the game on the PriceStar deal. He stopped at twenty-five and reached for his iPad, but hesitated, remembering the short, laconic speech by Cayetano's twenty-something computer tech.

"I loaded an app onto both of your cell phones. It records every number, conversation, email, and text message you send. That same app has also been placed on Mr. Collins's iPad and," the tech said pointing to Matt, "on the laptop we found in your hotel room. When you get back to LA, Mr. Collins, a man will meet you at your house at 6:00 a.m. He will install a device on your home phone, and he will follow you to work and install the same monitoring app on the laptop you use in your office and on your work phone. You will *only* use the phones and computer devices I just mentioned. If you talk to anyone who the chief thinks is a threat, or if you use any device other than those I just mentioned, well, I assume you know what will happen. One other thing, if you don't use the phones and computers, we'll know that too. Enough said."

Collins looked over at Matt, who was sitting in the seat across the aisle. His right hand was spasmodically tapping the armrest, and his left was locked in a tight fist. His eyes were fixed on darkness outside the window. Two guards were sitting in the row of seats behind them, and another three were in the row in front. Sienna was Cayetano's ace in the hole, but he wanted to make sure they remembered this fact on the plane ride to Mexico City.

Collins grabbed the iPad, attached the keyboard and started typing the to-do list and the contacts he'd have to connect with to tie down the PriceStar deal. By the time the jet began to descend, thirty minutes later, he'd written ten pages of notes, interspersed with questions, names, contingencies, and alternatives.

He glanced up at Alex Sanchez, the man sitting in the first row of seats. The short, almost frail Mexican accountant seemed an odd fit for the Cayetano drug gang, but then so did Gregorio. It didn't matter. He'd been told that Sanchez had to accompany him to every meeting on the deal, and he had to be in on every conference call.

Collins had initially been concerned Sanchez's presence would require an awkward explanation, but his background solved the problem. Sanchez had worked for a recognized international accounting firm, first as an auditor, then in their financial consulting division. Everyone working on a bankruptcy as big as PriceStar would expect the largest secured creditor to have a financial adviser on its team. Things would get more difficult when the backroom horse-trading between lawyers about attorney fees and case control took place, but he would deal with that then.

When the plane landed in Mexico City, Matt and Collins stayed in their seats, as instructed, until one of the guards waved them forward. Their bags were waiting on the tarmac. Gregorio stood off to one side. Collins suspected he wanted Sanchez to be the point man until cooler heads prevailed.

Sanchez walked over to Collins and Matt, followed by two of the guards. "Gentlemen, this is your itinerary." He gestured politely toward one of the guards. "Mr. Esposito will go with Miguel. He has the ticket for your flight to Grand Cayman. The flight leaves in three hours. Miguel will bring you to a private club in the airport where you can shower and change and get something to eat before your flight. Mr. Collins, you and I will be flying to Los Angeles together on a United Airlines flight. It leaves in ninety minutes. Do . . . do you have any questions?"

"No, but I need a minute with Matt alone." Matt was staring blankly at a Delta flight taking off from the tarmac about a mile distant.

Sanchez's face tightened, and he glanced back at Gregorio, who was talking to one of the guards.

"Look, it has nothing to do with the deal," Collins said. "I just need to make sure his head's in the game."

Sanchez hesitated, glanced at the blank look on Matt's face, and nodded.

Collins walked over to Matt. "Matt," he said quietly.

Matt continued to stare out at the airfield.

"Matt, I need your head in this game. I *can* get this deal done, and we can . . . *no, we will* get Sienna back, but we gotta do it together."

Matt stared back at him. He was listening, but it wasn't good enough. Unless Matt could fire up Nigel Kendrick and allay any suspicions he had, the deal wouldn't happen, or it wouldn't happen fast enough.

Collins grabbed the lapels of Matt's suit, and spoke in a cold, hard voice, his face two inches from Matt's. "What's my name?"

Matt stared at him, anger coming to his eyes. "What? What is this—"

Collins slammed his fists into Matt's chest, while still holding onto the lapels of his jacket. "Wrong answer, bozo. *What's my name?*"

Rage flared in Matt's eyes. "Get off!"

Then a look of understanding appeared on his face. He remembered the speech Mike Stone, the coach of their high school team, had made when they were two goals down after the second period during the state championships. At the end of the speech, Stone had roared over and over again, "My name is invincible. What is your name?"

"Your name . . . your name is invincible," Matt said quietly.

"Now, what's your name?" Collins growled.

"My name . . . my name is invincible," Matt answered without feeling.

Collins shook him again. "Say it like you mean it!"

Rage flared in Matt's eyes, and he growled, "My name is invincible!"

Collins released Matt's lapels. "Right answer. Okay, here's what I need you to do. When you get to Grand Cayman, tell Nigel you stumbled onto a killer deal. Tell him it will put 300K into his pocket within 120 days if he can get CerTrust back in good graces with CIMA within three days. Tell him he'll get ten grand in cash the minute that's done. Get me wire instructions, and I'll get you the money by tomorrow afternoon."

Matt nodded, and Collins continued, hoping Matt was lucid enough to remember the instructions. "I'll get Sanchez to approve a wire of ten million into CerTrust's account as soon as it's legal again. In the meantime, I'll work on the legal and bankruptcy aspects of the deal in LA. Nigel has to be the face of the hedge fund, so I need you to make him understand he's got to be sober, at least until five every day."

Matt nodded and looked over Collins's shoulder.

Sanchez was walking toward them. Matt stepped closer to him and said in a desperate voice, "Declan, can you really do this thing?"

Collins nodded. "Yeah, I can do it."

Los Angeles Airport

Collins waited for Sanchez just inside the passenger gate. Gregorio had stayed in Mexico City. The accountant had been seated eight rows behind him on the plane, and he was still making his way up the jet bridge, behind a man in a wheelchair.

Collins had spent the three-hour flight continuing to work on a flowchart of the PriceStar deal. The tasks diagram was starting to look like a spider's web. As he mentally walked through the series of minefields standing between him and getting the deal done, a wave of exhaustion washed over him. There was just too much to do in too short a time. *We are so screwed*, he thought.

"What is my name?" Collins said to himself, as Sanchez approached him. He silently whispered in response, "Invincible."

He pulled a flash drive out of his pocket and handed it to Sanchez. "Take this. There are two files on it. One is a program called Kryption Nine. It's made by a Russian outfit. There's no back door, so the Feds can't get in without the password if they happen to get their hands on an encrypted document or file. The password is my first and last name, spelled backwards, four-seven-six, the year the Roman Empire fell. If you type in the wrong password more than three times, the content is wiped. So remember it. Upload the program to your laptop. The second file is a ten-page flowchart that details what we need to do to get this deal done. It's encrypted."

Sanchez nodded.

Collins handed him a business card. "Write your email down on this card."

He waited while Sanchez pulled a pen from his suit and wrote the address on the back the card.

"We can communicate by email, but we encrypt every sensitive message or document being exchanged using the Kryption Nine program. I will be in the office tomorrow by 10:00 a.m. I'd be there earlier, but I have to meet with your . . . surveillance man. I suggest we meet at 10:15 and walk through who is doing what. I emailed the diagram to Donna; she's my office manager slash senior paralegal. Last week I asked her to bring in a temporary paralegal to close a bunch of old case files. The temp can handle the lower-level work on the PriceStar deal. We'll need the support. It's going to get real complicated real quick."

"Should you be using a new paralegal? Why not the one you have?"

"Simple. Donna has worked with me for ten years. She'll know something's out of whack in five minutes. A new paralegal won't have that history."

Sanchez hesitated and then nodded. "Yes, that makes sense."

"Good. I'll see you in the morning," Collins said, and he started toward the exit, not waiting for Sanchez to respond. He stopped abruptly three yards away and walked back to Sanchez. He glanced around quickly to confirm no one was within earshot.

"Before you or Gregorio come to my office, I need to know one thing—does anyone on this side of the border, as in US law enforcement, know you and Gregorio are associated with the . . . cartel?"

Sanchez hesitated, and Collins pressed him.

"I need to know, Sanchez. Some of the clients that I represent are tax cheats under federal indictment. They are often under surveillance by the Feds. If you or Gregorio get picked up on video, they may run your faces through their system. If you are in that system, this deal gets blown out of the water."

Sanchez glanced around before answering in a whisper, "We have been very careful. Mr. Cayetano has insisted we stay outside the . . . organization. Our surnames . . . they are not the names of our birth. Gregorio and I, we are citizens of Argentina. Everything is clean. That . . . that is why we are valuable to Mr. Cayetano."

Collins sensed Sanchez was holding something back. "What is it you're not telling me?"

Sanchez hesitated again, this time for a longer period, before answering. "Gregorio . . . he has people on the inside of the United States government. They have told him that my name is not in any of the databases. Gregorio's name isn't either, yet, but his face showed up on a search a few weeks ago with a note indicating a possible link to Mr. Cayetano. The entry was not listed as a high-priority item, and there are millions of people on the system. So . . . I think we are safe."

Collins wasn't surprised at the Cayetano cartel's reach. Hundreds of computer techs and contractors worked on government databases. Top secret was a relative term.

He shook his head. "We are not *safe*. Here's how it has to be: We interface with Gregorio on the phone or outside the office in places that are safe. You do not mention him in the office. That hit you found on the federal system means someone's looking at him. We don't know how closely. We have to assume the worst."

"Yes, I understand, but . . . but you must not mention to Mr.

Cayetano or . . . or Nacio that Gregorio's name was found on the FBI database. They don't know. It would . . . it would not be good for them to know."

Collins was surprised at the fear in Sanchez's eyes. He stared at him for a moment before responding, "I won't."

SIXTEEN

Los Angeles, California

Anna glanced at her reflection in the mirrored wall of the elevator. The woman at the employment agency who managed Collins & Associates' temporary staffing account had told her the dress code at the firm was casual. She suspected her dark pants, closed-toe shoes, and off-white silk blouse might be too formal, but since it was her first day on the job, she'd decided to err on the conservative side. When she introduced herself to Michaela, Collins & Associates' blonde, college-age receptionist, Anna feared she'd way overshot the casual mark. Michaela was wearing designer jeans and an upscale T-shirt.

Anna felt less out of place when a short and slightly overweight woman in her late forties with close-cropped brown hair walked into the reception area. She was also wearing jeans, but she was wearing a designer blouse, like Anna.

"Hello, I'm Donna Mason, Mr. Collins's paralegal-slash-office manager-slash-everything else."

"Hi. Anna Fallon."

Teo had told Anna to use her first name in the undercover assignment but pick a different surname. This would keep her real identity secret but avoid the risk of being nonresponsive when someone called her. A web search of the name *Anna Fallon* would bring up a newly established LinkedIn and Facebook account describing an experienced paralegal who'd worked for a series of small law firms located in the Midwest before moving to Los Angeles.

"The boss will be here around ten. He will insist you call him Declan. I'd like to bring you up to speed on the new case you'll be working on, but he hasn't told me much about it. When I spoke to him this morning, he just said it was a bankruptcy deal, with complicated tax implications."

Anna followed Donna through the office, which she guessed was about two thousand square feet, to a small interior office with a small desk, a chair, and a file cabinet. A laptop, a phone, three pads of paper, and two pens were sitting on the otherwise pristine desk.

"Here is your domain. Coffee is in the room over there on the right. I'd introduce you to Stan and Dave, the two associates, and Sheila, the admin that they share with Declan, but they're in New York interviewing witnesses for a trial Declan has next month."

"Thanks."

Donna pointed to one of the pads of paper on the desk. "The Wi-Fi code, Westlaw username and password, and your firm email address are all listed on that pad there. Just make sure you shred that page after you memorize them."

"Thanks again," Anna said.

Donna gave her two thumbs up and a smile and walked away.

Anna quickly texted a message to a phone number that would route the message to Teo: "At new job. Waiting for the boss to arrive."

Teo immediately texted her back: "Good luck."

Anna glanced around the office.

Thanks, I'm going to need it.

SEVENTEEN

US Bank Tower, Los Angeles, California

Collins pulled into the underground parking structure, eased the Panamera into his reserved space, and reached for the iPad bag on the passenger seat. His hand froze above the black leather case. His iPad, cell phone, home phone, and office phone were all being monitored. Each device was an electronic chain subjugating him to the will of a ruthless enemy a thousand miles away. He stared at the iPad case for a moment longer, picked it up, locked the car, and walked to the elevator.

The guard behind the desk in the lobby waved as he walked by. "Good morning, Mr. D. Looks like you got some sun."

Without responding, Collins made the thumbs-up sign as he walked into the elevator. His throat was so dry he didn't trust his voice. He pressed the button for the fifty-first floor and breathed a sigh of relief when the door closed before anyone else entered. He stared back at his blurred reflection in the polished elevator door. The "tech" who installed the listening devices on his phone, laptop, and iPad earlier that morning, a tall thin man in his mid-twenties with an Eastern European accent, had told Collins he'd meet him at his office within the hour. When Collins walked into the reception area of the office, the man was already there.

Michaela gave him a wave and nodded to the tech. "Good morning, Mr. D. Mr. Sitrick is here to see you."

"Morning, Michaela."

Collins gestured toward his office. "This way."

"Mr. Sitrick" eased out of the deep leather couch in the reception area and followed Collins into the office.

Collins pointed to a door on the far side of the small kitchen. "The server is in there. The code is 1500ABC. The phone system is VOIP, so its runs through the server."

The man nodded and walked in that direction.

Collins continued to his office and was met halfway by Donna Mason. "I didn't know anyone—"

"It's a router upgrade . . . a security thing. No big deal. Mr. Sanchez, who works for the new client I mentioned, will be here any time now. Please put him in the big conference room."

Collins could tell Donna wasn't satisfied with the upgrade explanation. The computer rep who kept the firm's server up-to-date was a friend of hers, and the two of them considered office tech to be their exclusive fief. Collins couldn't fix that problem, so he tried to change the subject. "Can we meet later on the Sedgwick deal? I need to see what the timeline is for the tax opinion. Does this afternoon work?"

"Yes." There was a hint of annoyance in her voice.

"Great. Oh, and good morning." Collins forced a smile, then turned and walked toward his office.

"Same to you."

Collins kept walking as though he had a pressing matter to get to, and he did, but his real objective was to avoid Donna's questions.

"Declan?"

He slowed and looked over his shoulder.

"The temporary paralegal you requested is here. I thought she was supposed to work on indexing and boxing up old case files, but your last email mentioned a new case."

Collins stopped just inside his office door. "Yes, PriceStar. It's a complicated deal with a . . . short fuse. So that's going to be at the top of the list. Closing the old files will have to wait."

Donna nodded. "Fine. She's in the guest office. Her name is Anna Fallon."

Collins knew Donna still wanted to question him about the computer tech when she took a step in his direction. A call from Michaela on the office intercom gave him an excuse to wave and close his office door.

"Mr. D?"

"One minute."

As Collins walked over to the phone, a text pinged on his cell. He glanced down at the message: "Nigel and I are ready to talk. Dial this number."

Collins recognized the international code for the Caymans.

"Mr. D?"

"Yes, Michaela."

"Mr. Sanchez is here to see you."

"Bring him back to the main conference room."

"On the way."

Collins sent a text back to Matt: "We will call in a minute." He hoped Matt got the message.

Collins shook his head. *I gotta find a way out of this communication box.* He walked over to the conference room. It had a large window, which ran the length of the room, overlooking downtown Los Angeles. Sanchez was standing at one end of the table. He was wearing a dark gray suit and carrying an oversized briefcase. Collins could sense the man's unease, which he found surprising, since Sanchez effectively held a gun to his head, not the other way around.

"Matt just texted. He's standing by with Nigel Kendrick for a call on the status of the hedge fund in Cayman. I'll put the call on speaker, but I'm not going to say you're in the room. Nigel's a cagey guy. If I let him know you're here, he may have questions that neither of us can answer. I'll introduce you later . . . once this thing is off the ground."

Sanchez nodded and tapped the screen of his iPhone several times. Collins was certain the accountant intended to record the call.

Collins pressed the speaker button on the phone in the center of the table, glanced at Matt's text, and dialed the number. Nigel answered the call on the second ring: "Good morning, Declan."

"And good afternoon to you, Nigel. How is everything in beautiful George Town today?"

"Exceptional. You really should open an office here. We have need of a man with your particular set of skills."

"I'm not sure you have enough crooks in this town to keep Declan in business," Matt said.

Collins could hear the undercurrent of strain in Matt's natural bonhomie, but at least he sounded as if he was mentally in the game.

"It could be a part-time thing, then," Nigel said. "We could meet in the afternoons, after a hard day's work, of course, and have a nip of scotch or two. I know this bar on Church Street with a sublime view."

"I'll think about it, Nigel. Who knows?"

"Now, tell me, counselor, is this deal really going to be as lucrative as Mr. Esposito tells me?"

"It could be. There's . . . a big success fee if we get it done. Where are we with CerTrust?"

Nigel cleared his throat in a self-congratulatory manner. "Through my extraordinary efforts, and with a wee bit of help from Matt, of course, the deed is done. The hedge fund will be back in good standing with CIMA by tomorrow morning and it's been rechristened Fourth Street Limited, per your direction, sir."

Collins nodded in relief. It was only one step up a very steep ladder, but it was a critical one. "Great work, Nigel."

"Thank you, sir. Matt and I also transferred our ownership shares in the old girl to Caledon, Ltd., a newly formed Bahamian corporation. So, Matt and I now own Caledon, and Caledon owns Fourth Street. Now, as I understand it, the corporate daisy chain is going to get a wee bit longer?"

Collins tapped his pen on the white marble tabletop in front of him. "It is. A Belizean corporation is being formed today—Lysander Partners, IBC. Once it's formed, you and Matt will transfer your shares in Caledon to Lysander. Simon Rios, the corporate nominee for Lysander, will call you in about an hour. He'll fax you the docs you need to sign to make the transfer."

"How is the corporate governance going to work over here?"

Collins knew what Nigel was after. He wanted to know how he was going to get paid.

"You and Matt are currently the sole board members of Caledon. I'll fax over a board resolution appointing you and two other people to serve as the board of advisers to Lysander. The other two board members will be straw men for all practical purposes. Sign the resolution and put down the date and time. Then do the stock transfer to Lysander. Make sure to date and sign the docs so the sequence is clear."

"Understood. Would you care to tell me who will be the owner of Lysander?"

Collins hesitated for a moment and looked over at Sanchez before answering. "That's complicated, Nigel. Let's just leave it there. By the way, I need the wire instructions for Fourth Street's Cayman account. You'll get a 500K wire by tomorrow morning and another five million within two days."

Sanchez nodded.

"Who do I take my directions from?" Nigel asked.

"Me and Matt. We're the direct link to the money people at the bottom of the corporate ownership chain."

"I see," Nigel said hesitantly. "Well, I do trust you gentlemen, at least a wee bit."

"Relax, Nigel," Matt said in restrained voice. "We won't screw you over."

"Why, that's very comforting, Mr. Esposito."

"Now tell me, gentlemen, what is the investment deal we're doing?"

Collins pulled up the deal diagram on his iPad. "Let me walk you through it."

When the call ended, Collins said to Sanchez, "Okay, the hedge fund platform is set up. Now, we have to pin down the PriceStar secured debt position."

He hit the intercom button on the phone. "Donna, can you have the new paralegal come in? What did you say her name was . . . Ann?"

"Anna Fallon. She will be right in."

He walked over to the conference room door, opened it, and then returned to his seat. He checked off two of three items listed on the deal diagram and then began interlineating more lines.

There was a knock on the open door. Collins finished the line he was typing on the iPad and stood up. "Welcome to the team, Anna."

He walked over to the attractive, five-foot-seven-inch woman and held out his right hand, which she took in a firm grip. "Declan Collins."

"Anna Fallon."

Collins turned and gestured to Sanchez. "This is Mr. Sanchez."

Anna started walking around the conference table, but Sanchez met her halfway, and the two of them shook hands.

"It is my pleasure, Ms. Fallon."

"Anna, please."

"And I am Alex."

"Alex it is."

Collins was surprised and somewhat irritated at the friendly exchange. Sanchez was part of the cartel—the barbarians holding Sienna hostage. His politeness and genuine demeanor grated on Collins, but he suppressed his ire, knowing he would have to work with the accountant whether he liked it or not.

He glanced at his watch. He needed to connect with the Pace Cohen law firm before David Cohen went to lunch.

"Anna, I am sorry to throw you into this, but we need some information on a deal Alex and I are working on, and we need it yesterday."

"Of course."

"Here's the download. Bank of America has a seventy-million-dollar loan outstanding to a company called PriceStar. Pull up PriceStar's last twenty filings on the SEC's Edgar system, and see if any of them mention this facility. If the loan's in default, there may be a short write-up in a Form 8-K filing. Print out those filings. Also, run a search on Google and print out every article, blog, or blurb referencing PriceStar that's dated within the last forty-five days. Send me PDFs of those to my email address. Just send the emails seriatim as you find stuff, whether you think it's a big deal or not."

Anna stood up. "I will get right on it."

"Great, and thanks." Collins started to turn toward Sanchez, but he hesitated for a moment, and watched Anna walk out of the conference room. Her face seemed familiar, but he couldn't recall from where. He slowly turned back to Sanchez.

Sanchez glanced from the departing woman to Collins. "Is something wrong?"

Collins shook his head. "No . . . nothing. Okay, now we have to call the big guy, David Cohen, PriceStar's Chapter 11 attorney. We worked on a case together a year ago. I was called in to deal with an exotic tax problem with potential criminal implications. Hopefully he'll remember me."

George Town, Grand Cayman

Matt walked over to the window of the small second-floor office that was the new world headquarters of Fourth Street Limited, a formerly defunct hedge fund. He watched Nigel stroll across the street to a small bar the Brit deemed a "very reputable establishment." Matt suspected that just meant it was well stocked with the finer brands of scotch whiskey.

Nigel would be gone for at least two hours, which gave Matt plenty of time to call Declan to get an update. Matt reached for the phone and then slowly withdrew his hand. Every call was monitored, which meant he could not ask, and Declan could not answer, any of the questions that mattered. Matt glanced over at the laptop on his desk, knowing it was also off-limits. It had every software application he needed, and one he did not—the same program that was installed on Declan's computer.

Matt walked over to the framed map of the world Nigel had hung behind his new desk earlier that morning. The Brit had circled all the places he'd visited in red. It was quite an extensive list. Matt stepped closer to the map and held his index finger over Mexico and whispered in a desperate voice, "Where are you, Sienna?"

Maijoma, Mexico

Sienna awoke with a start to a shrill cry in the distance. It was a rooster. She pushed the coarse woolen blanket away from her face and stared at her surroundings in confusion. Then she remembered yesterday's nightmare. For several minutes, she hyperventilated, but it slowly passed. She sat up and put her bare feet on the cold, dusty stone floor. Her running shoes were just visible in the semi-darkness. She dragged them over with her right foot and rested her feet on top of them.

She desperately wanted to take a shower, but the narrow cin-der-block enclosure two steps away looked dirty, and more importantly, like the bathroom, it didn't have a door. After pondering her options, she decided her captors could sexually abuse her whenever they wanted. They didn't need to wait until she was naked in the shower. Despite the cold logic of the thought, she was in and out of the shower and fully dressed within three minutes.

For the next two hours, she alternated between pacing around the room and sitting in the single chair located in one corner staring at a discoloration on the far wall. The hundreds of questions she'd wrestled with most of the night kept returning, and she still had no answers. As she stood up for another circuit around the room, she suddenly realized there were only two questions that mattered: How long did they intend to keep her alive, and was there a way to escape? She was all but certain she knew the answer to the first question—not one minute longer than necessary. As for the second, if there was a way to escape, she intended to find it and take her shot, no matter the risk.

The sound of someone on the other side of the door to the room momentarily unleashed a paralyzing wave of fear, but it quickly ebbed and was replaced with a general numbness. There was nothing she could do. There was nowhere she could go.

When Arturo, the older Mexican man, opened the door, he gestured for her to follow him down the corridor that led toward the front of the building. Just before they reached the outside door, he opened a door on the right side of the corridor and gestured for her to walk down a narrow flight of wooden stairs to a dimly lit room below. Sienna hesitated for a moment and then eased down the stairs. She was led to a basement that appeared to span the length and width of the building above.

A kitchen area was located at one end. It was outfitted with an old stove, a sink, and two yellowed refrigerators. The rest of the room was filled with eight or nine rough-hewn wooden tables surrounded by a disparate collection of old chairs.

A Mexican woman in her mid-twenties wearing a dirty white apron over a dark blue T-shirt and blue jeans was stirring the contents of a large steel pot cooking on the gas range. When she glanced over her shoulder at Sienna, her eyes widened, and she quickly returned her gaze to the pot in front of her. The eight-year-old boy sitting on a stool to her right stared at Sienna until Arturo hissed at him.

The boy's eyes widened in fear, and he immediately averted his gaze.

Arturo pointed to the table nearest the kitchen. "Sit there. You will eat quickly."

Sienna nodded, walked to the worn table, and sat down. In spite of the dire situation, whatever the woman was cooking smelled good. Sienna's stomach grumbled. Several minutes later, the woman brought her a plate of rice and beans. The boy followed the woman with a worn plastic pitcher of water and a paper cup. Sienna glanced at the woman, who had a kind face. She avoided eye contact. After placing the food on the table in front of Sienna, the woman silently returned to the kitchen. When the boy hesitated and stared at her curiously, Sienna smiled at him, and he returned the smile. The Mexican woman saw the exchange and hissed at the boy. He quickly placed the cup and pitcher on the table and returned to the kitchen.

Arturo, who had been preoccupied looking at a clipboard attached to the wall, turned at the sound and looked from the table to the boy. Then he glanced at his watch and walked over to the table.

"You must be done in five minutes. The workers . . . you must leave before they come."

The urgency and fear in his voice surprised Anna. She quickly picked up the spoon on the edge of the plate and hastily ate the entire plate of food.

EIGHTEEN

Los Angeles, California

C ollins glanced up at the partially open door of his office. The new paralegal was standing there holding a sheaf of papers. "Uh . . . Anna, right? Please, come in."

"Yes, and thank you. Mr. Collins, I—"

"Declan. Please call me Declan."

"Okay, Declan it is. I reviewed the sources and the filings on the Edgar site. It's laid out in this memo. The more important documents are attached."

"Okay . . . that's great."

Collins took the documents and quickly scanned the one-page write-up.

"This deal is moving quicker than I thought. Let's go to the conference room. I need to call the Chapter 11 lawyer on the case. I tried him earlier, but he wasn't in the office."

Collins followed Anna to the conference room, reading the memo as he walked. "By the way, this memo is great."

Alex, the Latino man she'd met earlier, was sitting in the conference room working on his laptop when they entered. He stood up and nodded to her politely. Collins gestured for her to take a seat at the table, and he took the chair across from the conference phone in the center of the table.

"Anna pulled the data on PriceStar. The chatter on the bankruptcy blogs confirms David Cohen is the company's bankruptcy attorney. It also indicates that Corexion, a big player in the distressed debt space, is trying to buy B of A's debt position at a big discount. We need to get into that negotiation queue ASAP and outbid Corexion's offer, which I suspect isn't much. The head deal guy at Corexion is known as a relentless grinder. I'm going call Cohen and see what the story is. If it makes sense, Sanch—Alex, I'll introduce you."

Collins scanned the contacts on his iPhone and dialed Cohen's direct extension. A woman's voice answered: "Mr. Cohen's office."

"Hello, this is Declan Collins. Does Dave have a minute?"

"Can I tell him what case this relates to?"

"PriceStar."

"One moment, please."

A full minute passed before the woman came back on the line. "I'm sorry, Mr. Cohen is just on his way out to lunch. He will have to talk with you later today."

"Tell him my client is having lunch today with B of A to discuss a bid for the PriceStar senior loan position. I just wanted to know if he had any insights on the deal before the client makes a bid."

"One moment, please."

Thirty seconds later a gruff voice came on the line. "Declan Collins. What's it been, a year or two?"

"In that range."

"I don't have much time, but Monica tells me you have a buyer for the PriceStar debt piece."

"Yes."

"I think that train has left the station, or so I've heard."

Collins shook his head dismissively. "Well, you would know. The word is you're PriceStar's Chapter 11 guy."

"Is that right?"

"Yes, sir. Any comment?"

"Nope."

"Understood. So, you're not in a position to give me any insight into the pricing on the B of A debt."

"Uh, not really, other than to say I have heard someone else has an option on it. Like I say, that train may have left the station."

"Thanks for the input—and put me on your lunch calendar."

"I'm directing Monica to find a couple of dates that work. She'll send you an email."

"Very well then. Have a good lunch."

"I will."

Collins terminated the call and stared at the phone for a moment, before looking over at Sanchez. There was a stricken look on his face.

Collins waved his hand at the phone.

"Relax, it's BS. B of A is still looking for a buyer."

"How can you know this?"

"First, he took the call. Second, I know BS when I hear it."

A knock on the door allowed Collins to cut his explanation short. He walked over, opened the door, and Michaela, the receptionist, handed him three copies of Anna's memo.

"Three copies, Chief."

Collins took the copies and gave her a smile. "Thanks, M," he said and closed the door.

He handed Anna one of the copies and slid a second over to Sanchez.

Anna turned to Collins. "Mr. Collins . . . Declan, do you want me to—"

Collins nodded. "Yes. We're going to call B of A, and I want you to take notes. I particularly need you to get the names and titles of the bankers. I have a blind spot when it comes to names."

Collins tapped his iPhone several times, scrolled down to a contact number, and then typed a number into the conference phone keypad.

"Mr. McAlister's office."

"Hi, this is Declan Collins. Is Sean available?"

Collins pressed the mute button and glanced over at Anna and Sanchez. "This guy's a friend—another hockey bum. He's in B of A's corporate office in Boston. Hopefully he can get me to right person—"

A loud baritone with a pronounced Boston accent came over the speaker: "Declan Collins! Wait. Let me close my door. How the hell are you? What are you doing, drinking a beer on the beach?"

"No, it's only eleven in the morning here. Unlike bankers, lawyers don't imbibe until after the sun begins its descent."

"What a bunch of crap. So, how the hell are you? The last time I saw you was at the Flyers game, in what, 2016?"

"Doing great, and it was the Bruins."

"Bruins? That's right, damn. When are you getting back to this side of the country again?"

"Could be this week, if you can get me a meet with the right B of A exec."

"Who are you looking for?"

"Not sure. B of A is the senior lender to an outfit called PriceStar. I represent a hedge fund that wants to buy the position."

"PriceStar! That loan is with special assets. Oops!"

"Relax, Mac. Everyone knows PriceStar is sliding toward a cliff, which means B of A is going to take it in the shorts. Why do you think my vulture-fund client is circling?"

"See here, old son. B of A doesn't make bad loans."

"Yeah, right. Here's what I need my good buddy to do for me. Other folks are trying to buy that position, possibly as we speak, and I want to get my client in front of the B of A exec who's in charge of selling that loan ASAP."

"That's *if* the bank is selling it."

"Mac, the bank wants out. The loan is up for sale. Here's the deal: My client wants a look at this debt piece, and they're willing to wire five million of flash money into a B of A account, but only if they can meet with the guy at the bank who's in charge of the sale process this week—preferably tomorrow."

"Why the rush?"

"PriceStar's a wasting asset. If there's a deal to be done, it has to be done in days. Otherwise, there will be no there there."

"Got it. Okay, buddy, just let the Macster part the high weeds and see what he can see."

"Can you give me a time frame on this?"

"Pushy bastard. Within the hour."

"Thanks, Mac."

Collins ended the call, stood up, typed something into his cell phone, and then looked over at Sanchez. "Let's reconvene here when Mac gets back to me. Anna, in the meantime, can you pull up every bit of financial data you can find on PriceStar? Start with the most recent income statements and balance sheets in the SEC filings. Then pull whatever analyst reports you can find. Some of the more up-to-date reports will be prepared by private analysts, and we'll have to pay for those. Donna will give you a Visa card for that. Email whatever you find to Alex and me. I really appreciate you jumping into this deal."

"You're welcome," Anna said.

Collins looked into her eyes when she spoke, as if seeing her for the first time, and raised a hand as if he'd just remembered something. "One other thing, I may need your help on an . . . exotic private placement deal. A Latvian bank is involved, and there are Patriot Act problems. We can talk about it later. Code it on your billing entries as the Perez deal."

He turned to Alex. "We have to do our due diligence on the company before we make our bid for the B of A position, so it's going to be a scramble. Do whatever you can to get your arms around the company's financial picture. We'll need that data when we wrestle with B of A over the discount on the loan buy."

"Yes, yes, I agree." The Mexican was nodding furiously as he spoke.

"Okay, then, let's get to it!"

Coyoacan, Mexico

Gregorio stared at the woman sitting at one of the umbrella tables in the square below as she raised a glass of ice tea to her full red lips. She was in her early twenties, attractive, even beautiful. The sandals, worn jeans, and plain white blouse, coupled with the oversize bag at her feet marked her as one of the young artists seeking inspiration from Frida Kahlo's works. Although the woman could well be an accomplished artist, Gregorio knew the bohemian façade wasn't real. The Prada sunglasses, aristocratic Spanish features, and the bodyguard sitting discretely two tables away revealed the reality. The woman came from wealth and power.

She reminded Gregorio of the woman in a picture he kept in his Mexico City apartment. The would-be artist at the table outside was about the same age as the woman in the picture but not nearly as beautiful. The woman in the picture had the aristocratic cheekbones and blue eyes of her Russian mother, and the lustrous brown hair, aquiline nose, and darker skin of her father—a Mexican diplomat who could trace his lineage back four hundred years to a noble family in Astoria, Spain. Every time Gregorio looked at the picture of Selene Pena, his mother, her smiling eyes made him think of what could have been, what should have been, instead of the nightmare she'd endured for almost twenty years.

"Gregorio, I thought you had left. Can't you stay another little while?"

Gregorio turned to the woman behind him. His mother was only fifty-two years old, but she looked two decades older. Her face was still pretty, but the high and prominent cheekbone on the right side of her petite, quietly regal face had been broken by the hand of a man who wore a heavy bejeweled ring on every finger. Those rings had ripped three furrows in her cheek.

The cruel blow had not only broken her cheekbone and permanently marred her face; it had also damaged the retina in her right eye. Although vision in the eye could have been saved had the retina been quickly reattached, medical attention had been delayed for a week. The man with the golden rings wasn't interested in the welfare of the cadre of women he considered to be no more than his personal sex slaves.

"No. I must go. But I'll be back next week."

"Where are you off to?"

"Los Angeles."

"Very well, my sweet son."

Gregorio hugged the woman gently and left the apartment.

As he walked down the street, he glanced up at the window. His mother was looking out at the woman sitting at the umbrella table.

Gregorio glanced from his mother to the woman and back again and spoke quietly.

"Madre, I cannot return what he stole, but I *will* make sure he pays the devil's price for it."

NINETEEN

Los Angeles, California

The strike team's command center was on the tenth floor of an office building three blocks from Collins's office. The former tenant, a law firm, had filed bankruptcy two months earlier and left almost all of the furniture in place. Eric was holding open the door to the suite when Anna stepped off the elevator.

"How was your first day?"

"Not as bad as I thought it would be."

Eric glanced inside the door and then spoke in a lower voice as Anna walked by. "His eminence is waiting for your download with bated breath."

Anna smiled. Somehow Teo didn't seem like the eminent type.

Eric closed the door after her, walked across the opulent reception area, and pulled open a glass door on the other side of the room.

Anna walked into a large conference room with a long white marble table in the center. Two of the fifteen plush chairs situated around the table were occupied by Teo and Calder. She didn't recognize the man standing at the head of the table. He was dressed in a dark suit and reminded her of one of the fortyish models in the Rolex watch commercials. He didn't look up from his iPhone when Anna walked into the room, although she could tell he knew she was there. Calder broke the silence, a small smile playing across his face.

"So, what's it like to be a paralegal?"

"Harder than—"

"Let's get started, shall we?"

Anna looked quickly over at the Rolex man. "Of course."

"You must be Anna Torres. I'm Regge Carlton, Assistant US Attorney. We spoke on the phone several days ago."

Anna nodded. She wasn't about to be interrupted a third time. She glanced over at Teo. He gave her a friendly nod.

"Good to see you, Anna. Please, take—"

"Yes, do that. We're all anxious to hear what you've managed to discover." Carlton's tone was a mixture of condescension and subdued impatience.

Eric pulled out one of the heavy leather chairs for her and sat down in the next chair.

Anna nodded her thanks and sat down.

"Enlighten us," Carlton said as he eased back into his seat and pulled out a leather-covered legal pad.

She spent thirty minutes reviewing what she considered to be the day's material events and another forty-five minutes answering questions from Carlton. It was evident from the inquiries that he didn't believe Anna was capable of deciding what was material and what wasn't. Although Teo tried to abbreviate the process on several occasions, Carlton ignored or overrode his recommendations. After going over a point for the fourth time with Anna, Carlton eased back in his chair and spoke in a tone that was clearly intended to preclude differing opinions on the matter.

"It's the private placement—the Perez deal. That's how Collins is going to do it. Collins will initially capitalize the limited partnership or limited liability company making the underlying investment with legit funds. Six months later, the partnership or LLC will book a significant profit, when in fact it hasn't earned a penny.

"The incoming drug dollars will conveniently be used to fill this illusory profit hole. Sure, the cartels will pay a tax on the phantom profit, but not much after the bogus depreciation or depletion deductions Mr. Collins will design into the deal. Once the deal is closed, the drug dollars will be distributed as clean, usable profits. That, folks, is the alchemy in play here."

Teo nodded carefully. "Could be."

"Not could be—is," Carlton said without looking at Teo.

"What about an audit?" Teo asked. "The IRS will find out that the profit is bogus if they take a look."

Carlton scoffed. "Teo, Teo, the investments will be parked in Belize or some other foreign jurisdiction. The IRS will never go down there to check out whether the condo complex sold for ten million or fifty million, and even if they did, whoever Collins assigns to cook the books will have a second set of books, in Spanish, that will tie out to what's in the tax return filed by the limited partnership. And, news flash, the IRS isn't looking for people who overstate their profits. They're looking for people who understate them."

"You don't consider the bankruptcy deal—" Anna started.

"Forget about it," Carlton said.

"But what about Alex Sanchez? He—"

Teo shook his head. "We ran him, Anna. He's—"

"A citizen of Argentina, born and raised," Carlton said dismissively. "He works for a reputable accounting firm in Mexico City. He's clean. Here's how I see it: There's got to be a connection between the Perez deal and the Cayetano cartel, and you, Agent Torres, are going to find it."

Carlton looked directly at Anna and smiled when he spoke, but Anna sensed the threat in his directive. Regge Carlton was looking for a win that would advance his career, and he expected his newly adopted team to get it for him, or else.

Carlton glanced at his watch and abruptly placed his notepad into his black leather valise. "And now I must take my leave. We've made a good start. I won't be able to make most of these little chats, but I'm sure you'll keep me apprised Agent . . . Teo? Yes, Teo."

Teo nodded stiffly but didn't respond.

After Carlton had left the office, Eric shook his head in disgust. "What an arrogant—"

"Sack of shit is what you are looking for," Calder finished.

Anna let out the breath she'd been holding for the past hour and a half and laughed.

Teo smiled. "No comment. Our problem is that this sack of . . . whatever could well be the Attorney General in the future—the big boss. Unless we collectively want to be staffing the Alaska field office, we need to toe the line and make him happy."

Calder smiled and nodded toward Eric.

"Eric the Red over there might like the move, but that's a no-can-do for me."

US Bank Tower, Los Angeles, California

Collins stood in front of the window behind his desk staring at the sun fading below the horizon to the west. After the golden orb passed out of sight, he glanced at his watch and turned back to his desk. It was ten o'clock in Grand Cayman. He started to reach for the phone, intending to call Matt before it was too late, but stopped in mid-movement. The phone was bugged. He shook his head in frustration. Unless he found a way to get outside the communication box Cayetano's techs had set up, there was no way he could put together the resources needed to find Sienna and take her away from Cayetano. He needed access to people who were smart, capable, and absolutely trustworthy, and even with those assets, he would need a bucketload of luck.

As he flipped through the court calendar on his iPad, a name came up—Tony Lentino. There was a post-trial status conference in Lentino's tax fraud case. The judge had set the date in the original scheduling order, and it was still on the calendar for next Thursday.

Collins walked over to the window with the iPad clutched in his hand. *Lentino . . . Tony could help. The two of us have walked through this kind of minefield before.* Tony had been under intense surveillance by the FBI for over a year, and the two of them had worked out a system to avoid monitored calls. If Collins could replicate that, he could get around the Cayetano's surveillance. There was only one problem: When he called, Tony had to pick up on the verbal cue—"Tony L, Tony L, the man"—he'd used in the past, by agreement, to warn Tony the call was being monitored, or the whole effort could blow up in his face. Collins picked up his cell phone and stared at the screen for a moment before dialing Tony's number.

"Lentino."

"Hey, Tony L, Tony L, the man."

There was a momentary hesitation. "Declan! How ya doing, buddy?"

The pause and Tony's tone of voice confirmed he'd gotten the message. "Eh, just surviving. I ran out of that Tuscan Chianti you picked up—"

"The Luglio? Relax, you bum. Uncle T will get you another bottle."

"Thanks, but that's not why I called. I just wanted to give you heads-up on the status conference set for next Thursday."

"Status conference?"

"Yeah, the one Judge Metcalf has been continuing forever. It's going to get kicked out again, so don't worry about it, but we need to talk about making it go away permanently. There's a few post-trial cleanup issues we need to talk about to get that done, and we need to talk about getting my final bill paid."

Lentino chuckled. "You friggin' vampire. Yeah, okay. Have Donna call me to set up a date."

"Will do. Okay buddy, I gotta get back to the trenches."

"You work too hard—drink some wine, take a break."

"Yeah. Good night, Tony."

Collins hung up the phone and exhaled slowly. Tony had gotten the message. The chime from his cell phone interrupted his thoughts.

"Declan, it's Mac at B of A."

"Whoa. What happened to banker's hours?"

"You tell me. That world's gone, chief. I've been working my ass off since the day I took this job. In the next life, I'll sign up to be a big deal LA lawyer. I hear it's an easy gig."

"You hear wrong, brother. What's the deal with the PriceStar loan?"

"You were right about it being on the sale block. I spoke to the head of special assets. They're trying to move that credit out the door before the company goes bankrupt, but so far, they only have a bunch of letters of intent. The bank's not crazy about any of them, but I was told, and you didn't hear this from me, that the department intends to enter into a lock-up with one of them by Friday. So, if you want to get in this game, you need to get out to Charlotte ASAP, and you need to come with a big check. That last point is key, Declan. If you can't show proof of funds, the bank's going to ignore you. Think five million in flash money, at least, and proof that the rest of the cash is sitting in a bank account ready to go."

Collins glanced at his watch. It was seven o'clock. "Hold on a minute, Mac." He pulled up a travel site on his iPad and looked at flights to Charlotte. There was a red-eye later that evening. The next screen indicated that there were seven available seats.

"Mac, I'll be there tomorrow morning, with a client rep. I need you to get me a meeting with the head of special assets. I will have an LOI in hand. My client wants that loan."

"Declan, I'll do my best, but—"

"The five mil is already on deposit, Mac. If we're the buyer, you'll be a hero. I'll call you at eight when I arrive. Get me that meeting, buddy."

"I'll get you the meeting, but only if you promise to get back to Boston for dinner and a game."

"Done."

Collins hung up and tapped a speed-dial key on the phone. "Donna, its Declan. I need you to get me and Sanchez on the 11:30 flight from LAX to Charlotte tonight. If they have first class, great. If not, I'll take whatever they have."

"Okay. I have your information, but I'll need—"

"I'll have Sanchez call you with his information. One other thing. If there's a . . . plausible way I can avoid sitting in the same row as Sanchez, do it."

Maijoma, Mexico

Sienna lay in the narrow bed staring at the far wall. The light from the moon was just visible through the small cracks and holes in the corrugated wall. She glanced to the left automatically, expecting to see the luminous face of the pink clock her dad had given her when she was seven years old. There was nothing but blackness. The clock was a thousand miles away in her college dorm room. As she drew in a heavy breath, she remembered something her dad had said to her after she'd come across the finish line dead last in her first track meet: "Sienna, you're never defeated until you decide to give up." Tears came to her eyes, and she brushed them away. She had no intention of giving up.

As she closed her eyes in the hope of getting back to sleep, Sienna heard a noise that seemed so close by she feared someone was in the room with her. She froze, listening intently, her breath held in check. A moment later, she heard it again. It was a stealthy footfall on the other side of the corrugated steel wall. She slowly exhaled as she heard a third step. Whoever was on the other side of the wall was pausing after each step, as if listening. She eased out of the bed and moved with exaggerated care closer to the wall, until her ear was an inch away from it.

She softly ran the tips of her fingers over the steel until she found a small crack, lowered herself down to the level of the aperture, and stared out into the darkness. When she didn't see anything, she considered whispering a plea for help, but she decided against it. If it was a guard, she could pay a terrible price. She turned her head and placed her ear to the crack and waited. A moment later, she heard three more steps, and then it was quiet again. Minutes later the person on the other side of the wall walked quietly away, leaving her alone again.

Sienna stood up and slowly let her breath out. After the person outside had stopped moving again, she had heard a familiar sound— two thumbs tapping out a text message on a mobile phone. The man in the black silk shirt was wrong. Someone in the compound did have a cell phone, and that person had found just enough of a cell signal to send messages to someone on the outside.

Charlotte, North Carolina

Collins followed Sanchez into the back seat of the limo as the driver loaded the bags into the trunk.

The driver stepped into the car a moment later. "You're going to the Marriott at City Center?"

"That's it," Collins answered.

Collins glanced over at Sanchez. "Okay flight?"

"Yes. It was fine," Sanchez said.

"Good, we don't have a lot of time. I prepared a letter of intent for the loan acquisition on the plane. As soon as we get to the hotel, I need you and anyone else who needs to weigh in on it to send their comments as soon as possible. We need to get it over to B of A before the meeting."

Sanchez hesitated and then said, "I will look it over right away, but we may need some time to get approval before we present it to the bank."

Collins shook his head. "We don't have that time. We are behind in this game, and we have to catch up. You need to reach out to whomever else needs to approve this within the next hour and get them on board. Otherwise, we will lose this thing."

"Sí, I mean, yes, I will get Gregorio. I will get everyone on it right away."

There was a noticeable undercurrent of fear in Sanchez's response.

Collins dialed a number on his cell phone and prayed McAlister would pick up.

"McAlister here."

"Mac, I'm in Charlotte. Where are we?"

"Welcome to the great state of North Carolina."

"Thanks, Mac. Now what about the meeting?"

"Relax, the Macster came through. You've got a meeting with Tamara Wilson, head of special assets, at 10:00 a.m."

"Thanks, Mac. I owe you big time."

MacAlister chuckled. "B of A's CEO lives in Boston, and his grandkid plays on the hockey team I coach, so people think I'm connected. It's BS, but hey, they don't need to know that."

"Can you tell me anything about Ms. Wilson?"

"I've only met her once, but the scuttlebutt is she's tough, smart, and ambitious—cute too. Beyond that, I don't have a clue. I'll text you her email. Send her a confirmation on the meet. I gotta run. Remember, you owe me dinner and a Bruins game."

"You got it, buddy."

Collins ended the call and turned to Sanchez. "We're on at ten. That gives us an hour and a half to get the letter of intent in shape and email it over to the B of A rep before the meeting."

———

After revising the letter of intent four times based on Sanchez's and Gregorio's comments, Collins signed the document and emailed it to Tamara Wilson. He glanced at his watch. They had twenty minutes to get there. The cell phone on his hip chimed as he reached for his jacket. It was Matt.

"Declan, what's the story? Have you been able to tie up the deal?" Matt's voice was hoarse, and he sounded groggy, as if he'd just woken up, or more likely, he'd never gone to sleep.

"Matt, no time. I'm in Charlotte about to meet with B of A on the debt buy. I need you to confirm that five million hit Fourth Street's B of A account, and I need to know whether Fourth Street received the forty million from the . . . investor."

"I confirmed the five mil wire this morning. The forty million didn't get here."

"What! Are you shitting me? Why not? Don't answer. I'll call our . . . friend and find out what's going on. Gotta go."

"Declan, can you get this—"

"Yeah, I can, and I will. Tell Nigel I need him to stay by the phone and to stay away from Johnny Walker Black until at least three today. I need him at the top of his game. The B of A exec we're meeting with is Tamara Wilson. I need you find out every scrap of information about her that might help me. Feed it to Nigel. He's a master at working people."

"Okay. I'm on it."

"Good. Gotta go."

Collins ended the call before Matt could say anything. The subdued desperation and exhaustion in his friend's voice scared the crap out of him. This was sudden death overtime for real, and the other bidders for the PriceStar debt were already halfway down the ice.

The other teams also had an inherent advantage. B of A would be inclined to sell the loan to a familiar face with a recognized name, even if Fourth Street's offer was higher. That's why they needed the forty million in the bank today.

Collins called Sanchez, who was waiting in his hotel room. "Alex Sanchez here."

"Where's the forty million?"

"The forty—"

"Where is it?" Collins couldn't restrain the anger in his voice. "We're going into a meeting with no proof of funds. That doesn't work. I need to talk to Gregorio, now."

"I may not be able to reach—"

"Then get me on the phone with the big boss. I'm walking out the door now. Meet me in the lobby. If this thing dumps, it's on you and Gregorio, not me."

"Wait, wait! I will—two minutes!"

Collins felt a moment of satisfaction as well as surprise at the desperate fear in Sanchez's voice. It was almost as if he and Gregorio were also under imminent threat from the drug lord they served.

Sanchez stumbled out of the elevator into the lobby two minutes after Collins arrived and hurried over. He looked like a man with a gun to his head. Collins felt an instant of satisfaction. *Welcome to my nightmare, Sanchez.*

"Gregorio will call you."

"Good, let's head over. B of A's HQ is three blocks down."

Collins's cell phone buzzed as he turned toward the door.

"Mr. Collins."

Gregorio's voice was calm, as always, but Collins could sense the same element of fear he could plainly see in Sanchez's eyes.

"Where's the money, Gregorio?"

"I apologize. The . . . logistics were more complicated than I thought."

"Gregorio, I need to prove that Fourth Street, Ltd., has the ability do this deal in about thirty minutes. How do I do that?"

"I'm working on that."

"Work harder. Without that cash our offer for the loan goes into the shredder. I'm texting you Nigel's number. Coordinate with him. I need proof of funds."

"Understood."

Collins ended the call and weaved between two women who were meandering down the sidewalk pulling rolling suitcases behind them. He glanced over his shoulder. Sanchez was dabbing at his face with a large white handkerchief and struggling to keep up. Collins pointed to the lobby door of the building next to B of A's headquarters. Sanchez hurried after him.

"This is not the building."

"I know," Collins answered and pulled open the door. Collins walked to a deserted corner of the broad lobby and waited until Sanchez reached him. He glanced quickly at his watch and then looked at Sanchez.

"Have you ever done this before?"

Sanchez dabbed the sweat running down his forehead with the handkerchief. There was a confused look on his face. "What do you mean?"

"Have you ever played the role of a principal in a big deal-negotiation session?"

"Well . . . no."

"I have. I do it all the time. So I'll control the conversation. Here's the big picture. The bank wants to get rid of this loan—real bad. You'll hear a lot of posturing from B of A's special assets rep to the contrary, but it's all BS. The bank has the weak hand, not us. Their asset is declining in value daily, and they can't do a damn thing about it. So they have the sale pressure; we don't.

"We are also a cash-flush hedge fund in a cash-poor market, which means everyone's begging for our money. That means we can afford to be selective. In sum, when we walk into the meeting, we act like we hold all the cards—and we will if I have confirmation of cash availability when the bank exec asks for it."

Sanchez nodded and swallowed uncomfortably.

"Good. Now, here's the tactical game plan. After the introductions are over, but before the grinding begins, I'll tell the B of A folks that you have to take a five-minute call at about 10:30 and make the obligatory apology for the interruption. Then I'll explain Fourth Street's interest in the distressed debt space and go into detail regarding why this particular loan is of interest to the fund. The bank will then trot out their BS about wanting top dollar, and—"

"What is this BS?"

"Bullshit like 'we already have a buyer, but we'll listen to what you have to say, just in case they fall out of escrow,' or 'we're not really interested in selling the loan, but that could change.'"

"Oh, yes. I see."

"After this spiel, just nod cordially and then glance at your phone. You will then stand up, apologize for the interruption, and explain you have to take the call. You tell the B of A rep the meeting can continue because I have the full confidence of Fourth Street's investment board. Then leave. Go outside, call Gregorio, and get me confirmation that the forty million is in a bank account I can refer them to. Pretend to talk for five minutes if you have to and then return."

"Mr. Collins, why the call? I can—"

"I need time to get in their face."

"Is that wise? I—"

"We have no choice. We need to jump to the head of line on this deal, but we don't want them to think we are willing to overpay. So, I need to walk them through the numbers on this thing, which are bad and getting worse, and then put a bigger carrot on the table than what others have offered. To make the deal even more attractive, I will offer to close the deal on an expedited basis. B of A's quarter closes in two weeks. The bank probably wrote this loan way down six months ago. Every dollar we pay them over that sum is pure profit. That looks good on the department's quarterly report and on the bank's 10-Q."

"I see. But why is it that I—"

Collins glanced at his watch as he cut Sanchez off. "Have to be out of the room? People expect lawyers to be jerks, but if there's a principal in the audience, they feel compelled to push back. With you out of the room, I can get in her face and get away with it. I also want to paint you and the investment board as a group of newbies who are relying on me to get the deal done, or not. Describing you in that light when you're sitting there doesn't work."

Alex hesitated and spoke haltingly, "I don't mean to be difficult, but I think Mr. Cayetano will want me in the room."

Collins stared at Sanchez for a moment before responding. "Alex, what Cayetano wants, what he needs, is this deal! I can get it. You can't. Either we do this my way or this thing crashes and burns, and we *both* suffer the consequences."

Sanchez eye's widened, and he nodded.

Collins gestured toward the exit. "Good. Let's do this thing."

TWENTY

Mexico City, Mexico

G regorio put the cell phone in the inside pocket of his suit jacket and walked over to the stained and broken mirror hanging on the concrete wall of the aging warehouse. After straightening his azure necktie, he returned to the steel folding table that had been his post for the last ten hours.

Five hundred thousand dollars in cash was stacked on the table in five neat bundles. It was the last batch. Over twenty million dollars had been stacked, sorted, and placed in shrink-wrapped packages in increments of one hundred thousand dollars by a team of trusted clerks over the last six hours. The cash would be deposited in over twenty smaller banks located throughout Mexico and Central America—banks that didn't cooperate with US law enforcement. The two banks receiving the largest deposit totals were Banco Seguro and Banco Real, which were located in Panama and didn't provide banking services outside the country. Both banks were on a US government money laundering watch list.

At noon the day before, Banco Seguro and Banco Real had each issued a letter of credit for twenty-five million dollars in favor of the Banc of Panama, which was also on the US watch list. After hours of interbank negotiations, First Cayman Bank, located in Grand Cayman, agreed to issue a forty million cash advance to Fourth Street's account backed by a fifty-million-dollar letter of credit issued by the much larger Banc of Panama. Gregorio had received a text confirming the deposit three minutes ago. He glanced down at his watch. It was 8:22 a.m. PDT, which meant it was 10:22 a.m. in Grand Cayman. Gregorio exhaled slowly, trying to ease the tension headache pounding between his temples. *We have survived another day, Alex.*

Gregorio placed the six remaining stacks of bills on the table into a steel box, placed a small padlock on the box, and then pressed the red key on the black remote control sitting next to his computer. The heavy carbon steel bolt on the door behind him eased out of its slot with a quiet whine. A small, hunched-over old man wearing a worn brown suit pushed open the door from the other side and walked over to the table, pulling a steel cart behind him. Gregorio nodded at the box in front of him.

"This is the last, Ernesto. Log it in, put it on the truck, and have Tomas and his men lock the place up. Tell the driver I'll be out front in a minute."

The man nodded, jotted down the number on the outside of the steel box on the clipboard he held in his other hand, and lifted the box with some difficulty into the cart. Then he turned and walked back into the darkened room, pulling the cart behind him.

Gregorio waited until the door had closed before calling Sanchez. Sanchez picked up on the first ring.

"Gregorio?"

"Yes, Alex."

"Is it—"

"Yes. Fourth Street's account will show a forty-million-dollar balance as of three minutes ago."

"Thank the Virgin Mother. I thought I would have a heart attack. I cannot take much more of this."

Gregorio could feel the restrained hysteria in his friend's voice.

"I know, Alex, I know. How are the negotiations going?"

"The woman banker. She says the bank is not particularly interested in selling the debt, but Collins says it's just a front. He's instructed me to stay out of the room for fifteen minutes while he . . . what does he say . . . 'gets in their face.'"

Gregorio smiled in spite of the headache. "I suspect he will do just that."

"I am afraid he will overplay his hand, Gregorio. We could lose the deal!"

"We have to trust him, Alex, at least in this. He knows this business. Now quickly tell me what has been going on—all of it. Mr. Cayetano will want to know."

Charlotte, North Carolina

Collins sat in the large conference room and listened patiently as the tall, attractive blonde woman on the other side of the marble table repeated a shorter version of the prepackaged speech he'd heard ten minutes ago. Although Collins enjoyed Tamara Wilson's Southern contralto, he knew the factual picture she was describing was not the reality. As he waited for her to finish, he mentally honed his response. He could easily rebut almost every point the banker had made, but he had no intention of doing so. The game plan was not to win the argument. It was to persuade. Tailoring the pitch to the mark was a key part of that game, and Tamara Wilson was a hard target.

Collins had read Wilson's bio ten minutes before he walked into the room. The thirty-eight-year-old Wharton grad managed a twenty-billion-dollar portfolio of troubled loans secured by almost every possible form of collateral. She was bright, tough, and ran ultramarathons when she was not getting bad loans off B of A's balance sheet. Her stylish but conservative business suit, serious demeanor, unflinching blue eyes, and confident presentation were cool, confident, and all business.

"As I said, Declan, the PriceStar loan is for sale, but right now the price is par. We believe we have sufficient collateral to recover what we have advanced. Any discussion of a discount at this stage of the negotiations is premature."

Collins nodded politely, leaned forward, and responded in a tone that was friendly and reasonable, but one that also suggested he was only mildly interested in making a deal.

"Tamara, PriceStar's most recent financials reflect a negative EBITDA burn of five million a month, the company's inventory is limited, and in many stores it's what the trade vendors call 'broken,' five major leases are in arrears, and the company has about a month's worth of cash left. Absent a near-term plasma loan, as in within the next two or three weeks, PriceStar will collapse, leaving you with hundreds of stores full of crap. If that happens, the word on the street is the bank will lose 90 percent of its principal."

"I think you overstate—"

"Now, I know you've met with Black Oak, RGD, and Corexion on this deal, and we both know those vulture funds pride themselves on leaving absolutely nothing on the table. I would guesstimate they offered twenty mil for your sixty-million-dollar revolver. We also both know they will try to recut that deal at least twice during the due diligence period and then again fifteen minutes before you close."

"I'm not at liberty—"

"I know, I know, and I'm not asking you to. What you need to understand is Fourth Street wants to get into the distressed debt space in the near-term, and dollars have been allocated for the purpose. That means the fund is . . . probably willing to pay more for the position than the other players. Fourth Street's only problem is time. It needs to place its funds before the end of this quarter. That's why the fund gave you an offer with an opening bid of thirty million. I know that beats what you've been offered, and unlike the other bidders, I can tell you Fourth Street won't try to recut the deal prior to closing unless the latest financials are way off. However, this buyer's deal is time sensitive. Today is the day."

Wilson's cold blue eyes displayed almost no reaction. She glanced down at her laptop and tapped the screen several times quickly. After a few moments, she looked over at him with an expression that did not yield any clues as to her real thoughts.

"Let's agree to disagree on the quality of the collateral and the status of our borrower and focus on Fourth Street. The bank doesn't have a lot of confidence in your client's ability to perform, and that will be a big factor in their decision-making process. To be blunt, show me the money."

Collins had suspected this was going to be the make-it-or-break-it issue, and sure enough, it was. The bank wasn't going to spend the time and money putting a deal together unless they knew the buyer could perform. The almost inaudible ping of an incoming text drew Collins's attention to his iPad: "Bank of Cay will conf 40M available. B of A can call Stan Kearny at bank. See email I forwarded to you from bank."

Collins looked over at the woman. "Fourth Street has five million sitting in an account at B of A right now. Grand Cayman Bank will confirm Fourth Street has ample funds immediately available to satisfy the balance of the offer. I am emailing you the name of the banker at Grand Cayman to call right now."

"Mr. Collins, the availability of funds in a foreign bank—"

"Thirty million will be parked in a B of A account within one business day of the date you execute the letter of intent I sent you. What is the likelihood you will see a penny of Black Oak's money before the day you close?"

"Black Oak is a billion-dollar fund out of New York. We know they can perform."

"And the morning after you sign our deal, you will know we can as well, and you will also be getting a substantially more attractive price for the asset."

"You're sure about that?"

"Sure enough to commit to suffering through one of your ultra-marathons if I'm wrong."

The comment drew the first smile from the woman's otherwise implacable exterior. Collins returned the smile. There was a quiet knock on the door to the conference room, and then Alex Sanchez reentered the room.

"Let me apologize again, Ms. Wilson, but it was unavoidable."

The blonde woman's icy demeanor was back in place as she stood up and reached across the table and shook both men's hands. "No apology necessary. Mr. Collins and I have used the time productively.

It's been a pleasure, gentlemen. We shall let you know by the end of the day."

Collins waited until she was at the door before asking, "About the marathon or the deal?"

The woman didn't turn around when she answered, but Collins could hear the smile in her voice. "Both."

Sanchez restrained himself until the two men were weaving through the foot traffic on the sidewalk outside the building.

"What . . . what do you think?"

"I think we're now the front-runner."

"How do you know?"

"I don't, but I can read people, even the ice queen back there. I can sense our offer is millions better than the other players. The only issue is can she get comfortable with our ability to perform. We need to get Nigel to call his guy at Grand Cayman Bank and have him ping Tamara Wilson to confirm the availability of a wire."

Collins dialed Nigel's number, and he picked up on the second ring. Matt must have been working on him. "Nigel, it's Declan. Do you know a Stan Kearny at Grand Cayman?"

There was a slight hesitation. "Why yes, I do. Spoke to the chap about an hour ago. He says Fourth Street has a forty-million-dollar credit available. You're quite the magician, Declan."

"Good. I need you to call him and turn on the charm. I'm texting you Tamara Wilson's email at B of A. Tell the Grand Cay banker we are going to wire thirty million to B of A tomorrow and we'd like him to call Tamara to confirm the wire instructions. If he hesitates, tell him Fourth Street intends to do a significant amount of business in the distressed debt space, and we're looking forward to doing a lot of that business with his bank."

"Relax, Declan. I know the man. He's a young Canadian transplant. Quite ambitious. I'll call and chat him up a bit. I may even invite him for a round of golf at North Sound."

"Good. But you need to make that call now."

"Yes, yes. Good day, my friend."

Collins dodged between two Japanese businessmen and hustled

across an intersection before the last ten seconds of the crosswalk count. Sanchez broke into a half jog to catch up.

Collins turned to Sanchez as he walked through the door of the hotel. "The next step is to get PriceStar's bankruptcy lawyer to support our play to be PriceStar's post-petition lender."

"How do we do that?" Sanchez gasped.

Collins entered the lobby of their hotel, walked into an open elevator, and punched in his floor number.

"The way everything is done in bankruptcy—through a bribe."

Sanchez's eyes widened. "We bribe him?"

"In a manner of speaking. We offer to leave money on the table to pay his fees as part of the deal."

TWENTY-ONE

US Bank Tower, Los Angeles, California

Anna arrived at Collins & Associates at 8:00 a.m., an hour before it opened, in the hope of talking to Donna Mason about the Perez deal before Collins arrived. Donna walked in at 8:05. Anna waited two minutes and then walked over to the small kitchen to get a cup of coffee. On the way back to her office, she stopped outside Donna's door.

"Oh, hi, Donna."

"Anna. You don't have to be here until—"

"I know. I have to pay some bills, so I came in a little early."

"What fun. How's the grind so far?"

"Great. This PriceStar thing is really interesting."

"It's definitely moving fast. I spoke to Declan this morning. He said the negotiations with B of A went well."

"Is he coming in today?"

"Oh yeah. He'll be here in an hour. No choice."

"Why?"

"The mysterious and imperious Mr. Perez called and told him to clear his morning calendar."

"Clear—"

"Yeah, as in the king is coming, so make way. What a jerk. I haven't even met the guy, and I hate him."

"Sorry, Donna. I wish I could help."

"You can. Declan has added you to the Perez case team."

"Great."

"No, it's not *great*. Declan tells me this guy is a social Neanderthal. Expect to be insulted."

"Okay, not great."

"If he gets too out of control, Declan says he'll rein him in, or at least try to."

"Why does Declan want this client?"

"Money. Perez is apparently made of it. Declan told me the guy is giving him a fifty-thousand-dollar retainer for a simple consult. The guy is bringing in another 100K next week."

"Wow!"

"The real wow is not the figure. Declan gets big retainers whenever he takes on a criminal case. This, on the other hand, is a simple consult, and the retainer was paid in cash."

"Cash?"

"Cash."

Anna hesitated. *Carlton was right. Perez must be Cayetano's front man.* "Bigger wow. Any idea what the case is about?"

"It's some kind of tax-leveraged private placement deal involving a lot of foreign cash. Bottom line: It's a cash-cow case."

Anna nodded. "Speaking of which, I'd better get those bills paid before the day starts."

Anna emailed an encrypted message to Teo detailing her conversation with Donna Mason about Perez as soon as she returned to her office. Teo responded a moment later: "We need more information on this guy. He doesn't show up in the system."

"What about his car? We can get the license."

"No good. He came in a limo owned by a commercial outfit. He rented it for the trip."

Anna glanced up from her computer and saw Declan Collins walking toward his office. Donna Mason followed him.

Anna sent a last email to Teo: "Collins just walked in. I'll give you an update after the meeting. Gotta go."

"Good luck."

Anna walked over to the kitchen hoping to overhear what Declan and Donna were talking about through Collins's open office door. When she walked by, Donna was standing in front of Collins's desk.

"You look like you haven't slept a wink."

"I didn't."

"You should have cancelled the meeting with Perez."

"No, that's the one thing I can't do."

"Declan, there's a half a million in the firm's general account. We're not going broke."

"I know, but trust me when I say Perez is a guy who . . . I have to take care of. Enough said."

"Okay."

"Your email said that you wanted both me and Anna in the meeting."

"Yes. This guy is very demanding, and I don't trust him. I need both of you in the room as witnesses."

Donna exhaled in irritation.

"He should be here any second now. Put him in the conference room and tell him I'll be back in a minute."

Collins walked out of the office to the men's room in the hall carrying a copy of the *Daily Journal*. He walked to the stall at the far end, closed the door, dropped his pants, and sat down on the toilet. He opened the paper on his lap and then listened for a moment. There was no one else in the restroom. He reached under the toilet paper dispenser and found the key taped to the bottom. He opened the dispenser and found the small cell phone that was taped to the inside cover. Lentino had gotten the message. Collins turned on the phone and opened the message app.

"T"

"Here."

"Mexican drug cartel is hlding Sienna, Matt's sis. Matt and I hve to launder big $ in a US deal or she's dead."

There was a momentary pause before Tony's response: "Thyll kill her anywy."

"Know. Need a wy out."

"How."

"We met the big boss in Mx. Ramon Cayetano. Chk him out."

"Done. What else."

"I need a team of hvy hitters on stndby to get her back once I find her."

"Got it."

"These are bad gys—smrt bad guys. No mistkes or Si dies."

"Relx. Gtcha back."

Collins heard someone open the outer door to the restroom, and he quickly typed a last message.

"Done."

Collins rustled the newspaper on his lap as he inserted the phone back into the dispenser, closed it, and reattached the key to the bottom. Collins looked under the door when he finished. He recognized Sanchez's polished wingtips near the sink.

Maijoma, Mexico

Sienna walked another slow circuit around her room before sitting back down on the bed. She shook her head back and forth trying to keep herself awake to see if the man with the phone would come back, but it didn't do any good. She was exhausted.

Arturo had finally yielded to her repeated requests for the right to exercise once a day after she'd told him she had arrhythmic heartbeat and would suffer a stroke unless she walked regularly. It wasn't true, but it had moved the needle. She'd been allowed to walk two miles around a circuit encompassing the eastern half of the compound. She was a sprinter on her college track team, and the walk should have been easy, but the combination of a week of sleepless nights, the sun, and the exercise had left her so drained she couldn't stay awake any longer.

As she lay back on the bed and closed her eyes, Sienna heard stealthy footsteps on the other side of the wall, just as she had the night before. She eased off the bed and walked quietly to the large pipe that ran up the side of the far wall. Earlier in the day, she'd carefully examined the six-inch-wide iron cylinder and picked out the foot and handholds she could use to climb up to the vent in the wall near the ceiling. She quickly found the first foothold and pulled herself up using the lip of a connecting joint. As she pulled herself upward a second time, a bolt nicked her exposed ankle. She grimaced at the pain but continued to climb. Two more exertions placed her even with the vent.

At first, she didn't see the man in the darkness below, but then he stepped out from under the eaves of the wooden shed ten yards from her building. She'd walked by the shed earlier in the day on her exercise circuit. The man took a small step forward, staring intently at the phone in his hand. After glancing around furtively, he took another step, his eyes still glued to the phone. Sienna knew what he was doing—looking for a cell signal that would enable him to send a text to the outside world. That meant a cell tower must be located within forty to fifty miles of the compound.

She watched the man repeat the process over and over again until he found the signal and quickly tapped a message into the phone. As soon as the message was sent, the man returned to the protective shadow of the shed's eaves. A moment later, he came back into the open without the cell phone and made his way across the compound, moving stealthily from shadow to shadow.

Sienna eased her way down the rusted pipe, probing for footholds. When her foot finally touched the floor, she stood there for a moment gasping for breath, her mind focused on coming up with a way of getting her hands on that phone. Juan, the guard who followed her as she walked around the exercise circuit, was old and overweight. After the first loop, he'd allowed her to get so far ahead she'd been out of his sight for almost a minute and a half at certain points. *If she could get to the phone for sixty seconds and send a text seeking help, it could bring a rescue.* The text would pass through a nearby cell tower—a tower within fifty miles. That might be enough for the FBI, or whoever was looking for her, to find her location. It might be her only chance at staying alive.

US Bank Tower, Los Angeles, California

"Anna?"

Anna looked over at the intercom on her desk phone.

"Yes."

"Perez is here. Declan wants to meet with us before we meet with Mr. Sweetness and Light. I'll meet you in his office."

"On my way."

As she walked across the office, Anna glanced at the large swarthy man in his late sixties visible through the open door of the conference room. His eyes roved over her body, as if deciding whether this particular piece of fruit met the grade. She looked away, trying not to react, but the distance between her office and Declan's suddenly seemed much farther.

Donna was waiting outside Collins's office. She noticed the look on Anna's face. "Ignore the jerk. I suggest you keep your eyes on your notepad in the meeting. That's what I intend to do."

"Good advice."

Unfortunately, my job is to observe this jerk and figure out what his story is.

Donna knocked on the door to Collins's office before opening it and walking in.

Collins was furiously typing on his laptop. He waived them in. "Morning, Donna, Anna."

"Good morning. How did it go in Charlotte?"

"Okay, I think. They didn't throw me out the door."

"That's something."

"So," Donna said, drawing out the word, "what's the plan with Perez?"

Collins took the computer off his lap and placed it on the desk.

"Here's the deal: Matt and I are behind on getting out a private placement deal this guy wants done yesterday, and he's here to bite my head off. I'm hoping he'll be less belligerent if you two are in the room."

Donna turned to Anna. "Matt Esposito is Declan's hockey buddy from Boston. He works for a broker dealer three blocks from here."

Collins nodded. "Yeah, Matt's firm will be the broker dealer on the deal."

Donna nodded.

Anna could tell by Donna's body language she didn't think much of Matt Esposito. "So . . . what should Donna and I do in the meeting?" she said.

"Duck and cover. I'll introduce you. After that, focus on taking notes. I'll do the rest. Michaela will interrupt us in about thirty minutes with an urgent call from the court. I'll use that as an excuse to cut the meeting short."

Donna folded her arms across her chest. "I think you should—"

"Dump him? I know, Donna. It's more complicated than that. Perez . . . he's not the kinda guy you can just walk away from."

Collins briefly glanced at Anna as he spoke, but she avoided eye contact. A moment later, he stood up and gestured toward the door.

"Okay, then, let's beard the lion."

Anna followed Donna out the door. She knew Collins was hiding something, but for some reason she suspected there was more to it than a desire to keep the details of his relationship with Perez secret.

George Town, Grand Cayman

Matt stared at the picture-perfect harbor scene visible from the veranda of the Prince George Pub. The mug of White Tip beer in front of him was untouched.

"Nice, eh?"

Matt glanced across the table at Nigel, as if he'd forgotten the man was there. "Yeah . . . it's amazing."

"Actually, I was commenting on that gorgeous creature sitting at the bar."

Matt looked over at the attractive brunette on the other side of the room. The woman noticed his look and a touch of a smile crossed her lips. Three days ago, trying to pick up the woman would have been Matt's mission for the rest of night. Now she was just another piece of furniture.

Nigel swirled the scotch whiskey in front of him and raised an eyebrow.

"You seem out of sorts, old son. What's the matter? Did you get dumped by yet another one of those LA lovelies?"

Matt turned back to Nigel. "No, no. I'm good. It's just the combination of jetlag and lack of sleep."

"Really? I'm inclined to think it's more than that, but I won't kick you while you're down. At least not too much."

Matt forced himself to respond. "Don't do me any—"

The cell phone on table vibrated. It was Declan. Matt grabbed for the phone. "Declan, where are we?"

"We're in the game. B of A has picked the top three bidders for the note. We're one of them."

"We didn't win the bid? Why not? We have to—"

"Matt, we're going to get the deal, we just have one more hoop to jump through. The bank's going to conduct a final three-way auction in NYC. I'll text you the address. I need you and Nigel to get on a plane tonight. It's happening at two tomorrow afternoon."

"Wait, shouldn't you—"

"I don't have time. Buying the senior debt position only gets us a seat at the negotiating table in the bankruptcy case. We have to get control of PriceStar's going-out-of-business sale to pull this off. PriceStar's bankruptcy attorney holds the key to that treasure chest, and he's not going to let it go cheap. You and Nigel need to get to that auction in NYC and buy the note, while I pin that down here in LA."

"Okay, okay. We'll be there."

Matt turned to Nigel. "We need to be in New York tomorrow afternoon."

"I see. Then we'd better get on about it. The last flight out is in about three hours."

Downtown, Los Angeles, California

Anna didn't get back to her apartment until eight o'clock. Her cell phone rang as soon as the door closed.

"Anna, it's Teo. I'm gonna put you on three-way so Calder and Eric can hear the download. Give us the rundown."

"Well, I met Perez. He's a piece of work. The guy went ballistic as soon as the meeting started. He kept saying, 'I gotta get the money into this deal now, and I don't care about the effing legal niceties. Just get it done.' After ten minutes of shouting, he insisted everyone leave the room but Collins. So I didn't get to hear much more than that. But I can tell you this, when Collins came out of that room fifteen minutes later, he was . . . shaken up."

"Anna, I need you to be granular on this. Carlton—"

"Teo . . . fine. When we entered the conference room, Collins tried to introduce me and Donna—she's the office manager—to Perez, and he started raging at Collins. His tirade went something like this, 'I don't want to know who they are unless they're going to bed with me. What I want to know is when this effing deal is going to close.' Collins tried to interrupt him, but Perez wasn't having it. He said, 'You're gonna get rich doing this deal, Collins, so get the effing thing done.' Then he screamed and yelled about the value of the Mexican peso going into the tank. In the middle of this rant, it was as if he suddenly realized Donna and I shouldn't hear what he was saying, so he stopped and told Collins we had to get out. Collins was pissed, but he agreed. Fifteen minutes later, the two of them came out of the conference room, and Perez left. Perez seemed to have calmed down somewhat by then, so I assume Collins must have told him what he wanted to hear about the timing of the deal. However, like I said, Collins looked shaken up."

Calder made a low whistle. "I suspect he told him to make it happen or he'd end up dead."

"Anna, this is Eric. Can you get a copy of the private placement doc on this deal? That would tell us a lot."

"I'll try, but I don't think it'll help you even if I could access the file. Donna told me all of the Perez files are encrypted."

"We can beat most encryption programs," Calder said. "There's a back door."

"If you can safely get the file, Anna, do it," Teo interjected. "Put it on the flash drive Calder gave you. Was the Sanchez guy there today?"

"No, but he and Collins were on the phone three times. I think they were talking about the B of A debt acquisition deal. Donna said it looks like they have a good shot of being the winning bidder. Other than that, it was proofreading, drafting letters, and trying to help Donna with trial-prep work."

"Great work. Check in with us tomorrow."

"Thanks, Teo."

TWENTY-TWO

Santa Monica, California

Collins exploded out of bed, his heart pounding like a jackhammer trying to smash a hole through his chest. In the fading dream, he'd been running through the empty streets of LA pursued by pack of wolves, but no matter how fast he ran, they were always just one step behind him. He ran a hand through his hair. It was soaked in sweat.

He grabbed a bottle of water from the refrigerator and spent an hour alternating between the wall climber machine and the set of dumbbells located in the second bedroom. After stretching for ten minutes, he shaved and took a shower. The cell phone beside the sink rang as he was in the midst of drying off. He wrapped the towel around his waist and picked up the phone.

"Good morning, Mr. Collins."

"Good morning, Ms. Wilson, and Mr. Collins is my dad. I'm Declan."

"Very well, Declan, congratulations. Fourth Street was the highest bidder in the PriceStar loan auction. Bank of America is willing to proceed with the sale, subject to certain conditions."

"Which are?"

"The most important one is velocity. Fourth Street must agree to complete its due diligence and close within thirty days, no extensions."

"We'll get it done."

"No, 'I need to check with my client first?' Impressive."

"No, ma'am. A good lawyer must have client control."

"We'll have to meet for a drink when this deal is done. This Southern belle would love to know why y'all are so hot to get your hands on this loan."

"As I said, Fourth Street views this deal as an opportunity to make its mark in the distressed debt space. As for the drink, you're on."

"Very well. I'll send you the loan assignment docs within the hour."

Declan couldn't risk a dig. "No proof of funds question?"

"We confirmed you were good to go last night. We wouldn't be having this conversation otherwise."

"Just making sure."

"No need, Declan Collins. Tamara Wilson was born sure. Get me those contracts back ASAP."

"I will, Tamara Wilson. I surely will."

Collins laid the phone down on the hand towel lying beside the bathroom sink, closed his eyes, and raised his right fist. He squeezed until his fingers hurt and his arm was shaking. He slowly exhaled and unclenched his hand. The face staring back at him in the mirror when he opened his eyes seemed noticeably older than the face he was used to seeing. After staring at his reflection for a long moment, Collins slowly made the sign of the cross. It was something he hadn't done in a long time. Then he picked up the phone.

"Sanchez, I need twenty-five million dollars. We got the B of A loan."

"Gracias a Dios!"

"Yeah, roger that. But remember, we're only halfway there. We need to cut a deal with the unsecured creditors."

Sanchez was dismissive of the problem. "That should not be difficult. They are out of the money. The B of A debt is secured by a first-priority lien, and our debt exceeds the value of the collateral. If they don't cooperate, we can threaten to foreclose on the collateral, leaving them nothing."

"That's the real world, Sanchez. This is bankruptcy. The people who play in that space are experts in the fine art of extortion. Trust me, we still have a few more steep hills to climb."

Mexico City, Mexico

Ramon Cayetano's home in Mexico City was a twelve-thousand-square-foot mansion encircled by a fifteen-foot-high brick wall. Scrolls of barbed wire lined the top of the wall, and armed guards accompanied by dogs patrolled the inside perimeter. The four-thousand-square-foot steel-and-concrete-reinforced bunker in the basement, which served as Cayetano's office and his saferoom, was structurally designed to be bombproof. However, the furniture and décor of the room were modeled after the smoking room in one of London's oldest gentlemen's clubs.

As Gregorio waited patiently for Cayetano to finish his review of the cash take from last month's drug sales, he inwardly scoffed at the incongruous decorative motif. Ramon Cayetano was anything but a gentleman, despite his five-thousand-dollar suits, ruby-studded gold rings, and thousand-dollar cigars. Nacio Leon, who was sitting in a plush leather chair steps away, came visibly closer to the mark, with his white linen suit and aristocratic looks, but Gregorio knew this was an illusory veneer. A hired killer, no matter the pedigree, was still just another thug.

Cayetano's brusque voice interrupted Gregorio's mental ruminations. "Gregorio, tell me what this American lawyer, Collins, is doing with my money."

"Yes, sir. Mr. Collins has arranged to take control of the corporate shell of a failed hedge fund, Fourth Street, Ltd. We . . . you own this entity, indirectly, through a Panamanian bearer corporation. Using this shell as a front, Collins recently acquired the senior loan secured by all of the assets of PriceStar, the bankrupt American retail chain."

Gregorio pointed to an envelope he'd placed on Cayetano's desk a moment earlier. "The shares of stock in that envelope confirm your ownership of this entity."

Gregorio hesitated a moment to allow his boss to ask questions, but the Cartel lord just flicked his hand through the waves of cigar smoke. "Continue."

"Collins is negotiating with PriceStar's lawyers to get control of PriceStar through a bankruptcy plan of reorganization. His objective is to persuade these lawyers to allow people under our control to run a massive going-out-of-business sale during the bankruptcy case throughout PriceStar's network of stores. As part of this sale effort, our people will overstate the sales by one hundred million dollars. We will then backfill that hole with the dollars we're bringing across the border. If all goes as anticipated, the . . . illicit dollars will become clean, legitimate sales proceeds that can be used for any purpose."

"And what about taxes? How much will I be gouged by the IRS and the other bloodsuckers?"

Gregorio was amused by the man's hypocrisy, but his face remained impassive when he answered. "Collins has a plan to shield the phantom hundred-million-dollar gain from taxes by washing it against PriceStar's existing net operating losses. It's . . . a very complicated scheme, but it . . . should work."

The drug lord stared at Gregorio for a long moment before turning his gaze to Nacio. The hired killer was caressing his nails with a gold nail file. Nacio didn't look up when he spoke.

"It is, as you say, very complicated, but then, Collins is . . . a clever man."

Cayetano growled a response. "Maybe too clever. What will it cost and when will it be done?"

"The cost could be as high as twenty cents on every dollar we bring in, or as low as five cents on the dollar. It should take about two months, maybe three."

Anger flashed in Cayetano's eyes. "Tell me, Gregorio, what will you do to keep the costs down, so my money is protected?"

Gregorio swallowed heavily, realizing the lethal nature of the threat, but he nonetheless answered in a calm voice. "PriceStar will make a cash profit on the sale, if it's done right, and we will receive a percentage of the recoveries obtained from third parties on PriceStar's litigation claims. Alex and I will do everything we can to limit the costs charged by the vendors supplying merchandise for the sale and to cap the fees charged by the lawyers."

"And what of Collins? Do you trust him to do this thing?"

"I spoke to Alex this morning. He says Collins is playing by your rules. He also says the man is quite the genius when it comes to making deals."

"You tell Sanchez not to let his guard down for a second. If this man is as smart as you think, he will try to find a way out of the trap he is in. You and Nacio are to go to LA to see this does not happen."

"Nacio?"

Nacio smiled at Gregorio's surprise.

"Yes. Nacio will meet you in LA, in two days. He will be there with a team to watch Collins and the broker when he comes back from Grand Cayman. You will tell Nacio if you see or hear anything that might be suspicious."

"Yes . . . yes, sir."

"Good. Now go."

"Yes, sir."

Nacio followed Gregorio out of the room to the stairs leading up to the main floor of the house.

"I will call you when I arrive," Nacio said with a smile that never reached his eyes. "Maybe we will have dinner together."

"Yes . . . just let me know when. I know a good restaurant or two there."

"I'm sure you do. Until then."

As the two men emerged from the basement, the two armed guards at the top of the stairs nodded respectfully to Nacio, but they ignored Gregorio.

"Stay safe, Gregorio," Nacio said with a cold smile as Gregorio walked out to the limousine waiting to take him to the airport.

Maijoma, Mexico

Sienna's designated exercise circuit was a dirt path that formed a horizontal square encompassing the eastern third of the compound. One leg of the square ran along the base of the building where she was being held captive. The second, third, and fourth legs ran along the base of the wall enclosing that part of the compound. She was allowed to walk around the roughly four-hundred-yard distance three times every afternoon.

Each trip around the route allowed her to scan the wall enclosing the compound. It was ten to twelve feet high. The older sections of the wall were made of adobe and stone. The newer parts were rough-hewn wood that was worn and rotted in places. Crude watchtowers had been built into the corner and middle sections of the wall. Sienna knew from the conversations she'd overheard when eating breakfast that the towers were manned by armed men after dark. What she didn't know was whether the guards were there to keep people out or to keep people in. She suspected it was both.

The building where she was being held was situated on the southeastern corner of the exercise path. The storage shed where she believed the man had hidden the phone was just around the corner from that building. Juan, the guard who reluctantly followed her on each circuit, had fallen forty yards behind after her first lap around the square. He was out of sight when she turned the corner. Sienna jogged to within five yards of the shed and stopped for a minute, pantomiming catching her breath while surreptitiously scanning the dilapidated structure in the hope of finding a clue to where the guard had hidden the phone. It had to be here—there was nowhere else he could have hidden it. Minutes later, she heard Juan trundling around the corner, and she turned and continued her walk.

Sienna steadily increased her pace when she walked around the loop a second time, gradually expanding the distance between herself and the guard behind her. When she came around the corner near the shed the second time, she sprinted to the door and dodged inside. For a frustrating moment or two, she couldn't see anything as she waited for her vision to adjust to the darkened interior.

The single room was full of dusty boxes, rusted tools, and buck-ets of paint that hadn't been touched for years. As she scanned the room, counting aloud to herself in a whisper, she realized there were a hundred places the phone could be hidden. She would never find it in time. Then she looked down at the dirt floor for the outline of footprints in the dust. There were none. The man with the phone had never entered the shed.

Sienna walked out of the shed, confused. What did he do with the phone? Then she saw the holes in the eaves just under the lip of the roof. If the man had never entered the shed, they had to be there. She reached into the hole in the first eave but found nothing. As she moved to the second eve, she heard Juan's heavy step. She ran to the track, dropped to the ground, and unlaced the laces on her right sneaker. A moment later, Juan trundled into view, huffing and puffing, and sweating profusely.

As soon as she finished retying her laces, she started around the circuit again, increasing her pace so there was an even greater gap between herself and Juan. As she came around the corner of the last building and readied herself for a sprint to the shed, she saw Matias, the man in the black silk shirt. He was standing in the middle of the dirt path waiting for her.

TWENTY-THREE

Los Angeles, California

mpeccably dressed in a dark gray Zegna business suit, Gregorio opened the door to the suite on the tenth floor of the Beverly Wilshire Hotel and gestured for Collins to enter.

"Please come in and sit down."

Collins nodded, restraining the anger that arose whenever he saw Gregorio. Sanchez was standing by a marble table in the main room wearing the same brown suit he wore every day. Gregorio gestured toward the table. A crystal pitcher was sitting on a tray in the middle surrounded by glasses.

"Please sit and have a glass of iced tea."

The invitation reminded Collins of the lunch he and Matt had shared with Gregorio before their Armageddon meeting with Cayetano, increasing the cold rage simmering within him. Collins suppressed the emotion. He had to get through this. There was no other choice.

He walked over to the far end of the table where he could see both men, but he didn't sit down. When he spoke, it was in a controlled, matter-of-fact tone. "Pace Cohen's law office is five blocks away. Sanchez and I will be meeting with David Cohen, PriceStar's lead bankruptcy lawyer."

Collins turned to Sanchez. "Before we walk into that meeting, I need you to understand how this has to go down. Think of it as a parley between the generals of two armies before a battle. Cohen's army is manning the walls of the city we need to take control of.

Let's call that city PriceStar. Cohen knows we can take the city by siege, but he also knows a siege will take time and money, and it will leave PriceStar a burning ruin. So we need to convince him to give us control, or at least partial control, of PriceStar without a siege. We are going to have to pay a price for that privilege."

"Privilege? I'm sorry, Mr. Collins, I don't understand your analogy," Gregorio said politely. "We are the senior secured creditor. Our debt is secured by a lien on all of PriceStar's assets, and the liquidation value of those assets is less than what we are owed. Unless my understanding of American commercial law is deficient, neither the unsecured creditors nor the stockholders of that company will receive a penny in a liquidation. They should just—"

"Hand us the keys?" Collins finished. "That's not going to happen. They know the company is losing five million to ten million of cash a month, or more, which means PriceStar's balance sheet, like the city in my analogy, is being burned down. So, if they can drag this out in a bankruptcy for six months or more, which they can do, we lose somewhere between thirty million and sixty million of value by the time we finally get our hands on those keys. Bottom line: We write the check necessary to get the keys to the city."

"This is . . . an abuse of the system," Sanchez said, shaking his head. "We're going to pay them for not destroying millions of dollars of our collateral!"

Collins pointed his index finger at Sanchez. "Bingo."

Gregorio face tightened, and he spread his hands out on the table in front of him. "Mr. Collins . . . the man we answer to is not going to like—"

Collins stepped closer to Gregorio and emphasized each word as he spoke. "There is no other way."

He then hesitated for a moment before continuing, "But we'll extract something from them in return that . . . should be worth the price."

"And that is?"

"The use of PriceStar's net operating losses to shelter the phantom gain created by the incoming dirty money."

"Net operating losses? Señor Collins," Sanchez said, shaking his head, "I'm not the tax expert like you are, but I know large profitable American corporations used to buy shell corporations with accrued net operating losses on their balance sheets and use those losses to wash out the profits generated by the buying entity. This . . . this was a very good way to reduce corporate taxes, but your Congress and IRS changed the law. Now a company's net operating losses all but evaporate when there is a change of ownership or . . . a change in the control. So, as soon as we take control—"

"That's right. As soon as we take control." Collins glanced at his watch. "That won't happen until after PriceStar has used the losses to wash out the phantom gain we're going to create. We will bury findings in PriceStar's plan of reorganization and in the order approving the plan ratifying this tax treatment. We will also have PriceStar take the same position in the final tax return filed by the bankruptcy estate. If Cohen goes for it, it's a big win."

Gregorio looked over at Collins. "How big?"

"If we assume a 20 percent average corporate tax rate on the one hundred million dollars of phantom gain, twenty million dollars."

Sanchez's eyes widened. Then he leaned forward and said conspiratorially, "Won't the IRS see this is a just an illegal scheme to evade taxes?"

"We're avoiding, not evading," Collins said laconically. "And yes, outside of a bankruptcy, the IRS would probably audit the crap out of us and challenge our use of the net operating losses. That won't happen in a bankruptcy. The IRS only has a short time to object to a Chapter 11 debtor's tax returns, and if they don't object, it's game over."

"And why are you so sure that the IRS won't audit PriceStar's returns before the objection period expires?" Gregorio said.

Collins shook his head. "I'm not, but I know the chances are in the slim-to-none range. The IRS is not going to bust its hump going after a company that's circling the drain when it can go after a company that can afford to pay."

Sanchez nodded. "Yes . . . yes, this makes sense. I can see it."

"Mr. Collins," Gregorio said quietly, "if PriceStar's management controls the company during the sale, how are we going to . . . launder one hundred million dollars in front of their collective nose?"

"We bribe them—legally. We get the judge to approve a bonus program for PriceStar's key execs. Half of the bonus is earned if they stay on through the sale period; half is discretionary. We tell them that getting the second half requires one thing—cooperation. We make it clear that our people will run the IT and accounting departments during the sale, and our people will prepare the final tax returns. And yes, we will get someone with PriceStar to sign them. As for the mechanics of bringing the drug money in through the back door, it's all doable as long as we control PriceStar's IT and accounting departments. When the sales figures are reported by PriceStar's local stores, we gross them up by, on average, 1.7 million dollars a day. We use your drug money to fill in that hole when we make the daily bank deposits. We start small, at first, but once the sale is in full swing, we ratchet it up. Over time, we walk in the whole one hundred mil."

Gregorio and Sanchez remained quiet. Sensing their skepticism, Collins made a dismissive gesture. "Relax. Remember what I told you when we first met. These sales are organized chaos. Inventory is pouring in the back door and racing out the front. Cash is flying every which way. No one really knows whether the sale is a success until it's over. By then, PriceStar's reorganization plan will be confirmed, all of the outstanding shares of stock will be cancelled, and the company will be out of bankruptcy. Once the stock is cancelled through the reorg plan, PriceStar is a private company. So, the corporation won't have to report the results of the sale to the public. Yes, the grossed-up sales figure will show up on PriceStar's tax return, and yes that return will show the gain being washed out by the net operating losses. However, as I said, the only one looking at that, the IRS, is not going to notice. When it's all over, your people pocket the excess cash as clean money."

Gregorio stared at Collins for a moment before nodding his reluctant acceptance.

"Good," Collins said with finality. "However, you will have to supply the personnel to get it done—the IT people and the compliant cash couriers."

Sanchez wrung his hands. "Gregorio, there are hundreds of stores! That's a lot—"

"You put together one courier for every ten stores," Collins said. "Call them roving auditors. They show up for each cash pickup and dump an extra sack of dirty cash in the truck. That's ten to twenty trips a day."

Gregorio nodded after a long silence. "We have the people to do it."

Collins started toward the door. "Get those people ready to go, Gregorio. This is going to happen fast. Sanchez, let's go. It's time to cut a deal with the enemy."

———

Collins explained his negotiating strategy to Sanchez as they walked from the hotel over to the Pace Cohen office. He finished his monologue just as they entered the lobby.

"Wait, please wait, Mr. Collins," Sanchez gasped. "I have some questions."

Collins glanced down at his watch. They had five minutes. "Shoot."

"I think I understand your game plan, but . . . do we really need this Charles Dennison to participate in the negotiations? This man sounds like he's looking for . . . for a fight."

Collins nodded. "He is. That's his role. He's an ultra-expensive, take-no-prisoners litigator. You hire him and his law firm when you want to destroy the other side. The bankruptcy lawyers upstairs hate him because he doesn't play by their rules, and he routinely sues the other side's lawyers when things really get down and dirty."

Sanchez's eyes widened. "But I thought you said we had to do a deal with these people?"

Collins lowered his briefcase to the polished marble floor and glanced around the lobby. "We do, but it has to be a deal that works for us. Here's the picture we want to present. We tell the bankruptcy lawyers we represent a hyper-aggressive offshore hedge fund—a vulture fund with no intention of playing by the good-ole-boy rules the bankruptcy lawyers are used to. That's why they hired a mad dog like Dennison. We tell them the client made this choice over our objection."

"Over our—"

"Yes. We want them to think you and I are wrestling with Dennison for control of the client, and if they push too hard, Dennison will get the upper hand. They know if that happens, Dennison will drive the bus and everyone in it over a cliff. By the way, he's done that before. For him, crash-and-burn endings are totally okay."

Sanchez's eyes widened as he extended a hand in a cautionary gesture. "I . . . I'm not sure—"

Collins waved away his objection. "Relax, Sanchez. It'll work. You have to understand the driver in this negotiation. It's the professional fees. Pace Cohen's primary objective is to make sure there's enough money to pay their fees and the fees of the other professionals who they bring into the case. As long as we agree to cover that nut—and it will be a big one—everything else is negotiable."

Sanchez stared at Collins skeptically. "I thought the American bankruptcy system was designed to liquidate assets so creditors could get paid."

Collins glanced down at his watch as he answered. "It is, but the suits always get paid first. So here's how we play it. Dennison will take the lead. Things will get hostile real quick. Just before the whole thing blows up, I'll suggest we take a break. During the break, David Cohen will pull me aside and try to cut a deal. I'll give him the term sheet I showed you earlier, and we'll get the deal done. Now let's get up there."

The ultramodern decor in Pace Cohen's lobby was opulent but not palatial. It was as if the law firm's senior partners realized, reluctantly, that a firm catering to financially distressed companies should make some effort to restrain its own financial excess.

Collins walked over to the female receptionist who had the same cold but attractive air as the surrounding decor.

"Collins and Sanchez. We're here for a meeting with David Cohen."

"Good morning. I will let his assistant know you're here."

"Thanks."

Collins heard the elevator open behind him, and he glanced in that direction just as Charles Dennison strode out.

"Declan Collins! What's an upstanding barrister like you doing in this disreputable neighborhood?" Charles Dennison said.

Although Collins hadn't seen Dennison in over a year, he recognized the cultured Boston accent. The lean six-foot-two man standing two steps away looked like a British diplomat who'd just popped across the pond to negotiate a trade agreement. His full head of gray-white hair framed a thin aristocratic face, a narrow aquiline nose, and penetrating blue-gray eyes. The dark blue Saville Row suit projected respectability rather than combativeness, but Collins knew otherwise. As he shook Dennison's hand, Collins knew he was gripping the hand of a human rapier just waiting to strike.

"Chip. Good to see you."

"And you as well."

Collins turned to Sanchez. "This is Alex Sanchez. He's an SVP with Fourth Street."

Dennison stepped forward and shook Sanchez's hand. "The pleasure is mine."

Sanchez nodded. "And mine, as well."

"Very good, then if the plan is the same, let's have at these greedy scoundrels. Speaking of scoundrels, here's Mr. Cohen," Dennison said with a supercilious smile of pleasure.

Collins turned around. David Cohen was standing outside the door of the large glass conference room on the other side of the reception area. The balding fifty-five-year-old lawyer was just shy of six feet, and unlike Dennison, he carried an extra thirty pounds on his waistline. Although Cohen's dark blue suit had been expertly tailored to hide the paunch, the lawyer had thwarted the effort by wearing a dress shirt that seemed a half size too small.

Collins could tell by the hint of ire in Cohen's cold brown eyes that he'd heard Dennison's comment, just as Dennison intended.

"Let's get started, Collins," Cohen said derisively as he turned and walked into the conference room. "I don't want to waste any more of my client's time unless you have something better to offer than that piece of trash Dennison sent over yesterday."

"What's that saying about not wasting your pearls?" Dennison mused in a voice just loud enough for the departing Cohen to hear.

The knives were drawn. It was going to be a long morning.

———

Anna glanced down at her watch as she stepped out of the elevator into the reception area of the Pace Cohen law firm. It was exactly twelve o'clock. She'd texted Collins a moment earlier advising him of her arrival, just as he'd directed. The loud and angry voices coming from the conference room across from the circular receptionist's desk immediately drew her attention. Although the conference room's frosted glass doors were closed, she could hear one man shouting in a loud voice with a heavy Brooklyn accent.

"Listen, you wiseass schlock, you can't sell any of the clothes in those damn stores without my say so! They're all on consignment, and I have a lien."

A male voice with a Boston accent responded scornfully, "Clothes? You mean rags, don't you? As for your so-called consignment, it might have been worth a damn in the last century, but not in this one. Ask your counsel; he'll tell you the bank's lien is first in line. So, take what's offered, or walk with zero."

Before the other man could respond, she heard Collins's voice. "Let's take a break. Shall we?"

A loud exchange followed. A moment later, Collins emerged from the conference room with Sanchez and a distinguished-looking man wearing a dark blue suit. The man was smiling in pleasure despite the cacophony he'd left behind.

A short elderly man wearing a mauve blazer and beige pants emerged from the other door to the conference room and started toward Collins and his companions with a slow shambling gate. His thin red face and the wispy tufts of white hair made him seem like a wizened elf in an apoplectic fit.

"Who the hell do you bastards—"

A second balding man dressed in a dark suit intercepted the older man. "Bernie! Wait! I'll deal with this."

The older man shook off the lawyer's hand on his shoulder and snarled, "Screw that. I'm not doing a deal with that arrogant bastard!"

The lawyer stepped in front of the old man, blocking his access to Collins, and pointed toward a door down the hallway. "Bernie, the rest of the creditor's committee wants to talk this over. Come down the hall to the other conference room."

"Talk! I've heard—"

A second figure came up behind the old man and rested his hand on the irate man's shoulder. The smaller man went silent and listened grudgingly as the man spoke in a placative voice.

"Bernie, we've known each other for thirty years, and you persuaded the creditor's committee to hire me because you trust me, right?"

The other man reluctantly answered, "Yeah, that's right."

"Then trust your old friend to do his job, okay?"

The man's calm, friendly voice worked its magic.

"All right, all right, but if this Chip character says one more word I . . . I—and what the hell kind of name is Chip anyway? What's his middle name—Wood? He can't pull this kind of crap!"

The tall man nodded appreciatively as he guided the other man down the hall. "I know, I know. Let's take a minute with the committee before we break for lunch."

"Anna."

Anna was so intrigued by the conflict she didn't realize Collins was standing a step away from her.

Collins gestured to the man standing beside him. "Anna, this is Chip Dennison. He's co-counsel with the firm on this matter."

The man shook Anna's hand in a firm but respectful grip, a smile coming to his distinguished face. "It's my pleasure, Anna. I look forward to working with you."

Anna nodded. "And I with you, Mr. Dennison."

"Chip will do fine, Anna."

"Of course."

Anna turned to Sanchez. "Hello again, Alex."

Sanchez nodded politely. "It is very good to see you again, Anna."

Despite his polite demeanor, Anna could tell Sanchez was upset, but Collins didn't seem concerned.

Collins turned to Dennison. "Chip, I want to talk to Cohen alone. You've bounced him off the walls enough this morning."

Dennison's smiled widened. "And here I was just beginning to enjoy myself."

"I know. That's what I'm worried about."

"Very well then, counselor, Anna, and Alex, I will bid you adieu for now."

Anna returned Dennison's smile. Collins nodded.

After Dennison left, Collins glanced over at the conference room down the hall where loud voices could be heard within despite the heavy glass door. Then he turned to Sanchez.

"In a few minutes, David Cohen will come out, and we'll have a one-on-one meeting. Anna will be in the meeting, but you, Sanchez, will stay out."

"I don't understand. I am the principal. I should—"

Collins shook his head. "Not if you want to get the deal done. Remember how we played it in Charlotte with B of A. This is a different situation, but the dynamic is similar. If you go in there, Cohen will just posture to try to move the needle his way. If I go in there, we'll get the deal done. Don't worry, I'll come out and get your final approval, but that's how it has to happen."

"And Anna . . . why is—"

"Two reasons. One, she's part of your legal team, and two, Cohen just got divorced, and he considers himself a ladies' man. If Anna's in the room, he'll be less belligerent."

Collins turned to Anna with an apologetic look on this face. "Sorry, Anna, but—"

"I understand. You're playing every card you have."

Collins gave her a nod of thanks. "That I am."

Sanchez hesitated for a moment and then reluctantly nodded his consent. "I understand."

A moment later, Cohen came out of the conference room down the hall. His face was grim. He looked over at Collins, pointed to a door at the end of the hallway, and walked in that direction without waiting for a response.

Collins turned to Anna and gestured for her to go first. "Let's get this done, shall we?"

Anna nodded and walked down the hall to the open door. Collins was a step behind.

Cohen was sitting at a conference table staring at a pad of paper. He didn't look up when he spoke. "You really screwed this—"

"David Cohen, let me introduce you to Anna Fallon," Collins interrupted.

Cohen looked up. His look of irritation evaporated after his first somewhat restrained scan of Anna's face and physique. He stood up and stretched out his hand, an ingratiating smile on his face. "Hello, Anna. Welcome to Pace Cohen."

Cohen leaned close to Anna as he shook her hand and spoke in a conspiratorial tone, nodding toward Collins. "Do yourself a favor and try to ignore everything this guy says."

Anna smiled politely but said nothing.

The tightness in Collins's chest eased a little. The emotional needle, at least, was moving in the right direction.

"Anna is a paralegal, David. She will be taking notes on the deal we're going to do."

"Deal—what deal? That piece of crap Dennison, pardon my French, blew up any deal!"

Anna sensed Cohen was playing a game.

"That's rather unfair. Chip only had nice things to say about you."
Anna had to restrain a smile.

"Don't give me that BS, Collins. You know the guy's a jerk. He
has to go or—"

Collins held up a placative hand. "David, here's my problem. My
client's a hedge fund and Dennison's their guy, and they've done the
math. That's what they're good at. They know the unsecured creditors are dead if we don't make a deal. What they don't understand
is the bankruptcy . . . variable. I'm working on that, and I think I
can get us to a place that works for you and the committee. Here's
what I think I can sell to them. You file the bankruptcy case with
the pre-negotiated plan. My client brings in its own outfit to run a
going-out-of-business sale, from start to finish. That way they control the cash, and they own the result. Your firm drafts the plan and
disclosure statement. We leave one million on the table for the other
creditors and for legal fees. The committee gets all of the avoidable
transfer recoveries, which could be another five to ten million, but
we get 40 percent of whatever they recover on those claims net of
fees and costs."

"So my firm is supposed to file this case without retainer?"
Cohen said caustically.

Collins spread his hands out on the table in a gesture of accommodation. "I said we'd leave a million on the table. You can use
some of that to pay your fees."

"That's crap. It'll take at least two to three million in fees to get
this case through plan confirmation, and that's on the cheap. I need
at least three million on top of that for the unsecured creditors plus
the recoveries on the litigation claims. Otherwise it will never sell."

Anna was stunned by the attorney's fee estimate.

"We'll front 500K in legal fees and leave 500K on the table for
the unsecured creditors and limit our piece of the litigation recoveries to 30 percent."

Cohen shook his head. "Not happening. A million-five for the
fees, up front, and two million for the unsecured creditors, and you
get 10 percent of the recoveries."

Collins leaned back in his chair and spread his hands on the table.

"Look, we both know bankruptcy work is thin right now, so a 700K retainer will look good to your partners."

"One million, and you carve out another 500K from your collateral for our fees, and your piece of the avoidance recoveries is limited to 5 percent," Cohen snapped back.

Collins leaned forward as if he wanted to make sure his voice didn't carry outside of the room. "This is a hedge fund, David. They're in the business of taking other people to the cleaners, not vice versa."

"Look," Cohen said in a friendlier voice, "if the unsecured creditors get a million five, plus another six million from the avoidance claim recoveries, that's a 10 percent recovery."

Collins stared at Cohen for a long moment, and then said, "I'll try to get it done, but here's the deal: One, whatever comes to my client from the going-out-of-business sale is their business, good, bad, or indifferent. You don't even get to look at the numbers."

"What! How the hell does that work? We have to file the final tax returns!"

Collins shook his head. "No, Fourth Street's people will get that done. Don't worry, we'll get PriceStar's outgoing CFO to bless them. You take the money we leave on the table for the attorneys and the unsecured creditors, set up your liquidating trust to pursue the litigation claims, and leave my client alone."

Cohen looked at Collins, hesitated a moment, and then said, "Fine. I'll try to sell it. There's nothing but crap in those stores, but hey, if your client can turn it into gold, go right ahead. But tell me, why?" The suspicion in his voice was plain. "Why does your client want the ups on an iffy sale and the right to do the books and records?"

Collins smiled conspiratorially. "Come on, guy, this a hedge fund, not a public corporation. If they knock it out of the park running the sale, the managers will find a way to pocket a big piece of the ups. If they take a bath, they'll want to keep it quiet, so it won't affect next year's sales pitch to their Chinese and Saudi investors."

Cohen gave Anna a smile as he stood up. "Got it. Go to lunch, Collins. Let the master do his work. I'll have this sold by the time you get back."

TWENTY-FOUR

Maijoma, Mexico

Sienna could sense the cold rage beneath Matias's emotionless visage. His eyes held Sienna's for a moment, and then he turned to face Juan. Matias slapped the back of his hand into the palm of his other hand as Juan stumbled forward.

"Move faster, you pig!"

Sienna could hear the fear in Juan's response.

"Sí, Señor."

Then Matias turned back to her. "Sienna, that is your name?" He posed the question in the same quiet, atonal voice she remembered, but there was a dangerous edge to it. She struggled to keep any hint of fear from reaching her voice. She wasn't wholly successful.

"Yes."

"Do you remember what I told you when we first met?"

"Yes."

"Good."

There was a long silence during which Matias's eyes bored into her own—his gaze cold and unmerciful.

"It seems, Sienna, someone has been using a cell phone within this compound."

"I don't have a cell phone," Sienna said without hesitation. "You know that. I was searched twice when I arrived."

"So you were. But then cell phones come in very small sizes, and a desperate woman could find a place to hide one."

She could feel her face redden. "I don't have a phone," she rasped out in anger.

Matias's eyes roved over her body. "Your quarters are being searched. A woman will come to you when it is done. She will search you—everywhere. Pray we do not find a phone."

He turned without another word and walked back toward the main building.

When Sienna raised a hand to brush the hair back from her forehead, it was shaking uncontrollably.

She was allowed to return to her room three hours later. Holes had been cut in every one of the walls and the mattress she'd been sleeping on had been replaced with a new one. After washing quickly in the darkness and making her way to the bed, she lay down and closed her eyes. The kind Mexican woman from the kitchen had been assigned to search her. She told Sienna in a whisper that if she did not do as they said, Matias would hurt her son. The experience was invasive and demeaning, despite the woman's apologies.

After the woman left the room, she could hear Matias grilling her about the search. At one point, she heard him slap the woman's face and threaten the life of her son if she'd made a mistake. The woman's cry of pain and the desperate fear in her voice sent a wave of fear washing over Sienna. She knew beyond a shadow of a doubt that Matias would kill her the instant the cartel no longer needed Matt and Declan's help. She had to find a way out of the compound before that happened.

Hours later, she awoke with a start and stared into the impenetrable blackness. She waited for her eyes to adjust before easing out of the bed and quietly slipping on her running shoes. After listening for the sound of someone waiting outside the door for several minutes, she crawled over to the pipe in the corner of the room and said a prayer of thanks for the dark, overcast sky.

Sienna glanced back at the door again, drew in a breath, and started up the pipe. When she reached the top, she pushed on the polystyrene panel above her head until it separated from the steel frame with soft pop. She froze for a moment to listen and then pushed it aside.

The opening allowed her to continue up the pipe to the point where it disappeared through a two-foot hole in the roof. Although mesh had been nailed over the hole, a gap large enough for her to wriggle through was just visible in the darkness. Sienna pushed aside the remaining mesh and stuck her head through the hole. She struggled to catch her breath as she scanned the roof and the area below.

The pipe was connected to a crude rainwater cistern on the roof. A second overflow pipe ran from the top of the cistern down the side of the building to the ground below. The shed where the man had hidden the phone was ten yards away from where the pipe reached the ground.

Sienna climbed through the hole onto the roof and started down the side of the building, using the outside pipe as a ladder. She dropped into a crouch when her feet touched the ground, and she scanned the surrounding area, gasping for breath. No one was there. She ran over to the shed, stood on her toes, and reached into the darkness of the second eave she'd missed in her earlier search. As her arm extended into the rough wood aperture, she heard a scurrying sound and yanked her hand back, her heart pounding in her chest. She despised rodents, and Dr. O'Brien, the head of the Doctors Without Borders team, had advised the staff that some of the rats in Mexico carried a potentially deadly form of hantavirus.

After drawing in several breaths and glancing around the area once more, Sienna reached into the eave again, expecting at any moment to feel the sharp teeth of a rat biting her hand. The eave was empty. She moved on to the next opening. When her hand was only partway into the wooden hole, she felt two square metallic objects. She patted the first and then the second. The guard had hidden two small phones in the eave!

She grabbed the closest phone and pulled it out. It was a cheaper model, but it would do. She turned it on and said a prayer of thanks when the entry screen didn't request a password. She scrolled through the apps on the phone. Her breath caught in her throat when she saw the Google Maps application. She tapped the screen and stared at the location. The nearest entry was a place called Maijoma.

She glanced around quickly before opening the message app. She started typing Matt's cell phone number but stopped after the area code. The men who'd taken Matt and Declan prisoners would have taken their phones. If she sent a message it might go to a member of the cartel. She typed in the phone number of her best friend, Grayson Manning. Grayson worked in LA and had met both Matt and Declan.

"Grayson, its Si. Need help! Life in danger, no BS! Being held near Maijoma MX in a bg wooden compnd in open valley. Find Matt or Declan, IN PERSON, no phone or text. Give them message – wrt it out. Find me!!! It's me. I remember your pk poodle. Hurry!"

When Sienna pressed the send message button, nothing happened. No signal! She walked over to where the man had been standing when he'd found a signal the other night and tried to send the message again. Still no signal! She started walking in a circle slowly, when nothing happened, the hysteria and frustration she felt became almost unbearable. She glanced around, and her eyes found a man stealthily making his way between the buildings that led to where she was standing. It was the guard.

"No, please, God, no!" she whispered.

She took another step and found the signal. A second later the message transmitted. Sienna deleted the message and ran to the eave. The guard hadn't seen her, but he would in a moment. She replaced the phone in the eave, ran to the pipe and frantically scrabbled to the top. The man entered the area below her just as she reached the roof. She froze, and the man looked around suspiciously, as if sensing her presence. Then he turned his back and moved stealthily to the eave where she'd just replaced the phone.

Sienna eased across the roof, pushed aside the wire mesh, and crawled back through the hole. Before starting down the pipe to the room below, she glanced down. Three men were walking into the dirt square between the buildings. She recognized the man in the lead. It was Matias.

The guard had just pulled the phone from the eave when he realized they were behind him. He wheeled around, froze for a moment, and then grabbed for the gun in his belt. Matias must have expected the move. He fired one shot, and the man clutched his stomach and stumbled forward, dropping his phone. Sienna covered her mouth, smothering a gasp of horror. The dying man fired a second shot at the ground in front of him a moment later. Matias fired two shots in rapid success, hitting the man in the chest. He stood motionless for a moment and then fell forward into the dirt. One of Matias's men reached down and picked up something from the ground. It was the phone.

The man looked at the phone and turned to Matias. "It's destroyed."

The man had taken the time to put a bullet through the phone even as he was dying. He must have known Matias and his killers would track down whomever he'd called and kill them.

For a moment, Sienna thought Matias was going to shoot the man holding the destroyed phone, but he curtly waved him away. "Send it out to Ernesto at base camp to investigate. Whoever he called dies."

Matias walked over to the body of the man on the ground and kicked him viciously in the side before turning and walking back toward the headquarters building. After several steps, he slowed and scanned the surrounding area, as if he realized he was being watched. Sienna froze. After a moment, Matias turned and left.

Sienna climbed quietly down the pipe. She was halfway down before she realized she'd failed to put the ceiling tile back in place. She struggled back to the top and edged the tile back into its steel frame and made her way to the floor. By the time she reached the bottom, she was gasping for breath and shaking with fatigue and fear.

She drew a breath and walked over to the bathroom and washed her hands and face in the sink, trying to be as quiet as possible. She lay awake most of the night trying to repress the memory of the guard's lifeless body falling to the ground.

Downtown, Los Angeles, California

Anna watched Declan Collins as he emerged from the restroom on the other side of the restaurant and walked back toward the table where she was sitting. Collins stiffened as he walked by a table where a Latina, about her own age, was eating lunch with a male companion. The woman was beautiful in an exotic, seductive way, and it was clear she knew it. The woman's male companion, who was facing away from Anna, was wearing an expensive and well-tailored dark blue suit and a pair of sunglasses.

Although the woman didn't look up at Collins as he passed by, the touch of a smile crossed her face. It was as if the two of them knew each other, and they were making a point of hiding their relationship. At first, Anna suspected Collins and the woman may have had a romantic relationship in the past and were attempting to keep it secret from her present lunch companion, but Collins's body language didn't read that way. His face froze, and although he hid it well, there was cold rage in his eyes. As Anna watched Collins ease his way across the restaurant, she realized the man across from the woman had turned his head in her direction. He was staring at her through a pair of Panthère de Cartier sunglasses. She recognized the miniature gold panther heads on the outside edge of each lens. Anna continued to scan the restaurant. When her gaze reached the man's table, he looked away, but she sensed he was still watching her.

She had only seen the man's strikingly handsome face, but it was enough. Despite his smile, relaxed manner, and expensive clothes, he had a threatening aura, like a razor-sharp knife.

Collins nodded at the menu as he sat down. "Did you see anything you liked?"

Although his tone was casual, there was an undercurrent of tension in his voice.

"No . . . I mean, not yet. Is . . . everything okay?"

Collins smiled stiffly and made a dismissive gesture with his hand. "Everything's fine, just stress. Fourth Street is pressuring me to get the deal, but, of course, they also want to pay a bargain basement price. Layer on top of that PriceStar's massive daily cash burn, which neither side wants to eat, and . . . well, it becomes real simple. We get this done today or—"

Collins's cell phone interrupted his response. He glanced down at the number. "It's Cohen. I have to take this. Can you order me the spinach salad with blackened salmon? I'll be right back."

Anna smiled. "I'll make it two."

As Collins walked out of the restaurant talking on the phone, the handsome Latino man watched him without moving his head. Then he glanced over in Anna's direction, as if to assure himself Collins intended to return. When Collins returned to the table twenty minutes later, the man followed his progress.

Collins gestured to the two plates on the table. "Let's eat. We've earned it."

Although Anna wanted to hear about the phone call, she was also ravenous, and the food looked delicious.

After several mouthfuls, Collins asked, "So, do you want to hear the news?"

"Yes!"

"The debtor and the creditors' committee will do the deal, but there's one hiccup. The old guy from New York, Bernie, is holding out. He's been a player in the rag trade for fifty years. His father was sort of the godfather in Manhattan's garment district back in the day. The other committee members don't want to offend him by doing the deal without his consent. Cohen says he's thinks the committee will eventually agree to the deal, but the problem is—"

"You can't wait," Anna finished.

Collins smiled. "We've only been working together for a couple of weeks, and you're finishing my sentences. That's not good."

Anna returned his smile. Despite the pressure being put on her by the strike team, she was starting to enjoy working with Collins.

She also found herself questioning the premise of the investigation. Something was going on, but Collins didn't seem like someone who was willing to commit a federal crime to make a quick buck, no matter how big the payoff.

Collins tapped the iPhone on the table. "I called Sanchez and gave him an update when I was outside. I have to meet with him after lunch and work on the memorandum of understanding with Cohen based upon the assumption that we'll be able to get the deal done. I'd like you to go back to the office. I'll send you the draft as soon as it's done. It's going to be a rush job, so do what you can to clean it up ASAP. Feel free to drag Donna in as well. We need that finalized in record time. But most of all, I need Cohen and the creditor's committee to say yes to the deal. Let's pray for luck."

"One prayer coming up," Anna said in mock solemnity. "But it will cost you extra." She glanced over at the Latino man. He was walking out of the restaurant. There was an amused look on his face.

Collins glanced over at her, and their eyes met for a moment. "Thanks, Anna."

She was surprised at the feeling in his voice.

When they were waiting for the bill, Anna reluctantly asked, "Is there anything I can do to help you on the Perez deal?" She knew Carlton would grill her about it later that day.

The muscles running along Collins's right jawline tightened visibly. "That's a complicated transaction. I . . . I have to do most of the drafting myself on that one. I wish that wasn't the case, because it has to close soon. Perez is driving me nuts. There's a second leg to this deal that's . . . as I say, complicated."

"What's the second leg? Maybe I can help with that," Anna replied, trying to infuse her voice with an innocence she didn't feel.

Collins's shook his head when he answered. "I . . . I can't talk about it. I know you'd never tell anyone, but, it's just one of those matters where any disclosure would . . . would have severe consequences. Perez is not a man to cross."

His words were tinged with a hint of apprehension and regret. It was if he was warning himself to step warily.

Los Angeles, California

Bernie Edelman slowly climbed down the concrete stairs from the fifth floor of the parking garage adjacent to the hotel on Santa Monica Boulevard. He could have had valet park his rental car, but he made a point of walking whenever he could, and he knew the exercise would calm his nerves. The other members of the committee had pressed him hard for a yes vote on the deal offered by the hedge fund, and he knew it was a fair deal, given PriceStar's condition. He just couldn't get over his rage at the hard sell made by that son-of-a-bitch Dennison. He'd let the bastards on the other side stew for a while. No one was going to get the best of Bernie Edelman.

He heard someone coming down the stairs behind him. He slowed down and glanced in that direction. A Latino man was walking down the flight of stairs above carrying something in his right hand. The man was wearing Cartier sunglasses, and he was very well dressed. As he drew closer, Bernie decided to compliment the man on his exceptional taste in clothes—and then everything went black.

Intercontinental Hotel, Los Angeles, California

Sanchez opened the door to the hotel room on the first knock, as though he'd been waiting a step away. Collins walked past him to the conference table where Gregorio was sitting. His eyes were fixed on Collins. Sanchez was on Collins's heels.

Collins glanced down at his watch as he spoke. "Cohen should call by two, but it could be later. We just have to wait. If we call him, he'll take it as a sign of weakness and try to extract another round of concessions. While we're waiting, I need to crank out the memorandum of understanding with the deal points and the individual task assignments. We're going to have to run a hundred miles an hour once we get the word."

"Do you believe they will do the deal?" Sanchez's voice was both fearful and anxious.

"They'll do it," Collins answered curtly as he walked around to the other side of the table and set up his laptop.

Thirty minutes later, Collins emailed the document to Anna. She sent him an email seconds later: "I'm on it."

He nodded and pulled up the task assignment list and started adding additional tasks and questions to be resolved. The chime of Gregorio's cell phone interrupted his concentration. Gregorio looked at the screen of the phone and nodded to Sanchez. Both men rose quickly, walked into the bedroom across the way, and closed the door. They returned ten minutes later. Although Gregorio hid his emotions well, Collins sensed his unease, and Sanchez looked as if he was going to be sick. Neither man offered an explanation.

Cohen didn't call until four thirty. By that point, the tension in the room was stifling. Collins answered the call on the third ring. "Hi, David, where are we?"

He listened silently for several moments. Then his eyes widened, and he said abruptly. "He fell! Is he—"

Several minutes later he nodded, his face grim. "I understand. Okay. Does 9:00 a.m. tomorrow at your place work? Good."

The room was deathly silent when the call ended, until Sanchez gasped in a frantic whisper, "Did they reject the deal?"

Collins looked over at Sanchez, his face grim. "No. The deal is a go. The one holdout on the committee is no longer . . . a problem."

Collins turned to Gregorio and stared at him for a moment in silence. Gregorio's eyes remained fixed on the table in front of him. When Collins spoke, it was devoid of emotion.

"I just sent you the assignment sheet and deal timeline. Get your people ready to go. Sale preparations begin next week. Fourth Street's . . . contractors will have to be in place by Saturday. We can meet tomorrow morning, early, to go over the mechanics."

Sanchez nodded. "I will come to your office at seven. Gregorio can dial in."

Collins shook his head. "No, I'll come here. I have to meet Cohen at nine."

He turned and started packing up his laptop, not waiting for a response. As Collins walked through the lobby of the hotel, he glanced across the room at the bar. A well-dressed man wearing a distinctive pair of Cartier sunglasses was sitting there. Collins stiffened but kept on walking. It was Nacio Leon. Collins could only see a part of his profile. There was a smile on his face.

TWENTY-FIVE

Library Tower, Los Angeles, California

Collins called Anna on the way to the office. "Thanks for turning around the deal document so fast. It looks good."

"Thanks. Are you sure you don't need my help tonight?"

"No, I'm good. I'll call you in the morning about ten. Get some rest. This is going to get crazy."

"Crazy works for me," Anna said, a hint of amusement in her voice.

"Good night, Anna." *You have no idea, Anna. You have no idea.*

The middle-aged parking attendant in the guardhouse at the front of the underground parking structure waved to Collins as he started down the ramp and jogged over to the car. He remembered the man's name as he opened the window. "Mr. Collins, sorry to hold you up, but I have a message."

"No problem, Ari. What's up?"

"A woman stopped by an hour ago. Grayson, that was her name. She asked you to meet her at the Starbucks up the street. She was pretty, Mr. Collins. You should go. You work too much."

For a moment, Collins couldn't connect the name to a face, then it came to him—Grayson Manning. She was Sienna's best friend. He'd met her several times at the dinner parties Matt held at his house in Pasadena.

"Thanks, Ari. Thanks a lot."

Collins parked the car and walked back up the ramp to the car exit, ignoring the sign on the wall that said no pedestrians. He didn't want to take the elevator to the lobby and walk out the front door. One of Nacio's men would have someone there ready to follow him.

The Starbucks was a half block down the street. He spotted Grayson as soon as he walked through the door. She was a tall, athletic redhead. She'd been a top water polo player at USC. As he approached the table where she was sitting in the back, he remembered her easy smile and ready laugh from the last time they'd met. She seemed to have lost both of these attributes. Her face was grim, scared.

She stood up quickly and spoke in an urgent whisper. "Declan. Thank God you're here. We have to talk. It's about Sienna."

Declan's heart began to pound as soon as she spoke the name, but he forced himself to smile and gestured for her to sit. "It's great to see you—"

"Declan, this is serious," Grayson said in an urgent whisper. "I was going to call the police, but Sienna told me to come to you. If she's just jerking me around, I swear—"

As Declan quickly sat down, he glanced around. No one had followed him into the coffee shop, and the nearest person was three tables away.

"Wait, wait! You received a text from Sienna? When?"

Grayson's brown eyes widened at the intensity in Declan's voice, as if it confirmed her worst fears. "What is going on? Is Sienna in—"

"Grayson, listen to me!" he whispered. "You and I have to keep up a front in this conversation. Assume we're being watched. I'm going to take your hand for a moment, and you are going to give me a smile."

Grayson hesitated, but she forced a smile when Collins reached across the table and gave her hand a quick squeeze.

"You cannot tell anyone what I'm going to tell you. If you do, Sienna could die. It's just that simple. Okay?"

"Okay," Grayson answered in a whisper, her voice cracking.

"Here's . . . here's where we are. Sienna's been kidnapped by a group in Mexico. It . . . it happens more frequently than people think. We're negotiating with the kidnappers. Everything is moving forward, but we have to keep this buttoned down tight until we have her back."

"Is the FBI or the police handling it? Do you need money? My dad can help. He's—"

"We're good on the money, but thanks, Grayson," Collins said politely. "And yes, the police and FBI are involved, but in the background. I hired a special outfit to do the negotiations. They deal with kidnapping situations down there all the time. They will get this done. Sienna will get home safe. Now, tell me about this text."

Grayson stared at Collins for a moment in shock and then grabbed for her phone. "I'll forward it to you. What's your cell number?"

"Grayson, wait. I can't do that. There's a risk. The kidnappers sometimes hack the principals' phones when this happens . . . to gain an advantage. They . . . they're very sophisticated. Please, just tell me what it says."

Grayson reached into her coat pocket, pulled out a sheet of paper, and handed it to Collins. "I wrote it down exactly, just in case the text was deleted."

Collins read the message four times, memorizing its contents and then slid the paper back across the table. His mind was racing in ten different directions, weighing options, variables, and consequences. This was the break they needed.

He leaned forward and spoke in an even more subdued tone. "Grayson, can you do me a favor?"

"Yes, yes. I'll do anything to help Sienna."

"Take your phone to Tony Lentino. He runs The Arrezzo. It's a club about—"

"I know where it is."

"Good. Tell Tony I need him to find the cell tower where that text originated from. Tell him Ivan can find that out. Tell him I need to know yesterday. They'll only need your phone for a minute or two, and then you're done."

"Declan, isn't this something that the police or FBI should do?"

Declan sensed the doubt—suspicion—in her voice. "A big part of what I do is criminal law. There are ten thousand members of the Mexican mafia in LA County alone, and these people almost certainly have links to the kidnappers in Mexico City. The members of that community have ears in a lot of places, including law enforcement. That's why . . . that's why I brought in an outside outfit. Believe me, these guys are specialists. They have the inside track. You have to trust me. Matt and I are going to get Sienna back, alive."

"Sienna . . . she said you were the smartest guy she'd ever met. So . . . I'm going to trust you, but you have to promise me you're going to get her back, Declan."

The desperate intensity in Grayson's whisper was like a sharp lash across Collins's back.

"I will get it done."

Grayson nodded and stood up, as if she had just left a team huddle and was now ready for the next round of play.

"Oh, Grayson, if anyone asks you about this meeting, tell them you were asking my advice. Say a friend had a DUI, and you wanted to know what she should do."

"Uh . . . okay."

"Remember, take the phone to Tony Lentino. Take it tonight, and tell him to have Ivan find the cell tower where the text originated."

Grayson nodded and stood up. "I'm on my way there now." She turned and left.

Collins ordered a venti black coffee to go. It was a going to be a long night.

Irvine, California

Gabe Mattson parked his black Ford Explorer in one of the hundreds of empty spaces in the middle of the parking lot and walked to the two-story building forty yards away. There were thirty other similar buildings in the complex, but it was eight o'clock on a Sunday night. Only a few buildings had lights on within.

The small sign on the front door of the building read "Failsafe Exports, Inc." Failsafe was a Nevada corporation in the business of providing elite soldiers to customers throughout the world. Failsafe's human assets trained nascent armies, provided security in high-risk venues, and, on occasion, executed off-the-books military operations for governments seeking plausible deniability after the operation hit the news.

The door opened when Mattson was five yards away, revealing a tall man dressed in khaki hiking pants, trail running shoes, and a nylon T-shirt. The man's face was shrouded in darkness, but Mattson recognized the outline of the tattoo on his formidable right forearm. Devlin Campbell was ex-SASR, the Australian version of the British SAS.

"You're late, Mattson. That means you're buyin' the first round tonight when we're done here."

Mattson smiled and shook the man's outstretched hand. "There was a wreck on the 405 just past San Clemente."

"There's always a wreck on the 405. You Americans don't know how to bloody drive. Come on. The colonel's in the back."

Mattson smiled. He'd worked with Campbell on two assignments in Afghanistan and one in Indonesia. He followed the Australian down a long dimly lit corridor to a room with no windows at the back of the building. The old wooden conference room table in the middle was surrounded by six chairs. A seventy-five-inch television screen dominated the wall at the far end of the table.

A man with a full head of gray-white hair was sitting in a chair next to the big screen. He was staring intently at an iPad, listening to a man with a thick Scottish brogue explain the finer points of successfully putting on rain-soaked golf greens. When Mattson entered the room, the man turned off the program, walked over, and shook his hand.

Colonel George Bissom, US Army, was five-ten and rapier thin. He walked with a barely noticeable limp, a souvenir from the first Gulf War. He'd spent forty years working on the intel side of special operations missions, and he enjoyed his work, almost as much as he enjoyed playing golf.

Mattson shook the colonel's hand and gestured to the iPad. "Plan on playing in the rain, Colonel?"

The colonel smiled. "St. Andrews next week. Gotta get ready for it. Speaking of getting ready, let's get to it. I have a late dinner in an hour."

Mattson nodded. "Works for me, but I have to tell y'all, Langley hasn't given me a lot of input on what this little meetup is about."

Campbell put a hand on his shoulder. "Take a load off, old son, we'll get you there."

Mattson sat down in the nearest chair, and the colonel began to pace in front of the television screen.

"Here's the nub of it, Mattson. We have what I would call a convergence. The Pentagon does not have much interest in your run-of-the-mill Mexican drug cartel. However, one of these gangs, the Nauyacas, has made common cause with a group we do have an interest in—Al Qaeda. It seems they recently formed an informal relationship. Al Qaeda wants entry into the US of A, and the Nauyacas have agreed to guide them across the border for a hefty price and a little help with irregular warfare tactics. Some of Al Qaeda's battle-hardened fighters will be flying into Mexico City next week to help the Nauyacas gain supremacy over another cartel."

Campbell chimed in, "Read that as annihilate."

Mattson gave a low whistle. "That sort of ups the ante."

"Indeed it does," the colonel said as he executed another circuit.

"And here's the convergence I mentioned. The attack that nearly wiped out the Mexican contingent of your strike force last month was planned by an Al Qaeda operative with the code name Abdul Haq."

"And you know this how?" Mattson said, raising an eyebrow.

"Let's just say we grabbed a loose communication feed and traced it back to the Nauyacas HQ. And by the way, Abdul appears to have convinced the Nauyacas to undertake a second mission—in San Diego. An even bloodier mission."

The colonel hesitated a moment and took a sip from a cup of coffee Mattson suspected had grown cold before he showed up.

"Now, as to why you're here. The powers that be have decided to make an example of the Nauyacas. They want to dissuade the other cartels from traveling this same path. So, we're prepping an op to hit these folks and hit them hard. You, Mr. Mattson, will be the lead on that op."

Mattson leaned back in his chair. "There's going to be a lot of blowback from the Mexican government if we undertake that kind of op on their side of the border."

The colonel nodded. "Very true, but this operation will, superficially at least, look like an inter-gang gunfight, which happens all the time down there."

Mattson raised his hands in a concessionary gesture. "If you say so."

The colonel smiled. "Have faith, Mattson. This isn't my first rodeo." Then he tapped the power button on the television screen behind him. "Now, let's take a look at our prospective field of battle."

The satellite image on the screen showed a motley cluster of buildings surrounded by a ten-foot wall in the middle of a broad plain. A range of low hills ran east to west just to the north of the compound.

"This here," the colonel said, stepping over to the screen, "is where a cartel run by Ramon Cayetano packages up cocaine, weed, meth, you name it, before it's shipped to a network of warehouses in towns and cities along the border. From there, it's all coming into the US of A one way or another."

Mattson leaned back in his chair. "Are we hitting the Cayetano cartel as well?"

The colonel shook his head. "No, but that little rathole in the desert is about to get a visit from the Nauyacas and Abdul Haq. They intend to relieve the Cayetanos of their precious wares and wipe out everyone unlucky enough to be inside those walls when they show up. It will be a very bloody affair, I suspect."

Mattson's eye's widened. "When's this supposed to go down?"

"The intel's not clear, but it will happen within the next sixty days."

Mattson leaned back in his chair. "I gather you intend to take advantage of this rendezvous?"

The colonel nodded as he slowly clicked through a series of images of the site. "We do, that we do."

Most of the images showed guards dispersed throughout the camp and workers being escorted from one part of the compound to another, but one image showed a woman walking alone followed by a single guard.

"What am I looking at?" Mattson said, his eyes focusing on the female figure.

The colonel pressed a button on the remote and the size of the image increased dramatically. Although the image was blurred, Mattson could clearly see the woman was young, had blonde hair, and was wearing a T-shirt with an indiscernible logo.

The colonel turned to Mattson. "Not sure. She could be one of the big bosses' women, or . . . a hostage of some kind. One thing is for sure, if she's there when the Nauyacas show up, God help her."

Santa Monica, California

The sun was just rising over the mountains to the east as Collins sprinted to the top of the hill two blocks from his condominium. He slowed his pace to a walk at the top, gasping for breath. After three more steps, he stopped, waiting for his heart rate to slow. It took several minutes, which was surprising. He typically cruised through a five- to seven-mile run three times a week, after spending thirty minutes working out with the weights in the extra room.

At the end of each run, he made a point of charging up this hill with everything he had. On most mornings he wished the hill was higher and longer. Today, he almost didn't make it to the top. He knew what the problem was—stress and lack of sleep were wearing him down. He also knew it would get worse before it got better, if it ever did.

He glanced at his watch and forced himself to walk the rest

of the way up the street. He had a call scheduled with Matt and Nigel in about an hour to discuss the B of A debt acquisition. Gregorio and Sanchez would be on the call as well. If everything went according to plan, after the call, Gregorio would call Ramon Cayetano and obtain authorization to release the balance of the purchase price to B of A.

Although Collins didn't expect any problems, he knew from experience that acquisitions often failed the day before the closing or on the day of the closing. The price of backing out in most cases was the loss of a deposit. In this case, the price would be a lot steeper. Sienna would be killed, and he and Matt would almost certainly follow her into the grave in short order.

After taking a shower, he dressed in a dark gray suit. He'd been up half the night generating the proposed work assignments for the bankruptcy case and drafting the agency agreement allowing Gregorio's people to run PriceStar's going-out-of-business sale. The game plan had a lot of moving parts and uncontrollable variables. The two biggest variables were the bankruptcy case and the sale. Cohen had to get the bankruptcy plan drafted and approved in an extremely expedited time frame, and Gregorio's people had to secretly comingle one hundred million dollars of drug money with the incoming sale proceeds. They also had to book these bogus collections as legit sales on PriceStar's computer system. Despite his assurances to Gregorio and Sanchez, a lot of things could go wrong.

As he stared at the visibly tired face in the mirror and straightened his tie, Collins spoke in a voice tainted with anger and regret. "The next time you come up with a killer money laundering scheme, keep it to yourself, jerkweed."

The ping of the event alarm on his phone drew his attention to the kitchen counter. He walked over to the phone and typed in the conference call number and password. It was still five minutes before seven, but he wanted to make sure he was the first person to dial in. He had to take control of the call as soon as everyone dialed in and make it as short as possible. Four minutes later, Matt and Nigel signed on.

Collins spoke calmly but quickly. "Gentlemen, the two represen-
tatives from Fourth Street, Gregorio Pena and Alex Sanchez, will
soon be on the phone. For a number of reasons, I need to manage
the call, so follow my lead on this."

Before they could answer, a ping signaled a new participant had
joined the call.

"Good morning, this is Gregorio Pena and Alex Sanchez."

"Gregorio and Alex, this is Declan. Matt and Nigel are on the
phone as well. I have to be in Century City in an hour. So I'm going
to skip the pleasantries and ask Nigel to give us an update on where
we are."

Nigel cleared his throat. "Yes, very well, let's get on with it. I
just received a call from Kedrick & Baines, Fourth Street's solicitors
in Grand Cayman. They've tidied up Bank of America's assignment
documents, and we expect to close the loan acquisition this afternoon. We do, of course, need you to authorize the last bit of funding.
I assume we will receive that this morning."

The combination of Nigel's upper-class British accent and the
absolute confidence in his voice seemed to take the edge off the pointed
inquiry, but Gregorio received the message loud and clear.

"You will receive authorization within the hour, Nigel," Gregorio
said smoothly.

"This is Alex Sanchez. Is Fourth Street in full compliance with
the Cayman Island legal authorities, and is it also authorized to do
business in the United States?"

"Yes," Nigel answered. "Matt and I have all that in hand. We
have our certifications from the Registrar of Companies in Cayman,
and Matt and Declan sorted things out with the Securities and
Exchange Commission—isn't that right, Matt?"

"Yes, New York counsel filed an 8-K last week updating the
records. We're good to go."

Collins silently exhaled after Matt finished. This was the first
time Matt had been on the phone with Gregorio since Sienna's
kidnapping and his own near-execution in Cayetano's villa in
Mexico. Having known Matt for thirty years, Collins could sense

the underlying antagonism in his subdued voice, but he suspected Nigel could not.

"Matt, once the closing happens," Collins said, "email me a PDF of the final assignment documents and send a certified copy by FedEx. I'll need them for the bankruptcy lawyers in the PriceStar case."

"I'll get it done, Declan."

"Great, Matt. When are you coming back to LA? I'll need your help with going forward with the deal logistics. There's a lot of moving parts."

Collins didn't need Matt's help on the deal, but he wanted him in LA. The two of them needed to come up with a rescue plan once they pinned down Sienna's location using the text message.

"I can be there the day after tomorrow. Nigel and I have to work with the Kedrick firm tomorrow on post-closing matters. After that, I'm clear."

Gregorio cleared his throat. "Are you sure it would not be preferable for Mr. Esposito to return to the Caymans from New York? The regulators there—"

"Oh, don't worry about that lot," Nigel interrupted with blithe confidence. "I've dealt with them for two decades. If anything pops up, I can settle the matter. After a drink or two, the clerks generally come around. You gents go on ahead and put your house in order in the City of Angels."

There was a long silence. Rather than let it drag on, Collins took the issue out of Gregorio's hands. "Very well, then. I think we should adjourn for now."

"That would be quite satisfactory. Cheerio, gentlemen." Nigel responded so quickly that Collins suspected he was late for his morning cocktail.

He breathed a sigh of relief after the call ended. Gregorio might not like how it had turned out, but it was done.

He glanced at his watch. He had thirty minutes to get to Cohen's office.

Los Angeles, California

Gregorio and Sanchez were waiting for him in the lobby of Pace Cohen's office building when he arrived. The two men had called him on his way to Century City and insisted upon meeting him before he spoke with David Cohen. He guided them to a quiet corner before asking tersely, "Are the attorney fee estimates I sent you acceptable? You didn't get back to me on the issue last night."

"Señor Collins," Sanchez started hesitantly, "our . . . principal thinks they are high, but he will agree to them if . . . if you can assure him that the plan of reorganization vesting ownership of PriceStar in Fourth Street will be approved by the court within forty-five days."

Collins shook his head. "That's impossible. The rules require sixty days, and that's a bare minimum. My guess is one hundred days is a doable time frame."

A look of fear crossed Sanchez's face. "Ay, Dios! It has to be faster!"

Gregorio stepped forward. Although his face was impassive, Collins could sense his unease. "It can be done on a more expedited basis. The rules allow you to shorten time for good cause."

Collins shook his head. "It can be shortened, but the judges don't like to expedite plan confirmation proceedings. It—"

"Has to be done," Gregorio said adamantly, his voice laced with an undercurrent of tension and fear. "We must get it done, or . . . or we will *all* suffer. Do you understand?"

The threat almost unleashed the simmering rage Collins harbored toward Gregorio, but he realized something had changed. Gregorio and Sanchez were visibly afraid. Sanchez's left hand was twitching so uncontrollably that the small man shoved it into his pocket. Gregorio's fear was less visible, but it was there. Ramon Cayetano must have moved up the timetable and made it clear the penalty for failure would be painful, if not fatal.

Collins slowly exhaled. "That kind of deal velocity will require Cohen's firm and committee counsel to throw major resources at this case. They may do it, if the price is right. Those fee estimates I gave you just went up. I suspect it will take an extra five hundred thousand dollars or more in professional fees to get a plan confirmation order entered within forty-five days, and we will need to throw an additional bone to the creditors' committee."

Sanchez crossed himself and again muttered, "Ay, Dios."

Gregorio nodded, his face grim. "If that's what it takes, do it."

Collins nodded and turned toward the elevators. He called over his shoulder, "Stay off the phone. I will need to get you to okay the final details as soon as I call."

After two hours of grinding negotiations with Cohen, the three-way deal between Fourth Street, PriceStar, and the creditor's committee was finalized. The price had been an extra million all-in.

At the end of the meeting, Cohen promised Collins he would have a plan and disclosure statement on his desk, along with financial projections from PriceStar's financial advisers, within four days. The Chapter 11 plan would be filed a day later. As for the going-out-of-business sale, it would be initiated within a week, assuming the judge was cooperative. The money laundering operation was about to begin.

TWENTY-SIX

Los Angeles, California

t 11:45 p.m. Collins stepped out the back door of his town-house, walked south to Palisades Avenue, and then two blocks east to Ocean Avenue. The limo was waiting for him on the corner. The driver didn't say a word during the thirty-minute drive downtown.

The car pulled off the Santa Monica Freeway onto South Alameda, drove north for half a mile, and pulled into a gated parking lot behind an old warehouse. The lot was encircled by a twelve-foot-high fence topped with scrolls of barbed wire. The limo stopped in the shadow of a concrete loading ramp.

A square, muscular man opened the rear door wearing a black T-shirt and jeans. His face was hidden by a large pair of sunglasses, which looked incongruous in the darkness, and his bulging forearms were covered with tattoos. He pointed toward a stairway leading to the loading dock.

"This way," he commanded. There was a threat in his guttural voice.

Collins scanned the surrounding area as he walked toward the building. He recognized the location. It was about a mile from the federal court on Temple Street. The street was lined with ware-houses. A line of homemade tents put up by the homeless ran the length of the road. If they intended to kill him, this was as good a place as any.

He followed the driver up a worn set of concrete stairs and

across the loading dock to a battered steel door. The driver pushed open the door and gestured for Collins to enter the darkened space within. Collins stepped through the door and waited on the other side as the man closed and locked the heavy door behind him. As soon as the door was closed, an overhead light came on revealing a cavernous concrete space half the size of a football field. The expanse was empty but for a few scattered wooden pallets and two overflowing trash bins.

The man with the tattoos gestured to a light visible from an open door on the other side of the building. "Over there."

The threat in his tone was still there, but it was suffused with contempt, as if Collins was somehow a coward for not resisting his directions.

Collins walked across the concrete expanse, listening for the sound of movement behind him. He heard nothing other than the sound of his own footfalls on the dusty floor. A figure appeared in the doorway when he was three strides away. He recognized the lean figure. Nacio Leon's face bore the same look of amusement he remembered from the meeting in Mexico, a look that didn't reach his cold, dark eyes.

Collins stopped a stride away from the man he was certain had killed the head of the creditors' committee less than a week ago and returned his stare. Nacio was wearing the same dark blue suit he'd worn in the restaurant last week and the same sunglasses, but he'd added one more distinctive accoutrement: the hand resting against his left thigh held a nine-millimeter. Collins owned two nine-millimeter handguns, and he'd been trained to use the weapons by an expert. He was fully cognizant of how much damage a single bullet from the gun in Nacio's hand could inflict upon the human body.

Nacio stepped closer and raised the gun in a slow arc in front of him. He stopped when the muzzle was the width of a playing card from the center of Collins's forehead.

"This is a Beretta 92FS. I'm told you own a Glock 17 and a Springfield XD. Both fine weapons, but this one . . . it has a better feel. One should be at ease . . . when experiencing the pleasure of taking the life of an enemy . . . or even, a friend."

A smile came to Nacio's face. Collins knew the Mexican killer was goading him. Collins stood motionless, waiting for the explosion from the Beretta. He knew he would be dead before his body dropped to the cold, dusty floor beneath his feet. The two of them stood there in silence for a long moment, and then Nacio waved him past, as if he was bored with the deadly game.

"Go. That way."

Collins looked past Nacio and saw Gregorio standing in front of a partially open door. Collins walked over to the door and followed Gregorio into a room he suspected had been cleaned and renovated just for this meeting. The walls were freshly painted and a plush oriental rug covered the concrete floor. The wooden table in the center of the room was old, but it was polished to perfection. When Collins looked closer at the walls, he realized they were metal. The room was a Faraday cage designed to block any electromagnetic signals from penetrating the space.

The only light came from the brass banker's lamp in the center of the table. Cayetano was sitting at the far end in semidarkness. Gregorio sat down next to Sanchez on the left side of the table. Collins could sense the undercurrent of fear emanating from the two financial mandarins.

Two men dressed in black, unmarked combat fatigues stepped out of the darkness behind Cayetano and walked toward Collins. They were armed with submachine guns equipped with suppressors. The black balaclavas covering their faces left only their eyes exposed. The man in the lead said curtly, "Arms up."

Collins raised his arms and remained stationary while one of the armed men patted him down and waved a portable metal detector over every part of his body. The wand made a sharp beep when it was waved over his right pocket. The man stepped back and pointed to the table.

"Empty it there. Use your left hand."

Collins reached into his pocket, pulled out a flash drive, and laid it on the table. The guard ran the wand over Collins's body a second time, and it was silent. The two men turned to Cayetano, who nodded, and they left the room with the flash drive. Nacio came in a moment later, closed the door, and walked to the space on Cayetano's right.

Collins slowly lowered his arms and faced the drug lord. There was a long silence as the old man lit a cigar, drew in a mouthful of smoke, and exhaled. Then his eyes rested upon Collins. "Tell me, Declan Collins, what are you doing with my money?"

———

As Anna looked at the unbroken line of cars on the freeway from her apartment window, she remembered staring out another window decades earlier. Her family had lived in an old apartment building off Queen's Boulevard when she was six years old. Each morning she would watch the subway trains stop at the elevated platform visible from her bedroom window before they continued on to Manhattan. As she watched the riders' faces, she'd been struck by how much they were alike in one respect: no one ever smiled. Not even her father, an accountant, who boarded that same train every morning.

Years later, when she was working with a special operations unit in a place that was hot, dirty, and very dangerous, one of the ex-Seals had asked her, "Why'd you sign up for this crap? Hell, you could be in an air-conditioned office in Manhattan sipping chai tea right now." Anna remembered her response with amusement. "Because I wanted to smile when I went to work." The answer had drawn a collective laugh from the other members of the unit. The reality was more complicated than that. But it was close enough.

She turned around and looked over at the iPhone resting on the coffee table several feet away. Carlton's supercilious lecture was coming through the speaker loud and clear.

"There's a lot of eyes on this case, folks. So, if you don't get the ball across the finish line, there will be repercussions. You need to think about that long and hard."

Teo tried to break in. "The investigation is—"

"Bogged down," Carlton interrupted. "So you, Agent Torres, need to be more proactive. Press Collins about the private placement deal and this character Perez. We need to drill down on that."

Anna suppressed her anger when she responded. "I will do what I can, but if I push too hard—"

"Then don't, Agent Torres," Carlton said with the hint of a threat in his voice. "Push just hard enough. Now, that's all the time I have. Get on it."

A moment later, a recorded voice said politely, "The host has ended the conference. Thank you."

Anna punched the off button on the cell phone, sat down on the couch, and leaned back into the cushion behind her head. Her momentary respite was cut short by the vibrating cell phone. She reluctantly put her wine glass back on the table and picked up the phone. It was Teo.

"What a bunch of crap!" he said. "This guy doesn't know the first thing about undercover work."

"He may not, Teo, but he's the boss, or at least he thinks he is."

"I'm not going to let you get in a bad spot just because this clown wants his day of glory to come a week or two sooner."

Anna shook her head dismissively. "I'm not worried about Collins. He may be involved in criminal activity, but I don't think he's dangerous. I'm just worried he'll figure out I have my own agenda if I press him. He doesn't miss much."

"Do what you think is best. The agent on the ground almost always has the best insight. And don't . . . don't assume Collins won't go rogue once he realizes his next suit is going to be orange and he's going to have to wear it for a long while."

Teo's comment bothered Anna, and for a moment she was tempted to defend the lawyer. She stifled the temptation, knowing it would trigger warning bells with Teo. "Understood."

"Anna, is everything okay?"

Despite her answer, Anna could sense the deeper inquiry in Teo's question. "Yes. It's all good."

"Roger that. Get a good night's sleep."

"That I will."

Anna pulled on her running clothes and took the elevator down to the exercise room. It was empty. She walked over to the treadmill and chose the intermediate hill program. As she pounded out three miles, the memory of the scene in the restaurant returned over and over again. What struck her as odd was the look on Collins's face as he walked by the fashionable Latino couple. Collins knew them, and they knew him, but they didn't acknowledge each other, and for some reason, seeing the couple in the restaurant had unnerved Collins.

As she cruised through the last leg of the run, the answer hit her like a sharp poke in the solar plexus. Collins didn't just know the couple—*he knew their presence in the restaurant wasn't an accident.* He didn't confront them because they were watching him, and there was nothing he could do about it. But if they were surveilling Collins, why didn't they try to keep their presence a secret from him?

As the treadmill slowed to a stop, the disparate tumblers spinning in Anna's head fell into place. The couple had been sending Collins a message: We're watching you, and we want you to know it. That meant the man and woman at that table, not Collins, held the power in whatever relationship was in play. Anna reached for her cell phone. She had to tell Teo. He needed to know who else was involved in this game.

———

Collins was awakened by the sound of his cell phone vibrating on the night table beside his bed.

"Collins."

"It's nine o'clock. I thought you worked for living." It was David Cohen.

Collins glanced at the time on the phone. They'd kept him in the warehouse asking questions until three in the morning. Cayetano kept asking the same questions over and over, as if he expected a different answer.

"It was a late night," Collins said hoarsely.

Cohen chortled. "I just might have an idea who kept—"

"You don't," Collins said curtly. "What's up?"

"The plan and disclosure statement are done. We incorporated the tax treatment sections you sent over. Also, the committee approved the docs as well so we're good to go, assuming you don't screw around with them. To get this thing done on your time frame, I'll have to ask the court to preliminarily approve the disclosure statement at a hearing on shortened notice, say on Thursday, and then get it finally approved at the plan confirmation hearing."

"There's a risk—"

"I know the risk, Collins. The judge could decide the disclosure statement doesn't include adequate information at the confirmation hearing. Yeah, that would push the whole timeline out sixty days while we re-solicit votes on the plan with an updated version of the doc. I get it. It won't happen. This judge runs a rocket docket. He'll love the plan concept, and the docs are bulletproof."

Collins hesitated a moment before agreeing. He had no choice, given the expedited schedule Cayetano was demanding.

"Done. I'll get you my comments."

"Good. Also, the motion seeking approval of the going-out-of-business sale will be heard at the same expedited hearing. I sent that over too. As I recall, you wanted your team to take over the accounting and IT departments during the sales process. That's all in the motion. I don't think we'll get any pushback from the judge. Your client pays us and the unsecured creditors what we agreed upon whether or not the sale gets cocked up, so why should he care? By the way, PriceStar's CFO is available to meet with your finance guy this afternoon on the accounting switch-over. I'll text you his number."

"Got it."

"Get those documents back to me, Collins. This train's leaving the station."

"You'll get them."

Collins pulled up his emails on his phone and forwarded the plan and disclosure statement draft to Gregorio and Sanchez with the admonition, "I need your comments before noon. PriceStar's CFO will meet with Sanchez and your IT people this afternoon. Here's his number. Can you make those deadlines?"

Seconds later Sanchez replied, "Yes."

Collins put the phone down and walked over to the porthole window on the far side of the room. It was the only one that offered a partial view of the beach through the space between the two buildings on the far side of the street. The idyllic scene in the distance offered him no comfort. He had less than thirty days to find and rescue Sienna. Once PriceStar's reorganization plan was confirmed, she was dead. They all were.

The cell phone rang again. For a moment Collins considered ignoring it, walking out the door, and running somewhere—anywhere but here. He walked across the room and picked up the phone.

"Collins."

"Declan, it's Tony Lentino."

For a moment, Collins was confused and then terrified. If Tony had forgotten his phone was bugged the game was over.

"Tony—"

"Relax, the Feds aren't chasing me. I'm paying my taxes. In fact, I'm paying way too much in taxes! But I still gotta talk to you, right away. The accountant says I got a big cancellation of debt income problem, whatever the hell that is. He's says you may be able to solve it. I got the draft tax return and his notes. I know it's not much notice, but I gotta get this off my back. Can you meet at Seville for coffee this morning? I'm buying."

Collins hesitated and then feigned reluctance. "Okay. But I don't have a lot of time. I'll be there in an hour."

"Done. Thanks, buddy; I owe ya."

An hour later, Collins walked into the small coffee shop a block off Santa Monica Boulevard. He spotted Tony sitting in a corner booth in the back. He walked over and slid into the worn vinyl bench seat. Tony pointed to the cup of coffee and the blueberry muffin close to the wall.

"Those are yours."

Then he leaned forward and spoke in a low voice. "Here's the skinny. We found her. At least we're 90 percent sure. This Maijoma, Mexico, place is about forty-five miles from the US border. It's due south of the Big Bend Ranch State Park in Texas. We know she's there, because the call came through a cell phone tower in Ojinaga, Mexico, about thirty miles across the border."

Collins exhaled slowly, trying to ease the tension gripping his chest. "Okay, now we just have to find the compound she described and get her out of there. That could be—"

Tony glanced around the restaurant, before looking over at Collins with a satisfied smile on his face. "Relax, paisan. I got this. I know a black ops guy. Met him back in New York at a club over twenty years ago. I helped him get started in the biz after he left the Marines. I trust him like a brother. He's gonna organize a rescue. It ain't gonna be cheap, but he can get it done."

"Tony, this is serious—"

"Shiitake? Yeah, it sure is. But you have to trust me on this. I had a lot of other lives before I got into the entertainment biz. Spent four years in the Marines and five years after that as muscle for some folks in the business of making money the old-fashioned way—gambling, vice, and drugs. You wanna get someone away from people like this, you need a team of hard-asses, the kind of dudes who kill other people for a living. That's what this guy does, and he's a pro. He's been doin' this crap for over thirty years."

"Tony, we have to find her first. We can't—"

"Have a little faith. My guy contacted somebody, a former black ops buddy in the DEA. He asked him whether this Cayetano's drug outfit had any known facilities near the cell tower. Well, they do. It's a big drug-packaging plant. They put the crap into smaller containers so it can be smuggled across the border."

Tony glanced around again and tapped the envelope in front of him. "I got two satellite photos of the place in this tax return. Not bad, eh? Take a look."

Collins pulled the tax return out of the envelope and paged

through it slowly as if he were assessing its contents. The first photo was a high-altitude view. A square structure was just visible in the middle of a barren plain surrounded by low hills. A dirt road connected the structure to a larger secondary road several miles away.

The second photo was much closer. Four walls enclosed five or six buildings of various sizes. Cars and trucks and a few figures were visible. The last photo brought the viewer right down to ground level. The twelve- to fifteen-foot-high wall surrounding the compound was in a state of disrepair, but it was still an impediment to egress and ingress. The larger holes in the wall were filled with what appeared to be barbed wire. All of the figures walking around were men, and several of them were carrying rifles. The overall impression conveyed was that of a primitive, decaying prison. A prison that held Sienna, if she was still alive.

Collins slowly shook his head. "How are we going to get her out of there?"

Tony leaned forward and spoke in a gruff whisper. "This guy I told you about, Dante Romano, he and his team will get it done. He's a bad dude—an elite sniper with a lot of combat experience. The other guys on his team are topflight mercs. They can do this thing, but . . . like I say, it's gonna cost you."

Collins nodded. "We'll pay the fee, Tony. I just need to know how they're going to do this. This . . . this thing has to be planned, and I want to see that plan before it's a go."

Tony smiled. "They're already working on it. I gave Dante 20K to get started. All in, it's going to run you about 300K—half up front."

Tony tapped the account information handwritten on the bottom of the last photo.

"Here's the wire instructions. And . . . Declan, you gotta know how this works. These guys get paid whether she comes back dead or alive."

Collins stared at Lentino for a moment and then pulled a pen out of his pocket and wrote the account information on the napkin beside his plate.

"I'll get them the money. I have a rainy-day account with a

hedge fund in New York. It's held under the name of a limited liability company. The wire will go out this afternoon. We don't have
a lot of time, Tony. This thing has to happen in the next month at
the latest."

Tony's eyes widened. "Crap! Are you kidding me?"

"No. The bad guys accelerated the schedule. I'm pretty sure
they'll keep her alive as long as they need me to make the deal happen, but once it closes, in thirty days, Sienna's done."

"Okay, I'll talk to them. I'll do what I can."

Collins nodded and held out his hand. "Thanks, Tony. I have
to go."

Tony gripped his hand and leaned close. "Declan, you know
these bastards will nix you and Esposito as well when the deal is
done. You know that, right?"

Collins nodded. "Yeah, Tony, I know. Trust me, staying alive is
on my to-do list as well. It's one line below getting Sienna out of that
hellhole alive."

Tony released his hand. "Roger that."

As he walked out of the restaurant toward his car, his phone
rang.

"Collins."

"Declan, its Matt. The loan deal closed. Everything's a go on that
piece of this thing." The strain and fear in his voice was palpable.
"How are we doing on the next—"

"We're getting it done, Matt. We're getting it done."

Maijoma, Mexico

Sienna waited four days before risking another climb up the pipe to
the roof. Before starting down the side of the building, she carefully
scanned the area below. At first, she didn't see anyone and started to
crawl forward. A moment later, the flash of a cigarette lighter illuminated a guard, and she froze. Sienna recognized the man's brown
Stetson hat. He'd been with the man in the silk shirt when the guard

with the phone had been executed. Sienna suspected he was waiting to see if the dead guard had an accomplice.

When the light of his cigarette went out, the man's silhouette faded back into darkness. Sienna waited, unmoving, for what seemed like hours. As dawn approached, the man's left boot became visible, and several moments later his entire leg. He was sitting on a stool on the far side of the shed.

About a half an hour before sunrise, the man stood up, stretched, and scanned the area one last time before walking toward the center of the compound. Sienna hesitated, weighing the risks of climbing down the exterior pipe and trying to get a message out before the sun rose or waiting another night or two. She decided to wait. She needed to watch the guard's routine for several more nights to see if it remained the same. If it did, she would be forced to try to get to the phone as soon as he left, send a message, and then get back through the hole in the roof before the compound came alive at sunrise.

Two nights ago, she'd heard a woman screaming for mercy on the far side of the compound. Her screams had continued for almost an hour and then abruptly stopped. Sienna suspected the only mercy the woman had received was unconsciousness or death. She didn't intend to suffer that fate. She intended to get out of this hellish pit alive.

TWENTY-SEVEN

Los Angeles, California

ollins walked into the men's restroom at 10:00 a.m. Thankfully, all of the stalls were empty. He entered the stall where the phone was located, closed the door, sat down on the toilet, and opened the toilet paper dispenser. The phone was still taped to the lid. He pressed the "on" button and waited for what seemed an eternity for the screen to light up. After typing in the access code, he tapped the text icon. Lentino had sent a text less than an hour ago.

"Can you meet at the club at 11:00 tonight? The TGs want to go over logistics and timing."

"Send me an email demanding a meeting ASAP," Collins texted back. "Say you have to find a way to get the court case closed or you won't be able to get financing on a second club opportunity. Make it sound frantic. I'll haggle with you in the back and forth but will eventually agree."

A moment later the response came back. "Done."

Collins turned off the phone and put it back in the dispenser, closed it, and replaced the screw.

When he emerged from the bathroom and walked back to the office, Sanchez was in the lobby. For a moment, he assumed someone had discovered his secret communications and Sanchez was there to confront him, but he rejected the thought. If the phone had been discovered, the confrontation would have been with Nacio, and it would have taken place in a remote location.

Collins nodded to Sanchez and greeted him warmly for the bene-fit of the receptionist. "What a pleasant surprise! Come in."

As they walked back to his office, Sanchez nodded politely to Anna, whose office door was open. She smiled back. Collins closed his office door behind them.

Sanchez pointed to the phone. "Gregorio is calling. We need to talk."

Collins pressed the flashing light on this phone. He didn't wait for Gregorio to speak. "Gregorio, PriceStar's going-out-of-business sale begins tomorrow. I assume your people are in place."

"They are. Our IT people control and have exclusive access to PriceStar's point-of-sale system at the store level and the company's accounting system."

"And you will have assets in the stores when the cash pickups happen? Remember, we don't control all of the armored truck ser-vices who pick up the cash. So—"

"We have to get the extra bag of cash waiting for them when they arrive and change the receipt logs to show the additional pickups. Arrangements have been made," Gregorio said quietly.

"You have a man in all of the stores?"

"No, just in the busiest locations. We have another fifty who will be on the move. The store managers know they're coming, and they will make sure to move fifty additional bags of cash each day into the trucks. I've done the math. It all works."

"It had better. You can manipulate the data on the computers, but the cash pickup and cash deposit records will be in the hands of the armored car services and the depository bank. An extra hundred million has to—"

"It will, Mr. Collins." Sanchez stepped forward, wringing his hands. "It will."

Collins stared at Sanchez for a moment. *It had better*, he thought. *Sienna's life depends upon it.*

Sanchez lifted his right hand almost apologetically and spoke in respectful voice. "Mr. Collins, what about the plan of reorganiza-tion and the disclosure statement? Are they—"

"I spoke to Cohen this morning. The creditors' committee will approve the final version of the disclosure statement today, and they'll ask the judge to approve the doc on shortened time—midweek."

Sanchez's eyes widened. "Will he do that?"

Collins shook his head. "No guarantee, but he should. He understands the cash burn, so he gets the need for speed."

Gregorio interjected. "On the cash burn, Mr. Cayetano—"

"A million a week. I know!" Collins said, his voice harsh and louder than he intended. "And this thing is going to take another four weeks, so you're looking at four to five million at least. Then you'll have to front another million for windup costs. That's the price of admission. I can't do anything about it."

"I see."

Collins could sense the barely restrained fear in Gregorio's voice. He glanced over at Sanchez, and the smaller Mexican wouldn't meet his gaze, but he could see that the uncontrolled tremor in his right hand was back.

Collins raised a hand in a placative gesture. "Tell Mr. Cayetano we'll pick up some money from our piece of the litigation recoveries after the plan is confirmed. If he's lucky, the entire cost equation will be a wash. It could take a year or two for those recoveries to come in, but it will happen. I can send you an analysis backing that up if you need it."

Sanchez grabbed for the lifeline. "Gracias! Yes, that would be so much appreciated. Can you say when . . . when you—"

"This afternoon. It's an internal litigation doc prepared by the creditor's committee. It needs to stay confidential. Now, is there anything else?"

Sanchez nodded as he spoke. "Yes . . . no, I mean yes, we will keep it secret, and no we have no more quest—"

"Actually," Gregorio interrupted, "there is one more." After a long pause, he continued, "Mr. Cayetano wants to know exactly when Mr. Esposito is coming back to Los Angeles. He worries . . . you may not have enough help."

Collins walked to the window and stared out at the sun dancing on the windows of the building across the way. Cayetano wasn't worried about his manpower problem. He wanted to make sure his targets were lined up for the kill at the end of the month.

"He'll be flying in tomorrow at three."

———

Collins glanced in the mirror and noticed the dark black van five cars behind him on La Cienega. It was the same van he'd seen parked a block from his house on several occasions. He suspected that Nacio or some of his people were tailing him.

For a moment, he considered calling Lentino and telling him he couldn't make it, but he rejected the thought. The meet had to go forward. The going-out-of-business sale was going full bore, and the plan would be confirmed within three weeks. From Cayetano's perspective, his usefulness was coming to an end. The only question was when and where Nacio intended to kill him and Matt. He glanced in the mirror again. Although it could be tonight, he suspected the drug lord would wait until the plan was confirmed by the court. At that point, the sale would be almost over and his team would be fully in control of PriceStar. That gave him about three weeks, maybe four. After that, any day could be his last.

Collins put on his turn signal and drove past the limos lined up in front of Lentino's club to the gated service entrance in the back. The guard saw him waiting for a break in the traffic and pulled the heavy steel gate open. He shot through a small gap in the two lines of onrushing cars, drawing an angry horn from a Mercedes Benz. He glanced in the mirror and saw the black van drive by.

He parked and locked the car in the only space left and walked through the open back door. The hallway just inside the door that led to the stairs up to Tony's office was dark, which was unusual. He waited for his eyes to adjust. When they did, he realized he wasn't alone. A man was standing, motionless, just past the stairwell. One of his hands was behind his back. His beard and mustache were neatly trimmed, and a full head of hair ran almost to his shoulders.

The man was at least six-four, 220 pounds, and from what Collins could see, there wasn't an ounce of fat on him.

The man held his right index finger up to his lips, gesturing for silence, and drew a cell phone from his pocket and held it up. Collins handed over his cell phone. The man deposited it in a square box on a table against the wall. Then he pulled a square wand-like instrument from under his jacket and ran it over every inch of Collins's body. It gave a small squeak when it passed over the pen in his pocket. Collins handed it over. The man ran the wand over the pocket again, and it was silent. He put the pen in the same box as the phone, closed the lid, and gestured for Collins to follow him.

He walked to the pair of swinging doors that led to the small loading dock on the far side of the building and pushed them open. When they walked onto the dock, Collins stopped in confusion. It was pitch black. The man in front of him pulled something aside and said quietly, "Two big steps forward."

Collins obeyed the instruction, and the man followed him, pulling what Collins suspected was a black curtain back into place. The man stepped past him, bent down, and pulled a door upward, revealing the interior of what appeared to be a delivery truck. Tony Lentino and three men Collins didn't recognize were sitting at a table in the back of the truck, lit by a ghostly blue light.

Collins stepped inside, and the man behind him followed. Nobody said anything until the door behind him had been closed and locked tight.

Tony lifted the Peroni in front of him and waved Collins forward. "Come in, come in. I want you to meet one of my oldest friends, Dante Romano." The man sitting in the semi-darkness on the far side of the table stood up and extended his hand. Collins took in the man's thinning head of near-white hair, brown eyes, aquiline nose, and sun-bronzed skin. Two pencil-thin scars crisscrossed on his left cheek, one running from his ear to his chin and the second straight down past his eye to his jawline, giving his otherwise friendly face a hint of the man's violent past.

Dante shook Collins's hand and pointed to the man standing

behind Collins. "You met Dieter. This is Nick and Pat." Nick had olive skin, a bald head, deep-set brown eyes, and a broad, flat nose. The dark brown beard covering his strong jaw was tinged gray in spots, and a narrow scar line was visible on the left side of his face. Although he was about five inches shorter than Collins, his broad shoulders and bulging arms made him seem larger.

The other man, Pat, was a tall, lanky redhead with the physique of a high jumper. He smiled as Collins approached and spoke in a western drawl. "Pleasure, counselor."

Collins shook his hand and turned back to Romano. The look in his eyes was friendly but cautious. Collins could sense he was being carefully weighed by the ex-soldier. He hoped the other man came to the right conclusion. He needed these guys. They didn't need him.

Lentino came over and gave him a hug and then waved at the heavy steel walls surrounding the table. "How about this SCIF, eh? It's a lot more secure than that piece of crap in the attic we used during my criminal case. Not even the CIA can get a sound bounce outta this baby."

When Collins sat down, Dante walked to the head of the table and spoke in a calm voice tinged with an accent Collins recognized as unique to Providence, Rhode Island.

"Here's the two-minute sales pitch. Pat and Nick are green berets. They have about eight years of experience in the field. At least a year or two of that was in a combat theater doing actual fighting. Pat was in Afghanistan and Nick in Iraq. I go way back. I was a scout sniper with the Marines in the first Gulf War. After that I worked for the CIA as a contract employee in a whole bunch of places you'd never want to go.

"A decade ago, I started a small company that specializes in rescue operations—getting people out of bad spots. Most of the time, it's straightforward—snatch, grab, and go. No guns, no fight, no blood. That's the way we like it. That's how a well-planned and well-executed op is supposed to go down. When things get to what we call 'bang,' something's gone wrong."

Dante hesitated for a moment and put his hands down on the table and looked directly at Collins. "When we get to that place, people get hurt or die, no matter how good they are, and no matter how much firepower they have. Pat, Nick, Dieter, and the rest of the team do *not* want to be heroes. They want to be survivors. If the job's doable, we'll get it done, but the odds have to be stacked in our favor."

Collins nodded, his mouth suddenly dry as a bone. "You're telling me you can't get her out."

Dante shook his head. "No, I'm not saying that. We have SAT photos on the place where the girl is being held. There are over fifty men in that compound—men armed with automatic weapons—and we don't know where they're keeping her. Even if we infiltrated the place without being seen, we'd have to go through five or ten buildings trying to find her. All we need is one stray eyeball and we're in a firefight. If it goes down that way, we'd be lucky to get out alive ourselves."

Collins slowly shook his head, a growing weight pressing on his chest. "There's no way . . . no possible—"

Dante leaned over the table and interrupted him, speaking in a flat, hard voice. "Yes, there is a way, but . . . she has to get outside the compound."

Collins stared at the other man. "Outside? How? She's a prisoner!"

Dante pushed a grainy black-and-white photograph across the table. "Not always. They let her out to exercise at about noon every day. She also may have found a hole in their system."

Collins stared down at the two-foot-square photo. It showed the interior of the compound. A figure with long blonde hair was just visible on a dirt road that ran along the base of the wall. Another figure was walking about fifty yards behind Sienna wearing a baseball hat.

"Where . . . how did you—"

"Not your business, counselor," Dante said. "All I can say is the intel is recent and accurate."

There was a long silence, and then Pat stood up and pointed to an edge of the picture. "Do you see this . . . this corner where the two walls adjoin? They piled up what looks like a bunch of broken crates. If she can get on top of those, she may be able to climb the rest of the way to the top and get over. There may be better options. The wall is only ten to twelve feet high. If she can find one or two footholds, she can get to the top and pull herself over."

Collins looked at the dark wall and tapped the top of a section across from Sienna. "We can't get a rope over the wall? If I can tell her where and when, that would help her get over the top."

Dante pulled another large grainy photo out from underneath the first one. The shot was taken from a higher altitude and showed the north side of the compound and the surrounding countryside. Dante gestured to Nick. "Your turn."

Nick stood up and stared down at the photo for a long moment before tapping the blurry line of objects about fifty yards outside the wall.

"There are two or three boulders here. You can't see them too well, because of the trees and scrub brush that's grown up around them, but they are there. That's the best cover. The forty- to fifty-yard stretch between there and the compound is open—a killing ground."

Nick moved his finger to one of the wooden guard towers. "The guard tower here . . . it's just a shack built atop the wall, but if the guard is there, he will have eyes on this stretch of ground. We only want to risk crossing that space when Sienna is already there and ready to go. If we go to the wall early, just to throw a rope over, we double the risk of detection. That's a bad move."

Collins stared at the photo, then looked over at Dante and said with quiet intensity, "What you're telling me is . . . Sienna . . . you want Sienna to cross that killing ground and get to you."

Pat returned Collins's stare and said in a slow drawl, "Yes, but we'll have eyes on the guard. If he even looks in that direction, we'll take him out."

Collins shook his head. "Look—"

"Declan," Nick intervened, "we're okay going to the wall to get

Sienna if we have eyes on her. In a perfect world, we grab her and get back to cover without getting spotted. If we get spotted and it becomes a fight, we can maintain fire supremacy for two, maybe three minutes. After that it becomes a shit show. So . . . she has to come over that wall."

Collins understood the situation and the outline of the op, but he didn't like either. "How many men will you have?"

"There will be five of us. Four on the ground. The fifth is the helo pilot. He'll also be the communications anchor."

Collins tapped the satellite photo showing Sienna walking along the base of the wall. "I need you to walk me through this plan, step-by-step, as if I were not just one of the members of your team, but the most critical one. Sienna is not just my best friend's little sister; she's like my little sister. We were, and are, that close. I have to know that every detail is covered and every risk weighed."

Dante nodded and sat down in the chair across from him. "Then let's have at it."

When Collins left the room four hours later, he knew the hardware, the flight route, the call signals, the approach route, the evac route, and the risks—or least as many as the four of them could conjure up. Dante's plan was a good one. Simple, but well-planned. There was only one problem. They needed to contact Sienna so she could get over the wall at the designated date and time. That missing piece was totally on her.

———

Collins pulled up to the curb outside the Tom Bradley International Terminal, and Matt jogged over to the car. He put his carry-on bag in the back seat and climbed into the front seat. Collins glanced over at his friend before pulling back out into traffic. His face was drawn and pale, and he'd lost at least twenty pounds since they'd parted company in Mexico three weeks ago. His suit, which Collins knew had been tailored by the best, looked as though it was at least a size too big for him.

"Declan, what is—"

Collins raised a hand in caution, and Matt lapsed into silence. Collins drove out of the airport circle, down Century Boulevard, and pulled into the parking lot of the Hyatt Hotel.

He looked over at Matt. "Let's get a cup of coffee."

Matt followed him into the café located in the rear of the lobby, and they both sat down. Collins scanned the surrounding area for several moments before looking over at Matt.

"Assume both of us are bugged at all times unless I say otherwise."

Matt's eyes widened. He glanced around furtively and said in a whisper, "Here?"

Collins shook his head. "I don't think so, but I can't be sure."

He glanced around a second time and spoke in a quiet monotone. "The deal is on track in the bankruptcy court. It's moving faster than I thought. The plan could be confirmed in two, maybe three weeks. PriceStar's going-out-of-business sale starts tomorrow, and it will run for a month. Our part of that equation will take about three weeks."

"And Sienna?"

Collins nodded. "I'm working on that. I'll update you when it's safe."

They waited in silence as the waitress approached.

"An ice water and a coffee," Collins said.

"The same," Matt said.

As soon as the middle-aged woman was out of earshot, Matt leaned forward and spoke in a hoarse whisper. "I need to know what's going on. This shit is killing me!"

Collins stared at Matt for a moment and then an idea hit him. "Let's meet at the gym tonight, around seven. We can hit the steam room. It's safe to talk there."

———

When Anna walked into the reception area at 8:30 a.m., she could see Collins and two other men through the glass wall of the conference room. One of them was Sanchez. The other man looked like Matt Esposito. She remembered his picture from the file. As she walked to her office, Anna surreptitiously pointed the camera lens on her iPhone toward the room and snapped a series of pictures. After turning on her laptop, she texted the best shot to Teo with a short message.

"Can you confirm that's Matt Esposito?"

Moments later, she received an answer: "Yes. Carlton says Esposito will be in on the deal for sure. Find out everything you can."

Anna texted back: "Done." She turned to the file cataloguing project Donna had asked her to work on when Declan didn't need her on the B of A project. An hour later, she stood and walked to the door of her office where she had a view of the men in the conference room. Matt Esposito was standing against the wall of the conference room listening to Collins walk through something with Sanchez. Sanchez was looking at the papers Collins was pointing at, so he couldn't see Esposito's face, but Anna could. His eyes radiated hostility.

Anna walked back to her desk confused. Sanchez was just an accountant and a mild mannered one at that. The B of A deal they were working on together was a distressed debt transaction. It was a big deal for sure, and Collins had been stressed about getting it closed, but Sanchez had never been an impediment in the meetings she'd attended. If anything, he'd been just as stressed out about closing the deal as Collins. Why would Esposito dislike or even hate him?

Carlton had insisted that Esposito was the guy who'd dragged Collins into the Mexican currency deal with Perez. He was also convinced that the Perez deal was the money laundering scheme in play and the evidence seemed to indicate this assessment was correct. If that was the case, then why was Esposito involved in the B of A deal? What was his role in it? Could there be a crossover between the two deals, and was Sanchez in on it?

Anna's musings were interrupted by the intercom. "Anna, its Declan. Can you come into the conference room? I'd like you to meet a friend of mine. He's going to help with the Perez deal."

TWENTY-EIGHT

Riverside, California

J ose Estrella, the manager of PriceStar's SuperCenter in Riverside, California, looked down at the 170,000-square-foot expanse from his cluttered second-floor office. Hundreds of tables stacked high with everything from clothes to candy bars ran the length and breadth of the store. Each table had a big red sign in the middle advertising the once-in-a-lifetime bankruptcy discounts being offered to customers. Runners shuttled back and forth between the floor and the warehouse, bringing out just enough inventory to promote the illusion of frenzied sales and diminishing supply. The staff had already been forced to break up several tussles between frantic customers at the tables offering 50 and 70 percent discounts, and it was only noon.

Jose's gaze wandered to the giant banner fluttering above the cashier stations in the front of the store: "ADDITIONAL 10% DISCOUNT ON ALL CASH SALES!" He shook his head in frustration. Promoting cash sales didn't make any sense. They slowed down the checkout lines, complicated the reconciliation process, and increased the risk of theft, but the guys from Southwind, the lenders' agent, had insisted.

He glanced over at the area of the office that had been partitioned off for Southwind's on-site reps, Miguel and Javier. Promoting cash sales wasn't the only thing Southwind had insisted upon. They'd taken control of the accounting system and had sole responsibility for uploading sales and collections data to corporate. A friend had told him they controlled the accounting system at corporate as well. No one else had access.

Jose could understand the bank's interest in controlling the money and accounting, since it was their money at the end of the day. What he didn't understand or appreciate was their obsession with cash. They'd even brought in their own armored car service to make the daily pickups—an outfit Jose had never heard of. The whole setup was odd.

He glanced at his watch and waved to his administrative assistant, Meghan Arias. "Off to lunch, Meg. Back in thirty."

He said it loud enough so the two Southwind reps could hear him. There was no reaction. Meghan saw his look in that direction, and she rolled her eyes. Jose smiled and shrugged his shoulders as he opened the door to the stairway leading down to the sales floor.

He stopped by the glass cubicle up front bearing the faded "Head Cashier" sign and stuck his head in the door. "Cindy, how many bags of cash went out at noon?"

The small blonde woman frantically typing data into a computer held up four fingers. For a moment, Jose assumed Cindy had made a mistake, but she eliminated any doubt.

"That's right, four."

Jose made a low whistle, before turning and weaving his way through the crowd to the door that led to the loading docks. Two tractor trailers were backed up against the dock, and four forklifts were waiting to unload the incoming merchandise. Jose walked over to the worn black refrigerator on the far side of the dock and pulled out the brown bag holding his lunch. Tomas, the dock manager, waved to him from the far side of the dock, and Jose walked over to him.

"How's it going, T?"

The small, friendly man in his fifties, who'd immigrated from Guatemala thirty years ago, shook his bald head. "Crazy. These guys are throwing inventory at us. This crap is coming from everywhere."

Jose smiled approvingly.

"You're doing great, T. Remember, if we hit the sales target, everyone gets a hefty bonus."

"We'll get there," Tomas said, gesturing to the armored truck driving away. "They just picked up six bags of cash."

Jose shook his head. "Six? Can't be, Cindy said—"

"Heard the guard calling it in." Tomas spoke over his shoulder as he stepped quickly forward to steady a stack of boxes wobbling on the skids of one of the overloaded forklifts.

Jose made his way back to Cindy's glass cubicle. She was talking to one of the younger cashiers, but she turned around as he approached.

"Cindy, did you say four bags were taken out to the cash truck?"

Her brown eyes widened. "Yes. Is one missing?" She leaned forward and spoke in a whisper. "That guy Javier from Southwind went with the guards. Maybe he took one."

Jose shook his head. "No, no. Tomas thought they picked up six bags, not four."

Cindy scoffed. "Six? We've never had six bags in one pickup. Not even during the Christmas sales."

Jose waved off her concern with a gesture. "No worries. I'll check with our new bosses."

Jose called Javier's cell phone on his way back out to the loading dock. Javier's tone was always the same—abrupt and guarded.

"Javier, this is—"

"I know who it is. What is it?"

Jose looked up at the opaque window of the second-floor office area, wondering if Javier was looking down at him. He felt a flash of anger, and for a moment, considered making an obscene gesture in that direction, but he quashed the urge.

"Cindy Howe, the head cashier, says four bags of cash were delivered to the armored car service, but Tomas thinks it was six."

There was a long hesitation on the line. When Javier answered, his voice was even more guarded. "It was six. Everything's good."

Jose looked up at the window again. For some reason, he was all but certain Javier was looking down at him.

"Great, just wanted to make sure."

The Southwind rep ended the call without waiting for a response.

Jose had worked for PriceStar for over ten years, and he knew finding another decent job in the retail space would be difficult, but he
was looking forward to leaving. Working in the same office with the
Southwind people was not just unpleasant—it was also oppressive.

Los Angeles, California

Anna sensed Carlton's growing irritation as she described the events
of the past week a second time at his insistence. Halfway through
the recitation, he abruptly raised a hand.

"I've heard enough." Carlton leaned forward, his eyes boring
into Anna's.

"The meet with Perez tomorrow is critical. Tech will get you set
up with a listening device. I need to hear what's being said and I . . .
I want you to ask a few specific questions—questions that will make
them uncomfortable. We need a forced error in this game."

Teo shook his head. "A bug's okay, but if Agent Torres starts to
grill this guy about the deal, it will blow this op."

Carlton made a dismissive motion with his hand, as if brush-
ing off a fly. "Relax. I'll feed her the questions. They'll be the kind
of questions a rookie paralegal would ask. If Collins says the right
things, it might be just enough to get a tap on his landline and cell
phone."

Anna picked up the pen beside the pad of paper on the table.
"Can you give me the questions now?"

Carlton glanced at his watch. "No time. I have a meeting I need
to get to. I'll email them to you later tonight. You and Teo can do
a back-and-forth over the phone before the conference tomorrow."

Teo leaned forward. "That's not a lot of time. What's the ETA
for the questions?"

Carlton picked up his briefcase and started toward the door. For
a moment, Anna thought he was going to ignore the question, but he
stopped at the door and said over his shoulder. "Sometime tonight.
Could be late, but you'll get them."

US Bank Tower, Los Angeles, California

As Anna stepped off the elevator, she glanced down at the second button on the right cuff of her off-white blouse—the button embedded with the listening device. A matching button was sewn onto her left cuff.

She waved at Michaela as she walked through the reception.

Michaela waved back. "They're already in the conference room. Declan said to come right in."

Anna smiled. "Thanks."

She left her jacket and bag on the chair in her office and picked up a legal pad and a pen and then headed to the conference room. The shades were pulled down, but she could see the outline of the three men in the room. She drew in a deep breath and exhaled before opening the door.

The doors to the cabinet at the end of the room were open, exposing a whiteboard covered with a series of circles and arrows. The circle at the top was denominated "Banco De Norte" and the circle at the bottom "Citibank." The arrows connecting the two circles passed through another circle with the words "Bank of the Baltic" in the middle. For some reason, the name seemed familiar.

Matt Esposito and Perez were sitting on one side of the table tapping on iPads. Declan was at the end of the table closest to the whiteboard. He gestured to the chair across from Matt and Perez.

"Good morning, Anna. Take a seat. You're just in time."

Perez said a gruff "Good morning," as his eyes roved over her body. Esposito smiled and nodded, but the smile seemed forced. "Good to see you again."

Anna nodded. "And both of you, good morning."

Declan closed one of the doors to the cabinet, partially hiding what Anna knew had to be a visual depiction of whatever deal Collins and Esposito were putting together for Perez, and then handed Anna a sheet of paper with a list of corporate entities.

"Anna we're putting together a complex . . . tax-advantaged transaction for Mr. Perez," he said. "This is a somewhat unique transaction, so we may have to create a good part of the documentation from scratch. However, I believe these companies may have put together deals with similar attributes. If they have, I want to borrow from their docs. Some of them may be on the internet."

Esposito pointed to the list of the names on the sheet.

"Each of the entities on that list is a special purpose vehicle," Collins said. "They were formed by . . . less well-known investment outfits, so the deal docs may be difficult to find. They may be referenced in pending or past litigation cases. If that's the case, check out the court filings online."

Anna looked over at Esposito and tried keep the strain from her voice when she posed a version of one of the questions Carlton had given her. "There may be a lot of extraneous documents in these transactions that you don't want. Can you tell me more about Mr. Perez's transaction, so I can . . . try to get as close to the mark as possible?"

Esposito glanced over Declan, and Perez started to shake his head, but Declan cut him off.

"Anna, this . . . is a highly confidential transaction, so we're worried about someone stealing a march on us if it becomes public. We can't tell you the particulars, but I can give you the basic concepts and some words and concepts to use when you're doing the search."

Collins hesitated, his eyes focused on the pad of paper in front of him, and then he nodded as if reaching a decision. "Mr. Perez and his team have had great success in playing the spreads between thinly traded currencies around the world—basically arbitrage. The deal Matt and I are putting together for him will allow a group of investors to take advantage of that skill. It will also enable Mr. Perez to earn a much larger pot of profits by leveraging the other investors' capital."

He paused, and Anna took the opportunity to pose another of Carlton's questions. "Are the other deals I'm looking for US-centric transactions?"

Esposito shook his head and spoke a little too quickly. "These will be offshore deals, so no SEC filings."

Perez seconded this comment with grunt. "No SEC. Too complicated. Too expensive."

Anna drew in a breath and put out another feeler. "How do I find deals that have the tax-advantaged angle you mentioned?"

Collins wrote on the yellow pad in front of him as he spoke, ripped out the sheet, and handed it to her. "I know this is kind of a scattershot, but these terms and IRC sections may pull up something that will help us avoid one more minefield in the drafting process."

She nodded hesitantly. "How much time do you want me to put into this, and what is my timetable?"

Collins glanced over at Perez. "I would say twenty hours of research time. As a completion date, today is Thursday, so by Wednesday of next week. I expect there will be a lot of garbage in what you send over, but I also think some of it will be very helpful. Be more inclusive, not less, in what you send me."

Collins glanced at his watch and stood up. "I have a meeting in twenty minutes outside the office, so I need to run. Matt, are we done here?"

"Yeah, we're done."

Collins shook Perez's hand and gestured for Anna to follow him. When they emerged from the conference room, he pointed to Donna's office. "Donna will give you a separate laptop for this search. It logs on to the internet through the Wi-Fi set up by the virtual office outfit downstairs. It's slower, but it works. I . . . I don't want the firm's IP address coming up when you do this research. It could . . . alert other players in the market to what we're doing."

Anna turned to ask Collins a question about the privacy issue, but he'd already started toward his office, and she decided to leave it alone.

As she walked toward Donna's office, her thoughts were racing in multiple directions. She knew Collins wasn't telling the truth about the Perez deal, but it wasn't clear to her why he was being deceitful. She assumed it was because he didn't want to disclose the deal's illegality, but she sensed there was more to it. She froze just outside Donna's office. She suddenly recognized the name of the bank on the whiteboard—Bank of the Baltic. She also knew it was suspected of laundering money for several Russian oligarchs.

Los Angeles, California

As Collins waited impatiently in the lobby of Cohen's building for Gregorio and Sanchez to arrive, David Cohen walked into the lobby trailed by an entourage of younger attorneys. He spotted Collins and walked over to him, after gesturing for the rest of the group to go on ahead.

Cohen extended his hand, and Collins shook it.

"Collins! You're early. Come right up. We'll find you a conference room."

Despite the bonhomie, Cohen's eyes, as always, were carefully assessing him, as if seeking an undisclosed weakness.

"Thanks. I would, but I told my clients I'd meet them here."

"I understand. Oh, by the way, speaking of early, the judge accelerated the hearing a week. So were up to bat next Wednesday."

Collins felt as though a giant vice had gripped his chest. Once the plan of reorganization was confirmed, Cayetano wouldn't need him and Matt anymore. He might wait a week before ordering Nacio to eliminate them just in case any unanticipated issues arose, but there would be no reason to keep Sienna alive. *Romano and his exfil team would have to be ready to go in days! He'd also have to text Sienna the date and hope she got the message, otherwise Romano and his team could do nothing.*

"You okay? I assume that's good news."

Collins's eyes refocused on Cohen. "Yeah . . . yes, just had . . . a senior moment . . . there's something I have to do in another case today. Why was the hearing accelerated?"

"The judge had an eye operation scheduled three weeks out, but his doc said he had to get in there sooner. So we gotta button this package up next week or wait another month until he gets back. I told his clerk next week is good. You're okay with that, right?"

Collins answered reflexively. "Yes. The sooner the better."

Cohen smiled. "Thought so. See ya upstairs."

Collins nodded. "Yeah." His mind raced through the list of things that had to get done in the next week for everything to come together. For a moment he considered cancelling the meeting with Cohen but rejected the idea. If Gregorio and Sanchez advised Cayetano that he was dragging his feet, the reaction could be deadly.

"Mr. Collins?"

Collins was so tense he spun around too quickly in response to the inquiry and had to take another step to regain his balance. Sanchez and Gregorio were a stride away, staring at him.

Sanchez's eyes widened. "Is everything okay, Mr. Collins?"

"Yes, fine. We can talk on the way upstairs."

Collins didn't tell them the hearing had been accelerated, and he hoped it wouldn't come up in the meeting. It was a gamble, but there was nothing he could do about it.

An hour into the meeting, Cohen threw out a question that unnerved him. "Just as an aside, this Southwind Analytics out-fit—the guys you brought in to manage the cash collections on the going-out-of-business sale—who are they?"

Collins parried with a question. "Why? Is there an issue?"

Cohen's eyes bored into Collins and then traveled to Sanchez and Gregorio. Both men stiffened. Cohen leaned back in his chair, his eyes returning to Sanchez. "Let's just say I'm receiving reports from the stores that suggest these guys are a little on the scary side."

Collins made a dismissive motion with his right hand. "It's a miserable space, David. You called the outfit who ran the going-out-of-business sale in the Capital Retail case 'Ali Baba and the Forty Thieves.' Not exactly a ringing endorsement."

Cohen chuckled. "Nah, but it was accurate."

The meeting ended ten minutes later without any mention of the expedited hearing date on the plan confirmation. Collins walked quickly to the elevators, forcing Gregorio and Sanchez to match his pace. Once the elevator doors closed, he released the breath caught in his throat.

"Are you in a rush, Mr. Collins?" Gregorio asked.

His tone didn't carry a note of suspicion, but Collins felt com-pelled to offer an explanation. "Yes, to get out of there. Cohen never stops negotiating. That's who he is. If we delayed another minute, he would have grabbed us at the elevator and tried to extract another concession."

"I see." The tone of Gregorio's voice suggested otherwise.

As they walked out of the elevator, Collins gestured to an unoccupied space in the far corner of the lobby. Collins turned to Gregorio and Sanchez when they reached the spot. "What is Cohen talking about?"

Gregorio feigned ignorance. "I'm not sure what you mean."

"I'm talking about Southwind Analytics. What's going on at the stores?"

Gregorio shook his head dismissively. "It was nothing. Just a . . . difference of cultures, let us say."

"I see," Collins said, his eyes boring into Gregorio. "Where are we with the . . . additional deposits?"

Sanchez looked around furtively before answering. "We're good. Over thirty million in . . . outside cash has been picked up and deposited into the PriceStar bank account. We could have added more bags to the daily pickups, but we're following your advice and starting slow—although the pace is increasing. We should meet our . . . goal by the middle of next week. The week after that the plan of reorganization will be confirmed, and we will have total control of the company, right?"

Collins nodded. "Yes. Then you will have total control."

The words were like the tip of a cold knife touching the side of his neck. "Gentlemen, I have a problem in another case I have to resolve tonight."

Gregorio nodded. "Of course. We will call you in the morning, Mr. Collins."

Twenty minutes later, Collins entered the bathroom stall, unscrewed the top of the paper dispenser, and pulled out the phone. He sent a text to Tony: "Need a meet with the team tonight. Schedule has accelerated. Sienna has to be out next week. Need to text GO date to Sienna ASAP!"

He waited three minutes for the answer to come back. "Be at club by ten. Will send you another frantic email about a meet for cover."

Los Angeles, California

Anna moved the phone away from her ear to reduce the sound of Carlton's self-congratulatory crowing.

"I knew it! Collins plans to walk drug money into the country through that dirtbag bank in Lithuania, just like the Russian big dawgs were doing until we put the boot down on them. Well, it's not going to work. Old Regge is gonna grab those dollars as soon as they hit stateside. Then . . . then I'm going to put those two former ice rats in orange jumpsuits for the next twenty years! This is going to be big, folks, real big. And you can be sure I'll share the credit with the whole team. This kind of bust is going to make every front page and . . .well, let's leave it there."

Anna made a third attempt to get Carlton to listen to her concerns. "Mr. Carlton—"

"Call me Regge, Anna. We're all on the same team."

Anna internally scoffed at Carlton's belated attempt at comradery. "Regge, as I said, I'm concerned there may be something else going on here. Collins is clever, even a genius, when it comes to complex financial transactions. If he was going to structure an illegal transaction, he would . . . I believe he would be more circumspect, and his plan would be much more sophisticated. I think we may be—"

"Relax, Agent Torres," Carlton said dismissively. "I've taken down a lot bigger and smarter fish than Declan Collins. Trust me, we're running a game on him, not vice versa. It's the Perez deal. Keep your eyes on that ball and only on that ball, clear?"

"Yes, sir."

Teo called her after the conference call ended. "What a pompous ass."

Anna smiled. "To say the least. I just wish he'd consider the possibility that something else may be going on."

"What's gnawing at you, Anna? Spit it out."

"I just don't think Collins is careless enough to let an outsider, like me, learn that much about what he knows is an illegal transaction. This guy has been two moves ahead of everyone in the B of A acquisition, and his dealings with Cohen and the creditor's committee were brilliant. Why would he—"

"Simple," Teo interrupted, "he doesn't know you're anything other than a temp paralegal. So why should he worry? You said yourself the chart looked like a complex geometry equation. There's not a lot of people who would have any interest in figuring out that maze, and Collins would have every reason to assume you don't have the background to do so."

Anna reluctantly nodded. "I guess . . . maybe I *am* overanalyzing it."

"That's not a bad thing. Always keep an open mind when you're in the field. Always."

"Thanks, Teo. I'll check in tomorrow."

"Do that."

When Anna returned to her apartment, she took out a bottle of wine and filled a glass nearly to the top. After taking a long sip, she walked over to the window and stared at the band of light encircling the top of US Bank Tower. *What if we're wrong? What if Collins knows I'm an undercover FBI agent and he's running a game on me?*

―――

Tony and Romano were in the secure communications unit in the truck behind the club when Collins arrived. Romano pointed to the chair across the table from him. "Take a seat, counselor."

Collins walked over to table, but he was too wound up to sit down. "Here's the bottom line. The judge accelerated the plan confirmation hearing in the bankruptcy case. Once the order approving the plan is entered, Cayetano doesn't need me anymore, which means that order is a death sentence for Sienna."

Romano stared at Collins for a moment before responding. "Can you delay the entry of the order?"

Collins shook his head. "No. The proposed order will be uploaded to the CM-ECF system the day of the hearing, or at the latest, the next day, and the judge will enter it right away."

Tony leaned across the table. "Okay, what about this: We grab the two local guys who are part of the cartel, this Gregorio and Sanchez. We use them as bargaining chips."

Collins shook his head. "No good. Those two guys are scared shitless of Cayetano. My read is he would kill them without a second thought if this deal goes sideways."

Romano pointed a finger at Collins. "He can't just kill the girl. He's gotta kill you and Matt Esposito as well. Lining that up will take time. That may buy us a week or two."

Collins met Romano's eyes. "No, it won't. Nacio Leon, Cayetano's top killer is in town. He's been shadowing me for the last couple of weeks. In fact, I can guarantee you one of his men is parked just up the street waiting for me to come out. Anyway, I can't take that chance. We need to get Sienna out before next Friday. Can you work with that schedule?"

It seemed like an eternity before Romano responded. "We can do it. But only if you connect with the girl. She has to be able to get over that wall when the exfil happens, otherwise it's all a waste of time."

Collins nodded. "I'll . . . I'll get it done."

Romano stood up and walked over to Collins. There was a cold intensity in his gaze, and his tone was all business. "You do that. Here's the message. My team will be outside the northeast wall of that compound on Wednesday night, three hours after sundown. That's the wall with the antenna right smack in the middle of it. We will wait there until two hours before sunup. Then we're gone. She has to get over that wall within that time frame, clear?"

Collins let out a breath and reached for Tony's iPhone. He typed in the phone number Grayson had given him and typed the text message. He read it three times and then passed the phone across the table to Romano. The mercenary read it carefully looked up.

"Why'd you sign 'The Mick'?"

"That's what she used to call me in the old neighborhood. Everyone was Italian. I was the only one with an Irish name, so they called me The Mick."

An amused look crossed Romano's face as he handed the phone back. "Send it."

Collins pressed the send button and was gratified by the whoosh confirming it was sent. He watched the screen in silence for four minutes. There was no message indicating the text bounced back. He closed his eyes and said a quiet prayer. Sienna had to receive it and get over that wall next Wednesday.

Maijoma, Mexico

Sienna eased her head through the opening in the roof and scanned the shed and the surrounding area. She guessed it was about two or three in the morning. The sky was overcast, cloaking the area below in a pall of darkness. In one respect this was good; in another it was not. The darkness would make it more difficult for anyone to see her as she climbed down the pipe and ran across to the shed. On the other hand, if Matias or his men were waiting and watching in the darkness, she might not see them until it was too late.

She took in a big breath, climbed onto the roof, and started down the pipe. A minute later her feet touched the hardpacked earth below, and she dropped into a crouch. She stayed there for a full minute listening and scanning the area for movement before running over to the shed in a crouch. She reached into the eave where the second phone was hidden, pulled it out, and dropped back into a crouch.

When she pressed the power button, the screen remained black for a moment and a wave of fear raced through her. *The battery was dead!* Then the screen lit up, and she quickly put her hand over it to hide the glow. The new message icon flashed and she tapped it. Her breath caught in her throat when she read the message. It was from Declan. Grayson had done it!

She read the message twice before fully grasping its importance. They wanted her to climb over the northeast wall on Wednesday night. That was in two days! Someone would be there waiting to take her home. Tears began to flow down her face. She roughly brushed them away, looked furtively around, and read the message again. Declan had signed off with his nickname to let her know he was the sender.

She typed a message: "I will be there. Please come! Tell Matt I'll give him a slap if no one shows up." The last comment would validate her identity. She stared at the phone for another moment, and for a long moment nothing happened, and then a quiet whoosh confirmed the message was sent. A second later there was a responsive message.

"Got it! Be there and be safe, Mick."

Sienna started to type another message, but the sound of a woman's scream in the distance changed her mind. She glanced around again, crept over to the eave, and returned the phone to the hiding place. Then she ran over to the pipe and started back up to the roof.

Reston, Virginia

Colonel George Bissom glanced at the door of the all-but-empty coffeehouse as he stirred a packet of sugar into his second cup of coffee. He looked down at his watch. It was 3:00 p.m. If he didn't get on the road in the next thirty minutes, the drive home to Leesburg would take more than an hour.

He tapped the screen of his phone and pulled up the email from Mike Easton, the NSA liaison on the operation about to go down in Mexico, and read it a second time: "We need to talk ASAP. I'll meet you at the Metro Plaza Starbucks at 3:00 p.m. Hit me back if you can't make it."

"I know. I'm late."

Bissom looked up, surprised. Easton was standing on the other side of the table. "Sneaking up on me, eh?"

Easton's bald head was too large for his thin body, and the wire-rimmed glasses perched on the end of his long, thin nose lent him more the air of an aging history professor than a top NSA analyst.

"Sorry about that. It's an occupational habit. I'll tip over a chair or two on my way next time."

Easton's dry, raspy voice had just a hint of a Boston accent. "You do that. Now, pull up a chair and tell me about this ASAP thing."

Easton eased into the chair across from Bissom and adjusted his blue bow tie. The color seemed a bit odd to Bissom. It was the same color as the NSA man's suit.

Easton glanced around the room and then leaned forward, folding his hands on the table in front of him. "I'll get right to the point, since we both want to beat the traffic. As you know, we keep track of all sorts of data."

Bissom raised a mocking eyebrow. "Really?"

"Really. And not all of it is SigInt. Some of it is more mundane, such as the names and addresses of people who buy a sensitive compartment information facility."

Bissom nodded. "Makes sense. If someone buys an SCIF, they must be trying to hide something."

Easton smiled. "We do try to be masters of at least the obvious. In most cases, there's a legitimate explanation for the acquisition, but in other cases, there's not. For example, a night club owner in LA bought a top-of-the-line SCIF two weeks ago and had it installed in the back of a truck he parks behind the club. We sent this information to the local FBI office, and they just happened to know this guy, one Tony Lentino, a tax scofflaw who avoided a stretch in the federal pen due to the skills of a very expensive lawyer, Declan Collins."

Bissom glanced at his watch. "How does this—"

"Patience, patience. Here's the connection to your pending op. A week ago an exfil specialist called Dante Romano showed up at Lentino's place along with three of his mercs."

Bissom eyes widened, and he leaned forward. "Never met the guy, but the word is he runs a topflight outfit."

Easton nodded. "That he does. Maybe you can ask him for a few pointers when you meet him next week."

"Next week? How's that?"

Easton glanced around. "It seems the two of you intend to visit the same rundown resort in Mexico, at just about the same time."

Bissom scoffed. "That's BS."

"Maybe. But I think not. Four of Romano's mercs flew into a place called Lajitas a day ago—a golf resort near Big Bend National

Park. It's just a short hop from the Mexican border. They secured a permit from the park service to overfly the park and take pictures. The word is they're posing as location scouts for a nonexistent movie studio in Santa Barbara."

Bissom shook his head dismissively. "Mike, who knows why they're down there, or what they intend to do. It could be just a training op."

Easton unfolded his hands and brushed an imaginary piece of lint off his cuff. "I know why. On a lark, if you will, I checked the log on the surveillance file—the one with the satellite close-ups of the compound the Nauyacas intend to hit next week. Someone in the CIA pulled that file two weeks ago. I ran this guy's jacket. He worked with Romano on an extraction op in Iraq three years ago."

Bissom spread his hands out on the table in front of him. "Why would Romano be interested in that compound?"

"I had the same question, so I dug a little deeper and found the nexus. Do you remember the blonde girl who showed up in one of those satellite photos of the compound?"

Bissom nodded. "Sure do."

Easton brushed another imaginary piece of lint off his cuff. "Well, that bothered me. So I had a tech blow up that picture. The logo on the T-shirt the girl is wearing says Westmont College. I had a few of our techs run a search on Lentino and Collins—through social media and that sort of thing. Lo and behold, look what they found." Easton pulled a photograph out his pocket and pushed it across the table.

Bissom stared at the photograph. A blonde girl in her early twenties wearing jeans and a Westmont College T-shirt was standing between two men in their mid-thirties. The men were dressed in suits. The three of them were smiling.

Easton tapped the figures in the photo. "The man on the right is Declan Collins. The other fellow is Matt Esposito. Collins and Esposito went to school together. The girl in the middle is Sienna Esposito, Matt's sister."

Bissom stared at the photo for a long moment before pushing it back across the table to Easton. "Mike, I think I see where you're going, but there are a lot of missing pieces."

Easton shook his head. "Actually, there aren't. Homeland Security has a record of Sienna Esposito flying to Mexico to join a Doctors Without Borders unit working in Chiapas, Mexico. That unit left the area early due to risks posed by a local narco gang. There's no record of Sienna returning to the United States."

Bissom shrugged his shoulders. "Okay, maybe the girl decided to take an extended vacation. Who knows—"

"I know. I did a wee bit more investigating. Sienna didn't leave with the medical team. She left over a month earlier. A helicopter, supposedly hired by Declan Collins, picked her up and rushed her to the nearest airport so she could get home to see her critically injured brother. Unfortunately, that's not the reality. First, Matt Esposito wasn't injured. Second, Collins never hired a chopper in Mexico. And third, as I said, Sienna Esposito never returned to the United States."

Bissom's eyes widened. "That's Sienna Esposito in the compound in Maijoma."

Easton nodded. "The photo and facial rec say it's a 90-plus percent certainty. And yet, her loving brother and his best friend have never reported her missing. Why? Because—"

"They've hired Romano and his team to get her out," Bissom finished. "Jesus, Mary, and Joseph, this could become a real cluster."

Easton stood up. "It could, but I'm sure you'll find a solution. By the way, I never told you anything, I was never here, and you will not repeat any of this to anyone except to the extent necessary to delay Mr. Romano's intervention. Alienating my brethren over at Langley would be . . . problematic. Have a good night, Colonel."

TWENTY-NINE

US Bank Tower, Los Angeles, California

Collins reviewed the draft of the proposed order approving PriceStar's plan of reorganization one last time. The order confirmed the plan, and it made a long series of findings, including findings regarding the tax treatment of the gains being generated from the sale. Once the order was signed by the bankruptcy court, Fourth Street Fund, aka Ramon Cayetano, would become the sole owner of PriceStar. Cayetano would then have access to the 100 million dollars of drug money in PriceStar's bank accounts—money booked in PriceStar's accounting system as proceeds generated from the going-out-of-business sale. His scheme had worked. There was only one problem. The entry of the order confirming PriceStar's plan would be a death sentence for him, Matt, and Sienna.

A third email from Cohen popped up on the screen, demanding to know whether he'd signed off on the form of the order. He typed, "Approved," and reluctantly pressed the send button, knowing Cohen would upload the order to court within the hour. Since the confirmation hearing set for the following morning at ten was uncontested, the judge would sign and docket the order that day or the next day. He now had less than twenty-four hours to get Sienna out of that hellhole in Mexico or she was dead.

Collins glanced at his watch. It was 8:20 a.m. He'd reluctantly agreed to meet Matt at the coffee shop across the street in ten minutes. The meet was not a good idea—one of Cayetano's soldiers was parked in a car on the street outside his building—but Matt had been frantic.

Collins ripped a page off the notepad in front of him, wrote a message on both sides, and placed it in his shirt pocket. He pulled his suit jacket off the back of his office door and walked through the lobby to the elevators. Anna emerged from the women's bathroom in the hall just as he pressed the elevator button. Collins turned to face her.

"Anna, can you check the dollar conversion rate today against the Mexican peso and then do a quick search on where the market sees that price going in the next week? Perez's deal is going to close soon, so I need to keep an eye on the currency risk we could face in the next week."

She nodded. "Yes, of course. Is there anything else I should be doing?"

"Um . . . yes. Ask Donna to check on flights to Riga next week."

Anna's eyes widened. "Riga, as in the capital of Latvia?"

Collins nodded. "That's the one. I'm thinking of taking some time off. It looks like a nice spot."

Collins turned his attention to the phone in his hand, but he watched Anna through his peripheral vision as she walked back into the office. He noted that she turned in the direction of her office, not Donna's, when she crossed the lobby.

As he crossed the street to the coffee shop, Collins glanced to his right and left. The black Altima was halfway up the block. The Latino man behind the wheel looked in the other direction. Collins knew the driver would report the meet to Nacio. The only question was whether Nacio would consider the meeting threatening and react.

Matt was sitting at a table in the back. The dark-gray designer suit, Rolex watch, and power tie conveyed a message of wealth and success, but Matt's face told a different story. The dark shadows under his eyes and the oversize Band-Aid inexpertly pasted on the right side of his jaw suggested he'd recently been in a fight and gotten the worst of it. Collins held up a hand for silence as they sat down at the table. He pulled the handwritten note from his pocket and pushed it across the table. Matt's eyes widened as he read it. Then he glanced quickly around the room.

Collins drew a black Faraday bag from his pocket, put his phone in it, and held his hand out for Matt's phone. Matt handed him the phone and Collins placed it in the black bag as well and zipped the top. He flipped over the note and pointed to the writing on the second side: "Go to the restroom and use this RF detector to scan your suit, shoes, etc., for electronic devices." He handed Matt a small black device.

Matt picked up the device and walked to the men's room. He emerged three minutes later, sat down at the table, and pushed the detector across the table. As Collins returned the device to his suit jacket pocket, he said quietly, "Are we good?"

Matt exhaled as if he had been holding his breath a long time. "We're good."

"Okay, what's up?"

Anger flared in Matt's eyes and he answered in a hoarse whisper. "What's up? You said the final hearing is tomorrow. What's the plan to rescue Sienna?"

Collins leaned forward. "The exfil op is tonight. If all goes well, Sienna will be safe by morning."

"Tonight? Why didn't—"

"Because we didn't get the confirmation from Sienna until a day ago and setting up a hostage extraction operation while running a hundred-million-dollar money laundering operation at the same time is just a little more difficult than you might think."

"You couldn't just—"

"Call? No. Remember? They own these," Collins said, pointing at the phones in the Faraday bag on the table. And right now, they aren't getting a signal. So this conference has to be short. Let me talk, Matt, and you listen, all right?"

Anger flared in Matt's eyes again, and for a moment Collins thought he was going to lose it, but he recovered and nodded in agreement.

"Yeah, sorry. Tell me where we are."

Collins glanced at the door to the restaurant and scanned the street outside. No movement so far.

"As I said, the op goes off tonight. Once Romano and his people have Sienna, he'll call me on my cell. It will be a call for a DUI representation. I'll pass, but I'll promise to call him back with a referral. Then I will call you and ask you for the name of the lawyer who represented you in that DUI case two years ago. You will say you can't recall the name, but you will look it up and call me back. That call is your exit order. You grab your go bag and get out of there, Matt. I'll meet you—"

Collins stopped in mid-sentence. Tony Lentino was walking across the coffee shop toward them. The look on his face was grim.

Matt followed Collins's gaze. "What's Tony doing here?"

There was confusion and fear in Matt's voice.

Tony pulled a chair over from the next table and sat down. He looked over at Collins and tapped his right ear.

Collins shook his head. "No, we're good."

Lentino leaned forward. "We got a big problem. Romano just called. The FBI grabbed his team about an hour ago. Someone ratted us out, but shit, I can't figure out how!"

Matt exploded out of his chair. "What? How could that—"

Collins cut off the coming tirade in a harsh whisper. "Sit down, Matt! Remember, Nacio's man is just outside the door!"

Matt eyes strayed to the door, and he reluctantly sat down.

Collins glanced quickly around the restaurant and then looked over at Tony. "Walk us through it from beginning to end."

"I don't know a lot. The chopper pilot and three of Romano's mercs were staying at a hotel in Lajitas, Texas. It's right on the Mexican border. They were supposed to meet Romano at the airfield at nine this morning. It's about fifteen minutes away. When they didn't show up, he called the hotel. The guy at the front desk told him a swarm of FBI and ATF agents showed up and grabbed the three of them in the parking lot. That's it. That's all I—"

"What about Romano?"

"He's fine. He stayed with the chopper at the jump-off point in Terlingua."

"Tony, get him on the phone. We have to put this thing back together."

Tony pulled his cell phone out of his pocket.

Collins shook his head. "Not here. In the parking lot out back."

Collins left a twenty on the table and walked down the narrow corridor past the restrooms. A door displaying a prominent "NO EXIT" sign was located just around the corner. He pushed open the door and they walked out into a narrow lot behind the building used for deliveries.

Tony had Romano on the phone by the time the door closed behind them. "Dante, it's Tony. Declan wants to talk."

Collins took the phone. "Dante, we have to find a way to put this thing back together. Sienna is going over that wall tonight, and someone has to be there to meet her."

There was a moment of hesitation. "We need a minimum of three people to do this op. A chopper pilot, someone to go and get the girl, and at least one person as backup. Right now, I'm missing two of those assets."

A wave of frustration and rage washed over Collins. He'd designed and executed a nearly impossible money laundering scheme and concurrently arranged a secret exfil operation to save Sienna while under constant surveillance by her kidnappers. *How could everything get blown up by a random event at the last minute? Sienna would be left standing outside the walls without a rescue!*

As the magnitude of the disaster they were facing began to overwhelm him, Collins remembered the mantra he'd insisted Matt repeat on the tarmac in Mexico: "My name is invincible."

"No," Collins said, his eyes locked on Matt and Tony, "those assets are available and they're ready to go. I'm an IFR-qualified chopper pilot with over a thousand hours as the PIC. As for shooters, Tony and Matt are qualified as marksmen with AR-15s, and I'm a better shot than both of them. We will be there in four hours."

"Counselor, you can't just—"

"Romano, if no one is there to meet Sienna, she dies tonight. If she stays in the compound, she dies tomorrow. I'm going to be outside that compound tonight, with you or without you. Now, will you help me or not?"

There was a long silence before Romano responded in a growl. "How about this, you find a way to get your butt to Terlingua, Texas, in four hours, and maybe we'll have something to talk about. Oh, and try to avoid getting your ass scooped up by the goddamn FBI on the way."

"We'll be there," Collins said and ended the call.

Collins turned to Tony. "You don't have to do this—"

"Button it, paisan," Tony said gruffly and turned to Matt.

"We're gonna do this thing, right, Esposito?"

"Shit, yeah."

There was no hesitation in Matt's voice, only desperate rage.

Collins looked at the two men for a long moment before saying, "Okay then, let's do it. Tony, I need your phone. I have to charter a jet to El Paso and line up a second flight from there to the airstrip in Terlingua. We're going to need desert camouflage wear, boots, that kind of thing. We need to find a place on the way to LAX. There's no time for . . . damn, how could everything turn to shit so quick?"

Collins stood motionless for a moment, his mind frantically racing through the sequence of events that had to be lined up within a nearly impossible time frame for this to work. He shook his head slowly, momentarily overwhelmed.

Tony slapped him roughly on the shoulder. "You get the transport. I know a place in Inglewood where we can pick up the military gear, and yeah, it's on the way. My Rover's parked on the street out front. Let's go."

Collins turned to follow him, and Matt grabbed his arm. "Wait, you said one of Nacio's guys is out front!"

Collins stared at Matt in confusion for a moment.

"Declan?"

"Yes, the car." He pointed to the building behind them. "Tony, pick us up one block over, in front of that building. We'll cut through the alley."

Tony pumped his fist in the air as he walked away. "This is going to be one kick-ass rodeo."

As he turned and started toward the next block, Collins said quietly, "Yeah, and we're the three clowns about to take on the giant bull."

———

"Riga! I knew it!"

Carlton's voice was so loud Anna held the phone away from her head. She was thankful nobody was in the office next to hers.

"Learn from the master, folks. Learn from the master. I'm going to put Declan Collins away for so long that rink jockey is going to need a walker when he gets out."

Teo jumped in. "The Bureau has an open investigation looking into that bank. We should use them as a resource. They might—"

Carlton waved away the suggestion. "And risk a leak days before we bring the hammer down on these guys? Not a chance."

Anna knew Carlton wasn't worried about a leak. He was worried about someone stealing a part of the credit and the press coverage he expected to receive when Collins's arrest was announced.

Teo pressed Carlton again. "The deputy director will expect us to coordinate with the other strike team, and—"

"And we will, Agent Ortega. I will handle that personally, at the right time. Are we clear?"

The threat in Carlton's last inquiry was clear.

There was a long pause. "Crystal clear."

Teo's voice was calm, but Anna could hear the undercurrent of anger.

"Good. That will do it, team. Keep up the good work."

A moment after Anna hung up, the phone rang. She glanced at the number on the screen, expecting to see Teo's number, but it was Donna's cell number.

"Hello, this is Anna."

"Anna, it's me, Donna. I just got a call from Declan. He's on the way to the doctor."

"What! I just saw—"

"He said he has some kind of stomach bug, or food poisoning."

"Do you know where he's going?"

"No, he said he was so cramped up he didn't want to talk or drive. He took an Uber to wherever he's going. He wants you to call Sanchez, the guy you're working with on the B of A deal, and tell him the five o'clock meeting today is off. But he doesn't want you to call him until 4:30, just in case he recovers and gets back to the office in time for the meeting. He said that twice. Are you good with that?"

Anna nodded. "Yes. I'll call after 4:30."

"I'll be in the office in an hour. See you then."

When the call ended, Anna looked over at Declan's office. He was fine when she spoke to him this morning, just before he entered the elevator. Although that bothered her, she was more troubled by his comment about taking a vacation in Riga, the location of the bank suspected of being involved in money laundering. It had seemed just a bit too flippant. *It was as if . . . he knew she would react to it.* She walked back to her desk and picked up her cell phone, intending to call Teo. After staring at the screen for a moment, she decided not to. The call would either spark an explosion from Carlton or a wave of derision, and in the end, it would accomplish nothing. She needed more than a mere suspicion before suggesting her undercover status was blown.

THIRTY

Terlingua, Texas

A plume of dust flew into the air when the four-seater Cessna touched down on the narrow dirt runway. The strip was located along the base of a valley bordered on both sides by low brown hills covered with a mixture of creosote bushes, cacti, rock, and sand. The pilot, a man in his sixties wearing a Texas Ranger's cap, pointed at the two hangars a hundred yards ahead.

"I'll drop you there."

Collins, who was sitting in the copilot's seat, nodded. "Thanks."

As the plane made its way down the runway, the pilot glanced over at him. "What are you boys huntin' down here, mule deer? You don't look like you do this sort of thing very often."

Collins answered wryly, "Well, there's a first time for everything."

The pilot laughed. "There surely is. Watch out for those damn snakes—diamondback rattlers mostly."

"Thanks, we'll do that," Collins said as his eyes found Romano. The merc was standing under the roof of a giant steel hangar with open sides about forty yards up the runway. The aircraft inside the shed was covered by a giant tarp, but the landing gear on the left side was just visible. It was a helicopter.

The Cessna came to a halt about thirty yards from Romano. Collins climbed out of the plane and turned to grab his bag from the second seat.

"I got it," Matt said as he stepped out of the plane, followed by Tony, carrying two bags. All three men were wearing the desert camouflage outfits and hiking boots they'd purchased at the army surplus store on the way to LAX.

Collins waved to the pilot of the Cessna and walked over to Romano.

The mercenary looked at his watch. "Four hours and twenty minutes. I'm impressed."

Collins nodded. "Thanks. We took a private jet to Midland and chartered the Cessna from one of the locals."

Romano waved to Matt and Tony, who were standing three feet away. "Get under the roof. Feds could be surveilling this place with one of those small drones."

Matt glanced up in the sky and then stepped quickly into the hangar. He turned to Romano. "Then we need to get outta here quick! We can't let them grab us too!"

Romano stared at him for a moment with no expression on his face. "Relax, I got someone watching the road. We'll get about forty minutes' notice if anyone who even looks like a Fed starts in this direction, and we have to wait for darkness anyway."

"What's the status of your people?" Collins asked.

"Locked up in El Paso. I spoke to the lawyer representing them. He said something's not right. The US Attorney hasn't charged them with anything, and the inside word is he doesn't intend to. For whatever reason, they just want to keep my guys locked up until tomorrow morning."

Romano stared at Collins for a moment. Collins knew what he was thinking. He shook his head, his expression grim. "There's been no leaks on our side, Dante. I didn't tell Matt and Tony it was a go until we met this morning, and they've been with me since I called you. And no, I don't believe the Cayetanos somehow figured it out on their own, or worse, bribed someone in the FBI."

Romano stared at Collins skeptically. "Then what kind of shit is going down here?"

Collins met his stare, knowing he had to get Romano to trust them. "I don't know. What I do know is that Cayetano's people do not know we're coming."

"You'd better be right, counselor. Because *if* we go—and that's a big if—and they do know, we're all dead."

Romano made eye contact with the three of them and then walked over to the tarp covering the helicopter. "Now, tell me why I should believe that a tax lawyer can fly this bird—a Bell 407AH. Tony told me you never served in the military."

"I didn't, but I make two million a year as a lawyer, so when I decided to get a pilot's license, money wasn't a problem. I took private lessons with the best outfits. I can fly jets, planes, and helicopters. As for the 407AH, I haven't flown that particular bird before, but I've flown hundreds of hours in the Bell 505, 214, and the UH-1."

"How's that?" Romano said, his tone rife with skepticism.

"I'm in two volunteer pilot organizations. We fly supply-and-rescue missions after natural disasters. I flew hundreds of supply missions after Hurricanes Katrina, Sandy, and Maria. I spent so much time in Puerto Rico after Hurricane Maria, I bought a place there. I know, I wasn't under enemy fire during any of these flights, but I've flown into and out of some pretty rough country, and a lot of those search-and-rescue missions were nap-of-the-earth. You can't find people lost in the back country unless you're right on the deck, and the landing zones we put down in were . . . pretty hairy."

Collins walked over to the helicopter, lifted the tarp covering the pilot's door, and slipped inside. The instrumentation was almost exactly the same as the other Bell helicopters he'd flown. Every bird had its own feel, but he was confident he could handle any nuances after a little time in the air.

Collins turned back to Romano. "Any chance I can take this up for bit before we start south?"

"I'm not sure we're going south, at least not in my bird. As for a training flight, can't do it without risking another raid by the Feds. One of them is still local." There was a hard edge to Romano's voice.

"That's bull—"

"Matt! Let it be!" Collins's voice was harsher than he'd intended, but getting into a fight with Romano wasn't an option.

"This bird is a decade old, Romano. In today's market, you could pick one up for a million five. The wire transfer deadline at my bank expires in one hour. Matt and I can each wire $750,000 to Tony's account. If I put this machine into the ground, Tony will give you the money."

Romano stared at Collins, an implacable look on his face. Then he slowly smiled. "If you put the machine into the ground, counselor, there's a good chance we're all dead. As for the wire, skip it, but I'll take a written IOU. If I survive the wreck, I'll need the money for medical care and to get a new chopper. You can make that IOU payable to Silver Lake, LLC. That's two words, both capped."

Collins held out his hand. "Can I use your phone?"

Romano reached into his back pocket and handed Collins a cell phone wrapped in a thick layer of rubber. Collins opened the email app and looked over at Romano.

"What's your email?"

"Roman@silverlakellc.com, but you can't send me an email through any of your accounts, remember? Your friends back in LA will see it," Romano grunted.

Collins nodded. "You're right, but I just happen to know the username and password for Donna's personal account—she's the admin who runs my office. I can trust her."

Romano chuckled. "Well, it's for damn sure she can't trust you, since you stole her goddamn email access."

Collins ignored the comment. Donna would be pissed off about his knowledge of the information, but that was an issue for another day.

He logged onto Donna's Gmail account, typed in Romano's email, and then typed the following message: "This email shall confirm that I, Declan Collins, am liable for all damages caused to that certain Bell 407 helicopter owned by Silver Lake, LLC, to the extent the damages are suffered during my use of this helicopter on November 21, 2018, through November 22, 2018. Executed under the penalty of perjury this 21st day of November 2018, in Brewster County, Texas."

Then he typed the exact same declaration right below it but put Matt's name in as the declarant. After sending the message to Romano, Collins typed a separate explanatory message to Donna referencing the emails and told her to keep the matter secret.

Collins looked over at Romano. "Tony will tell you that I'm good for it. So, are we in agreement that this operation happens tonight as planned?"

Romano nodded slowly. "I'm still workin' on that."

"Can I see the flight plan your pilot put together while you're pondering the matter?"

"That's a roger. Follow me."

US Bank Tower, Los Angeles, California

Anna walked over to Donna's office and knocked discreetly on the open door. Donna glanced up from her computer. The look on her face was a mixture of confusion, concern, and anger.

"Hi Donna. Any word from Declan?"

Donna looked down at her computer screen again and answered in an incredulous tone. "Well, according to this email, which came in two minutes ago, he's in Brewster County, Texas."

"Texas? That must be a mistake. How could he—"

"Get there?" Donna said. "I don't know, but I can tell you he's there, for sure."

Anna walked forward, so she could get a look at the message. "How do you know that?"

"Because," Donna said, tapping the computer screen, "this message is an indemnification contract, and it's signed under the penalty of perjury. It says the contract was signed in Brewster County, Texas. Declan is very careful when he signs anything under the penalty of perjury, trust me. I've worked for him for almost a decade. If he says he's there under the penalty of perjury, he's there."

Suddenly Donna shot out of her chair, her hand covering her mouth. "I wasn't supposed to tell you that! Promise me you'll keep it a secret!"

Anna nodded without thinking. "Of course."

Donna shook her head and whispered to herself. "Damn, I am so mad at him! He used my email to send the message to this guy Romano. How in the hell did he get the username and password to my personal email?"

Anna could feel her heart rate accelerating. She typed Brewster County, Texas, into the map application on her phone. It was on the Mexican border. Frantic thoughts raced through her mind as Donna continued to talk in an increasingly irate tone in the background.

"He must have chartered a jet from LAX or Van Nuys, but why? What's in Brewster County? I wonder if a client set up some kind of surprise outing. It's happened before, but he should have called me from the airport, and he shouldn't have lied to me about being sick!"

Anna wanted to run back to her office and call Teo. *What if the operation was blown and Collins was on the run? But if that's the case why is he writing up an indemnity contract and what is the story with the helicopter?*

"Donna, is Declan a helicopter pilot?"

Donna pointed to a picture on the wall of her office. "Oh yeah."

Anna walked over to the picture. It took her a minute to recognize Collins in the helmet. He was sitting in the pilot seat of a helicopter hovering over a house that looked like it was in the middle of a lake. A woman holding a child was sitting on the roof.

"He's part of a volunteer pilots' organization. Whenever there's a hurricane or other disaster he gets a call. That picture was taken right after Hurricane Katrina."

"So he might just be down in Texas on a volunteer mission or possibly with a group of friends?"

Donna threw up her hands. "I don't know what he's doing down there. It doesn't make sense. The plan confirmation hearing in the PriceStar case is tomorrow morning. I guess . . . I guess he's not going to it. I thought he was. I've been calling him to find out just what the hell is going on, but he's not picking up, or his phone is off."

Anna turned toward the door and spoke over her shoulder. "He may be out of cell range. I'm sure he'll call when he can. By the way, what was the name of the party he indemnified?"

Donna looked at the email. "Silver Lake, LLC. Why?"

Anna tried to sound nonchalant. "Just curious. Must be a local outfit that leases helicopters. By the way, I'm running downstairs to get something for lunch—can I get you anything?"

Donna shook her head. "No, I'm good, thanks."

Anna walked to the elevator and waited impatiently for the door to open. She glanced down at the screen on her cell phone and stared at the map of Brewster County. *What is Collins doing there?*

As soon as she reached the lobby, she found an empty corner and called Teo. He answered on the first ring.

"What's up?"

"We may have a problem."

Intercontinental Hotel, Los Angeles, California

Gregorio looked down at the fifty-plus-page spreadsheet on his computer. The report detailed the results of PriceStar's going-out-of-business sale. The six-week event had doubled topline store revenue, but the actual profit from the sale was modest. After the payment of all related sales costs and the agreed-upon dividend to unsecured creditors, the drug lord would recover thirty-eight million of the funds used to acquire the B of A loan and most of the legal fees he left on the table for the lawyers, but very little above that.

Anyone looking at the results would conclude he'd made a bad investment, but no one other than Gregorio, Sanchez, and Cayetano would ever see it. PriceStar's books and records and tax returns would show a 95-million-dollar bogus profit, net of costs from the sale—a profit solely attributable to the bags of drug money added to the daily store pickups. That cash was now clean, legit, and ready for use in the American economy.

Gregorio stood up and walked across the hotel suite to the floor-to-ceiling window and stared out at the city below.

"Well, Declan Collins," Gregorio said in a whisper, "it seems you and I have served our foul master quite ably in this venture. Now, all we have to do is survive. I wish you Godspeed in the next three days. You will need it."

The loud knock on the door to the suite startled Gregorio. He wasn't expecting anyone, and the only people who knew about the hotel room were Sanchez and Nacio. For a moment, he considered ignoring it but rejected the thought. Sanchez didn't have a key to the room, but Nacio did. If he was at the door, delaying his entry would only create suspicion.

Gregorio walked over and opened the door. Nacio and Hector, one of Cayetano's lower-tier soldiers, were standing there. For a moment, Gregory was almost amused by the striking contrast between the two men. Nacio was slim, debonair, and attired in a perfectly tailored suit. Hector, in contrast, looked like a bald, tattooed bull stuffed into a blue blazer purchased from a bargain basement store.

Gregorio stepped aside and waved the two men into the room. "Nacio? To what do I owe the pleasure?"

Nacio walked past Gregorio followed by Hector. His typical charming but feigned smile was missing.

"Where is Sanchez? We must talk."

Gregorio pulled the phone from his pocket and speed-dialed Sanchez. "Alex, please come to my room. Nacio is here."

Alex knocked on the door a minute later, but the silent interval seemed to last forever.

As soon as the door closed, Nacio spoke in a cold voice. "Collins and Esposito are missing."

Sanchez made the mistake of asking the obvious question. "Missing? Have you called his cell?"

Nacio stared at Sanchez, his cold black eyes conveying a quiet threat. "Do you think me a fool?"

Sanchez was frozen in fear. Gregorio answered Nacio's question. "No, of course he doesn't. I'm sure your team called their cell phones multiple times, Nacio, and, I assume, checked their home and office locations. That's why you are here."

Nacio nodded. "We did. His car is still in the parking garage, yet the idiot receptionist in his office says he's not there."

"I'm sure he's at court or in—"

"I am not," Nacio said coldly. "Why? Because Esposito is missing too, and his office also does not know where he is."

"What is it you would have us do?"

Nacio pointed at the table. "You will put your phone on that table and call his office, on the speakerphone. You will demand an urgent meeting. If they say he is unavailable, you will find out where he is."

Gregorio took the phone from his suit pocket and flipped through his contacts.

"Alex will call Collins's paralegal, Anna, on her direct line. We have worked with her. If she knows where he is, she will tell us, unless . . . unless she does not know."

Gregorio walked over to the table, dialed the number, and set the phone down. Nacio walked to the other side of the table. Anna picked up on the third ring.

"Anna, hello; this is Alex Sanchez and my business partner, Gregorio Pena. How are you today?"

"Very good, and you?"

Gregorio sensed a hint of restraint in Anna's voice. Gregorio glanced over at Sanchez's shaking hand and decided to take over the call.

"This is Gregorio, Ms. Fallon; we are both quite well. However, Alex and I must meet with Mr. Collins immediately. We cannot wait until five o'clock."

"I'm sorry, Gregorio. I'd like to help, but I don't know where he is. I haven't been able to reach him on his cell."

Gregorio placed his hands on the table and leaned closer to the phone. "Anna, I know there are times when . . . when you might, how shall we say, deflect a client because Mr. Collins does not want to be disturbed, but this is not such a time. We could lose millions of dollars . . . and possibly more . . . if we cannot contact him."

The phone was silent for a moment. Then Anna responded, "Gregorio, this is what I know. He came into the office this morning, but then he left to go to the doctor. We haven't been able to reach him since he left."

Gregorio looked over at Nacio, who was staring at the phone as if he intended to crush it under the heel of his shoe. He waved his hand curtly and turned away.

"Thank you, Anna," Gregorio said apologetically. "Please, please have him call Alex if he calls you. It is a matter of great urgency."

"I will, Gregorio. I will."

"Good day, Anna," Gregorio said and ended the call without waiting for her response.

Nacio was facing away from him when he looked over.

"Nacio, I don't know anyone else who—"

"I do," Nacio said with a cold smile as he turned and walked to the door. "And I am sure he will be very cooperative."

Gregorio swallowed heavily as soon as the door closed with a heavy thud behind the two men.

"What is going on?" Sanchez gasped in a whisper.

"It seems Mr. Collins has gone missing."

"What does that have to do with us? Do you think—"

Gregorio raised a finger to his lips and pointed to the door.

"Let's go to dinner, Alex. We have to discuss what we're going to do after tomorrow's hearing."

Presidio, Texas

Gabe Mattson waved to the US Customs and Border Protection officer from the passenger seat of the tractor-trailer truck as it crossed into Mexico. The officer nodded. A glance in the mirror confirmed the second tractor trailer was right behind him. The guards on the Mexican side of the border waved the trucks through. Two blocks from the border, a black SUV was waiting on a narrow side street. The driver of the tractor trailer, Tom O'Neill, a former Marine gunnery sergeant who'd worked with Mattson as a CIA contractor, waved, and the SUV pulled into the lead.

Mattson pointed to a small cantina by the side of the road. "Whaddya say we stop in there for a beer and chow on the way back, Gunny? Doesn't look half bad."

O'Neill looked skeptically at the worn exterior and dirty

windows. "I'll drink anywhere you want when this op is over, but I gotta tell ya, Chief, I think we're ridin' into a major shitstorm. Comm says there may be as many as fifty truckloads full of Nauyacas headed toward that compound, and these folks are totally armed up. They're not gonna be too impressed by ten dudes pulling up in an SUV and two old tractor trailers. And . . . well, I have to tell ya, those guys in the back of the truck seem like techs, not real soldiers. They'd better have something real special under that tarp. Otherwise, we might not be coming back."

Mattson chuckled. "Relax, Gunny. Those gents know business. As for firepower, trust me, even Tommy O'Neill is gonna be impressed."

O'Neill glanced over at Mattson. "Don't underestimate the Nauyacas, Gabe. They're bad to the bone, and they'll be armed up with AKs, Uzis, and maybe a few grenade launchers. Tell me we're gonna have some air assets in this fight."

Mattson shook his head. "Not a one. This op has to have a real small and plausibly deniable footprint. So it's ground assets and bullets only."

O'Neill took one hand off the wheel and made the sign of the cross.

"I knew I should have gone to confession before we left."

"Damn good thing you didn't," Mattson said with a chuckle. "That would have taken at least three days. Hell, I would have had to find another driver."

O'Neill smiled despite his anxiety.

Mattson smiled. "Relax. Old Gabe will keep you among the living."

"Yeah, but missing an arm or a leg, eh?"

Mattson smiled. "Have—"

Mattson's cell phone chimed. He glanced at the number on the screen and put the phone to his ear.

"Cedric, tell me, has Mr. Romano gone home now that we have his band of merry men locked up?"

"Not quite. In fact, I think he's bringing in some reinforcements."

Mattson sat up straighter. "You're shitting me, right?"

"I just got word from my contact at the ranch. Three guys dressed in military gear landed three hours ago in a private plane and met Romano at the airstrip."

"What? Three or four hours ago! Why—"

"Gabe, our contact is one of the hunting guides. The guy's out in the field most of the day. He only learned about it when he got back from the hunt."

Mattson clenched his right fist in frustration. "What the hell is the FBI agent in Terlingua doing about it?"

"Sitting in his motel, I suspect. Do you want me to contact him? His name's Dan Phelps. He's a newbie."

"No, no, we don't want the FBI getting wind of this op. Let me deal with it. Keep me up-to-date!"

"That's what I've—"

Mattson terminated the call and dialed Calder. "Hey, bro, I need you to contact the FBI through an untraceable line and leave an urgent message for one Agent Dan Phelps. Got a pen?"

"No, but I got a keyboard. Shoot."

"Tell Agent Phelps that Romano has found himself a new pilot and two new soldiers. So he'd better get his butt over to Terlingua Ranch with a search-and-seizure warrant ASAP."

"One anonymous message coming up."

United States Attorney's Office, Los Angeles, California

Anna was surprised when Teo told her to meet him at Carlton's office on Spring Street. Walking into the United States Attorney's Office when you're working undercover five blocks away is not a smart move, but Carlton had insisted.

The receptionist led her back to a conference room on the far end of the floor as soon as she arrived. Teo was already there. Before she could say a word, Carlton entered the room through a second door. His eyes locked on Anna, and he spoke in a voice laden with threat. "Where, Agent Torres, is Declan Collins?"

"We believe he's in Terlingua, Texas, a small town—"

"On the Mexican border," Carlton interrupted acidly. "How is it that you didn't know the target was on the run until an hour ago—getting from LAX to that shithole in Texas is a daylong trip!"

Anna met Carlton's accusatory gaze without blinking. "He walked out of the office to get a cup of coffee and instead drove to LAX and took a private jet from LAX to Midland. From there, he took a plane to Terlingua. It was a four-hour trip, door-to-door, not all day."

Carlton dramatically stretched out his arms. "Why didn't we know he was on the move? We have a tracker on his car."

"Because he didn't take his car," Teo interjected curtly.

"Then he's on the run. No question! Someone blew the op. Why, I can just see it now. My perp is drinking margaritas at some fancy resort in Mexico chuckling about how incompetent we are. That's just—"

Teo jumped out of his seat. "We didn't blow anything."

"He's not on the run," Anna said quietly.

Carlton wheeled on her. "And how, Agent Torres, do you know that?"

"There are more than five flights a day from LAX to Mexico and Canada. If he wanted to run, he could have taken any one of them, or a flight to anyplace outside the country, for that matter. For some reason, he wanted to get to Terlingua, and he wanted to get there fast."

Carlton stared at her for a moment. "Okay, then tell me why Collins is so hell-bent on getting to a crap hole on the Mexican border?"

"I . . . I don't know for sure. What I do know is he and Matt Esposito are both there. And—"

Carlton exploded. "They're both there?"

Anna ignored the interruption. "And they both signed declarations under the penalty of perjury there today, pledging almost every penny they both have to an outfit called Silver Lake, LLC, if Collins crashed a Bell 407 helicopter."

Carlton's eyes widened. "A helicopter! Who or what is Silver Lake? Is he training to be a pilot?"

She shook her head. "A friend of mine in the intelligence branch is looking into Silver Lake, and no, he's not taking lessons. Collins is a trained pilot."

"Maybe it's some kind of specialized training course," Teo said in a tone that suggested he didn't believe it.

Anna walked over to the window and stared down at the traffic on the Hollywood Freeway and shook her head. "No, there's something else going on here . . . under the surface. Something we're not seeing."

Her cell phone rang, and she looked down at the screen. "It's my friend in intelligence."

Carlton tapped the table. "Put it on speaker."

Anna accepted the call and tapped the speaker button. "Patty, it's Anna. I'm here with Assistant US Attorney Carlton and Agent Ortega. Sorry to put you on the spot. Did you find anything?"

"My pleasure, Anna, and yes, I did. The Bureau has a file on Silver Lake. There are several entities in the corporate ownership chain, but at the bottom of that chain is a guy called Dante Romano. He's an ex–special ops soldier. In the past, he's done work for the Pentagon in Somalia, Iraq, Afghanistan, you name it. But, based upon the little you told me, I think what you want to know about is his private operation."

"This is Assistant US Attorney Carlton. What do you mean, private operation?"

Anna could sense the irritation in Patty's tone.

"He rescues people in bad situations—intel assets, hostages, prisoners, that kind of thing," Teo said.

Patty chimed in. "Yeah, but with deadly force."

Carlton leaned back in his seat and waved dismissively at the phone. "We have what we need."

Anna picked up the phone and turned off the speaker. "Thanks much, Patty. I owe you one."

"Anytime, and good luck with Carlton. What a peach."

Anna smiled as she hung up. She was surprised at the scornful smile on Carlton's face.

"I've seen it a hundred times before. Another rich lawyer playing GI Joe. Planes, jets, parachutes, guns, you name it—just a pathetic effort to grow a pair. Don't worry. He'll be back in a day or two with a hangover and a flash drive full of pictures to show friends and family."

Anna shook her head. "Mr. Carlton, I think we're missing—"

Carlton waved away her response with a brush of his hand as he stood up. "Stay on the target when he gets back, Agent Torres. And the next time he decides to do something stupid, tell me in advance."

Anna was thankful Teo didn't react to the insult until Carlton left the room. "That arrogant shit! He needs to grow a pair, and a brain as well."

"I won't comment on that one," she said as she glanced at the time on her phone. "I have to get back to the office, Teo."

He nodded and followed her out the door. When they reached the reception area, he pointed to the elevators.

"I have to go upstairs and see someone on another case. Let me know ASAP when you hear from Collins."

"Got it."

When Anna got back to the office, she noticed Donna going through the mail on Collins's desk and walked in to see her. "Any news from Declan?"

Donna turned. "No. I suspect he's too busy crashing helicopters to talk to the rest of us common folk."

Anna laughed, and Donna joined her. As she turned to leave Donna's office, Anna noticed a picture on the wall of the office. It was partially hidden by the door. She moved the door and stared at the picture. It was Collins, Esposito, and a young blonde woman wearing a Westmont College T-shirt.

"Who's the college girl?"

Donna looked over. "Matt Esposito's little sister. She worked here one summer. Nice gal. I think she's in Mexico this semester. One of those Christian mission trips."

Anna froze in midstep. "What's her name?"

"Sienna Esposito."

"Was it a school trip or did she go with one of those charities? I . . . I always wanted to do something like that."

"It was set up by the school, Westmont College. She's working with a Doctors Without Borders unit."

"Thanks," Anna said as she turned and walked back to her office and closed the door.

She pulled up Westmont College's phone number and dialed it on her cell phone. "Good afternoon, this is Special Agent Anna Torres with the FBI. I need to speak with someone about one your students, Sienna Esposito."

Terlingua, Texas

Collins stared at the flight plan and the pictures of the landing zone laid out on the crude wooden table in the rear of the hangar. The flight plan was complicated. He had to fly across the border through what Romano said was a small hole in the US radar system. Most of the flight would be nap-of-the-earth to minimize the helicopter's radar signature. The dicey part would be the approach to Cayetano's compound in Mexico.

The plan was to fly along the far side of the range of hills just north of the compound, right on the deck, and then land behind a hill about a mile and half from the target. From there, they would hike, under the cover of darkness, to within fifty yards of the point where Sienna was expected to come over the compound wall.

When Collins looked up from the flight plan, Romano was standing five yards away staring at him.

"I called your flight references, counselor. All of your flyboy buddies tell me you're an ace pilot. That gives me half the enchilada."

Then he turned and pointed at Matt and Tony.

"Now, tell me why I should take a risk on the ground with these two as my backup?"

Tony waved off Romano's concern with brush of his hand. "Listen, paisan, I was in the Marines, remember? I know how to shoot—"

Romano cut him off. "Don't give me that paisan shit, Tony. You were in the Marines for four years twenty years ago. Since then, you've been running fancy clubs and chasing tail. As for your friend there, he's never served a day, and his weapon of choice is a cell phone. The HK417s in the back of that bird—the weapons you'll be carrying if we make this run—have twenty-round mags. If he or you get antsy and pull that trigger by mistake, I'm dead, or worse, I'm half dead, and the bad guys will cut off my balls with a rusty knife. That's not gonna happen. So here's what we're gonna do: You and Esposito have one hour to prove to me you know you can use those weapons, and more important, that you know how to follow orders, capisce?"

For a moment Collins thought Tony was going to push back, but he was wrong. He just nodded and responded in a reserved tone: "Got it."

"Good. Follow me."

Romano walked over to the helicopter, opened the second door on the pilot's side, and pulled out two deadly looking assault rifles. He handed one to Matt and the second to Tony. Then he handed each man a magazine.

"You do not load these mags until I say, clear?"

Matt and Tony nodded quickly. "Clear."

Collins started toward Romano, expecting to be handed a third weapon.

Romano held up a hand. "You're staying with the chopper. You'll provide comm support and overwatch with the M24."

"What if—"

"The rest of us get taken out? Then the girl's dead, and you fly home. Real simple."

Romano turned and walked toward the far end of the hangar followed by Matt and Tony. Collins could tell both men were shaken by Romano's comment. He was as well.

The manic pace of the last seven hours had kept his mind away from the reality of what they were about to do, but Romano's harsh admonition brought it all home. If everything went as planned, they'd be back in a couple of hours alive and well. If not, there was a good chance some or all of them would die.

Los Angeles, California

Anna dodged between two women blocking the sidewalk outside the US Bank Tower and jogged down the street to where Teo was waiting in a black suburban.

"Take the 101 north and get off at Sunset."

Teo nodded and pulled the SUV into the traffic flow. "Okay, what's going on, and where are we going?"

"The Arezzo. It's a club on the corner of Sunset and Cahuenga."

Teo raised a skeptical eyebrow. "A nightclub?"

Anna nodded. "That's it."

Teo pulled the SUV away from the curb and started down the street toward the freeway. "And why are we going—"

"Collins is not playing GI Joe in Texas. I think it's the real thing. Matt Esposito's sister, Sienna, is being held hostage in Mexico, and Collins and Esposito are preparing to fly across the border with this merc, Romano, and his team to get her out. And I think it's happening tonight!"

"What!"

Teo's tone was incredulous, but he hit the accelerator, rocketed past a cab moseying down the street looking for fares, and roared up the on-ramp to the 101.

Anna grabbed the handgrip above the door to steady herself. "I know it sounds crazy, but it all fits. Sienna Esposito, Matt's sister, was on a mission trip with a Doctors Without Borders unit. The unit was providing medical services in a remote area of Chiapas, Mexico. A week before she was supposed to leave, a helicopter flew to the site and picked her up. According to one of the nurses who was on-site, someone from the Mexican government called and said her brother, Matt, had been in a serious auto accident, and Declan Collins had hired a helicopter to bring her to the nearest airport so she could get back quick."

"Okay," Teo said skeptically.

"Teo, I put a call into Homeland Security, and they have no record of Sienna passing through customs on the way back into the country. I called the college. They said she never uploaded the term paper describing her mission trip, and it was due over a month ago."

Teo weaved past two trucks slowing down traffic ahead and jammed down the accelerator. He glanced over at her. "There's been no communication from the kid? None at all?"

"From Sienna, no. However, Matt Esposito did call. In fact, he called quite a few people and told them the same story: Sienna got sick in Mexico and was taking some time off."

Teo shook his head. "Anna, that's thin. If I take it to Carlton after today's session, it's not going to play well. No, let me say it differently: It's going to crash and burn. And why would someone take all this effort to grab this girl Sienna? What's the point?"

Anna grabbed the handhold above the door again as Teo zigzagged over to the Sunset Boulevard off-ramp.

"She's the leverage! Collins and Esposito are putting together the money laundering deal because they have no choice."

Teo glanced over at her, a skeptical look on this face. "So you say. Carlton is going to crap all over that without corroboration."

"That," said Anna, as she pointed at the neon blue "Arrezzo" sign affixed to the side of a square modern building, "is why we're here. Donna told me Tony Lentino, the owner of this place, was one of Collins's closest friends. She also told me Collins visited his club this week twice."

Teo pulled into the circular drive and parked in front of the empty valet stand. "Let's see what Mr. Lentino has to say."

The bouncer standing at the front door strode toward them, pointing at the car. "You can't park—"

Teo held up his badge. "Yes, I can. We're looking for Tony Lentino."

The bouncer stopped in his tracks. "Tony's not here."

"Where is he?"

The bouncer shrugged his shoulders. "Don't know."

Teo stepped to within a foot of the man and spoke in a tone that carried a threat. "Who would know?"

When the man hesitated, Teo held his cell phone up to the man's face as if it were a weapon. "You get me to someone who knows where Lentino is now, or I get a warrant and ransack this place from top to bottom."

The man pointed toward the front door. "Okay, okay. You can talk to Debbie. She's in the back. Use the door on the right that says 'Employees Only.'"

As Teo and Anna walked through the front entrance, the bouncer called after them. "You're gonna have to wait in line. Some guy from the IRS is already back there. He's looking for Tony as well."

Anna slowed when she heard the comment and glanced back at the bouncer, but he'd walked out of sight. When she turned around, Teo was five yards ahead of her striding through the open door. As she quickened her step to catch up, she brushed back the right side of her gray blazer and rested her hand on the Glock 19 on her hip.

Teo was already halfway down the corridor walking toward the partially open door at the end. Anna could just see the man in the office over Teo's shoulder. As the man turned his head in their direction, she recognized him and instinctively reached for the Glock. It was the man in the white suit from the restaurant.

"Teo, stop!"

Teo froze and grabbed for his service weapon. The man at the end of the hall was faster. He wheeled and fired without hesitation. As Anna returned fire, she heard Teo grunt in pain and stumble backward as he frantically tried to sight his weapon on the man. The man kicked the door closed. Anna ceased firing and walked forward in a crouch, her gun pointing at door. She whispered to Teo. "Are you hit?"

Teo nodded and gasped. "Yeah . . . but . . . I'm good. He hit the vest. Stay behind me and provide cover. We're going through that door."

When Teo's heavy boot slammed open the office door, Anna expected a fusillade of bullets, but there was no movement in the room. The only occupant was a middle-aged blonde woman bound to an office chair by thick gray tape. A piece of tape also covered her mouth.

Teo nodded at the door in the rear of the room. "We go after the shooter and come back for her."

Teo pushed the door open with his foot. It led to a small parking lot behind the building. It was empty. He glanced to the right and left of the door and walked into the lot. The shooter was gone.

He gestured to the office. "I'll call this in and get an ambo. See if the woman can talk. I want this guy."

Anna glanced at the three holes in Teo's shirt. They were all dead center and just inches apart.

She nodded and walked back into the office. The woman was staring at her through wide, terrified eyes. Anna holstered her weapon and stepped toward her.

"I'm with the FBI, ma'am. An ambulance is on the way." She pulled off the tape, trying to be gentle as possible.

As soon as she was free, the woman reached for the water bottle on the desk and took a long drink. After choking for several moments, she turned to Anna, the terror in her eyes replaced with rage. "Did you get that bastard?"

"No, he got away, but we will find him. Can you tell me what he was after?"

"Debbie. My name is Debbie, and yeah, I can tell you what the jerk wanted. He wanted to know where Tony. . . Tony Lentino is. Tony's the boss. He said he would kill me if I didn't tell him!"

Anna heard Teo come in the door behind her. "What did you tell him?"

"I told him Tony was in some godawful place in Texas helping a friend, Declan Collins, with something or other. I told him I didn't know what it was, but it was something really serious and time was running out."

"How did the man react when you told him that?"

Debbie eyes widened, and she glanced from Anna to Teo and back again. "He went ballistic. He put his gun to my head and asked me exactly where Tony was in Texas. I told him it was a place called Terlingua. I had to tell him! He would have—"

"It's okay, Debbie." Anna rested a hand on the woman's shoulder. "You did the right thing."

"LAPD and the ambulance are here," Teo said. "They'll take care of you, ma'am."

He gestured for Anna to follow him out of the room. The two officers from LAPD nodded to them as they walked toward the office. He didn't say anything until they reached the SUV. Then he exploded.

"Do you really believe Collins and this other bozo are planning to pull some kind of paramilitary operation across the border?"

Anna turned to Teo. "That is exactly what I believe, and by the way, don't you think you should go to the hospital to get checked out?"

"I'm fine," he said curtly. "Tell me, how are they going to cross the border with the kind of firepower they're going to need?"

"In a helicopter. Collins is an ace pilot."

"Anna, I just don't buy—"

"Teo, Collins keeps a bust of Hannibal on the wall behind his desk. The quote on that bust says, 'We will find a way, or make a way.' Collins is going over the border with that merc and his private army. They intend to free Sienna Esposito from whoever is holding her down there."

Teo stared at Anna, and she met his stare, not giving an inch. After a long moment, he nodded. "I still don't buy it, but I can see you do, and then some. I'm gonna call the SAIC in San Antonio. He's a friend. I'll find out if he knows anything."

He stepped out of the SUV, closed the door, and dialed a number on his cell. Five minutes later, he got back into the vehicle and roared out onto Vine Street.

"Find Carlton. You were right. Collins and his pals just flew across the border. The shit's going hit the fan now."

———

Nacio punched the speed dial code on his phone as he raced away from the Arrezzo in the black Ferrari.

"This is Eduardo. How can I—"

"It's Nacio. Get me Cayetano."

"Mr. Nacio, he has guests—"

"Eduardo, if Mr. Cayetano is not on the phone in less than a minute, I will put a bullet in your head as soon as I return. Are we clear?"

Several moments passed, and then there was a click signaling the transfer of the call to Cayetano's secure line. When the drug lord came on the line, his voice was cold and reproving.

"What is it, Nacio?"

"You need to contact Matias at the compound."

"Why?"

"Collins is coming for the girl."

Cayetano's scornful laugh struck Nacio like a lash. "Coming? Nacio, the lawyer is in Los Angeles with you. He could never—"

"He's not here. He disappeared five hours ago. He hired a private jet out of LAX, and now he's in Terlingua, a border town in Texas. Terlingua is a one-hour helicopter flight to the compound, and Collins is a skilled helicopter pilot."

"What? This is absurd. How could he know where the compound is? And even if he did, he would never have the cojones to attack it. He's just a rodent who plays at being a man."

"Mr. Cayetano, what I know is that Collins is on the border, an hour away from the compound, the night before your big deal closes, and he may have hired men who are not mere rodents to help him with this rescue. Men who kill for a living, like me."

Nacio tried to keep the anger from his voice, but it came through in the last part of the exchange in full measure. There was a long hesitation, and then the drug lord spoke in a grudging tone. "Very well, I will call Matias. You can be assured *he* will not let the girl escape."

The rebuke stung. Nacio hung up without another word.

THIRTY-ONE

Terlingua, Texas

Collins eased the Bell 407 off the ground an hour after sunset, circled the ranch once while gaining altitude, and then headed south. He glanced over the instrument panel quickly, surprised by the muted noise made by the rotor blades. Romano, who was sitting in the seat to his left, noticed the look on his face.

"They're called blue-edged blades. Expensive, but they really cut down on the noise."

Romano pointed at a small caravan of cars racing down the road toward the ranch in the distance, led by a police car with flashing lights. "Speaking of noise, it looks like we got off the ground just in time."

"We'll have to find someplace else to land on the way back," Lentino said from the second seat.

"Got that covered," Romano said quietly. "Right now, let's just focus on getting there and back."

Collins glanced over his shoulder at Matt. "We'll get back. All of us."

Intercontinental Hotel, Los Angeles, California

Gregorio spoke in a somber voice as he stared out at the Los Angeles skyline, lit with a million lights.

"It is time, my old friend, for us to put our plan in play."

Sanchez, a step behind him, shuffled nervously. "We play a dangerous game, Gregorio. I fear Nacio will find out. He may already suspect—"

"Have faith, Alejandro. We have borne pain, ignominy, and the defilement of those we hold most dear. The good Lord will not deny us our vengeance or just recompense."

Gregorio drew his cell phone from his pocket. "As for Nacio, we are not his targets, at least not today. Nacio is a proud man, and he has been made a fool of. He will not rest until Declan Collins is dead."

Sanchez silently made the sign of the cross.

Maijoma, Mexico

Two miles out from the landing site, Collins pulled on the night vision goggles affixed to the top of his helmet and pointed to a dry riverbed, bordered on both sides by steep banks.

"That's our pathway in according to the flight plan."

Romano, who was also wearing goggles, nodded. "Roger that. Let's see if you can fly this bird ten feet above that arroyo without getting us killed, counselor."

Collins flew the chopper into the center of the arroyo and weaved along its length until they were a quarter mile from the site marked by the GPS coordinates as the landing zone.

Romano pointed ahead. "I recognize the topography. The LZ is just ahead. Slow it down and ease up the side of the hill. We can't overshoot. That hill ends about four hundred yards past the LZ."

Collins eased the chopper out of the arroyo and along the base of the hill until he spotted a narrow strip of flat ground ahead. He lowered the chopper until he felt the skids touch the ground in the blackness below. He eased off on the power, and the chopper came to rest. Romano was out the door before the blades stopped spinning, the stock of the HK pressed against his right shoulder, the business end pointing at the ridge of the hill off to the right.

———

Mattson watched the line of pickup trucks and SUVs from a rise about two miles to the north. The convoy was traveling east on the dirt road toward the Cayetano compound. None of the vehicles had their lights on despite the darkness. He lowered his binoculars and glanced over at O'Neill. The ex-Marine was four yards away, watching the column through the night vision scope atop his M-107 sniper rifle.

"I count forty-two vehicles. Seven, maybe eight, have light machine guns in the back. What's your read on those, Gunny, M240s?"

"Yeah, maybe an M249 as well. I can't tell with all the dust they're kicking up. If they get a chance to unleash those bad boys on us, we're gonna be in a world of hurt. Six hundred rounds a minute times eight. My fifth-grade brain tells me that's—"

"Not going to happen," Mattson said as he eased back from the crest of the hill. What's that you Catholics are always saying? 'Have faith.'"

As O'Neill followed Mattson back down the hill, he said wryly, "That's in God, not Gabe Mattson."

Mattson chuckled. "Trust me, Gunny, six hundred rounds a minute is just not going to cut it in this dustup. Now let's get downtown so we don't miss this soiree."

Mattson pointed to the black SUV. "You're with Sully. Get to the overwatch position and provide cover until we start in on these folks. Don't worry. You won't be there long. Once those boys in the back pull the trigger, it'll be game over in less than five minutes."

O'Neill shook his head skeptically. "If you say so."

Mattson climbed into the driver's seat of the truck and chuckled as he watched O'Neill get into the SUV. "Trust me, old son, we're going to bring a rain of steel down on these folks like you've never seen."

———

Collins climbed out of the cockpit, eased the door closed, and walked around to the other side. Romano was already making his way up to the crest of the hill, his HK at the ready. Matt and Tony followed in his wake, HKs pointed at the ground. Romano had made it clear the fire selectors on their weapons were to remain in the safe position until he ordered otherwise, and they were not to fire unless he gave an explicit command. Collins had been instructed to stay with the chopper until directed otherwise.

As Romano closed to within ten yards of the crest, he raised his right fist, and Matt and Tony froze in place. Romano dropped to his knees three yards from the top and scrambled the remaining distance on his hands and knees. After scanning the area below for what seemed like an interminable period, Romano waved Matt and Tony forward. He also pointed down the hill at Collins and waved him forward as well.

As he approached the crest of the hill, Collins dropped into a crouch and eased up on Romano's right. Matt and Tony were on his left. He could see a dimly lit cluster of buildings surrounded by a crude wooden wall, about seven or eight hundred yards away. The compound was situated on a broad sandy plain covered with low brush, intermittent clusters of boulders, and an occasional tree. Collins suspected he was looking at what had been a flood plain at some point in the past.

The dirt road visible on the west side of the compound appeared to be the only way in or out. Collins knew from the maps he'd memorized that the road intersected Route 67, the main road running north to the United States, about eight miles to the west.

Romano pointed to the end of the wall facing them with the satellite antenna on top of it. "If Sienna follows the plan, she'll come over the wall to the left of that satellite dish in about an hour."

Then he turned to Matt and Tony and pointed down the gentle slope of the rocky hill in front of him. "We're going down that hill, moving from cover to cover. Follow my lead. Once we get to the valley floor, we'll make our way over to that rock—the big one that looks like a giant loaf of bread. That's about fifty yards from the wall. When we see her coming over, I'll go get her. You two will provide cover if I need it. You will not fire unless I tell you to. If you have to fire, your objective is to keep the enemy's head down, no more. If some of those rounds find a home, so much the better, but what I want is suppressive fire on anyone trying to zero in on me and the girl. Clear?"

Matt and Tony responded as one: "Clear."

Romano nodded and glanced over at Collins. "You've got the big picture from up here, Collins. Your job is to let us know about what we can't or don't see. There's an M24 sniper rifle in the back of the chopper. Bring that up here, and I'll set it up. That wall is about eight hundred yards out. Unless you're a better shot than I think you are, all you can do is distract the bad guys if things get desperate, but that may be enough.

"I'll adjust the MOA on the scope. If you have to adjust it again after you've taken a shot, it's a quarter MOA for each click. You do not shoot unless I give the order. Clear?"

Collins nodded. "Clear."

Romano returned his nod. "Then let's get this done and get our butts back home in one piece."

Twenty minutes later, Romano, Matt, and Tony reached the bottom of the hill undetected and halted for a moment. Romano's voice came over Collins's headset. "We're starting across the plain. Keep your eyes on that wall, *not on us.* You see movement, I want to know."

"Got it."

Chastened by the warning in Romano's voice, Collins trained the night vision binoculars he was holding on the wall of the compound and slowly swept the top. He could see figures moving around within the compound from his elevated position, but he didn't see anyone on the wall. After what seemed an eternity, Romano came back on the two-way.

"We're a hundred yards from the wall behind a giant rock. Find us."

Collins scanned the plain below and found the rock. He could see Tony and Matt crouching beside Romano at the base of a six-by-four-foot boulder. "I see you."

"Good. Tony and Matt will stay in this position and provide cover. I'm moving up to those two trees about forty yards from the wall."

"I see them."

"Good. Get your eyes back on the wall, and remember, every two minutes you sweep the whole northern perimeter."

"Got it."

Collins turned the binoculars back to the wall and continued to slowly sweep the section of the wall with line of sight on Romano, Matt, and Tony. Every two minutes he scanned the entirety of the compound from one end to the other. After completing the sweep and returning his focus on the nearest part of the wall, he hesitated for a moment, and then scanned the other end of the compound.

It took him a several moments to discern what he was looking at through the green night vision image, and then it hit him with a jolt: A long line of vehicles was approaching the compound from the west. None of the vehicles had their lights on despite the darkness. He adjusted the magnification dial on the binoculars and focused on the lead vehicle. It was a Ford pickup truck with four men in the back. One of the men was standing behind something that protruded over the cab of the truck. It looked like a machine gun.

Mesmerized, Collins stared at the column for several moments before sweeping the top of the wall again. There was no sign of movement.

Collins pressed the PTT button on his headset. "Romano, a line of trucks is approaching on the road from the west. They're filled with armed men."

Romano was silent for a moment. "It must be transport for an outgoing shipment. The distraction may work to our advantage."

"Most of the trucks are pickups, and some of them have light machine-gun setups in the back. Also, none of the vehicles have their lights on."

There was another silence. "Keep your eyes on the wall. Romano out."

Collins nodded and scanned the vista below looking for movement. The approaching column bothered him.

Maijoma, Mexico

Sienna dropped to one knee and scratched another line on the dusty concrete floor in front of her bed. There were eighteen lines in all, each one marking the passage of ten minutes. She'd begun counting as soon as the gas generator in the front of the building roared to life, signaling the onset of darkness. If her count was correct, her rescuers were waiting on the other side of the compound wall. She glanced around the room that had been her prison for over three months, drew in a breath, and exhaled slowly. It was time to make her escape.

She walked over to the pipe running up the wall in the corner and put her foot on the bolt that served as the first foothold. The sound of a key being inserted into the door behind her froze her in place. For a moment, she considered trying to scramble up the pipe before the door was open, but she knew there wasn't enough time. She stepped away from the pipe and walked to the middle of the room. A moment later, Juan entered. His tone was curt. "Come, Matias wants to see you."

For a moment, the words wouldn't come, but she forced them out, placing a hand on her stomach. "I'm feeling sick . . . *enferma*. Can I meet him in the morning?"

"No. Matias says now. I take you to a new place at the other end."

The words lanced through Sienna like an invisible sword forged from ice.

She stood up and walked toward the open door, her mind racing through the options. *Should I go with Juan and risk being trapped in new quarters or run for the wall as soon as we are outside? Can I scale the wall and get over the top before one of the guards shoots me?*

As she approached the door that led to the dirt path between the buildings, she steeled herself for a sprint to the northeast corner of the wall, fifty yards away. Then she noticed the two guards waiting just outside the door. They were Matias's men, and unlike Juan, who was unarmed, they were carrying AK-47s. Sienna had written a paper on the ubiquitous weapon a year earlier for a history class. She knew there was no chance she would survive a dash to the wall with those guns pointed in her direction.

She followed Juan down a dirt path toward the large warehouse at the southeast end of the compound—the direction the screams came from late at night. She knew the path intersected with the main dirt road bisecting the compound, running from east to west. Thirty yards ahead, she could see a man standing in the middle of the road smoking a cigarette. She couldn't see his face, but she knew it was Matias. With each step she became more frantic, knowing it was unlikely she would ever be able to get over the wall to rendezvous with Collins and Matt unless she could break away now.

A tear of frustration slid down her right cheek. As she reached up to brush it away, Sienna heard male voices scream, "*Ataque!*" over and over again. She glanced in the direction of the scream and heard a loud rapid-fire cacophony coming from the other side of the wall. Sienna had heard automatic weapons fire once before, when she was at a gun range with Matt outside Las Vegas. She recognized the terrifying sound immediately. As she stared at the rough-hewn watchtower on the western edge of the wall, it was riddled with bullets, and one of guards fell backward into the compound, screaming in pain.

Matias stared at the wall for a moment, incredulous, before turning and bellowing orders to the men standing behind Juan with the AK-47s.

"Jose, Miguel, to the wall. We're being attacked! Juan, lock the girl in the toolshed and get to the wall. Now!"

The armed men behind her sprinted toward the wall, and Matias ran into the building on his left with a large antenna on the roof. Juan grabbed Sienna's arm and began to pull her toward a small building with no windows on the right side of the road. After being pulled along for three strides, Sienna pulled up short and covered her mouth as though she was about to vomit. "*Enferma!*"

Then she dropped to her knees and pantomimed retching and surreptitiously grabbed a handful of dirt. When she stood up in response to Juan's impatient yank, she threw the dirt in his eyes, shook off his grip, and sprinted down the road toward the northeast corner of the compound. As she raced past the nearest building, she could hear Juan coughing behind her. A moment later, she heard Matias's voice scream in rage.

A year earlier, Sienna had set the school record at Westmont College in the sixty-meter sprint. As she raced toward the wall in the distance, she knew she was running faster than she had on that day.

———

As Collins swept the length of the wall again with the binoculars, a guard appeared in the wooden guard post located on the western end of the north wall. The guard pulled out a cigarette, lit it, and took a leisurely draw before scanning the ground outside the compound. At first, the guard stared at the approaching column of trucks in silence, as if it was expected, and then he roared out a warning. The lead truck in the approaching column reacted to the warning by pouring fire into the guard post. A moment later, the entire column began enfilading the walls of the compound with automatic weapons fire.

Collins tapped his PTT. "Romano, that column I told you about is attacking the compound! This is some kind of coordinated assault."

"Roger that. Keep an eye out for the girl. The attackers are not our problem . . . at least not yet."

As Collins swept the compound again, he caught a glimpse of a figure racing through the compound—a figure with long hair. When the figure disappeared behind a building, he focused his binoculars on the next point where the runner would be visible, a point dimly lit by a stream of light coming from a nearby building. When the woman ran through the light, Collins recognized her. It was Sienna. Collins spoke into the headset.

"Romano, she's coming your way on the run!"

Collins scanned the area behind Sienna and saw three men running after her.

"She's being pursued, I—"

Romano cut him off. "What's her ETA to the wall, and how many guys are on her tail?"

Collins scanned the distance to the wall and walked the scope backward. He saw Sienna flash by another opening.

"Ten seconds, and there are three men forty yards—"

Collins heard Matt interrupt the exchange. "We gotta get in there!"

Romano shut him down. "Button it, Esposito. Stay in your position. Collins, get on the M24 and wait for my order."

Collins scrambled over to the M24, dropped into a prone position and put the stock up against his shoulder. He scanned the inside of the compound through the scope until he found Sienna. She flashed by another gap in the buildings and then ran parallel to the wall for ten yards before leaping for a handhold. She had already reached the top of the wall by the time the first pursuer arrived. The man was running so fast he slammed into the wall. The impact shook the wall, and Sienna lost one of her footholds. For a moment, she just hung there, desperately trying to find another foothold. A second later, another man ran up to the wall.

He put the scope's crosshairs on the second man when he pulled a gun from his waistband and pointed it at Sienna. He exhaled slowly and pulled the trigger before inhaling. The bullet hit the ground three feet behind the man, kicking up a puff of dust. The man wheeled around in confusion. Collins pulled the bolt back, cycled in another round, adjusted his aim, and fired a second shot. This time the bullet found its mark, punching through the man's upper body.

He scanned the area for the second man, but he'd taken cover behind one of the buildings. When he scanned the wall looking for Sienna, she was nowhere in sight.

Romano came over his headset. "She's over the wall. I'm going to get her. Collins, talk to me! Tell me about the shooters on the wall."

Tony responded to Romano's inquiry. "There are five shooters in the guard tower in the middle of the north wall, and more are coming. They're in a gunfight with the new guys, but once you come out into the open, they'll have a clear line of sight on you."

As Tony was speaking, Matt stood up and yelled to Sienna. "Sienna, it's Matt. We're coming to get you!"

Two of the men in the guardhouse on the north wall reacted immediately, pouring fire in the direction of Matt's voice. The bullets raked through the brush and trees in the area and skipped off the top of the boulder where they were hiding.

Romano, who was forty yards away from Sienna, roared at her: "Stay there until I tell you to move!"

Collins tapped the PTT on his mic. "Romano, she's safe there. The shooters in the guardhouse don't have a shot until she moves away from the wall toward you, but she can't stay there. They're bringing a ladder up to the wall on the inside. I may be able to fly the chopper around the east side and pick her—"

"You won't make it," Romano said. "There are too many shooters, they're too close, and there's no time. No, we provide covering fire when she makes the run. It's dark, they're not pros, and they're in a fight with the new guys. She'll make it. On my order, everyone provide covering fire."

Collins stared at the open stretch of ground, visualizing Sienna falling, riddled with bullets. He watched Romano calling out to Sienna, and he could see her nod.

Romano's voice came over the mic. "On my mark. One, two—"

Collins tapped the PTT button on his headset. "Wait!"

"Collins," Romano growled, "every second we wait brings more shooters to the wall! Don't you see—"

"I do see, Romano, but I also see something else. Five trucks full of bad guys are coming along the north wall to take on the shooters in the guard tower."

The men in the guardhouse on the north wall turned their attention to the approaching line of trucks and a separate firefight exploded.

"Romano, do it now!"

Collins watched Romano run forward at a crouch and reach Sienna's position without drawing any fire. A moment later, the two of them started back across the forty-yard stretch.

Romano roared into the mic, "Covering fire!"

Matt and Tony rose as one and fired at the guard post on the north wall on full auto. The men in the guardhouse dodged behind the wooden wall, now taking fire from two directions.

Collins lined the sights of the M24 up on the guardhouse, waiting for a head to appear, but then he remembered the second man who'd been chasing Sienna, and scanned the top of the wall further to the east. The second man was on the top of the wall pointing his gun in Romano and Sienna's direction. Collins fired a round without hesitation, knowing it would be off the mark. The bullet struck the wall two feet below the man's position, and he flinched but got off a shot. Collins's next round hit the man in the neck, and he fell back into the compound.

Collins scanned the ground below, fearing either Romano or Sienna would be down. The open area between the wall and the spot where Tony and Matt were hiding was clear. They were back under cover, but now they were facing an even more formidable threat. The trucks coming along the north wall had killed everyone in the guard tower, and now they were racing toward the spot where Romano, Sienna, Matt, and Tony were hiding. They must have seen Matt and Tony's gunfire and assumed it was another force from the compound.

Machine gun fire from the lead truck, which was still over seventy yards away, raked the ground yards from Matt and Tony. The gunners on the second and third trucks poured another long burst into what was left of the guard tower and then followed the first truck.

Collins tapped the PTT on his headset and yelled into the mic, "Romano, you gotta get out of there or you'll be cut off!"

Even as he screamed the warning, two of the trucks peeled off and started to flank Romano's position. Collins fired a round at the driver's side window of the first truck and the glass exploded. Seconds later, the ground six feet to his left erupted as bullets scoured the ridgeline.

He scrambled backward, dragging the M24 with him. He grabbed the steel box of bullets and sprinted in a crouch to a location thirty yards to the right, scrambled back up to the top, and positioned himself beside a refrigerator-size rock. He frantically scanned the scene below through the scope. He could see Romano peering over the top of the rock. Tony, Matt, and Sienna were crouched behind him. They were momentarily protected by three large boulders, but their path back to the chopper was blocked by one of the trucks with the mounted guns. Two other trucks were intermittently peppering the top of the rock with fire.

The man operating the machine gun on the third truck had the barrel pointed in his direction. A second man on the truck was scanning the ridge with a pair of binoculars, looking for his position. The man with the binoculars pointed to a spot off to his right, and the man on the gun poured a stream of bullets into the spot, throwing clumps of dirt and a cloud of dust into the air.

Collins zeroed in on the truck closest to Romano's position and put the crosshairs on the gunner's center mass and adjusted the scope. As he began to squeeze the trigger, bullets ripped into the ground to the left of him and began to walk toward his location. He rolled away from the fusillade and scrambled to the right, trying to get behind the protection of the ridge and find another position, but he was too slow. A bullet slammed into the M24, knocking it to the ground. A second slug slammed into his right side.

His armored vest stopped the bullet's penetration, but the force of the blow knocked the wind out of him. He gasped frantically for breath, grabbed the M24, and crawled just below the ridge to the other side of the rock. Every time he pulled his right knee forward, a lancing pain sliced through his ribcage like a white-hot knife. The bullet must have cracked a rib.

Collins eased back up to the top of the ridge, pulled the M24 to his shoulder, and glanced through the scope. All he could see was blackness. As he reached up to brush off whatever was blocking the front aperture, his hand stopped. The front of the scope had been blown off by an incoming bullet. He would have to aim without it.

Collins stared at the scene below. The men in the trucks were clos-ing in on Romano's position. Alternating bursts of fire poured out from the guns on the back of the three trucks in the lead. He could hear the sound of laughter and the blare of music floating across the plain as they closed in. Enraged, he pulled the M24 to his shoulder, hoping to draw their fire onto his position, giving Romano, Tony, Matt, and Sienna a chance to escape. The spotter on the fourth truck saw the movement through his binoculars and gestured toward his position. He pointed the weapon in the man's direction and pulled the trigger. The bullet struck the side of the truck, but otherwise did no harm.

He rolled behind the rock, pain lancing through his chest as another fusillade of bullets scoured the rocks in front of him and the ground to his right. He crawled to his left, after chambering another round, determined to try to kill the men on the trucks below even if it cost him his life. As he reached the crest and zeroed in on the truck again, a stream of light, accompanied by a roar that sounded like a million angry bees, lit up the entire valley.

The stream of light came from a rise three hundred yards away from the northwestern corner of the compound. When the light touched down on the two vehicles at the rear of the line, they dis-integrated as if they were being shredded by an unending shower of bullets. As the stream of light chewed its way through the column of trucks like an insatiable demon, the men in the cars and trucks at the other end of the column frantically tried to escape the approaching nightmare, but they were too slow. Within less than two minutes, the blizzard of incoming fire had devastated the entire attack force.

One of the gunners in the trucks firing upon Romano's position wheeled his gun around and began to fire at the source of the incom-ing fire, what Collins realized was some kind of high-tech weapon. The stream of light went dark for several seconds, and then there was a single explosive crack. The gunner on the truck was thrown backward as if struck by a giant fist. A moment later, the white stream of light streaked across the plain below and swept across the trucks attacking Romano's position. Bullets ripped through the vehicles with such horrific rapidity that the vehicles and the men inside them seemed to disintegrate before his eyes. Then it was suddenly dark and deathly silent. Nothing moved in the plain below.

Collins scrabbled over to where his binoculars were lying on the ground, crawled back to the ridge, and scanned the spot where Romano, Sienna, Matt, and Tony were located. When he couldn't see them through the cloud of dust kicked up by the hail of bullets, he frantically tapped the PTT on his mic.

"Romano, come in. Romano, are—"

"Roger. We're here, and we're all okay."

A wave of relief washed over Collins, and he exhaled the breath he'd been unconsciously holding.

Romano's voice came over the mic again. "Tell me what you can see."

Collins scanned the trucks for movement. There was none. Then he scanned the rest of the plain below, ranging over the line of destroyed trucks on the west side of the compound. A number of the trucks were on fire; steam was floating up from others. Shredded bodies covered in blood were sitting in the vehicles, lying in the flatbeds, or lying on the ground. No one was moving. He scanned the road to the west and saw the tail end of a tractor trailer truck disappearing into the distance.

"You're clear."

"Roger that. On our way back. Watch our six."

Punta Maldonado, Mexico

Ramon Cayetano paced furiously back and forth in his underground office, enraged at his inability to reach Matias in the packing compound or Nacio, Gregorio, and Sanchez in Los Angeles for the past three hours. With each passing minute, the punishment he vowed to exact on all four became more savage. As he reached for his cell phone yet again, it began to vibrate. He didn't recognize the incoming number. He hesitated for a long moment, knowing his location would be disclosed to whoever was on the other side of the line if he answered. When he punched the receive button, his rage ratcheted up another level.

"Mr. Cayetano, it is Gregorio. I—"

"Where have you been? I warned you and Alex a long time ago you would suffer if I could not reach you when I called!"

"I am sorry, sir. We were robbed at gunpoint on the way back from dinner. The thief took our phones, and the police insisted we come with them to make a report. We could not get new—"

"Fools. Fools! I will have you both killed!"

"I am sorry, sir. I will make amends. The package—did you receive it?"

"The box?" Cayetano growled. "Yes, I did, and I could not open it. It requires a code."

"Again, I must beg your forgiveness, sir, but if you will have the package brought—"

"It is sitting on the table in front of me. Now, tell me what is in it and then give me the code to open it!"

"Bear with me, sir, this operation has been . . . very, very successful, and all of your money is now in a single foreign bank account. With that much money at stake, I wanted to make sure that you, and only you, received the username and password allowing access to the account. You need to make sure no one else is in the room, Mr. Cayetano. If they were to—"

"Silence!" Cayetano growled, as he tapped the speaker button on the phone and sat down at the table. He placed the small titanium box on his lap and drew out his reading glasses. The electronic screen and keypad on the front of the box glowed a cold blue. The drug lord knew if he didn't type in the code in the exact order, a vial of acid within the box would be released and the information within would be destroyed.

Cayetano yelled at the phone on the table. "No one is here but me, Gregorio. Now give me the code!"

"The code is *t-a-s*, capital *L*, capital *X*, *f-e-r*, number 4, and letter *u*."

Cayetano tapped in the code with care and slowly lifted the cover. The box was empty.

"What is this? There's nothing in it."

Gregorio answered in a quiet voice. "Yes, Mr. Cayetano, there is. It's taped to the inside cover of the box."

Cayetano pushed the cover open further and the light from the nearby lamp illuminated two photos taped to the inside of the box. Cayetano stared at the photos for a moment without recognizing the faces. Then he remembered. One woman was Gregorio's mother; the other was Alex Sanchez's mother.

"What is this—a game? I will have you—"

"It is not a game, Mr. Cayetano—vengeance never is."

A high-pitched sound came over the phone and there was a flash of light. For a moment, Cayetano thought the lower part of his body was on fire. He shoved the smoking steel box to the floor, revealing the carnage below. The lower half of his body from his groin to buttocks was a bloody shredded mass. The drug lord opened his mouth to let out a scream of rage, but he was unable to utter a sound as he slumped to the floor.

THIRTY-TWO

Terlingua, Texas

No one said a word until the helicopter was twenty miles from the compound, racing northward at five thousand feet. It was as if they feared breaking the spell that had enabled them to escape the nightmare behind them. Romano was the first to speak. He turned to Collins and smiled. "There's a whole lot of helo pilots, counselor, but there are damn few who can say they pulled off a successful rescue operation, under fire, on the wrong side of the border. You just joined a rather exclusive club."

"I'll skip the next membership meeting, if you don't mind," Collins said dryly.

Romano chuckled and pointed at the lights in the distance marking the approaching border. "Remember, we can't land at the ranch. Those folks we saw on the way out were the FBI. There's a whole group of them waiting for you."

Collins glanced over at him. "How do you know?"

"Just got a text."

"From who? The guy at the ranch?"

Romano shook his head. "Nope. We have an unknown guardian angel. This guy texted me just before the metal storm started in on the bad guys back there."

Collins glanced over at Romano. "Metal storm?"

"Yeah. The gun that took out those trucks. It's a high-tech machine gun that can pump out more than a million rounds a minute. The bullets are triggered electronically."

Romano glanced down at his phone and raised an eyebrow. "How about that? It looks like our guardian angel wants to talk to you. Take off your headset for a moment."

Collins took off his headset and put on Romano's phone link. "Who is this?"

There was a low chuckle. "I'm the dude who just saved your ass. You can thank me when we meet. Fly the Bell to the private airport at Presidio, an hour north. I'll meet you there."

Collins hesitated. "Why . . . why should I trust you?"

The man on the phone chuckled again. "Like I said, I just saved your butt, so at least you know I don't want you dead. What you don't know is what I do want from you. Well, let me lay a few cards on the table. We have this common problem—Nacio Leon. Mr. Leon wants the three of you dead. Yes, the girl is on his list too. And he's not going to rest until he makes that happen. So, you folks can either go to ground for the rest of your lives and pray he doesn't find you, or you can help us bury his ass before he gets to you."

Collins's mind raced through the possibilities. If he landed, he and Matt would be taken into custody by the FBI. If bail was denied, which was possible, they'd end up parked in a cell for months, and despite the extenuating circumstances, there was a chance the two of them would have to do federal time. Sienna, however, would go free, giving Nacio an easy target. On the other hand, if he met the mystery man on the phone, without any assurances, they could end up dead. He decided to find out a little more about their unknown benefactor, without asking for the information directly.

"I need a flight plan for that, and I'll be picked up by radar when I come across the border. That means I'm going to pick up a tail immediately."

"A flight plan was uploaded five minutes ago. As for being forced to land, I can guarantee you'll be left alone as long as you head straight to the Presidio airport."

The answer confirmed what Collins suspected. The man on the other side of the phone worked for the government. He suspected the caller was CIA.

"Then I'll see you at Presidio," Collins said.

Los Angeles, California

Anna printed out a map of the area surrounding Terlingua, Texas, drew a rough circle around the location, and then walked into the drab conference room on the fourth floor of the FBI's Los Angeles headquarters. Teo was leaning over the conference table talking into the starfish-shaped phone located in the center. "You're telling me we can't track the helicopter, is that it?"

The voice on the phone was polite, but there was a subtle undercurrent of antagonism in the tone. "This is the border patrol, Agent Ortiz. We keep people out of the country, not in. The TAR system picked up the chopper on its way south. As I said, it crossed the border about twenty-five miles south of Lajitas. It was moving fast and low. We lost contact with it about a mile in. The pilot was almost certainly wearing night vision tech, and there are plenty of canyons running southward that he could have used for cover."

"But you will pick him up on the way back, right?"

The border patrol agent chuckled. "You sure he's coming back?"

Teo glanced over at Anna, raising an eyebrow for a moment. She nodded.

"Yeah. We think this is an in-and-out run."

"You know, it might help if the FBI told us folks down here on the frontline why that chopper was crossing the border in the first place."

Teo drew in a heavy breath and exhaled slowly. "Sorry, that's not my call. I just need you to call me and let me know when he comes back across the border."

"I just put a note on the corkboard, Agent Ortiz. You're at the tippity-top of the list."

The answer didn't make Teo happy. "Much appreciated, Agent Calhoun," he said dryly and terminated the call.

He turned to Anna. "Whaddya got?"

Anna walked over to his side of the table. She put the map down and tapped the center point. "This is the airport at the ranch in Terlingua. The agent on-site talked to the property owner. The helicopter was a Bell 407. It has a flight range of about 370 miles. That means their destination must be within 180 miles, max, but . . . there's not a lot there."

Teo stared at the map. "There's gotta be something. Ask research to get us whatever satellite photos they have of the area and have them check with the DEA, NSA, and CIA."

Anna nodded. "I already did, but that's tomorrow morning at the earliest. That—"

"May be too late," Teo finished. "I know, but there's nothing for it. We can't move until Carlton gives us the go-ahead, and the self-proclaimed magic man is not answering his phone."

Anna grimaced. "Apparently, we're not at the top of his list anymore."

Teo growled, "We never were."

Anna sat down at the table and pulled a laptop out of her backpack. "I'm going to use the time to write this up."

Teo nodded. "Good idea. When this gets reviewed by the big boys back in DC, it's going to have to be buttoned down real tight. I'm going upstairs to try to see what the research people have come with."

Anna waved.

Two hours later, Teo walked back into the conference room with an irritated look on his face. "Carlton's on the phone." Teo tapped the blinking light and the speaker button.

"Carlton here." His tone was curt and impatient.

Teo put both hands on the table and leaned toward the phone. "Sorry to interrupt, Regge, but there are big developments, and decisions have to be made. Collins crossed the Mexico border in a helicopter two hours ago. We believe—"

"So you blew it. You—"

"We didn't blow anything," Teo said icily.

"No? Then why is the perp on the run? Do you know how much time and money—"

Anna glanced at her watch and interrupted him. "We don't believe he's on the run."

"Then what the hell is he doing in Mexico?"

Teo leaned even closer to the phone and spoke in a near growl.

"Do *not* shout at Agent Torres. She's going to walk you through the facts, and you are going to listen, or we're going to call the director's office and let him deal with this problem."

Carlton was silent for a moment. When he responded his tone was laden with sarcasm. "I'm all ears."

Teo turned to Anna and gestured toward the phone. She nodded, drew in a breath, and exhaled slowly. "Matt Esposito has a sister, Sienna. Four months ago she went on a mission trip to a remote village in Chiapas, Mexico. She was helping a Doctors Without Borders unit. A week before she was supposed to return, she received a message. The message said her brother was in a car accident and his friend, Declan Collins, had hired a helicopter to take her to the nearest airport so she could fly home. Sienna packed up her stuff and got on the helicopter."

Carlton interrupted, "Where's this going?"

Anna held up a hand to head off Teo's response. "Here's where it's going. The message was bogus. Her brother was fine, and Declan Collins didn't send the helicopter. Even more important, Sienna Esposito hasn't been heard from since she was picked up, and yet her loving brother never reported her missing. Thankfully, one of the nurses took a photo of the helicopter when it landed. We have that photo. The photo picked up the guy who helped Sienna with her bags. His name is Nacio Leon, the Cayetano drug cartel's top enforcer. The FBI believes this guy has killed over thirty people, including one of our own agents."

Teo leaned forward and tapped his chest. "He also put three bullets into me an hour ago. But for the vest, I would have been added to his list of kills."

Carlton interrupted again, but he was more respectful. "Okay, all of this is interesting, but I'm still not connecting the dots."

Anna stepped closer to the table. "Ramon Cayetano grabbed Sienna as a hostage. He's using her as leverage to force Collins and Esposito to orchestrate a massive money laundering operation."

"So, you're telling me Perez is working for the Cayetanos?"

Anna shook her head in frustration. "No! The money laundering is somehow connected with the B of A loan and the bankruptcy case. That's why Collins went over the border today. That case is going to be wrapped up tomorrow. Once that happens, the Cayetanos no longer have a need for the girl."

Carlton scoffed. "Let me see if I understand this. You're telling me Collins is on some kind of rescue mission. Is that it? Look, I appreciate the enthusiasm, Agent—"

The intercom from the front desk drowned Carlton's voice out. "I have an urgent call from Agent Calhoun. He's with Border Patrol."

Teo put Carlton on hold and punched the other blinking red light. "Agent Ortiz here."

"Agent Calhoun here. Your boy just came back across the border, Agent Ortiz."

"Can you track him now that he's on this side of the border? We need to talk with the people in that bird as soon as it lands."

Calhoun chuckled. "That's your department, Agent Ortiz. He's no longer a border problem."

Calhoun ended the call without waiting for response. Teo shook his head in frustration and punched the hold button. Carlton was still talking: "As I said, Collins is a rich lawyer, not GI Joe. If he went across the border, he's on the run, and he's not coming back."

A satisfied smile came to Teo's face. "Sorry, Regge. You're wrong on that one. Collins's helo just came back across the border."

Presidio, Texas

When the Bell 407 landed on the tarmac of the small airfield on the outskirts of Presidio, Texas, Tony Lentino jumped out of the chopper, dropped to his knees on the concrete, and spoke solemnly: "Jesus, Mary, and Joseph, thank you for saving my sorry Sicilian ass. I know I don't deserve it, but I'm going to keep all those promises I made in the middle of that shitstorm . . . I mean, I'll do my best."

Sienna walked over to Collins when he stepped out of the helicopter and stared at him for a moment, tears streaming down her face. Then she wrapped her arms around him and spoke in a hoarse voice filled with relief and exhaustion. "I knew you could do it, Declan. I knew it. I can never thank you. I just—"

Romano interrupted her. His tone was urgent. "Collins, we've got company."

Collins returned Sienna's hug and turned in the direction Romano was pointing. A tall, lean African-American man in his fifties was walking toward him, wearing jeans, hiking boots, and a black leather aviator jacket. As soon as he spoke, Collins knew it was the man he'd spoken to on the phone.

"Declan Collins, I presume."

He stopped a stride away and held out his hand. The bemused expression on his face took the formidable edge off his square jaw, penetrating eyes, and short iron-gray hair.

Collins nodded and shook his hand. "Yes, and you are?"

Romano answered the question as he walked up beside Collins. "Gabe Mattson. We met—"

"In an unpleasant place that I suspect we'd both like to forget, Captain Romano," Mattson finished as he shook Romano's outstretched hand.

Mattson's attention returned to Collins. "Although I'd like to spend some quality time with you folks, the FBI will be here very shortly, and we have some decisions to make. Here's my take on your options, gentlemen. You can stay here, wait for the FBI, and sort out this whole quagmire with those folks over the next year or two. Or you can gas up the Bell, and Romano and another pilot, who just happens to be waiting inside, can fly everyone but Mr. Collins to a safe and sufficiently remote location of your choosing. I'm sure Mr. Romano knows a spot or two."

Romano nodded. "I do."

Mattson smiled and continued, "Under the same option two, Mr. Collins comes with me to a nearby bar, and we try to reach an understanding on a matter that only he and I need to know about."

"What happens if we don't reach an agreement?" Collins said quietly.

"Then you make a call to the FBI, and it's back to option one. Under that scenario, Gabe Mattson simply goes away."

As Mattson spoke an Avgas truck pulled up and started to refuel the Bell. Collins's mind was racing. Too many variables were unknown for him to decide, but he had no choice. He turned to Romano. "Can you get Sienna, Matt, and Tony to a safe place? I'll cover—"

Romano interrupted him. "Consider it done." He looked over at Mattson and back to Collins. "Good luck, counselor. You're going to need it."

Mattson nodded to Romano and gestured for Collins to follow him. As they walked to the modest two-story building fifty yards away, a handsome Asian man wearing a flight suit passed them. Mattson gave him a friendly nod. "Have a safe flight."

"Will do, sir."

Mattson walked to the door at the southern end of the building, opened it, and stood aside so Collins could enter. Collins hesitated for a moment, turned, and looked back at the Bell 407. Sienna and Tony were already inside, and Matt was just about climb in. When he saw Collins, a smile came to his face and he raised a fist. "That was a gino, bro; that was a gino."

Collins smiled and waved, in spite of the tension he still felt in his gut. Then he walked into the building. Mattson gave him a questioning look.

"A gino is a goal. We played hockey together . . . in another life."

Mattson walked over to an old refrigerator in the corner of the drab office and pulled out two bottles of beer. He opened them with a pocketknife, handed one to Collins, and sat down in an ugly plastic chair against the wall. He pointed to a similar chair a few steps away.

"Actually, it was two ginos. You got yourself there alive, and you got back alive. Now, I'm going to ask you to go out and get one more goal for team. That'll make it—"

"A hat trick," Collins finished, as he sat down in the second chair. "Enlighten me. It can't be any worse than what I've been through."

Mattson stared at Collins for a moment. "Killing a man at 800 yards with a sniper rifle is one thing. Putting a bullet into him when he's five yards away is something else. That's how you're going to have to put down Nacio Leon."

Collins stared at Mattson for a moment. Then he said quietly, "How do I find him?"

Mattson chuckled. "You don't have to. He's coming to you. Apparently, Mr. Nacio knows where you're hiding out—or more accurately, where you *will* be hiding out: the Especiale Hotel in Matamoros, Mexico."

Collins shook his head. "I don't understand."

Mattson punched a number into his cell phone and put the call on speaker.

"I'll let a friend of yours explain it to you."

"Hello, Mr. Collins."

It was Gregorio.

———

Sienna looked over at Matt as the Bell 407 ascended and banked northeast. Tears were running down his face. Sienna had never seen her brother cry. He'd even kept his outward composure at the funerals held for their mom and dad, although she knew he'd mourned their loss as much as she did. He'd wanted to be strong for her.

Matt roughly brushed the tears from his eyes when he realized Sienna was looking at him. "Who are you looking at?" he said with mock gruffness.

Sienna smiled. "My big brother. I love you, Matt . . . even if you're kind of a jerk."

He smiled and then acted offended. "Who are you calling a jerk? I just saved your ass."

Tony Lentino, who was sitting to her right, shook his head and said with mock derision, "I knew I should have shot you back there when I had the chance, Esposito."

Sienna and Matt laughed.

Tony leaned forward and tapped the shoulder of man in the front passenger seat, the man who'd come to Sienna's rescue when she came over the wall. "Romano, what's the story with Declan? Why isn't he coming with us?"

Romano turned in his seat, nodded to Sienna, and looked over at Tony. "Can't say for sure, but I get the sense there's still some unfinished business your buddy has to take care of before this thing is over."

THIRTY-THREE

Heroica Matamoros, Mexico

Collins sat in Room 301 of the Hotel Especiale, a one-story adobe affair on the outskirts of Matamoros that was anything but special. The walls in the room were yellowed and cracked, the floor was covered with brown linoleum, and the shade covering the single window was enfiladed with holes. The only furniture in the room, other than the wooden chair that Collins was sitting in, was a narrow bed covered in a frayed multicolored blanket. Unlike the rest of the room, the bed was distinctive in one respect: there was a coal-black Glock 17 and three spare magazines resting on the pillow.

Collins remembered Mattson's parting admonition as he stared at the gun.

"Your reservation is for Room 302. There's a bag under the mattress. In it you'll find a Glock 17, three spare magazines, and a key. Walk around the room a bit, turn the light on and off, and sit on the bed. Make it sound as if you're settling in for the night. Then quietly move to the room directly across the hall—Room 301. The key will open the door."

Collins nodded to himself as he mentally walked through the rest of Mattson's instructions.

"The guest who is supposed to be staying in Room 301 is not scheduled to check out until the next morning, but he won't be coming back. Stay as quiet as a church mouse until Nacio shows up. He'll bring at least one Cayetano soldier with him. When they bust in the door to Room 302, wait a second until they're inside and then empty the first magazine through the door—all seventeen rounds. Spread the shots over a four- to five-foot span. Aim at gut level. Don't worry about the door. The wood is thin. The bullets will punch right through. Then eject the first mag, put in the second, and keep shooting as you pull open the door and go into the hall. Empty the rest of the magazine into Nacio and his henchman. At least one head shot for each, just in case they're wearing vests.

"Put your toe into their ribs real hard, to make sure they are dead. Once you *know* they're dead, go back to Room 301. Pick up the spent mag, put it in your pocket, stick the Glock in your belt, and leave through the back door of the hotel. There's a Holiday Inn three blocks north. Ditch the Glock and the magazines on the way. Catch a cab from there to the Matamoros airport. Go to hangar four. A jet will be waiting to take you to a safe place."

The burner phone in Collin's pocket vibrated. He glanced down at the incoming text.

"Nacio plus one on the way."

He glanced through a hole in the tattered window shade at the narrow street below. The flickering light from the cerveza sign over the bodega at the end of the block illuminated two men walking down the center of the deserted street. They made no effort to conceal their approach, but then why should they? It was two in the morning, and Collins's room was on the other side of the hotel. The clerk at the front desk would have told them that. He also would have told them the American had gone to bed hours earlier with a bottle of Johnny Walker Red. Collins couldn't blame the old man for his lack of discretion. Dying to protect a guest wasn't in his job description.

Nacio was wearing a white linen suit, a matching Panama hat, and a pair of Cartier sunglasses despite the time of night. He was holding a gun in his right hand. Although Collins couldn't see the weapon clearly at this distance, he was certain of the make and model—a Beretta 92FS. Nacio had pressed the business end of the gun against Collins's head less than a month earlier. The killer had been denied the pleasure of pulling the trigger because Collins had been deemed a necessary asset then. Now he was a liability. Tonight Nacio intended to finish the job.

Collins didn't recognize the second man, who walked a step behind. He was shorter and broader than Nacio, and he wore a long black T-shirt and jeans. The light from the bodega illuminated the tattoos covering his bald head and thick forearms. It also revealed the deadly looking twelve-gauge shotgun resting on his right shoulder. Collins recognized the model—a Kel-Tec KSG. It carried twelve shells.

As soon as they passed out of sight, Collins walked over to the bed and picked up the Glock. He stuck the magazines in his belt, within easy reach, and positioned himself three feet from the door. He aimed the Glock and waited, struggling to control his breathing.

Two minutes later, he heard soft footfalls coming down the hallway. They stopped outside his room. A rivulet of sweat ran down the side of his cheek and trickled down his neck. A second later, he heard a heavy boot smashing open the door to the room across the hall. A series of explosions followed. Collins exhaled slowly and began firing through the door in front of him, spreading the shots in a pattern as Mattson had directed.

The third round drew a scream of rage and pain. Collins could tell the scream did not come from Nacio. Collins continued firing, and more screams followed, but they were all from the same person. When he counted twelve shots, Collins expanded the width to a pattern of four and five feet, punching holes in thin plaster and wood walls to the left and right of the door. On the seventeenth shot, he heard a grunt of pain from outside the room. This one he recognized. It was Nacio.

As he ejected the empty magazine and reached for a second, two bullets slammed into his chest. The vest he was wearing stopped the nine-millimeter rounds, but it didn't stop the impact. He felt as though he'd been hit with a baseball bat. Another round passed so close to his temple that Collins felt a breath of air caress the side of his head. He threw himself to the floor and rolled to the left, scrabbling for another magazine. As he slammed the magazine into the Glock, he kicked the chair on his right as hard as he could. The chair smashed into the wall and a hail of bullets from the hall ripped through it. Collins emptied eight shots through the wall in the direction of the incoming fire. Two were spot on where Nacio's last shot had punched through, and three were spread out on either side of the spot.

When Collins stopped firing, the only thing he could hear was his own heavy breathing. He knew Nacio could be lying in wait outside the door, but he had to get out of there. He stood up, walked slowly over to the door, took in a breath, and yanked it open, holding the Glock at the ready.

His eyes found the shorter man. He was sprawled out in the room across the way, unmoving. When he turned to look in the other direction, he felt the barrel of a gun press against his left temple.

"So, Mr. Collins, we meet again."

Collins turned his head ever so slowly to the left.

Nacio stared at him, a cold smile on his face. Blood was pouring down his left arm from a wound in his shoulder, and there was another wound in his thigh. Two bullets had hit him square in the chest, but his vest had stopped them.

"Yes, Mr. Collins, I am alive, and although I am wounded, I will live. But you will not. So let me say a final—"

There was a subdued cough, and a hole appeared in the center of Nacio's forehead. For a moment, the killer just stood there, the smile still in place. Then he slumped to the floor. Collins slowly turned his head to the right and stared down the hallway. Anna was walking toward him with a gun in her hand. It was a Glock 19 with a suppressor affixed to the barrel. She stopped in front of him and stared at him for a moment, before nodding at Nacio's inert body.

"You live an interesting life, Declan Collins. I was under the impression the practice of law was a bit more sedate." Then she turned and started back down the hallway. "Come, now, unless you want to spend the rest of your life in a Mexican prison."

Two cabs were waiting in front of the hotel. Anna pointed to the one across the street. "That's yours. The driver knows where to go. Get rid of the Glock and the magazines on the way."

Collins stared at her, unmoving.

Anna glanced at her watch. "Now you have four minutes."

"I have a question."

"Shoot."

"You're not FBI, are you?"

"No."

"CIA?"

"That's two questions, but let me answer this way: Employment in the special ops world is not binary—in government or out. There's a stable of off-the-books assets that are used by the shadow agencies in international ops. I just happened to fit the bill for this one."

Collins nodded slowly.

As she unscrewed the suppressor from the gun in her hand, she looked over at him.

"My turn. How did you know I was undercover? All in all, I thought I was pretty convincing as a paralegal."

Collin smiled. "You were. It was pure luck. I was walking into the LA Gun Club when you were walking out, three, maybe four months ago. The range master is a friend of mine. I asked him about you, and he said you were a better shooter than me. He said you were FBI. I didn't recognize you when you first showed up at the office, but then—"

"You remembered," Anna finished with a smile. Then she pointed to the cab across the street. "Go."

Collins walked across to the cab and climbed into the back seat. As he reached for the car door, Anna turned and said, "Au revoir." There was an amused look on her face.

THIRTY-FOUR

Los Angeles, California

Reginald Carlton stared uncomprehendingly at John Wilkerson, the head of the Office of the United States Trustee, the subdepartment of the Justice Department charged with supervising bankruptcy cases. The two men were sitting in a conference room.

"What are you talking about? PriceStar's accounting records don't exist? How is that possible?"

Wilkerson spread his hands in a placative gesture. "The management firm brought in to manage PriceStar's going-out-of-business sale says the electronic files were destroyed through a complicated hacking operation."

"What about the backup copies and the paper copies?"

Wilkerson shook his head. "PriceStar rejected the contract with their cloud storage provider during the bankruptcy, so they expunged the electronic backup version. As for the paper copies, the bankruptcy judge authorized their destruction."

"He what?"

"Mr. Carlton, the records were being held in a leased warehouse. Once the sale closed, no money was available to pay the lease. It was rejected as part of the reorganization plan. The destruction of the records was ordered to avoid having the records ending up in a dumpster. Remember, we are talking about employee records with social security numbers and bank account records. They had to be destroyed. Document destruction orders like that are common."

Carlton exploded. "That's a bullshit system! Wait, wait . . . the tax returns. The last tax return—that would have to be fraudulent. It would include the bogus cash walked through PriceStar's going-out-of-business sale. We can get these bastards for tax fraud!"

Wilkerson looked uncomfortable. Carlton stood up and put his hands on the conference room table, hovering over Wilkerson.

"What? Is there some other crazy bankruptcy practice in play here?"

Wilkerson looked down at his hands. "The bankruptcy judge approved the tax treatment provisions in PriceStar's plan of reorganization. The IRS never objected. And the tax return was sent to the IRS under a provision of the bankruptcy code that gave the service sixty days to object. It's a scream-or-die provision. Since the IRS didn't object, the returns are deemed accepted. You can't undo—"

Carlton smashed his fist into the table, spilling a cup of coffee at the other end. "The hell I can't! I'm going to lay this whole scam out. I intend—"

"To ruin your career?"

Carlton spun around and stared at the man standing in the doorway. It was Michael Sontag, the SAIC of the FBI's Los Angeles office. "I can see the headline in the *New York Times* now: 'One Hundred Million Dollars Laundered Under the Nose of an Elite Task Force Under the Leadership of Assistant US Attorney Reginald Carlton.' Why, I'm sure they'll just love those memos documenting Agent Torres's repeated effort to get you to focus on the real laundering scheme instead of the private placement deal Collins employed as a decoy. Mr. Perez performed his assigned role in that little scam quite skillfully, but then he is a high school drama teacher."

Carlton eyes widened. "What! What are you talking about?"

"Perez, the mysterious Mexican national who you insisted was the moving force in Collins's secret money-laundering operation, is a retired drama teacher. He was paid a thousand bucks per meeting to follow a script given to him by Collins. The guy thought it was an employee-training exercise. We checked him out. He doesn't even have a parking ticket to his name. As for the dirty money washed through the scheme, it was wired to twelve separate offshore accounts shortly after the order confirming PriceStar's plan of reorganization was entered. The accounts are in jurisdictions beyond the reach of US law.

"In sum, if you go big and loud on this disaster, Mr. Carlton, it will be on the front page of half the newspapers in the country, and the reportage will not be . . . kind. You may even get dragged before one or more Senate oversight committees. Or you could just close the file."

There was a long pause, and then Carlton spoke in a hoarse voice. "Like you say, it's time to close the file."

THIRTY-FIVE

Nassau, Bahamas

Collins sat at a table in the farthest corner of the veranda attached to the hotel bar. The back of his chair was positioned against the three-foot-wide pillar supporting the roof overhead. A whisper of wind from the ocean a hundred yards to his left tugged at the ends of the single sheet of paper in front of him. It was a copy of the shortest contract he'd ever read. Its one and only sentence read: "Declan Collins ('Collins') hereby assigns all right, title, and interest in the claims he holds against Proteus Acquisitions, LLC ('Proteus'), for the sum of twenty-five million dollars (US), and Proteus agrees to pay this sum to Collins, in cash, on the above referenced date." Collins's signature appeared at the bottom of the contract. Gregory Pena had signed the contract on behalf of Proteus. Twenty-five million dollars was now on deposit, in Collins's name, in a newly opened account at the First Bahamian Bank.

He took a sip from the scotch whiskey in front of him, his second. A wry smile came to his face as he considered the name Gregorio had chosen for the buying entity, a shell corporation formed in the Cayman Islands. Proteus was an ancient Greek sea god who could change his shape and color at will. Gregorio had surely done that.

He had considered killing Gregorio at least once a day during the past three months. His conversation with the perfectly mannered Mexican at the Presidio Airport had changed all that. The exchange was seared into his memory.

"Hello, Mr. Collins. Mr. Mattson tells me we don't have much time, so I would ask you to listen to my tale of woe, before you render judgment. My mother and Alex's made the mistake of going to work for a man named Ramon Cayetano many years ago when they were young. They had no idea he was a drug lord, and the wages offered were very good."

There was a hesitation on the phone, and Gregorio's otherwise calm and urbane voice took on a different tone when he continued, a tone laden with restrained anger and sadness. "Cayetano had a practice of hiring bright young women—women who were pregnant. He knew their condition made them vulnerable. He also knew their children would serve as ideal hostages once they were born. Once these two wonderful young women were trapped within Cayetano's web, he turned them into his personal sex slaves. Alex's mother died one night from one of Cayetano's beatings. Her body was dumped in the sea off the coast by a local fisherman.

"My mother had to endure Cayetano's barbarity for another two years before he tired of her and sent her away. Others, so many others, suffered a similar fate.

"The fate inflicted upon these women was cruel and unforgivable, but it was not Cayetano's cruelest blow. You see, he kept their children as hostages. This assured their silence. Some of the children were kept as servants. Others, who showed more promise, like Alex and me, were sent to boarding school. We did well, knowing any failure would bring terrible retribution. In time, we were brought into the Cayetano organization as accountants, and later as his personal financial advisers.

"Unbeknownst to Mr. Cayetano, I found my mother after he sent her away. She was working as a dishwasher in a small cantina located in one of Mexico City's worst barrios. I secretly moved her to a new location, outside his reach, when I had the money to do so, but she was not the same . . . she was never the same. I vowed revenge for his wrongs, and I waited until I had the opportunity."

"And Matt, Sienna, and I became that opportunity," Collins interrupted coldly.

"That is where you are wrong, Mr. Collins. Your friend, Matt, stumbled into my nightmare on his own. You see, I was not the one who brought your brilliant money-laundering scheme to Mr. Cayetano. Nacio did."

"That's bullshit!" Collins exploded.

"No? Ask Mr. Esposito. We met at a private party. I have no idea how your friend managed an invite, but he is a clever man in his own way. I was standing by the bar with Adriana. She was Nacio's date that night. I was holding Nacio's drink while he went to the restroom. It was then that Mr. Esposito approached. We'd met earlier in the evening and spoken briefly. I'm sure he would have ignored me but for Adriana. He was drawn to that woman like a moth to the flame.

"Oh, Mr. Esposito worked assiduously to secure her favors. Unfortunately, Adriana was unimpressed by his serial boasts and blandishments, and there were many. At some point, he began to describe the money-laundering concept in your screenplay, presumably in the hope of impressing her with his mental prowess. He was quite drunk, and quite desperate. By then, Nacio had returned, but he didn't interrupt. He stood behind me checking his emails and listening very carefully. Nacio saw the opportunity."

Collins interrupted him. "Nacio is just a hired killer, Gregorio. Only you could have—"

"Explained it to him? You underrate him. Nacio has a master's in business administration from the University of Barcelona. He is a sociopath, yes, but a brilliant one. It is he who told Mr. Cayetano about your scheme. Although I suggested it was too complicated and risky, Cayetano was adamant. He ordered Nacio to kidnap Sienna—and no, I was not told of this in advance, although there would have been nothing I could have done to stop it even if I had known. You must remember, my life and Alex's life have always hung by a thread."

"And so you agreed to be the puppet master."

"Alex and I were puppets, too, Mr. Collins, and this puppet did not leave you to your fate. Two years ago, a friend of mine from

Harvard Business School contacted me. Apparently, a CIA agent who had been investigating Mr. Cayetano's affairs had gone missing. His name was Michael Sontag. That name doesn't mean anything to you, but it should. He is the son of the special agent in charge of the FBI's Los Angeles office. I told my friend I knew nothing about it, but I said I would make discrete inquiries about the matter. I did not, for obvious reasons.

"Nothing came of it until six months later. I was working in one of Mr. Cayetano's warehouses checking the cash counts when I overheard one of the guards tell him Nacio had turned over an American CIA agent to the Nauyacas. I suspect the man was half-dead from being tortured, but Nacio had wanted the death to be attributed to the rival gang, and it was. I contacted my friend and told him what I'd heard. A week later, Gabe Mattson sat in the seat next to me on a flight to Mexico City. We have been working together, for the most part, ever since. You will note, I did not let Mr. Mattson know about your rescue effort until it was already underway. And, as you know, it is a good thing that I did."

"That's all well and good, Gregorio, but you never did a damn thing to help Sienna, or Matt and me, for that matter."

"You are wrong, Mr. Collins. Mr. Cayetano wanted to kill Matt two weeks ago, since he was no longer necessary. I persuaded him to wait. As for Sienna, ask her how she was able to contact you from the compound in Maijoma. She will tell you that a guard made calls each night outside the room where she was being held prisoner, a guard who hid two phones in the eave of a shed, where she could find them. He worked for me.

"Ask Romano's mercenaries whether they were tipped off about the FBI raid on their hotel before it happened. They were. They simply moved too slowly. Like you, Mr. Collins, I was under the knife every day, along with Alex, but I did what I could. You are welcome to hate me, but know this, you would all be dead but for my help."

Collins remembered hesitating before asking Gregorio the next question. "How did you know Nacio would be looking for me at this hotel in . . . in Matamoros?"

Gregorio answered in a cold voice. "Mr. Cayetano was ripped to pieces by a bomb delivered yesterday. His end was too long in coming, but come it did. Nacio's men found the burner phone you hid in the bathroom stall . . . with a little help. The last text on that phone was a room reservation sent to you by the Especiale Hotel. I made the room reservation and insisted they send it via text to that phone."

There was a long hesitation before Gregorio continued. "Yes, Mr. Collins, I knew about the phone. Sanchez thought he heard someone texting in one of the restroom stalls outside your office one morning. When you were the only one to come out immediately after that, he told me. I stopped by after hours and found the phone. I kept it to myself . . . otherwise you, Matt, and Sienna would be dead. So, you see, I am not as bad as you would like to believe. Now, Mr. Collins, I will leave you to your fate, one that is now solely in your hands. Good luck."

Collins's recollection was interrupted by the noise of the chair across from him being pulled out. Gabe Mattson sat down. He was wearing white shorts, sandals, and a bright yellow Tommy Bahama shirt.

"From what I hear, counselor, you're now a rich man."

Collins leaned back in his chair. "That I am, until the Justice Department gets an asset freeze order and persuades the Bahamian government to turn over this high-value fugitive. Then I'll be disbarred, incarcerated, and poor."

Mattson chuckled. "Don't be so sanguine."

A waiter put a bottle of beer down in front of Mattson. After taking a long pull, he pointed toward the beach. "Let's take a walk."

Collins followed Mattson across the beach to the edge of the water where no one was within earshot.

"Don't worry about that business back in LA. I suspect it's all going to work out fine."

Collins shook his head but didn't say anything.

"What you need to think about is what you want to do with the rest of your life, and I can tell ya, Declan Collins, you have a real future in my line of work."

Collins smiled in spite of his sour mood. "So that's why you're here. This is a recruiting trip."

"That and an opportunity for some well-deserved R & R. Hell, boy, I've been working my fingers to the bone keeping your damn butt alive."

Collins smiled wryly. "Not as hard as I've been."

Mattson picked up a rock from the beach and threw it into the surf and then turned back to Collins, a puzzled look on his face. "I've got a couple of questions for you. Anna told me how you figured out she was undercover, but why did you bring her in on the money-laundering scheme? Carlton could have jumped on you a lot sooner than he did."

Collins stared at a sailboat in the distance for a moment. "Once I realized she was undercover, I used her as . . . an instrument of misdirection. It was a risky game, but one I had to play."

Mattson chuckled. "'An instrument of misdirection.' I like that. You used this Perez guy and his nonexistent private placement deal to distract her from the main event."

Collins smiled. "His name is Stephen Scalisi. He's—"

"A retired high school drama teacher. I'm told the AUSA's office went ballistic when they discovered you bamboozled them with that ruse. Where the hell did you find this guy?"

Collins smiled. "Scalisi is a genius. When he was younger, he coached some of the most successful young actors on speech, diction, and stage presentation. Whenever I have a tough case, he critiques my closing argument beforehand—the inflections, movements, expressions, that sort of thing. We meet in the big conference room on the first floor of the building, not in the office, so Donna and the rest of the staff had never seen him before. He was on calendar for a meeting the day after I realized Anna was an FBI agent. So I put together the ruse, as you say. I asked Scalisi to play the role of a difficult client as a training exercise for the staff. He agreed. I also told him that I needed him to keep his identity secret and that there was at least one member of the staff who would make it her mission to discover it. The guy loved the challenge . . .

and I paid him a big bonus. Like a lot of things, it just happened to work out."

Mattson chuckled again. "Yes, counselor, we surely have a spot for you in the big leagues. Hell, you might even get to work with . . . a highly skilled asset formerly known as Anna. I bet you'd like that."

Collins smiled. "I just might."

Mellieha, Malta

Gregorio walked across the broad wooden deck encircling the ocean side of the palatial villa and stared down at the vista below. White sand beaches rimmed a sea of blue that seemed to extend forever. The real estate broker had promised him the property offered one of the finest views of Ghadira Bay. She had been right. It was breathtaking.

The stack of papers on the table behind him was ruffled lightly by the caress of the pleasant Mediterranean breeze.

"Gregorio, if you're not careful, those papers will blow out to sea."

He glanced over at his mother. She was sitting in front of a large easel at the other end of the deck wearing a white artist's smock and a broad yellow sun hat. The paintbrush in her hand was poised delicately above a broad canvas. There was a contented smile on her face.

Gregorio glanced over at the bearer shares beneath the glass of scotch on the table.

"You needn't worry, Mother. They have already served their purpose—served it well, indeed."

The End.

ABOUT THE AUTHOR

S. Alexander O'Keefe was born in Providence, Rhode Island. He is a graduate of Dartmouth College and Fordham University School of Law, and he practices law in Newport Beach, California. Mr. O'Keefe and his wife, Cathy, live in Irvine, California, and have three children.